BOOK TWO

THE WORLD OF DAEGRIES SERIES

THE ALLIANCE OF THE GRIM

M. K. BROWNING

M. K. Browning
ISBN: 978-1-961703-03-2
Printed in the United States of America

First Publication: January 2025 Howling Wolf Press

The Alliance of the Grim

To the Reader

This novel, like the other books in succession, is not a stand-alone story. Book two, *The Alliance of the Grim,* is the second in The World of Daegries series. There are several books expected in this series.

The World of Daegries
The Magik Scarf – Book 1
The Alliance of the Grim – Book 2
Working Title Twin Terrors – Book 3
TBD – Book 4

You can also read a free short story on my website when you sign up for the email newsletter! www.mkbrowning.com

This book is dedicated to...

...my husband and children, who have been first readers and advisors––and my grandbabies, who are the reason for everything I do.

Acknowledgments
This book would not have been possible without:

My critique crew, Ellen Holder and Michelle Fulmer

My favorite café where I write almost daily, thank you. Lake Wales Latte Lounge Coffee and Book Shop

My family at Moon Dreamz Metaphysical Shop. You guys keep me going.

My beta readers, Liz, David, Deb, Brian. Thank you so much for the attention you have given this book!

Contents

King Eldon's Map
Blighted Vale
Snowclips
River
Greater Daegries
Draksroy
The Heightlands
Dragyn
River
The Meadowlands
Lesser Daegries
Wildlands
Mers
The Farmlands
Ogres
Swamplands
River

Prologue

During the days of the eighth age, an age of advancement for the region, Mudden folks crafted items of great curiosity. Even some motorized vehicles, although no one knew where that knowledge came from.

A certain townie discovered that if she followed folks around, she could find out interesting things about the town and what was going on in it by asking the right questions.

It is thanks to her nosiness and ability to write that we now know all of the story about what happened around then. It all started when strangers began to appear around town. Overly large folk with big eyes and long fingers who crossed the Mudden road passing through, never staying long.

On a bright and sunny August day, one such creature was stopped and questioned by Mudden's own constable, Murray.

"Here now," Murray said in address. "What is the meaning of your travels through our town? You don't look like you belong here."

"Ach, we do not, 'tis true," the creature replied. "We're leavin' home. Our path crosses yours, but only for a time."

Murray lifted an eyebrow. "What is your name?"

"Danube, sir." The creature pointed one of his long moss-colored fingers at the female and child beside him. "And this is my wife and our child as you can see. We're ogres from the swamplands over to the east."

"Why is it that you must leave your home? I would think you are better suited there than here," Murray said, frowning. He didn't mean to sound so off-putting, but the creatures had a swamp stench that he wanted away from.

"Evil is afoot, sir. We're not takin' any chances on being its dinner."

Murray frowned even more and crossed his arms. "Evil, you say? What sort of evil do you mean?"

The ogre grew tired of the questioning and waved back over his shoulder. "The sort you'uns has never seen. Excuse us, your honor, but we've got to get on. Evenin' might catch us in a dangerous place."

And he took his lady's hand, and they continued trudging across the main street of Muddentown and disappeared over the hill leading to Old Stony, the river.

That noontide, Tobias Hopesinger, who went by Toby, sat with his friends at the bar of a little tavern and inn called Headstrong, situated on the western side of Mudden. It was named after the proprietor, Bricard Headstrong, an award-winning fighter for his special headlock maneuver. Bric was a stout man with a barrel chest and muscular arms. Toby sometimes wished he had a body like Bric, but he wasn't willing to put in the time chopping wood or beating opponents in the ring.

The talk turned to the weather as it usually did.

"It's so hot, it's burning up the crops all around," Hopesinger said.

"No rain in weeks, and none seems like it's on the approach," Bric agreed, shaking his head. "Just like last year."

Constable Murray opened the door and entered, closing it quietly behind him. The talk died instantly. The lawman sat at a table near the door and waved to Bric to bring him a drink.

Another man, a thin, hollow-cheeked fellow who had booked a room for the night, turned from his place at the bar to address the other two. He kept his eyes downcast and his voice low. "Has anyone seen anything strange happen in these parts because of the drought?" he asked.

"Don't know what you mean by strange," Toby replied, his gaze appraising the stranger. "Unless you mean strange like dust devils spinning up with no wind to drive 'em."

"It sure is bad," another said. "No rain for weeks. Starting to affect the crops and everything else."

"Costs going to rise," Toby added.

The stranger nodded half to himself. "How long has it been dry like this?"

Toby looked at the other man. "What do you think, Chester? We ain't had no rain since right after the July Jubilee."

Chester nodded, giving the stranger the eye.

Bric looked the man over as well. The man wore a worn green cloak with a hood, even in this heat. His head was uncovered, and his graying tresses hung limply as though unwashed for a time. His clothing marked him as a traveler, dusty from trails unknown. Even his boots were scuffed and worn.

"What did you say your name was?" Bric asked.

The tall man flipped the hood to cover his head and most of his face. Then he stood. "I didn't."

He whirled around and in three quick strides was at the doorway, a staff tucked under his arm.

"He's about the strangest thing I've seen lately," Toby laughed as he took a heavy pull on his beer "Guess I should be going too."

Bric laughed with him and said, "Right. You don't want your girl to have to wait for you."

Toby made a face. "No, I don't. Gosh, I think I may need help reeling her in, Bric."

"She ain't said yes yet?"

Toby shook his head. He had been dating a young lady in town for some time, and everyone was mentioning to him how he needed to go on and propose. "I haven't exactly asked."

Chester cackled. "You need a potion or a spell or something. She's the most eligible woman in Mudden, and everybody knows you're the best man for her. Yet the two of you don't see eye-to-eye."

"Yeah, I guess something needs to move me into action, Chester. Maybe I'll go see that weird family over on the edge of town and get a love spell."

"The Ohs? Old man Oh died last year, I hear," Chester replied. He leaned back in his chair and gave them both a look filled with remorse. "Sure was sorry to hear it. They were nice folks even if they were weird."

"You havin' regrets over your part in the near lynching?" the constable asked, a curious look on his face.

Chester nodded. "Yeah. I mean they never did nothing to me. I was following Mister Wanderfoot's direction."

Bric poured Chester a whiskey and carried it over to him. "Wanderfoot's a rabble-rouser. He only cares about lining his own pockets."

Toby turned away from the pair and studied his own glass. The mob that attacked the Ohs' house years ago had been a terrible situation in

Mudden, and one that his own father had held him back from, fortunately. Otherwise, he would have been in the middle of it, wooden club and all.

Murray didn't say anything else, but sipped his drink.

Bric came back around the bar and wiped the top of it with a wet cloth. "Rabble-rousers rouse rabble, that's all."

Chester spoke so all could hear. "I didn't do anything that most of this town didn't do. That family was practicing magik. Everyone knew it. Killed their own kin, so they did. Sacrificed, sure as rain."

"Was no proof of that, Chester. They just up and left this part of Daegries, is how I remember it being told," Murray replied, voice reasonable.

The others remained mute. A shadow of someone moving away from the doorway fell across the room. Toby wondered if it was the stranger who had been asking about strange things in the drought.

Constable Murray plopped some coins down and went out of the bar, likely following the stranger. He was the law, after all.

Chapter One

Alyssa awoke in her bed, heart pounding and body drenched in sweat. The troubling dreams had started soon after her return with the scarf. Today, the dream of the drought-stricken farm and the shadowy portals stayed with her. Dark, swirling holes with humming air around them and a soft, eerie vibration within them haunted her day.

She held both of her hands over her face, remembering. As if still in her dream, the familiar whispering of faraway voices came to her ears. Terror and dread filled her, and she threw off the covers.

"I'll look to see if Granny is about," she said aloud, moving toward the kitchen. Her nightgown flapped in the quietness of the house as she went.

Pappy would be up and already at his potions pot. He was still a disembodied voice in a jack-in-the-box, but he could leave the confines of it in spirit and attend to things as he needed.

He also might have an idea on what her dream could mean.

The scarf, which had taken her on such a journey last year to find it and which she'd lovingly named Shadow, or Shad for short, floated right along behind her.

She padded barefoot into the kitchen, the wooden floor creaking in all of its usual spots. Granny stirred something steaming in her cauldron.

"What's that?" Alyssa asked with a yawn. "My stomach is grumbling."

Granny turned at her voice. With a heavy wooden spoon, she pointed at the chair. "Potato porridge. Sit down, and I'll fix you a bowl."

"How are you feeling?" Alyssa asked, watching Shad drape itself over a chair nearby.

Granny wasn't getting around too well these days. Her injured legs from the poison of the portal plants had healed, but the scars ached oftentimes, and Alyssa would rub them down with a salve made from rosemary and chamomile. It didn't seem to help the pain much, but it sure smelled good.

"I'm all right," Granny told her, turning back to the pot to scoop up a bowl of porridge.

"Where's Pappy?" Alyssa asked, taking the offered bowl. She sat at the wooden table in the chair where Shad had situated itself.

"At his desk, most likely. Reading some spell book or worse."

Granny's voice had a strange note to it, and Alyssa stared at her. "Why do you sound so annoyed about him?"

The old woman straightened and put a hand to the small of her back. She turned to Alyssa and handed another bowl to her. "That one's for me. And I ain't annoyed. I'm what they call 'quitting'. I've quit worrying about that old man. He's been dead once and might likely die again through his own actions if he ain't careful. I'm not going to grieve him again."

Alyssa dug into her porridge and stopped asking questions. Granny was in a mood, and to keep questioning her would only bring an avalanche of trouble. She didn't want to hear again about how bringing her Pappy back, even half-way, was a crime against nature, and likely to be the end of the world.

A few weeks later, autumn arrived with a hard wind. Alyssa patrolled in front of the portal plants on the farm. The green patch before her looked to be new ones coming up, although slowly. How they were growing with no fertile soil and no water, she didn't have a clue. She fretted and muttered. Shad lay nearby on the ground, sunning. The wind blew the scarf's ends, and it rippled.

A wide black hole like a cave-mouth gaped open behind the new growth, and she stared into it wondering when she would have another nightmare about it. Pappy had said she had an overactive imagination, and that was likely why she dreamed about such things.

In times past, she had stabbed into the hole with a long stick, but it seemed to end a few feet in, giving her arms a good jarring.

This day, as she stood there, a wave of cold air struck her. Peculiar, she thought. Something that would be nigh on impossible, and so out of place considering the hot drought they had been having for so long. *Cold air? In this heat, where would that come from?*

She peered into the hole, wished for a stick to poke it with now, and smelled a foul scent. Gagging, she staggered back, nearly tripping over Shad. She bit back a wave of nausea and pinched her nose closed.

Nothing in Daegries had that smell. Nothing on this side of the dirt anyway. *What has done gone and died in there?*

As she watched from a few feet away, the air before the hole wavered violently like the pattern of the world was being shaken. It made her dizzy to watch it. Shad wrapped around her legs protectively.

Then something flashed repeatedly inside the hole. A flash of color at the top, then the bottom and, to her great surprise, someone flew out of the hole and collapsed immediately upon landing.

Alyssa stared, blinked, and stared again.

"Edegast?" she whispered.

At first, Alyssa was so startled that she didn't understand what she had witnessed.

"Edegast!" she cried, hurrying to him.

He was out cold. His long green robe bore dirt and something that could only be described as worm vomit. It smelled as foul as the air she'd been breathing.

What on earth is he doing here? Her mind went back to their first meeting at Needlemount Castle where he had played magik games with her and turned the two men who were ruling over the castle into rats.

When she reached down to check if he was still breathing, he opened his eyes.

"Alyssa?" he said, recognizing her. "Oh, thank the gods and goddesses."

"Yes, it's me." She helped him sit up. His hair and beard were matted and dirty. "What in Daegries has happened? And even more, how did you come through that hole?"

"Get me to the house. I'll explain all."

Alyssa pulled Shad from her legs, and the scarf fluttered before them, waving itself like a cloth fan.

She yelled for Pappy and Granny as she neared the door. Her grandmother appeared first, stepping gingerly down the steps from the porch.

"For the love of Kasu, what's going on?" Granny asked, taking one of Edegast's arms.

Pappy, still a disembodied voice due to Alyssa's first spell, landed in a flowerpot on the porch and said, "Edegast the Green, that's what." His voice sounded hollow and echoed in the clay pot. "Better get some chamomile tea brewing, Gert."

Alyssa and her family spent the next hour waiting while the wizard got cleaned up. They were anxious to hear the story he bore. Shadow flopped onto the ground at Alyssa's feet.

After Edegast had finished and reappeared cleaner and fresher, he sipped two cups of tea and ate a thick chunk of Granny's cornbread. He finally sat back, peered at them, and cleared his throat to speak.

"Ahem. Now, I suspect you are waiting to hear what has transpired that would cause my sudden appearance from out of that dark hole."

Pappy, now in his toy jack-in-the-box, bounced up and down. Granny and Alyssa nodded.

"Very well, I shall tell it. And quite a shaky tale it is, too."

He leaned forward in his chair and clasped his hands together, taking a deep breath.

"Before you get started, sir," Granny interrupted. "Can I ask you somethin'?"

He tilted his head a bit and nodded.

"I ain't too sure about much, but I *do* know for certain them Mudden folks'll be out here snooping in every nook and cranny if they saw you. Did you go through town before hopping into that hole? Were you hiding in it?"

Edegast took a moment to analyze her question. "No, I was not hiding in the hole, Mrs. Oh. I was traveling the realm, using it as a mode to get from one point to another, like a horse and buggy only...well, needless to say, I did not come through town at all."

She nodded and sat back with arms folded. Alyssa had never seen her at a loss for words, but it seemed this time that was the case. The teen was quite amazed at Edegast's words.

Alyssa asked, "You were traveling through the portal? What evilment is this?"

"There have been many portals to appear in the world of Daegries, many more than the one here at your farm, I am afraid. These places are not meant for good and may even be a plan by the Dark Master to overtake different parts of the world. As I am living proof, it is certainly possible to journey to and from, albeit uncomfortable traveling, oftentimes perilous."

Alyssa looked at her granny, and Pappy grew still and silent. Even Shad lifted a corner to give attention to the wizard's words.

"Dark Master?" Alyssa asked finally. "That sounds like a scary story told around a campfire."

Edegast lifted an eyebrow. His emerald eyes remained placid although his body tensed. "Not a tale at all, Alyssa. It is so, as certain as I am sitting in your parlor. The Dark Master, also known as Hektor the Pale, has arisen again."

"How do you know this?" Pappy asked, his voice a small sound from inside the box. "He was banished long ago, even before my time."

"I have witnessed terrible things from inside that portal and from without. When I say he is alive and well, I mean I have witnessed his masses of followers and seen their dastardly acts. There is trouble in the world of Daegries, and we have to do something quickly."

Alyssa looked at Granny's face, usually mild. Now, it was lined and aged and worried.

"Pappy, what do you think?" Alyssa asked, because she couldn't see his face.

"I don't know what to think, gal. The Dark Master has been a dreaded name for so long, few even believe he ever existed. He did become quite the tale to scare children. Least, I was scared when I was a boy. Many a time my old Pap told me to mind my magik or else be taken by Hektor."

Edegast frowned.

Alyssa argued, "So, he was a menace back when you were a boy, and he is back again? That's a mighty long life, Pappy. What is he, an immortal, like the elves?"

Pappy answered, "Good question. What about it, wizard?"

Edegast shrugged. "We know some of his history, including his youth as a witch's apprentice. But he spent a long time under the mountains in training with the Ferryman, learning a trade of ferrying the dead down the river to the Dead Lands far beneath the mountains. The first Ferryman grew aged and died, so Hektor took on the task. He worked for the god of the dead, Nikola. It is utterly possible that the god gave him special longevity, as he was um... well, valuable."

He sipped his tea and said, "Nevertheless, he has been forgotten as a real, live creature of the dark. And even those who ought to remember, do not."

He paused to stare at the box where Pappy's voice resided.

"I see you are still but a voice in a box," he told the mage. "Perhaps you will allow me to fix that for you."

Pappy bounced up and down. "I'd like nothing better, Edegast. I've done all I'm skilled to do. Seems like Daegries needs me to be whole and hearty to help things along."

"Hm. Indeed, we need every available magik-user with their wits about them," the wizard muttered. "But, before we discuss even more unhappy tales, I will restore you to your rightful state."

This met with some trepidation from Granny. She sat forward and blinked a few times. "Beg pardon?"

"I said, my lady, I shall restore your husband to his humanly state. I need all the help from magik-users I can get."

She shook her head as if to clear it from a fog. "But... he's dead."

Edegast peered at her and gave a small chortle. "Not at all, my dear. He passed away from this plane, but he didn't make the final journey to the plane of Everlasting. He's quite literally sitting here with us. He simply needs his physical form."

Granny looked at Alyssa as if seeking some sort of indication that what the wizard was saying was a bit of poppycock.

"All this time, I thought he was just a ghost," Granny said, wringing her hands.

Edegast shook his head, his beard moving side to side.

Alyssa patted her hand. "Sorry, Gran, but I tried to tell you he wasn't a ghost. Now if anyone can fix Pappy, it'd be Edegast."

Shadow, still and quiet, floated over and slid onto Alyssa's lap.

Granny stood and paced. "Well, who are you anyway, Edegast? I never clapped eyes on you before. I wouldn't know if you was friend or foe. And you wouldn't be sittin' in my house if my grandchild didn't act friendly-like toward you."

Edegast smiled. "Yes, well, you have been most proper and kind toward me, Mrs. Oh. I appreciate all of your ministrations on my behalf as I have been—" He looked down at his clothes. "Just shy of a scuffle with death. I am Edegast the Green, from the Snowclids. Knowledge Hall to be exact. Do you know of this place?"

She shook her head, seeming even more confused.

"It is the seat of learning in the world of Daegries. The wizards have long kept the Books of Knowledge and have been tasked with keeping them safe."

She moved back to her seat and sat heavily. "Wizards? Well, I'm sure you're a smart fella."

He chuckled and waved to Alyssa. "Come along, Lady Oh. Let us find the book with which to bring Pappy back to full power." He collected the jack-in-the-box on his way past.

They left the room but not before Alyssa saw her Granny Gert cover her face with her apron in dismay. Alyssa waved Shad to come along, and the scarf followed obediently.

Alyssa, quiet as a mouse, stood outside Pappy's tiny office. He had a wall of books on one side and a desk jammed into the far corner. She stood beside the doorway, leaning in.

Edegast set the jack-in-the-box in the desk chair and stood behind it. Shad floated onto a bookshelf and curled around and around until it made a ball.

"So, Sir Oh, is that tome given to you by Trudor still about?" Edegast asked.

"Yes, but I ain't never figured out how to use it," Pappy told him. "Else I'd be all the way here by now."

"That's quite all right. I know what to do." The robed man turned to Alyssa. "Where is it?"

She frowned. "Why do you think I have it?"

"Forgive me," Edegast drawled. "I *assumed* you had it. You did perform a spell from it, correct?"

She ducked her head a little. It wasn't a good idea to sass a wizard. She replied in a small voice, "Well, yes, but that was ever so long ago. I gave it back to Pappy."

The jack-in-the-box bounced up and down.

"Very well, Sir Oh. Please collect it for me."

The springs in the toy box pinged loudly, and it immediately went still. Pappy Oh had left the box. Shad lifted a corner of cloth to wave toward a shelf above giving the invisible man directions to it.

The book eased out of the slot where it was situated and floated to the desk. Pappy could do a lot of things out of the box, but inside of it, he was just a voice.

Pappy turned pages until he finally found the one he wanted. The toy box rattled and shook as he reentered it, and Pappy said, "Here 'tis. And here's the spell, far as I can tell."

Edegast nodded and bent over the book.

Pappy said, "I only figured out what to do wrong, Edegast. Alyssa used blood to work the spell, accidentally enough, true. But past that, couldn't ever figure anything out that made the spell go."

"I will need a few moments to decipher this. Alyssa, would you be so good as to bring me more of your grandmother's tea?" Edegast asked, turning toward her with a smile.

She nodded and backed away heading for the kitchen. Granny stood at the kitchen window, lost in thought.

"Gran, can I have more tea for our guest?" Alyssa asked.

She waved at the kettle sitting on the block of wood beside the fire. "You'll need to make fresh."

While Alyssa scooped tea leaves into the pot and added water from a nearby porcelain pitcher, she watched Granny closely.

"Granny, are you okay? You seem so distant and quiet."

The old woman turned toward her and crossed her arms. "This wizard coming here bodes ill all around, Lys. He shouldn't have done it. And coming through that hole? Somethin' is plain wrong with this situation. Far as we know, he could be someone posing as this Edegast fellow."

Alyssa's always active imagination blossomed.

"Oh. I'm not certain, Gran. I mean, he *looks* like Edegast. Even sounds like him, too. But with magik, anything is possible, I reckon. I'll double-check to make sure he is who he says he is."

She pushed the metal flange back over the fire and headed to where she'd left the men. *How does one tell if a wizard is who he says he is?* She didn't know, but surely, she would be able to tell, especially since she'd been a victim of his magik before.

Remembering this tidbit, she eased up to the doorway and allowed her seeking spell, without any glow, to wander the room. Soon, it found the wizard's magik and formed a silent circle over his head that appeared to her as a blurred vision.

Yep, that's Edegast. She recalled her magik with a tiny finger wave, and it flew to her.

Alyssa had spent a long time perfecting her own magik since she'd last seen the wizard. Maybe she'd have time to show him some of what she had learned. The Grim was partly responsible, as she had spent some time poring over it, trying out different spells with what she could already do.

Shad was still present in the room, which gave her a little comfort but, before she could even cross the threshold, a loud bang issued forth, and a bright orange light nearly blinded her.

"Pappy!" Alyssa screamed, feeling a cold wind blow over her. "Pappy!"

Granny Gert arrived at her elbow, shock on her face. "What in Daegries has happened?"

Together they inched forward, until finally they could see Shad twisting and sending the smoke out of the small room. Soon, both Edegast and Pappy reappeared, coughing.

"By the great goat's beard, you did it!" Pappy shouted, stepping lively. His hair and beard were snowy white and matched his bushy eyebrows perfectly. Same twinkling blue eyes, same thin gaunt frame. He patted himself all over, happiness puffing his cheeks out. Same old Pappy.

Then, his eyes welled with tears, and Alyssa wasn't sure if it was from smoke or something else. The old mage hurried over to Granny and hugged her close to him. "I'm here now, Gert. I'm back."

Alyssa grinned like a fool and shook his sleeve to reassure herself he was there. His clothing was exactly like when she had last seen him lying in his pine box, hands folded neatly over his middle. He looked almost as he had in life before. A bit grayer in his skin perhaps, but she was happy with that as long as he was alive.

Alyssa caught Edegast's eye as he peered closely at her grateful grandfather, and her smiled faded. The wizard shook his head and tugged his beard, absently. She walked to him, never letting her gaze fall.

"What is it?" she asked, quietly. "What's wrong?"

He tilted his head toward the kitchen. "Let's make that tea and let them get reunited properly."

Alyssa took a deep breath and followed him. Edegast patted Pappy's shoulder as he passed.

Once out of earshot, she grabbed heavy towels and pulled the flange away from the fire, removed the tea pot, and set it on a slab of wood that Granny had there for this purpose. "What about that spell are you afraid of?" she asked the wizard as she poured the tea. "I can see you ain't happy with the results."

She handed him the cup, and he thanked her before sitting heavily on a nearby chair. The room was stuffy from the heat of the fireplace, so Edegast pushed the sleeves of his robe out of the way.

"It is not that I am unhappy with the results," he said, looking into his cup. "It is more that I am unhappy the spell worked so well."

Confusion flooded Alyssa's mind. "What? I... why would you be unhappy about *that*? Didn't you perform the spell for success? I'm confused."

Edegast peered across the small house and saw Granny and Pappy talking together in the tiny room where Pappy worked his spells.

"No, I am quite pleased that your grandfather has returned to a full form at last; do not mistake me. It is a matter of the book he pulled down and the spell I used. The result may well change our world forever." Here, he took time to sip his cooling tea before going on. "In fact, Alyssa, the time has come to take the Grim and return it to Knowledge Hall for certain. The spell's power has made doing otherwise impossible."

"Return it? What do you mean?" She looked at him with a frown furrowing her brow. "Ain't that Pappy's book?"

"Not exactly. Many years ago, when we were just boys, Trudor, a great white wizard, gave it to him with instructions to keep it safe. I am not sure if an end date was placed with your grandfather, but since he still has it, perhaps not."

"Pappy never told me about any time that it was to be returned," Alyssa admitted.

"At any rate, I believe that Hektor has returned. In fact, his allegiances are in such numbers that every person in this world should be alert and in arms. The Grim would be safer now with the wizards in a fortified keep than here," Edegast said.

Alyssa felt her stomach twist. What was he saying? Her grandparents came into the room to join them for tea. For a while, Alyssa stayed busy pouring tea and offering biscuits that had been made that morning.

"We'll need a regular feast this evening," Granny said, smiling at Pappy. "It's high time we celebrated."

"Don't know why you've waited so long," Pappy said, patting her arm.

"Because it's hard to feel much for a voice that comes out of a toy box, that's why. It wasn't like you were here. It was real hard, is all," Granny said. "I'd still like to hear how that spell worked. I gave it the once over myself. Not like I understand the old language, but I tried."

"Another time perhaps," Edegast told her, standing. "For now, I believe Pappy should have a lot of rest, and some solid food. How long has it been since you ate?" he asked Pappy.

Pappy flashed a toothless grin. "Too long, if I'm bein' honest."

Edegast nodded with a smile. "Then that's an excellent place to start."

The wizard waited for the scarf to gather itself together and move to Alyssa's shoulder. "I will be taking my leave of you for now. I have other matters to attend to, but it might be prudent to remain out of sight, Sir Oh. You do not want the townsfolk to talk."

This made the family all look at each other with trepidation. How would they explain Pappy's sudden reappearance? How would they keep him hidden from their hired hand, Tony? Things shifted in the atmosphere of the Oh household. A resurrected Pappy would be unwanted excitement around Mudden.

The wizard moved toward the door. Alyssa walked him out and stood on the wide porch with the scarf draped over her shoulders. "You ain't going back into that hole, I hope."

He shook his head and pulled his robes tighter against the wind. "No. And I am not gone, really. I will speak to you again soon. Watch for me. Not at the hole, no." It was like he was half-talking to her, and half-talking to himself. He pulled his hood up over his head and strode

into the leftmost path, disappearing into the tangle of dying summer
flowers lining Granny's bower.

Chapter Two

Barely a month had passed when the town of Mudden flared with whispering.

Ladies gathered at their clotheslines to gossip, and menfolk chattered over a pint in the tavern; the strange family on the outskirts of town were once again doing things that warranted hushed conversation. The once-dead old man, Pappy Oh, had been seen hoeing a row in his garden. That was all it took for the townsfolk to rise up.

Murray, the constable, had to break up more than one fight over who would go out to the Oh farm and set them "straight" once again. He was pretty tired of all of the hullabaloo. It was bad enough that strangers were traipsing all across Mudden. Now this.

There was no mistaking the old man had indeed reappeared at the farm, though. It was validated by Tony, their hired hand. A solid member of Mudden society and a deacon at the local church, Tony would never lie.

The townsfolk were addled and not sure what to do with the news.

"Here, now," Murray scolded a pair of boys, dirty from rolling in the mud on Main Street. "Stop that this instant, or I'll take you home and let your mamas tend to you. Stop it, you hear?"

The boys did indeed hear and pulled away, red-faced. One had a bloody nose, and the other's shirt was torn. Murray brushed at the back of their clothes, knowing full well their mamas would be taking a switch to them over their antics.

"He said that the old man on the edge of town was going to come and get me," one said, wiping at tears.

"Did not!" yelled the other.

Murray shushed them, and right before he was going to give them a strong talking to, a hooded stranger crept down the street on the other side. The figure stayed in the shade of the buildings, his face averted. His tall frame moved easily, as though he was used to travel. The walking stick he carried bore his heavy weight as he turned the corner.

Three jaws fell slack at the shock of seeing him, a character entirely out of place in Mudden.

Murray left the boys with a command to stay put and not move. He hurried to the other side of the street and paused to look down the alley where the stranger had gone. But when he got there, the stranger had vanished into thin air. The boys joined him as their curiosity outweighed his command to stay in place.

"Where'd he go?" they asked in unison.

"Don't rightly know, but he looks suspicious wearing that long cloak in all this heat." He mopped his brow and shooed the boys away. "Go on home now. And not a word to your pa either!"

They muttered something and left.

He watched them trudge up the dusty street toward their homes. Why did that stranger seem so familiar? He mopped his brow again and tried to remember where he had seen such a spectacle. *This infernal drought! A man can't even think a good thought these days.* He gave up his pondering and turned into Headstrong.

"Get me a Sass," he told Bricard, who stood behind the bar.

The proprietor did as asked and gave Murray a long look as he handed him the amber liquid. "You look like you seen a ghost, Murray."

"Worse. More strangers crossing Mudden streets. This one looked like trouble."

"Why?" Bric's broad face went slack.

"Don't recall much, but think I've seen him before. Wearing a cape in this heat and drought, strode right purposefully into an alley." Murray stopped to wipe his sweaty brow.

"An alley? What happened then?" Bric asked.

"Well, that's the gold nugget question. He just up and disappeared."

Bric whistled low. "Uh oh. Yep, strangers doing strange things. Was he like that fella here the other day when you stopped in? Remember him?"

Murray's eyes narrowed. "Hm. Yes, I do, actually. Has he been back?"

"Possibly. I don't watch every patron who sits at my bar," Bric said with a shrug, turning away.

Why was Bric protecting the stranger? Bric always remembered his customers. It was almost an obsession. Murray drained his glass and slapped a wooden coin down on the bar. "Here, take this as down payment on my account. I'm worrying so much over this, I'll be back for more, I'm sure. Seems to settle my nerves." The constable shook his head and turned to leave.

Bric palmed the coin and overheard him mutter, "Guess it's about time to call on the Ohs." Murray turned to Bric and asked, "You hear the talk about the old man coming back to life?"

Bric shook his head. "Lots of talk goes around this town, Murray."

Constable Murray tromped out of the tavern leaving Bric to his bar rag and dirty mugs.

Lots of talk goes around this town.

The constable stood outside Headstrong frowning up at the glowering sun. "Go on, will ya? We're sick of sun and heat and no rain. You're bringing folks here that don't belong." He allowed his gaze to travel down the road toward the outskirts of town. "Making folks suspicious-like and liars, too."

As evening fell, Alyssa went outside to sit on the porch and listen to the frogs begging for rain. Their loud *ribbit, ribbit* blended into the noisy sounds of the crickets and other insects as they tuned up for their nightly serenade under the deepening purple sky.

It soothed Alyssa, who had listened to her grandparents sniping with each other most of the day. This was nothing new. They had always been grumpy. Pappy had finally retired to his study, and Granny had gone to tidy up the bedroom. Alyssa heard no sounds from there and assumed the old woman had dropped off to sleep.

Sleep would not come for Alyssa for some time, though. She still tried to understand the strange appearance of Edegast, and the dreaded tale that he would be back soon to finish. His hint about a dark master and desperate times had not landed in a fertile field. She didn't know what he was talking about.

"There's more to that wizard than he's letting on," she muttered to the nightfall around her. "That I do know."

"There always is," a deep voice replied from the direction of the sunflower patch.

Alyssa gripped the arms of the rocking chair, and she inhaled sharply. Shadow uncurled from where it had wrapped around her shoulders, and each of its woven ends stood up in attention like the antennae on a moth.

Edegast's face floated in the darkness as he snapped his fingers and put a flame to his rather ornate pipe. He strode up the steps and sat beside her on the other rocking chair of the porch, an aromatic stream of smoke wafting past Alyssa's nose.

"Edegast," Alyssa said, exhaling. "You're the master of surprises these days." Shad, the scarf, collapsed from her shoulders into her lap like a languid cat.

"I told you I would return."

"Where have you been?"

"Seeking answers."

"I'm at a bit of a disadvantage here. I don't even know the questions." Alyssa patted Shad nervously.

"Since you already believe that there is more to me than I am telling you, may I tell you a story? Call it a history lesson, if you will."

She nodded and then, aware that he might not see it in the darkness, said, "Yes. Of course."

He drew on his pipe. "Well," he said, exhaling. "It happens like this."

Alyssa leaned her head back against the rocking chair and listened.

"Long ago, when the World was young and wild, and before Mudden was even built, there was a strong river that flowed under the mountains, away up in the Heightlands."

Alyssa nodded and thought of the stream she'd followed to find the Haldor last year.

"The river flowed right under the mountains and carved out a whole place where inhabitants could live."

"The Haldor?" Alyssa guessed.

He puffed on his pipe. "Yes. The Haldor. But even they were unaware how far the river flowed. It carved itself even deeper down and under the mountains than they had explored, and that is something of note. Truly, few alive ever knew of its depth because the way to reach such a place was very treacherous indeed."

"Then how did you learn of it?" Alyssa sat forward, focused intently.

"Oh, I discovered the length and depth of it through maps that are housed at Knowledge Hall, not from anyone in my association. No, the discovery was made by one lone man who lived beneath the mountain. And he likely created the maps, if I am being honest. He was a businessman of a sort, named Hektor. He worked for the Haldor, ferrying their dead across the river and down to the Underworld. And a foul business it was, too."

Here, Alyssa relaxed. Edegast had told her and her grandparents part of this tale already. She released the scarf until it settled onto the back of the chair.

"That's an important job, I suspect. Why would that be considered foul? Doesn't everyone have to bury their dead?" Her mind quickly flitted to the crude burying spot they'd carved out for Pappy. Sad for sure, but not foul. Not like draining old Mrs. Slumtuggle's boil. That was nasty and foul.

Edegast turned toward her and took in a deep breath. "Foul is the first word that came to mind. If the old tales are to be believed, it was not only foul, but it was also considered unnatural. He had learned many things from the witch with whom he had apprenticed, including necromancy. It is a foul thing to play with the dead and bottle their spirits, only to bring them to life again as a creature that you can be in control of. He is called the Dark Master for a reason."

"Oh," Alyssa said in a small voice.

Edegast continued. "He had a longboat, and he piled the Haldor dead into it and floated them to the mouth of... well, let us call it the Dead Lands. Giving things a name can give them power. In fact, I will not speak *his* name again after tonight. I suggest you do likewise."

Alyssa didn't comment. Wizards had their ways, she knew. Besides, she had told the same thing to Lord Bryon's mother, Pianna, last year. Names were powerful. Even the names of places.

With an effort to get them back on a subject that she could speak to, she said, "That river was only a trickle when I saw it. Wasn't special at all."

"Yes, well, we will see about its uniqueness momentarily," he continued. He replaced his now-cooled pipe inside his cloak.

"Then what happened?" she asked, curiosity making her wiggle her foot.

"The Dead Lands are a place where the god of the dead accepted the Haldor and gave them their eternal resting place. Hektor, with his high intelligence and knowledge of magik, was only allowed so far into the Dead Lands and no farther. Hektor was never satisfied with his lot. He wanted more. He wanted to be the god of the Dead Lands. He thought Nikola was doing a poor job of running things, and Hektor brought an army against him in an attempt to wrest power away."

Now Alyssa leaned forward, fear creeping up her chest. Nikola, the Underworld God. She had heard his name all of her life. "Was this army made from... the dead?"

Edegast blew out a breath he had been holding. "Yes. A terrible ghastly army it was."

"Did he... did he... succeed?" She lifted her hand to her mouth afraid to speak the words.

"No. Nikola was too powerful and struck the dead army into the plane of Everlastingness. He also banished Hektor for three hundred years to the Beyonders past the Blighted Vale. He was not allowed to set foot on the land of the Greater Daegries. And Nikola made it his business to keep that edict enforced. He set guards at the border of the Beyonders and the Vale."

"That would slow him down a mite, I guess," Alyssa said, sitting back again.

He paused, listening to the hushed voices of the frogs and crickets. Finally, he continued, "Not really. It only made Hektor craftier. He spent the years practicing his magik and writing it down in his grimoire. And plotting his revenge."

"What was his plan? He wanted to take over the Underworld?" Alyssa asked, surprise lining her words. "The Dead Lands?"

Edegast nodded. "Yes. He intended to find a way to imprison the god, Nikola, and take over. But as the years have gone by, Hektor has been careless. In his mind, he gained power when he raised an army against Nikola and almost succeeded. But in truth, he only made Nikola reinforce his realm, go deeper into hiding from this world. When word reached Hektor that he would not again have a chance to act against the god, he went berserk. It is our belief that he lost his mind then, what small amount of it that remained."

Alyssa sat back and shivered a little. "Whose word? Who would have traveled to the Beyonders to tell him such a thing? Nobody would go there on purpose, Edegast."

"True, not on purpose. But this visitor was given a special dispensation. From Nikola. Especially to warn Hektor."

Alyssa lifted a brow. She couldn't imagine anyone who would have been allowed to get near the Dead Lands and a god, and then be *sent* to such a terrible place as the Beyonders. "Who?"

Edegast stood and looked out into the darkness. "The Witch who had raised Hektor. She was brought to Nikola, inanimate. But she was only in a state of extended sleep, under a self-administered spell to get her inside the Dead Lands. She wanted to speak to Nikola to beg for Hektor's return."

"And I suspect that is what happened," Alyssa said, touching the scarf draped over the chair.

"Yes. And her brief begging concluded with Nikola's threat to end her life and freedom if she did not do his bidding."

"What did he want from the witch?" Alyssa frowned.

"For her to take a message to Hektor. That there would be no escape from the Dead Lands if the ferryman didn't stop his planning and plotting. Nikola would see to it that Hektor remained there forever."

"So, the person responsible for raising Hektor to manhood was the one to deliver the news that he dreaded hearing." Alyssa digested the information out loud. "How did he react?"

Edegast made a sound of derision. "Very poorly, I am afraid. Hektor killed the witch. With his bare hands. Throttled the life from her and sent her body back to Nikola with a message of his own: free him, and he would trouble the god no more."

The evening sounds grew quiet around them as they both considered this.

Finally, Alyssa whispered, "That sounds like Hektor was planning something else."

"Yes. He wanted to be a Revenant, brought back from the abyss. Nikola could have given Hektor his wish, of course. He is a god, after all. But Hektor begged every day, to no avail. Nikola made it plain that his imprisonment, the three hundred years, would allow an entire age to pass before he returned and that perhaps he would change his ways."

"Is he an Elf, Edegast? He has lived a long time. A three-hundred-year imprisonment is far beyond what normal creatures live."

The wizard strode to the far end of the porch and listened. "No, he is not an Elf. But the tale isn't finished yet."

She nodded. "What are you listening for?"

"Spies. The wise ones only want this news shared with those who have to know."

"Then tell me, and let's be done. I'm sure I won't sleep this night," she said with a shiver.

He returned to his seat and turned to her, taking her hands. "The witch, fearing Hektor, as well she should have," Edegast said, "created an elixir that would bring a person back to life after being inanimate. She had it with her when she faced Hektor, and he killed her for it."

"So, he can't die?" Alyssa asked, alarm in her voice. While she didn't want her grandparents to ever die, not again, ever, this seemed like evilment of the worst kind.

"This was why I have been all over the realm of Daegries seeking answers. The only one who would have known the contents of the elixir was the witch. Now that time has passed, the god, Nikola, has created a veil over his dominion so that no one will ever be able to find him again. The only way to meet the Underworld God is literally to die. No one knows where the elixir is or even if it still exists. But the ingredients to the elixir and the spell to make it *are* in the Grim. We do not want that spread across the land. Can you imagine how many people would love to live again after death?"

Alyssa didn't know what to say, so she stared at Edegast. He released her hands and stood, listening.

"There is more, but I will tell it another time," he said, lifting his hood and taking the first step off the porch.

Alyssa heard someone stirring within the house. Either Pappy or Granny would be looking for her soon. Edegast stepped away, closer to the darkness from where he had come.

"You're not getting away as easy as all that," she whispered loudly to the tall wizard. "I want the rest of this story, and I have a few questions for you, too."

"Never fear, Alyssa, I am compelled and bound to tell it to you. I will return by and by."

And with that, he disappeared into the stillness of night beyond. When he was gone, the frogs began their noisy calls once again and the crickets chirped as loudly as ever.

Granny peered out at her. "Who are you sitting out there with?"

"Nobody, Granny. In fact, I'm about to come in and go to bed myself. What are you doing up?"

"Needed a nip of water. Come on in here, gal. Shut that door now. Don't let the bugs in."

Alyssa did as Granny asked. She paused in closing the door to the outside world and looked out at the night. She felt Edegast's presence. He was still out there; she was sure of it. But at least the wildlife seemed to think he was gone. The strange tale of Hektor the Pale stayed with her, though.

In a week or so, Edegast returned. He came in the heat of the afternoon, while Alyssa tried to train the scarf to allow her to ride it. Shad didn't seem to care for being called on to be a flying carpet and threw her off.

Disheveled and hot, Alyssa stood frowning at her magik scarf, trying to decide what to do, when Edegast strode up from the maze side of the farm.

"Edegast?" Her eyes beheld him, but her mind was still struggling with making the scarf behave.

"Yes," he said as he came toward her. "It is I. Come now, Shadow, what seems to be the trouble?"

The scarf flew to the wizard and perched on his shoulder.

"It's being very picky and won't let me to ride on it like a flying carpet."

Edegast's eyes twinkled beneath his bushy brows. "I daresay it does not wish to be a bird of prey."

Breathing heavily, Alyssa answered, "Of course not. Doesn't mean I won't convince it, though."

Edegast shooed the scarf away, and it fell across Alyssa's shoulders as sweetly as a kitten.

"Where have you been?" she asked the wizard.

"There and back again," he said, simply. "To Knowledge Hall, and back again. To here."

She didn't ask him how he had accomplished the feat so quickly. It was a terribly long way to the Snowclids. At least he appeared clean and not covered in refuse from the portal hole. Instead, she asked, "Did you find out more about the... um... *you know*?"

"Perhaps," Edegast answered. "Let us go within the house and speak."

He waved for Alyssa and Shad to go before him. They entered the Ohs' humble abode through the kitchen door. Pappy sat reading at the table, and Granny peeled the first of their fall apples into a big bowl.

Granny Gert stopped working and peered up at the wizard. "You're back," she said without any enthusiasm.

"Yes. On a matter of much importance. Might I possibly speak to you and our dear Pappy?"

She shrugged and set aside the knife and apple she had been working with. Pappy closed his book and carried it with him. They all went into the living room and sat.

"Sir Oh," Edegast began. "Might you have time to pack up the Grim for us? I intend to take it back to Knowledge Hall."

"What for?" Pappy asked, frowning. "I'm supposed to keep it here, safe and hidden. Nobody even knew it was around until the last year or so. I've done a good job, if I do say so."

"Oh, yes, my dear man. There is no question as to your care of our revered tome. The Grim is in high demand though, and it has been decided to send it home."

"High demand by who?" Pappy asked.

Here, the wizard tugged at his beard and looked at the floor. "By powers higher than I. The Grim must go North."

Alyssa recognized her pappy's stubborn look. His eyes narrowed, and his chin jutted out. "Don't get surly now," she told him. "Edegast has a bit of trouble on his hands."

"Be that as it may," Pappy said, setting his book aside and brushing at his tunic. "I've been told to keep that book safe all these years. I ain't letting it go without a good reason, even to a wizard."

Edegast took a deep breath and pointed at Shad. "Come here, my good friend."

The scarf obeyed.

"You may be the only magik item in this house that can help me to illustrate this problem." The wizard waved at the scarf. "Play dead," he commanded.

Shad flipped into the air in a dynamic twirl before falling into a dramatic puddle of follygrass cloth.

Alyssa stifled a giggle. Shad could playact quite well.

"I shall pick up where I left off telling this tale last time. Sometime in the last century, the Dark Master was freed from his imprisonment."

Alyssa raised an eyebrow. "You mean that three hundred years have already passed? That was ancient history you were telling me the other night then?"

He nodded. "It is a long, and convoluted tale, and there is much I do not know. I am telling you what I have found, and much of it is supposition. No one knew when the three hundred years started, so no one knew when it would expire, and preparing for it became something of a bedtime story. There is no way to validate any of it, so the only part I know to be true is this part, as my own father has told it to me."

The three people gathered before him leaned forward, listening intently.

"He was found wandering under the mountain where he used to ferry the dead. No doubt searching for the dominion of Nikola, but if you remember, Alyssa, Nikola has hidden his dominion. The Haldor found the Dark Master utterly emaciated and thought he was dead. They brought him to the wizards at Knowledge Hall to bury him in the catacombs beneath our castle."

"So that's how you folks came to get the Grim?" Granny asked. "He had it with him all along?"

Edegast nodded.

"Now, why would anyone bother with that rascal? He tainted a lot of Daegries with his dangerous foolishness," Pappy said. "Shoulda let him rot right there. That Dead God woulda took care of him right proper."

Edegast shrugged. "It was his last wish. He asked to be buried beneath Knowledge Hall and also that a Funerial be summoned to take him to his final resting place."

"Funerial? What's that?" Granny asked. Her eyes widened. "Seems like I might have heard of one of those at some time or other."

"Very likely, Lady Oh. It is a common accompaniment for the dead. Hektor was well known to the Funerials. He worked as a ferryman for the dead, remember. Now we know that he can control the dead, as well." At that, Edegast let out a worried sigh.

Alyssa motioned for Edegast to tell them more. "I'm getting gray over here, Edegast. What happened?"

"The wizards, along with the Haldor, could not refuse his final wishes, and so the Dark Master summoned a Funerial with his final breath. One appeared, verified along with us that no life remained. We felt it was appropriate to allow the Funerial to take the remains, as that is proper."

"Then what?" Alyssa asked, getting annoyed.

"This is where our story gets as murky as the Ogre's swamp."

Three sets of questioning eyes stared.

"The Dark Master can summon undead minions to do his bidding, we've discovered."

"What sort of dark magik?" Alyssa asked, blinking.

"A form that would enable the Funerial to take the body and disappear."

A few seconds passed as Shadow scurried behind the wall and disappeared, still playing the part.

"What about that elixir you were telling me about? Why didn't he just take that?" Alyssa asked, nerves twanging.

"I will get to that by and by. Firstly, he is alive. We know this because he has been seen by the Haldor wandering around, cloaked like a wizard. And secondly, concerning the elixir, the Grim, written by the Dark Master's own hand, holds details which explain how to bring someone back from the other side. You saw that yourself in the spell you used," Edegast told her.

"Thirdly, we know that the witch had the elixir. She was known in her part of the world for tinctures; it would be more than possible. She had to have taught him a few things. At least before he killed her."

Alyssa rubbed her arms. This tale was getting darker by the minute.

Edegast turned to Granny Gert. "Granny, how would you use an elixir if you had one, but only one?"

A little shocked, she dropped her gaze and thought a moment. Then she lifted her eyes and looked directly at the wizard. "I'd use magik to figure out the ingredients if I didn't know them. You only need a drop of an elixir to bring out the spell."

"Most excellent, my lady. The Dark Master did exactly that, we believe. It only took a drop of the liquid to return him to this plane. He didn't need the whole bottle. He was in a state of lifelessness, under a spell, as the witch had been. The spell was effective enough to fool the god of the Underworld, so we can assume it would have fooled members of the Wise, as well. Exacerbated by the Funerial's insistence that there remained no life..." he said with a shrug.

"But how did he get that drop of the elixir to come turn the spell around?" Granny asked.

"We can only assume the Funerial gave it to him, but perhaps it was someone else after they disappeared. Nevertheless, he is alive now."

"So, now what? He's back. But what does that mean exactly?" Alyssa asked, a little confused.

Here, Edegast sat back and placed his hands on his thighs. It seemed like his mind was made up about something.

"He is no fool. He studied forbidden texts while working for the underworld god. He experimented while banished. Something happened during that time that made him now a being of immense power but cursed with an eternal, dead existence. He is back, but not in his full form, just as Pappy was only halfway here, so is he."

Pappy straightened in his seat, rubbing his face with both hands. Finally, he said, "So, that's why Alyssa could bring me back at least partly. We ain't got the elixir, but the magik in that book was enough to get things started."

"Then how did you get Pappy back here?" Granny asked, suspiciously. "Did you give him some of that elixir?"

Edegast motioned for Shadow to return to the room. "No. Magik doesn't exactly work like that. Once magik is released, it can evolve and change. The spell that Alyssa released to bring Pappy back only needed one thing to be complete, and it was no elixir. Once I realized that, bringing him all the way back to here and now was simple."

They waited as Shadow returned to Alyssa's shoulder.

"The antidote had to be a magik equally as powerful, but for good. White magik against dark."

The group broke into exclamations, and questions flowed like melted ice.

"What did you do in Pappy's room? What magik exists in this house that would fulfill that part?" Alyssa said, speaking over the others.

Her grandparents quieted to hear Edegast's answer. "The Grim's spell could bring him partially back, but the magik in your scarf, Alyssa, was more powerful than even the elixir."

They all eyed Shadow, and a shiver went through it, ruffling the follygrass from end to end.

Edegast's voice faded as he mused aloud. "The Dark Master is filled with hatred now that he is back in some form. He plans to seek revenge on those who benefitted from his banishment. If Hektor could reach Nikola, he would make him a victim, of course. And especially the Haldors, and I suspect the wizards, as well."

"How can he be so dangerous when he isn't even fully here?" Alyssa asked.

"Right at this time, he is gathering power and followers even as a half-alive. Enough so that when he finds the Grim, he will be able to take the book and use it with a new elixir to perform a grand ritual that will merge the Dead Lands with the living world of Daegries, ensuring his reign of terror lasts forever. If that should be allowed to happen, then the living will become food for the dead."

There was no sound inside of the Oh house. The three family members sat silently, and every one of them jumped when Shadow sat up and floated through the air, out of the living room, and into Pappy's study. Alyssa could see it wrap itself gently around the still open Grim.

Chapter Three

Alyssa swallowed... and swallowed again. Her mind had frozen shut.

"So, if the Grim has the spell that he needs then I suspect that the Grim is mighty important," Pappy said, finally.

"Well, take it then," Granny Gert said with a wave of her hand. "Get it back to where it came from before we get saddled with some otherworldly company huntin' for it."

"You'll have to take me with you," Pappy said, lowering his gaze. "I was tasked with the accursed thing. I'll be responsible all the way through to the end."

"Over both of our dead bodies!" Granny exclaimed. "You ain't going nowhere without me!"

Edegast put his hand up for silence. The elderly couple growled a bit longer and cast mean looks at each other.

Finally, the wizard said, "No. Neither of you will be able to go with the Grim. Pappy Oh, you are too weak to make such a journey. And Granny, you are needed here to care for him."

Alyssa met Edegast's eyes. The log in the fire rolled over and shot out a stream of sparks hissing loudly.

"I'll take it back. If you will allow me, that is," Edegast said.

Alyssa collected the tome from the other room and tried to hand it to him, but the scarf behaved badly. It curled around the Grim protectively.

"Shadow, now you let loose of this book, you hear?" Alyssa commanded. "Edegast has to take it back home."

The scarf shivered all over and wrapped even tighter.

Alyssa pried the closest edge up and tried to wrest the book free. A tug-of-war ensued until Alyssa threatened the scarf with destruction. Shadow finally, slowly, released it.

"Don't be so onery," Alyssa said. "This book belongs to the wizards, really, and they have a right to have it back."

She hefted the heavy book in her hand and held it out on one palm, offering it to Edegast.

The wizard had remained silent throughout the incident, but now he hesitated, took a deep breath, and grasped the book by the spine.

The book twisted out of Edegast's grasp and fell from Alyssa's hand. Shadow slid down in time to catch it, almost as if it was a planned maneuver.

Edegast let out his breath in a long sigh and reached to collect the book from where it settled onto the scarf.

When he reached for it, Shadow wrapped around it and refused to let him have it.

"Well," the wizard said with a huff. "Apparently, the scarf is not going to allow me to take it."

Embarrassed, Alyssa tried to convince Shadow to release the book, but it refused resolutely. This time no amount of threats could affect the scarf's decision.

Pappy Oh tried to take the book, followed by Granny Gert. No one could get the book from the scarf.

Finally, Edegast told them to stop. "Shadow is not being petulant. It is truly protecting the Grimoire. There is nothing more that can be done. Shadow will go with me as the book's protector."

Alyssa cried out and flung herself over the scarf and book. "No! Edegast, you can't take my scarf. You have to figure out another way."

He tugged at his robes, amusement lighting his eyes. "You could go with us."

"Me?" she asked, looking up at him.

Edegast nodded. "You are able-bodied, and our leader has said he wants to meet with you and to witness Shadow. It will be a dangerous journey, but a necessary one."

In a few moments, the scarf floated back, unwrapping around the book and allowed Alyssa to pick it up.

"Guess I have to go now. This dang book and its keeper won't let no one else handle it."

The scarf wrapped around her arm.

"Shadow, release me this minute. You know I ain't going off without you."

Shadow relaxed and slid into her lap once more.

No one spoke for a while. Finally, Granny stood and wandered into the kitchen. Alyssa could hear her quiet sobs. Sighing, Pappy went to comfort her.

Edegast said, "We should make all haste, my dear. Winter is upon us already here in the lower Daegries, although you cannot tell it from this drought-stricken land. The snows are deepening in the Snowclids and if too much time passes, it will be months before we can safely arrive."

She closed her eyes and shook her head. "How do I get myself into these calamities?"

He didn't reply, and soon she headed to her room. She passed her grandparents and softly inquired if they would help her pack.

An hour or so later, Alyssa sweated inside a thick woolen tunic and breeches and milled about, ready to go. She carried a pack provided by Pappy with the Grim nestled inside. Granny sent with her a nice collection of food including corn pone that would keep well for days in the colder climate.

She thought about her bow and arrows and how wrong it felt not to have them. But she was traveling with Edegast, a wizard of great powers, and she knew a thing or two about magik, too. Her bow and arrows might not work as fast or efficiently as magik, but the scarf was her saving grace. It could move like lightning.

As if in response to her thoughts, Shadow draped around her neck, hanging on for dear life, refusing to remove itself even when she spoke roughly to it. The Grim was safely tucked in her pack, and as she looked around to make sure she had everything, she thought about what she was embarking on. "It might take time, and it might take energy," she said, "but I'm going to find my parents, if I can. I'll look for that phoenix. She said she'd help me."

Alyssa had spent time over the last year remembering the phoenix's words about her parents. But she had not found any way to travel to the Greater Daegries to look for them. Her grandparents would never permit her to go alone again. Now, with the wizard enlisting her aid, they couldn't stop her.

As they stood in the stuffy living room, Edegast promised her grandparents that she would be back in the spring. "I cannot promise her return before then, as the weather will preclude any traveling, I fear."

"If there is even a safe route by spring," Pappy mused. "You send word to us on how things are going, you hear?"

Edegast nodded, exhaling with a heavy sigh. Alyssa shrugged on a heavy, hooded cloak, pulling down on the sides so she could loop the catches.

"If we don't get a move on, I'll perish from the heat in this getup," she told the wizard, wiping the sweat from her brow as it dripped down her temples.

Granny, drying her tears, sniffed loudly and gave Alyssa a quick hug. "Mind your manners, now. You don't worry about us."

Before Alyssa could even reply, footfalls sounded on the front porch followed by a knock.

"Who's calling on us?" Granny whispered, a frown deeply etched on her face. Then, she yelled, "Who is it?"

"Murray," came a rough voice. "Constable of Mudden."

Edegast's brows crashed together over his nose. "Out the back!" he hissed. "Make haste!"

Pappy followed Alyssa and the wizard as they trudged through the kitchen and quietly opened the door leading out into the garden. Granny closed it behind them so it wouldn't slam and took off to let the constable in.

Pappy traveled as far as the bower and after a strong handshake to the wizard and a long hug to Alyssa, he said goodbye. "You're smarter than you know, gal. I'm real proud. I can't travel like I used to. When I was just a voice, out of the box, I was pretty swift, but... I'll send word somehow, even if it is on the back of a crow."

Alyssa, who had traveled with Pappy the last time she went on an adventure, wiped tears away and turned from her hearth and home to follow the back of the tall wizard. When she turned back a few steps later, Pappy was no longer there.

The travelers didn't speak for some time. In fact, they were almost to the tall grass of the Meadowlands when Alyssa asked Edegast where they were going.

The wizard answered as he sifted through corn stalks with his hands, looking for something. "To the lair of the gryphon king."

"What? Hold up, Edegast. I can't go to see that old ruffian!"

At these words, he stopped and turned. "Why not?"

"He and I are... unspoken enemies."

"Poppycock," Edegast said, moving ahead a moment before lifting his staff from the side of a thinning row of corn. "Ah, there you are. Hubert is a peaceable creature for the most part, Alyssa. There is no allegiance nor abhorrence in his homelands."

"Maybe not in *his* mind, but I ain't too fond of him. Last time we met, I told him that if I ever came this way again, it would be his undoing."

Edegast tucked his staff under his arm and gave her a peculiar look. "You did not mean that, surely. He is a king, after all. Now, there is nothing to fear. Leave your regrets here in this corn field, as they will not serve you. We must work together with all of the good peoples of the Daegries. We have an alignment with each other against a common foe now."

She shrugged, and they took off again. Quietly, she muttered, "Ain't going to be his play toy again; no sir, I ain't."

Edegast ignored her if he heard her at all, but she stiffened her spine anyway. King Hubert was not a nice creature, no matter what Edegast said, and she would be on her guard while in his presence. *Peaceable, my foot.*

They slipped silently among the tall wheat grasses of the Meadowland. Only a hot dry wind slapping the wheat against neighboring stalks could be heard. Alyssa was far too overdressed to be out in the heat. She called a halt, pulled the pack and cloak from her back and draped the cloak over her arm. Still too warm, but more comfortable, she replaced the pack and waved to Edegast to carry on.

While she tried to imagine cool winds and cold water, she remembered her first encounter with the gryphon. He'd acted so high and mighty; it had not been easy to talk to him. She hoped Edegast did the talking this time.

The pair passed the pavilion that Alyssa had taken refuge under on her last trip to this land.

Eventually, when Solly the Sun neared the far horizon, the wheat parted, and they found themselves in a tiny village built around a temple of sorts. The village included a tavern and inn, a blacksmith shop, and a mercantile. All the inhabitants lived in ramshackle houses on the outskirts of the village to allow room for trade in the village and less noise to the villagers.

Alyssa understood this reasoning; it was pretty much why her family lived where they did. Less noise and less interference from Mudden folks. As they walked along, the Meadowlanders shunned them, hiding inside their dwellings.

Most of these folk were known to be corn-dwellers, but it appeared to her that they lived closer to the water that filled the ditches near the temple. There was a small family of Deermice, a few Voles, and some Rabbits. She was amazed to see how human-like they appeared. She nodded to a Deermouse who wore an apron around her middle and hurried her young inside their straw house.

Alyssa wouldn't hurt them for love or money, but she did understand the strangeness of the world at the moment.

Edegast, seeing her curiosity, pulled his hood low over his head and waved for her to put her cloak on. He took Shadow and shoved it inside her pack. "No need to draw any attention to ourselves. These folk are in fear of everyone. Danger has already risen here, it would appear. Also, I think the king still has the fake scarf somewhere. No need to give him food for thinking. It wouldn't do for him to put the story together at this late date."

Alyssa had given the gryphon a fake scarf last year, once the real one had been found. If he had discovered her lie, she would likely have to pay a price on this visit. If not, and he found out her lie while she was here, it would not be good for her either. Hiding Shadow was the best idea, and she was ashamed she hadn't thought of it first.

Edegast strode up the steps on the outside of the temple, two at a time, and waited at the top for Alyssa to join him.

She marveled at how wide the steps were, and how the whitewash that had been applied on the wooden structure glowed in the late afternoon sunlight.

Her admiration for the building ended as soon as they went inside. It was nothing like a temple but a good deal similar to the castle at Needlemount. The red and gold banners hung from the pillars, and it held a great lot of heraldry in its furnishings, such as a coat of arms behind the large throne situated on a dais in the center of the room.

She allowed her magik to slip from her and wander around seeking other spells that might try to enchant them. There was nothing, and soon it returned to her.

There, on the gilt throne, with a jeweled crown on his head, sat the pompous King Hubert, royal bearing in the lines of his body, and eyes that twinkled with mischief, exactly as Alyssa remembered.

Edegast bowed low. "Hail, sire," he said. Then as he stood upright again, he said to Alyssa, "His Royal Highness, King Hubert the Gryph, Seventh of His Lineage, First Son of Gregory. Please bow."

Alyssa frowned. *As if I don't already know who this creature is!* She refused to bow, and stood instead, staring at her former enemy. "Howdy, King."

The vain ruler gawked at her, beady eyes blinking in disbelief. The eagle head tilted, the talons gripped the chair arms tightly, and he squawked, "Do you dare enter my castle and not bow? Impudence!"

"Yeah, I know," she told him, pulling her pack off. "You've said that before."

The gryphon tapped a talon, irritated. "Have we met?"

She stared at him with as blank a stare as she could muster. He seemed different. First of all, he was much thinner. And even though he could rustle his feathers the same as before, he didn't seem quite so sure of himself.

"Yeah, you know me. From last summer, remember? Sick granny, farm over near Mudden?" Alyssa asked him. "You seem a little off-color to me, oh, kingly one. Have you been sick?"

"I remember you now. I see your rude behavior remains, despite my warnings."

Alyssa laughed. "You'd be the one to know about rudeness, your kingliness."

Edegast put out a hand to stop her continued baiting of the gryphon. "Now, my lady," he said, voice soothing. "Let us not anger our good King. After all, he will be our mode of transport soon."

Alyssa turned to gape at the wizard. *Is he jesting? Nope. No jesting there.*

She played along for the time being and curtsied to the gryphon, murmuring something about his royalty. He took her actions to be those of submission and turned his attention to Edegast.

"So," he said, a note of disdain in his voice. "You've returned. I suppose you want to take advantage of my kindness once again. Where do you need to fly to this time?"

Edegast tapped the ground lightly with his staff. "Indeed, good king. I would appreciate it if you would fly the both of us with much haste to the Snowclids."

"And what will be my recompense?" King Hubert asked, not missing a beat. "I believe you know that my services come with a cost?"

"Ahem, yes," Edegast said, muttering a moment. "I am quite certain there will be something you may ask for that is not against the laws of Wizards or Men."

The gryphon king tilted his head, thinking. "Very well. I would like to be invited *inside* Knowledge Hall this time. Last time you sent me packing without even a by-your-leave."

Edegast took a deep breath. "My apologies, sire. You are most welcome. Our hall is tall and wide, and I believe even a king as magnificent as yourself will be able to enter."

Alyssa shifted from one foot to the other. She didn't doubt that the gryphon would fit, as he had fit into her small farmhouse. But Edegast's way of calling him overly large was well-done, she admitted. Their discussion explained how Edegast had been able to get around the world of Daegries without using the portals.

There's a game of words goin' on here, and I ain't privy to the game. I'll have to ask my friend about this later.

Edegast had agreed to let the creature into the castle. Was he even able to promise such a thing? And what did a gryphon want inside the wizards' castle anyway?

"Very well," Hubert replied, fluttering his wings a bit. "When shall this journey commence?"

"Now," Edegast answered, looking at his feet.

"*Now*?" the king exclaimed. "I am about to meet with my lords and earls. I cannot go *now*."

Edegast gripped his staff, red-faced. "When would be a good time, Sire?"

Alyssa's gaze went from one to the other as if watching a hay-bale-throwing contest. It was not a good idea to anger a wizard, but it was likely even more poor taste to insult a king in his throne hall.

"Tomorrow at the earliest, and that will only be if there is not more pressing business," Hubert answered, waving for a page to show them out. "Take them to rooms within."

As Alyssa pulled her pack back onto her shoulders, the gryphon king pointed at her and said, "We should have a word about your grandmother and that scarf soon, girl. All is not what it seems."

She nodded and followed Edegast and the page out of the hall as her thoughts turned chaotic. *He remembers!*

Sweat beaded on her upper lip, and she wasn't sure if it was from the overly warm temple or the feelings that Hubert created when he said something about her grandmother and the scarf.

Chapter Four

The page led them to divinely furnished rooms across the corridor from one another. The king was used to entertaining the best of his realm, apparently. Although Alyssa couldn't imagine the timid people that she'd witnessed staying in the royal court any longer than necessary.

Alyssa's room, decorated in shades of rose and lavender, had a lavish tray of fruit at the foot of an ornate four-poster bed. Her stomach growled at the sight of it.

She had barely removed her gear, freed Shadow, and selected a juicy apple when a sharp knock sounded on the door. She strolled to open it and allowed Edegast to enter.

"My apologies for intruding on your repose, lady Alyssa. I hope that your accommodations are pleasant," the wizard said, looking around at the room. "It was not my intention to ever have to stay here."

Alyssa spoke around a bite of apple. "The room's nice, anyway. Would you like an apple?"

"No, thank you. My constitution is not up to apples today." He made a sound of derision and began pacing.

She watched him for a moment or two before tossing the apple's remains into a bowl on the tray. She scooped Shad up from where it pooled on the pillows of the bed. She held it like a pet cat and stroked the follygrass.

Edegast never stopped moving though he watched her closely.

"What?" she asked finally, putting out a hand to stop him. "What has you walking the floor like you're trying to put a hole in it?"

"Time, dear lady. We are on a matter of utmost importance, and time is not on our side."

"You mean because of the Grim?"

The wizard whirled around and put his fingers to his lips. "Shh. We mustn't even speak of it!"

"Why? That fellow you told me about isn't in the gryphon's castle, is he?" She shrugged at Edegast's caution.

"Be that as it may, we do not know who might be listening, and we do not know who they are aligned with. In fact, Alyssa, it is better not to speak of anything pertaining to this dangerous situation until we are safely in Knowledge Hall."

"Fine. But please have a seat and let's rest. You're making me nervous."

He fluffed his robes out and sat. "You should keep the scarf in the pack whilst we are here. It would not be good for the gryphon to see it. In fact, he might want to pour out all of our belongings for examination. That would certainly be disastrous."

"He said something to me as we were leaving that makes me think he knows his scarf is not real." She looked down at Shadow before placing it back into the pack. "I'll see you later."

Alyssa sat on a chair with plush cushions and asked, "How do you know so much about this er... *situation* that we are not giving attention to?"

"I do not know anything certain," he answered. "I only listen well and put things in their proper perspective. There is much still to be learned, of course."

Alyssa nodded and pointed at the pack. "How did you know this *item* was the thing sought after?"

"Only since the spell was performed on your dear grandfather. It was suspected for some time, hence why the *item* went south. But there was no good way to find out for certain until now."

Alyssa stared at the wizard and noticed the fine lines that appeared around his eyes. Surely, he had aged overnight. "I can see this has placed a strain on your life."

"Indeed," he replied taking out his pipe and cradling it lovingly. He walked to the arrow slit and leaned against the stone. Alyssa hoped he wouldn't light the pipe. The thickness of his tobacco smoke would be choking with such a small outlet.

He paced once more, the pipe in his hand.

"Where is your staff? Aren't you worried about letting it out of your sight?" she asked.

He shrugged. "It has a spell of protection on it. Anyone who tries to use it will get quite a shock."

She nodded again. Perhaps it would be an actual shock, but perhaps it would be a surprise of another sort. No matter, she didn't ask more. She should probably learn some way to do the same to the scarf and the Grim while in her possession. Any deterrent was preferable to nothing at all.

Finally, he walked to the door and grasped the handle. "I will leave you then. I am only across the way. If you have any fears or anything upsets you, call out."

She thanked him and watched him go. Nothing she could think of in this place would frighten her. The king was the most obnoxious person in the castle, and his words from earlier worried her, but she was steadfastly not afraid of him.

Alyssa stared out at the approaching night through the arrow slit. The stars twinkled in the indigo sky overhead. A rap sounded on Edegast's door, and a voice said something about supper. The herald followed suit with Alyssa's door. She prepared to go, wishing desperately to take Shad, but she remembered Edegast's concerns and the gryphon's parting words.

She wondered then if Hubert had tried to make the fake scarf produce its magik, only to be disappointed. Considering that possibility, it would be a miracle if he let her leave without questioning, if not imprisonment.

She spoke to Shadow through the pack. "Now, you behave in there. Don't try to get out and don't cause any mischief. I'm hungry and the food is in the dining hall. But if I don't come back here in a short while, you do whatever the wizard tells you."

The pack settled into a flat lump, and after watching it for a moment or two, she left her room. Edegast stood outside her door waiting for her.

"Ah, food at last," he said, smiling at her. She wondered if he had taken a nap. He seemed calmer and more himself.

They traveled back the way they had come in hopes of meeting someone to give them directions to the dining hall. Finally, a serving man appeared and showed them the proper path. They soon sat at the king's oaken banquet table.

Alyssa had never seen so much food in all her life. There was a cheesy corn dish, potatoes in an herb sauce, and spiced pomegranates in a glaze. Hot buttery breads were served with a hearty stew filled with carrots and beans, too.

When she stuffed a bite of roll into her mouth, she thought how Granny Gert would love to have a roll like that. The fact that meat was missing at the feast was not lost on her. Last year, the king had said that his was a peace-loving kingdom. Perhaps that was extended to killing for food.

She remembered how he played with a tiny bunny that day, but no harm came to it, so perhaps he was a bit of a jester. Or that bunny was a child belonging to a family in the Meadowlands, and she was too nervous to notice the creature was dressed like a human.

Edegast ate tiny bites of the foods and kept a wary eye out for the entire room. There was no one in the hall aside from them. Not even King Hubert attended.

"Where's the gryphon?" he asked a serving man who poured steaming tea into their cups.

"On business," came the reply.

Alyssa sipped her tea and sat back. There was only so much one could eat at one sitting. She wished she could take a platter of it back to her room for later, but that likely would be frowned upon.

A herald stood outside the main entrance to the hall and shouted, "King Hubert, the Gryph."

Edegast stood and motioned for Alyssa to do likewise.

When the gryphon entered, he waved at them to sit. Alyssa looked at him closely. He definitely was thinner, and his claws were dull and unkempt.

"I trust that you have been cared for sufficiently?" he asked, seating himself.

They nodded.

He waved to the serving man to fill his plate. "It is so good to have company at my table once again."

"The food is delightful, Sire," Edegast said.

"Yes," Alyssa said. "Very tasty. How is it you have such wonderful vegetables with the drought?"

"Hubert stared at her, narrowing his eyes. "We harvest early and put the vegetables in a watering pot to keep them fresh and plump. Doesn't your grandmother do the same?"

Alyssa looked down at her plate and tried to control her heartbeat. "Y-yes, sire."

"I'd like to go and visit your family home again," he said, coughing a little. "Yes, there was much to learn there."

Alyssa fell silent. She didn't know how long the gryphon had been at her family farm, nor what all he had learned while there. Maybe old Tony had shared some farming tips with him, but Granny certainly would not have.

The gryphon tore into a roll of crusty bread with his sharp beak and was unable to speak for a moment. When he could speak legibly, he said, "You have traveled wide and often, Wizard. I would have the tale of who is crossing the Lesser Daegries headed to the sea, and why they are leaving."

This question caused Edegast to sit back in his chair. "You have seen this?"

The gryphon nodded, chewing thoughtfully. "They pass through my lands without permission. And a terrible mess they leave behind as well. My subjects are afraid to come out of their homes as these usurpers have stolen things from them."

Edegast swallowed a bite of potato. When he spoke, it was with trepidation. "I had heard the ogres were leaving the Daegries. I didn't believe it at first. But then, I caught glimpses over the last few months, so it was impossible to deny."

"Ogres?" King Hubert asked. "Smelly bunch of unfriendly beasts, they are. And messy, as well. They leave whatever they do not wish to carry further wherever it falls."

Aggravated, the king peered at Alyssa causing her to drop her gaze to her lap. "It would be nice to have a scarf that would protect me in battle, during all of this upheaval."

So, we're going to do this now? She took a deep breath and stared at the gryphon, trying her best to look calm. "Sire, you have a scarf. Don't you remember? I brought it to you last fall."

He harrumphed and coughed and did his best to find his voice. "Yes, I remember, but that is not the same one I lost. Did you give me the right one?"

"I gave you the one that was given to me by the elves. They are the scarf-makers."

"It doesn't work. You were lied to, and in turn, lied to me. I should overthrow your farm and take it from you as payment for such defiance of my royal decree."

Flames licked her face as her temper flared. "I ain't your subject, Hubert. You can't order me around with decrees and such. If your scarf won't do like you want it to, take that problem up with the elves."

She crossed her arms and glowered. "If you so much as step one claw over the line into the Farmlands, my Pappy will know about it, and you're going to be sorry."

Edegast interrupted their war of words. "Now, now, there is no need for these barbs, my friends. We are all in the path of great and terrible times of trouble. Let's not war amongst ourselves."

After that, King Hubert left the table and returned to whatever business he had to attend to while Edegast and Alyssa returned to their rooms. The wizard paused outside his door, and Alyssa thought he might have something to say, but he only smiled and bade her good night.

She closed her door and leaned against it. Exhaustion struck her full-on. Shadow wriggled to be let loose, so she went to the pack and freed it.

It flew at her wrapping itself around her like a hug.

"You're always so welcoming, Shadow. I appreciate it. I really do."

The scarf lifted one end to pat her face. She sat on the bed and pulled her boots off, one by one. She wondered why ogres were leaving the Daegries, and if she would ever see one. And she sent a heartfelt wish to her Pappy to keep the farm safe until she could get back.

The next morning, Edegast rapped on the wooden door, and Alyssa went to open it. She had been up for hours, unable to sleep in a strange place. Her dreams, however short-lived, had been filled with imaginary ogres being led by the gryphon kin. They turned into bugbears with long pikes in their hands, and mouths filled with jagged teeth.

Edegast was fully packed and held his staff as if ready to walk out of the castle and be on the trail.

"Oh," Alyssa said, surprise filling her. "I wasn't sure if we would leave today or if the king was playing with us. He seemed more interested in attending his council than flying us to the Snowclids."

"Yes, I have seen him this morning, and he is preparing now to fly us out of the Meadowlands. I still am uncertain as to whether he will carry us that far, however. He doesn't seem to want to be bothered. Your discussion of last evening about the scarf has put him in a foul mood."

"He didn't do much for mine either. Doesn't he understand the serious nature of your business?" she asked, repacking Shad and her other belongings.

Edegast stood in the doorway. "I am unsure of what he understands, truthfully. It is of no matter, however. We will allow his generosity to take us as far as he is willing to fly."

She remembered the gryphon king dropping her and Pappy Oh off on a mountaintop far away from where they needed to go last year. She didn't remind Edegast of the king's unpredictable behavior, since he'd had more to do with the gryphon than she had.

"I'm ready," she told the wizard, pulling the pack onto her shoulders and adjusting her coat. "We need food to take along in case he drops us off somewhere too far to get any."

Edegast shrugged. "Are you worried about food?"

"I took a long trip last year that was the hardest thing I've ever done. Food was hardly even thought about but, believe me, I would rather not attempt this trip or any other without a supply."

He grunted and waved for her to follow him. They strode to the dining hall where an abundant breakfast was spread out on a side table.

"You can serve yourself," Edegast told her. "Take as much as you like. I will seek someone to pack a bit of it for us for later."

While she ate a meal of boiled beets, savory cheese, and a luscious pile of berries, Edegast located a serving man and gave him instructions on what they needed.

In a short while, they were well fed, loaded with more food, and strolling out into the early rays of sunlight appearing over the castle.

Hubert strutted around the courtyard in front of the temple. He scratched in the dirt and shook his feathers, trying his best to look the part of a king. His crown was smaller and more fitted to his strangely shaped eagle head.

"Come along, come along," he told them. "I have much business to attend to, and it will be doubled by the time I return."

She didn't say anything, but wondered if Edegast had told the gryphon that winter might keep him in the mountains a lot longer than he wanted.

Chapter Five

The ride on the gryphon was cramped.

Edegast rode toward the rear which looked like a lion's tail, and Alyssa rode up front holding onto the golden chain around Hubert's neck. She was dangerously close to the sharp eagle-like beak, but so far, the gryphon had ignored her completely.

The two riders shivered and hunkered down lower trying to avoid the blast of cold air that swirled around and over them, and, for the first time, Alyssa was happy to have her warm clothes. She ventured a glance below and saw the river, Old Stony, beneath them. She followed the curving trail of it until it disappeared into the haze of the far away landscape.

There was no talking on the flight as the wind swooshed around them taking speech and hearing completely with it. Not as though either of them had much to say, anyway. Alyssa wanted to be excited to be going to the home of the wizards as she'd always hoped to someday.

The edges of the Meadowlands passed below, dotted with bundles of hay. The gryphon dove toward the ground in a sudden move that sent Alyssa pitching forward. Just as she was about to ask what the creature was doing, she could see her answer quite plainly.

Ogres (she presumed based on their appearance) made a direct path to the shore of the Silk Sea. They wore packs and warily hurried their young ones along with crude walking sticks.

Alyssa peered over her shoulder to see if Edegast was aware of the situation. His eyes were riveted on the scene below them. Then, unexpectedly, the gryphon dropped from the sky and landed.

"What are you doing?" Edegast demanded. "We did not ask to land here."

"You will go where I take you, Wizard," the gryphon said in a half-screech. "And at this moment, we are going here."

He stopped to allow them to disembark before hailing an ogre who appeared out of a stand of reeds.

"You," the gryphon said. "You, there. What is the meaning of your passage through this land? You have trespassed."

"Aye," the ogre replied, his gray eyes staring. "And a great deal more of us on the way."

"This is my land, Ogre. I am King Hubert the Gryph. Have you not heard of me? It is customary to ask permission before traipsing through a known realm. Why are you here?" Now the king stood at full height and sounded to Alyssa as royal-like as he could muster.

"I'll be off it soon enough, Gryphon. Fear not. It would not suit for a creature of the swamps to have to idle long on a grassy plain. There's nothing to eat here but... hay." His disdain was not lost on Hubert.

But the king allowed this insult to pass. "Nevertheless, I am still awaiting an answer to the question posed. What has sent you this way? The swamps of Og are that way," he said pointing behind them with a talon.

Alyssa gave Edegast a pained look that said the gryphon was being too forceful for the creatures and might be asking for trouble.

Edegast smoothly took matters into his own hands. "Good sir, I am sorry we have delayed your travels. In a quick moment, can you say as to whether you are going out to sea?"

The ogre nodded. "Yeah, we've crafted boats and taken them to the shores. Ready to sail soon. Evil's coming, nay, 'tis already among us."

"Evil? Such as?" Edegast asked, eyebrows drawing together like they were stitched.

The ogre took in Edegast's staff and shook his head. "Massive army of trolls, bugbears and the like. They hail from the north and their holes in the mountains. I wished for the rocks to fall on them, but there was no answer from the gods."

Edegast stroked his beard. "Yes, I understand. And did any of you capture any of them? Questions abound you see."

The ogre lifted his walking stick, half-covered in mud and pointed behind them. "Only one. He was about to perish. His words made no sense to us. Some foreign language he used. I will say though, these evil ones carry a mark, a sign if you will."

At this, the wizard stood straighter and gripped his staff until his knuckles turned white. "A sign? And what does that look like?"

The ogre grabbed his child's hand and pulled him away. "The mark of the monster that once was. The Dead One, who is alive again. The mark of the River of the Dead."

Edegast groaned and stood there watching the ogres disappear into the distance.

Alyssa asked, "What is the mark?"

Against closed eyes, he answered, "The memory of the sign fills my mind. Burned, etched into the flesh of every follower of the Dark Master. A crooked river flowing into a mountain."

Alyssa's jaw dropped at his words. The wizard opened his eyes and seeing horror on her face, looked away.

Hubert clicked his beak as well, rendered speechless. When he regained his composure, he said, "We could fly out over the waters and see where they go."

"That will not be necessary," Edegast replied. "We don't care where *they* are going. We would rather know where the nasty creatures they speak of are coming from."

"He just told you," Alyssa said. "The mountains in the north. Now what mountains he means, I ain't too sure about."

Edegast paced a moment before answering. "There are only so many mountains that could harbor a host such as he foretells. Unfortunately, we do not have time currently to divert to another task or I would go to see for myself."

Alyssa looked down at her feet. Wouldn't going to the area where the creatures were seen be important? Just as much as going to Knowledge Hall? She looked back to Edegast to see if his thinking had changed. It had not.

"Off with us," he told her, waving toward the gryphon. "We have little time to ponder matters. The snow flies in the Snowclids even now."

King Hubert flattened himself low to allow them to climb on again. Once they were seated, however uncomfortably, he began running and flapping his wings.

Soon, they were airborne again.

For a short way they followed the coast of the Silk Sea. The beach looked inviting in places with smooth sand and calm waves. Farther on, there were disturbed places, wild with windblown cliffs and crashing surf. Not a bit like its name, Alyssa decided.

Amazingly, this is where the gryphon decided to land again. He fluttered to the ground at the cliff's edge, next to a grove of trees.

"King Hubert," Alyssa said, tapping his neck. "What are you doing? This ain't where we're going."

He shook himself and fluffed his feathers, nearly unseating them. "No, but I need a rest."

He lowered to allow them to get off. Edegast grumbled to himself as he jumped to the ground.

"Gryphon, if you are playing me foul, I swear I will—"

"—you will do nothing, Wizard. This is a necessary delay. I am not used to being a creature of burden. Young Miss weighs nothing by herself, but the two of you have quite worn me out."

The pompous creature strutted about flapping his wings and pecking at the ground, slurping up a rather large worm. Alyssa shrugged when Edegast looked askance.

"I think he's been sick. And he does control this journey," she said by way of explanation.

The wizard pulled his cloak tighter around him and stalked off toward the cliff's edge. She assumed he was going to stare at the water and calm his anger. The weather had turned blustery, and the wind had the chill of a cool fall. Alyssa noted it and wondered how much colder it would be in the wintry mountains.

She made good use of the break to eat a bit of dried fruit, and some corn pone. Then she decided to rest. The tree she leaned against faced the cliff's edge, and even from her vantagepoint, she could hear the pounding surf.

Shad, inside the pack, thumped up and down to make Alyssa aware. *Must have figured something was up since we are not moving.*

She whispered, "Shadow, settle down. We ain't at liberty yet to set you free."

The pack flexed one last time and lay still.

As she readjusted everything, she had Edegast in her view. He paced back and forth along the cliff. One hand gripped his staff and the other waved back and forth while he muttered something.

Then, in a blink of an eye. The wizard was gone.

Alyssa stared so hard her eyes watered.

Gone into thin air!

Chapter Six

Alyssa struggled to her feet and stormed to the cliff's edge, peering over the side. Edegast was not bashed on the rocks below. Nor was he floating face down in the crashing surf. The cliff's edge had not given way suddenly either.

She cupped her hands around her mouth and yelled. "Edegast!" But the sounds of the sea drowned out her voice, and a small spray splashed against her face. She stared down onto the rocky coast, detecting movement. What had at first appeared to be seagulls, turned out to be something far more sinister.

There, sunning themselves on the rocks, lounged a bevy of sirens. Male and female. And Alyssa stood there dumbstruck, understanding why Edegast had disappeared. Near the water, the sirens were their most powerful. And although not known to have magik, Alyssa believed in her heart that they could do things in this environment that would make one think it was magik.

She turned back and strode to the gryphon.

"Edegast has disappeared," she said. "He was there and then he was gone."

Hubert shrugged and hopped to the nearest tree to sharpen his beak. "Wizards will be wizards," he told her in between rubs against the bark.

"But, but... that's not like him! And there are sirens down there!" She gestured toward the ocean.

The gryphon yawned loudly. "Never interfere in the path of those creatures." Then, he threw himself onto the ground. "I must have sleep. I have not slept for ages. The wizard will return once he has attended to his business."

Alyssa decided Hubert would only be a stumbling block to her quickly forming plan. She waited until the gryphon snored loudly before telling Shadow her plan. "I reckon that if I don't make it back in a little while, you just come on and get me."

The pack puffed up and wriggled as if to go with her, but she grunted and piled her belongings near the gryphon. The king would understand that she was not gone forever, but simply seeking the wizard.

"Guard that book good now, you hear?" she whispered to Shadow. The scarf poked its end through an opening in the pack and waved at her.

She found a jutting overhang that would hold her weight and began her descent that way picking her path carefully. A misstep would mean certain death, dashed on the jagged rocks below.

As she scooted and scrambled down, she kept a keen eye on the sirens. Did they lure Edegast away with their songs, or did he decide to pull his own disappearing magik out and use it?

She could only approach them and ask. She landed with a soft thud from the final drop and hurried toward massive boulders.

Quietly hiding in the boulders' shadows, Alyssa heard them talking and laughing.

"Oh, she thinks she is so smart!" one Mer-girl said.

"She's clever," the nearest male Mer-creature answered.

"But I am beautiful," replied the first, and they both laughed.

"Excuse me," Alyssa said, voice low. "Can I speak to you?"

Her sudden appearance scared the Mer people, and they scattered, jumping into the surf and climbing on rocks to get away.

"Wait!" Alyssa said, motioning for them to stop. "I'm not going to hurt you!"

A few stopped their movement to stare at her with glistening, cobalt-blue eyes. They flipped their fins like annoyed parlor cats.

"I-I'm Alyssa from the farmlands. I traveled here with a wizard, but he's gone missing. Have you seen him?"

At her words, a female leapt into the water from across the arch of rocks and swam around to where Alyssa stood, not quite in the water.

The siren had familiar raven-colored hair and slanted eyes. She lifted herself out of the water and slid onto a nearby rock.

"Alyssa Chance Oh," she said. "Do you remember me?"

Of course, Alyssa did. It was Lorelei, the siren who had gotten lost in the stream near Half Moon Manor, the home of Lord Bryon.

"Lorelei!"

"Yes, it is I," she replied, smiling but not showing all of her wicked sharp teeth. She seemed to be proud that Alyssa remembered her.

"Well, blow me to bits! How'd you get all the way here from where we last met?" Alyssa asked.

Lorelei laughed, the notes tinkly and friendly. "The same way I got to where we last met, only backwards!"

The other sirens nearby laughed too, but their laughter was hesitant and less friendly. They eased closer to Alyssa as if to protect their fish sister.

"What is a farm girl doing at the seashore?" Lorelei asked, her voice soothing like a purring cat.

"I'm on another adventure."

"I don't see your pop-up box. Have you lost it?"

"No," Alyssa answered. "Pappy didn't come with me. Hey, have you seen a wizard come through here? I'm on this adventure with him, and he's up and disappeared."

Lorelei laughed again and touched the large tooth hanging around her neck. "A wizard? Why, Alyssa, you should not keep such company." She paused before looking over her shoulder at the others. "Oh, but you do like to visit with dryads and such as I recall."

The fish people moved closer. "Dryads?" one asked.

"Tree sprites?" another asked. "Nasty."

They didn't seem fond of the creatures mentioned and, as Alyssa had nothing but good things to say, she backed away from the water.

"Well, it was good to see you, Lorelei. I hope you don't get lost again," she said as a parting word, backing out of the surf.

But something happened and the whole lot of sirens flowed toward her like a surf's surge and the next thing Alyssa knew, she was surrounded.

Cauldrons, that was fast!

She didn't know exactly what to do, but her current situation was dire. It would only take one strong merman to haul her into the water and hold her down until she drowned.

"Hey, now," she said, waving both hands at the crowd. "I ain't here to do no harm."

Lorelei crossed her arms and watched them, a small smile on her face. The nearest mermaid tapped her nails on a rock where she perched. They were long and hooky and tinted a slight green that matched the algae growing on the rocks in the water.

"I'm just looking for my missing friend, that's all," Alyssa said, wishing she had a weapon or, even better, Shadow. Even if it was only to cover her terrified shaking.

Lorelei finally spoke. "There is no reason to harm this one. She has earth magik in her, but she is less than easy prey."

"Are you certain you aren't saying that to keep her all to yourself?" the long-nailed one asked. She grinned, showing all her teeth, much like a shark.

Lorelei turned to glare at the mermaid and hissed. The sound was like a spray of water against the rocks. The others watched these two as they drew closer, hissing and showing teeth.

Alyssa turned and scrambled back up the rocks to the ledge as fast as she could muster. All the while she could hear the splashing and hissing of mermaids and mermen. She never turned back for fear of being included in the brawl.

When she arrived at last where the gryphon still snored, she was hot and disheveled. A few scratches on her hands and knees burned and stung from her hurried exit from the shore. They wouldn't follow her far onto land, and especially not as high up as she had climbed.

Unhappily, she realized that Edegast was still not back. The mystery of his disappearance bothered her greatly. Where did he go? And why? He seemed to be in such a hurry to get on the way to their destination; why would he vanish now?

She decided to wake the gryphon when the sky became darkened from Solly going to bed. The horizon turned purple and orange in sunset, and she rubbed her arms from the chill that blew in off the sea.

"King Hubert," she said, gently shaking the creature. "King, sir."

The bulk of half-lion, half-eagle barely moved. She took a deep breath and shoved him as hard as she could, nearly turning him over on his grassy bed.

"Harrumph... what is this?" he roared, coming awake. "Desist at once!"

She stepped back, a little scared at his outburst. She didn't want to be in firing range of his long claws or his beak.

"It's only me, King," she said softly.

He sat up. "Why have you accosted me so? I need sleep. I believe we have had this conversation—"

"Edegast is missing, and there are other dangers around. And night is coming, no less," she interrupted with a wave at the sky.

"The wizard will be back, as he is a man of his word. Gather firewood, girl. We shall stay here until he returns."

She closed her eyes and took a few deep breaths. Being ordered about by the gryphon went against all of Alyssa's boundaries, but they *would* need a fire.

Within a nearby grove, she shook some of the smaller trees to loosen dead branches. The small sticks would make good kindling to get the fire going.

Alyssa spoke to the trees as she went along.

"Don't be afraid, now. I know dryads live amongst you. I'm friendly with dryads. I won't hurt any of you. I only need enough wood to make a fire and keep it lit during the night."

Soon the trees swayed mightily, and not because of the wind. Branches small and large pelted the ground. Alyssa stood out of the way, waiting. When there were no more falling limbs, she gathered her bounty, thanked the trees, and headed back to where the gryphon sat.

He waved at her to make a fire. She built a mound with the kindling and called forth a bit of her own magik to light it. She got the small fire going and kept adding more branches until it blazed happily.

King Hubert placed a wooden box beside her. "You shall find dried fruits and vegetables in that. Put them on a flat rock on the fire and roast them."

She didn't have to look far to find a suitable rock and placed it on top of two sticks which burned away plopping the rock onto the embers. Once she placed the food on the rock, it heated, and a pleasing smell filled the air. When Hubert determined it was ready, Alyssa took it from the fire and spread it out on a cloth the king provided.

They ate from the ample supply of food, and Alyssa worried anew about the wizard. Hubert refused to say anything more about the matter, believing that Edegast was able to care for himself.

Soon, they grew sleepy from the food and the fire's heat.

Alyssa pulled out a blanket and curled up near the foot of a nearby tree, considering the woods to be her friends. The gryphon, as pompous as ever, declared he would sleep by the fire and take the first watch for the wizard.

Alyssa told him to be sure to wake her if Edegast returned. She felt certain the wizard would wake her himself if only to tell her what had happened. In a short while, she fell into uneasy dreaming.

When she awoke, Solly was quickly lighting the sky. Alyssa noted the fire had grown cold, and Edegast was not with them. The gryphon's soft snores came from a lump by the fire.

She yelled. "Wake up!"

He muttered and moaned and rolled over, blinking at her. "What in Daegries has happened that makes you bellow so?"

"You!" she yelled. "You have let the fire go out, and how would you know if Edegast came back, or called out for help? You were supposed to be watching."

Sirens take him!

Now, the gryphon had the good sense to look ashamed. "Apologies are in order. I am sorry, good lady."

Alyssa slammed tiny limbs onto the cold fire and called forth her magik. "Light."

When a tiny flame appeared, she added more branches. At last, she straightened and glared at Hubert.

"What are we going to do about the missing wizard? What do you think has happened?

King Hubert strolled to the cliff's edge. "He never told me of a plan to go out scouting. I think he was lured away by the ugly merfolk below."

"I tried to tell you that was a possibility. You agree with me now?" Anger sent her to her pile of belongings.

He paced back and forth, eyes riveted on the water's edge below. Her pack bounced around until she was reminded of Pappy Oh in his jack-in-the-box.

Shadow knew something, and she was going to have to free it to find out. But how to do that—

Her thoughts were interrupted when the gryphon stopped pacing. "I'll have a look around and see what I can see," he said. Flapping his wings, he lifted off the cliff.

Chapter Seven

*A*lone, Alyssa stalked over to her pack and pulled Shadow from it. The grateful scarf wound itself around her head until she was unable to even see.

"Shad," she mumbled. "Shadow, stop."

The follygrass scarf finally heard her muffled words and unwound itself.

"Shad," Alyssa said, quietly. "Do you know what has happened to the wizard?"

The scarf flattened itself out and lowered for Alyssa to climb on. "All my pleading for you to be a flying scarf and you refused. I'm grateful now you've had a change of heart."

Once she had pulled the pack onto her back and seated herself, the scarf lifted into the air. Shadow zipped down the cliff's side with Alyssa holding onto the sides for dear life. She saw no sign of the gryphon, and this made her even more worried. It wouldn't do to lose both of them. They slowed and floated into an underground cave.

Alyssa knew right away this was going to be a bad idea. The wet cave seeped moisture though her clothing until she shivered. She worried about the Grim and if the moisture was enough to damage it.

No time to look now, she thought.

Keeping her wits about her, they slithered through the cave above the trickling stream of water covering the floor. She noted water dripping down the sides, too.

When Shad slowed and lowered for her to get off, she stepped in a shallow puddle drenching her boots and making her even colder. Voices bounced off the cold walls of the cave, and she stilled to listened. They were not clear to her, so she scooped up the scarf, draped it around her shoulders, and inched toward the area before her.

Flickering torches were held aloft by mermen floating in a pool in the middle of the room. Edegast had been laid out on a raised floor of the cave, off to the side, out of the water.

The leader of the gathering, a flame-haired siren, held court with her tailfin in the water and her body on a ledge. She motioned for one of the mermaids to wake the wizard. Alyssa noted that his staff was missing, and dread went through her as she recalled his saying it had a spell on it. Such an occurrence would not go unpunished, she was certain.

To prevent retribution against her for being there and for being with Edegast, she tied Shadow around her middle and hissed, "Pretend to be a normal scarf."

The mermaid swam over to the wizard and slid out of the water to shake Edegast. She was nowhere as gentle as Alyssa had been with the gryphon, either. When this didn't bring the desired results, the creature took a long fingernail and dug it into his side.

Alyssa's heart drummed in her chest. Was he dead? He didn't even flinch from the nail.

The mermaid shook him again.

"Wake up, Wizard," the leader said loudly from her position. In fact, her voice reverberated in the cave until it seemed to shake Alyssa's entire body.

Edegast never moved, never moaned. How could anyone alive not react to that screeching voice, Alyssa asked herself.

She couldn't contain herself any longer. She had to know if Edegast was alive. Rushing into the pool area, Alyssa skirted the water and fell to her knees beside the wizard.

She had practiced her magik over the last year and knew how to place her hands over Edegast to determine his hurts. She did it almost instinctively now.

His body was full of fire. Not a fever, but a burning rage, and she was immediately repelled by it. She looked at the surprised mermaid. *Didn't she feel it?*

"What is the meaning of this? Who are you?" the siren leader demanded once she took notice of Alyssa. "Seize her!"

The mermaid gripped Alyssa's arm and tugged her toward the water.

Alyssa kept her head down and began incanting a spell to bring Edegast's mind back to his body. This was one she had learned after Pappy Oh had gone missing from his box and didn't tell Granny where he was off to. Sometimes she had to take things on her own shoulders, and that was one of those times. This was another one.

Before the mermaid could get her away from the wizard, Shadow lifted one end and gently placed it on Edegast in solidarity. Alyssa was about to punch the mermaid in the face and break free when Edegast inched an eye open and shook his head slightly.

He had been playing *possum*, a game she learned years ago to avoid early morning chores. Her Granny never bothered with her when she seemed so deeply asleep. Edegast had been fully awake the entire time.

Alyssa went along with the game. She jerked her arm out of the mermaid's hand, adjusted Shadow, shifted the pack, and dug in her heels. "Sorry sister, but I ain't going into that water with you."

Then she addressed the leader before the mermaid had a chance to grab her again. "I'm Alyssa, ma'am. I come from the land of Mudden, near the river. This man is my mentor, and we were traveling together when your people spirited him away to this place."

Suddenly, from the blackness of the other side of the room, a splashing could be heard and soon, Lorelei appeared. She came to the edge of the pool where Alyssa and Edegast were.

"We didn't spirit him, Alyssa. He came of his own free will. He slipped and fell on a rock. Is he...?" Lorelei asked.

"No," Alyssa answered quickly. "But he might as well be. What have y'all done to him?"

Lorelei looked over her shoulder at the leader who was preparing to join them on this side. "Tide, my regal, these are my friends. What has happened? Why would our people ever attack the likes of these? A wizard and a healer?"

Tide, the flame-haired siren, flipped her tail, indecision on her face. "Your friends? What does that even mean? Who can be friends with humans?"

"It is possible, your Highness. I encountered this female last year when I was lost. She never tried to betray me or do evil. I entrusted her with something, and she repaid me for it, kind for kind."

Tide is the Queen? This is getting more interesting by the minute!

"We do not allow strangers to know our location. He saw us. She can locate us."

Lorelei swam to the side where the queen sat. "He is a wizard, Tide. If we treat him or the girl ill in any way, there will be trouble."

Tide considered her words and stared at Alyssa. "What say you, Healer?"

"I wish no trouble. I only want to regain my friend and be on our way."

"What were you doing here?" she asked, pushing a strand of hair from her face. Her nails were so long that they curled on the end. "Whether you mean ill or not, you have discovered our lagoon. That is a punishable offense."

Edegast groaned loudly. Alyssa leaned over him and helped him sit. "Ma'am, we only want to be on our way again," she repeated.

Tide frowned and slid into the water, gliding to them. She glared at Alyssa. "I think not."

With that she opened her mouth and music began issuing out, the likes of which Alyssa had never heard. In a flash, their wrists were restrained with glowing seaweed, and they found themselves pinned against the cave wall, unable to fight against the siren's song.

Shad struggled against the spell, but Alyssa stopped it. The sirens didn't need to know he was a magik item. She'd dealt with their curiosity before. Instead, Alyssa tried to call forth her own magik, but nothing happened. She watched Edegast as his brow furrowed, and he appeared to go into a trance. It was to no avail.

Once he returned to the current situation, sweat dripped from his brow and a forlorn look came over his face. "We have to find a way to break this spell."

"Our magik won't work, but our brains are still intact," she said. "I ain't never seen a spell like this before."

"We will have to appeal to another side of the siren's world," he whispered. Then, he began to address the siren queen. "Your Majesty,

I know you have loved the world above the sea. There was a time when Mer creatures and humans had great friendships. Our realms were filled with laughter and love and hope. Why have you brought us to this melancholy cave, treating us as enemies?"

Her eyes were closed, and her mouth remained open as her music and song filled the cavern. But she heard Edegast, and his words caused her to falter. The music faded away.

Then, her face softened, and her voice was low. "Long ago, Wizard. It was so long ago. Back then, I loved a human, but he couldn't or wouldn't return my love. His world was on land and mine was under the sea. Our differences became too great. Since then, my heart for humans has grown cold and hard as this stone. My song is my salvation against another heartbreak."

"But you can love again. Vengeance and misery have consumed you, blinded you to even a possibility. Can you not remember the other time and how you felt? Let us go, and we will help you find your way back to goodness and peace."

Alyssa felt the restraints weakening. Shadow loosened as well.

Tide slumped in defeat. "You have reminded me that I still long for human companions. A treacherous heart I own. I am not under a misconception of love. But I am not under a failure to see wickedness either," she told him. "We have encountered strangers, and our fear has risen like the moon tide. I thought you were a part of it. Even a queen can be fooled, you see."

"Strangers? Evil wizards?" Edegast asked, lifting his bushy eyebrows.

"Evil humans, enslaving the lesser creatures," she answered, releasing them. "War is coming to your world, Wizard. Best be ready. We will not dally with you now, as the time for fighting is in its birth pangs. Our paths may join another way, and I would rather we were not enemies."

They stood cautiously, each too surprised at her words to say anything.

"Say nothing to others of where you found us. We have our own magik. We will find you. Until another day. Be gone," she said before plunging into the deep waters of the cave.

"Well, that's that," Alyssa said, shivering. "Where is your staff?"

"Someone took it, blast them."

"Let's look for it."

The other mermaids and mermen moved away from the pool's side, uncertainty on their faces. From a murky room beyond the cave pool, Lorelei swam forward carrying the staff.

"Take this," she ordered Edegast thrusting it at his feet. "It is painful."

"It should be," he answered, waspish. "It has been magiked."

"Alyssa, I feel that my debt is paid. I cannot save you again. Be forewarned in what Tide has said and beware my folk." Lorelei rubbed her hands as if the shock remained.

This amused Alyssa a little. She grinned at Lorelei and said, "And also to you, water woman. Beware the magik users, my folk."

Lorelei grinned and waved before swimming for her family and leading them away from the pool.

With that, Alyssa removed the scarf from her waist and draped it over her shoulder. Then she and Edegast turned and strode through the cave, leaving Lorelei and her water family behind.

When they were back at the mouth of the cave, high tide had come. Edegast instructed Alyssa to hold the staff until he could find footholds for them to climb up. She did so hesitantly until he assured her that she would not get a shock.

"Shadow can carry us up there a bit faster," she tried to tell the wizard, but he wasn't listening.

When the water crashed against their legs, she tapped Shadow and told it to fly them away. Edegast was not happy to be perched on a wriggling piece of follygrass but managed not to fall. Soon, they were atop the cliff again, scraped and wet. The gryphon was still missing.

"This is getting to be too much," Alyssa yelled, flinging herself from the scarf and ordering it inside the pack. "Not you, Shadow. I'm talking about that uppity gryphon."

"Where has he gotten off to now?" Edegast muttered.

"He was supposed to go out looking for you," Alyssa told him. "I suspect he is off watching ogres instead."

"He did seem a little fixated on them, didn't he?" Edegast asked, as he paced with his staff, thinking.

"Do you think Tide meant the ogres?" Alyssa asked, putting a finger to her cheek. "Is she talking about evil bringing war through them? But no, they ain't humans."

He stood a moment considering her words. "No. She has seen the signs emerging like the buds on the sunshine plant that foretell spring. Something is dreadfully wrong in the World of Daegries, and trouble is coming. And to her mind, the worst evil would be the humans who are a part of it."

His words sent a cold chill down her spine. They stood staring into one another's eyes for a long moment as if the other could read the fearful thoughts there.

Edegast and Alyssa stood on the narrow cliff's edge, their eyes fixed on an approaching storm. Gray clouds roiled in the distance, and flashes of lightning danced across the sky like ethereal serpents.

"Help lies that way," Edegast said, his voice carrying the weight of centuries. "But we won't make it there on foot, not with that tempest closing in."

Alyssa nodded, her blond hair billowing in the rising wind. "I reckon we have no choice but to call on Lord Bryon."

Edegast raised his staff, which was etched with intricate runes, and whispered an incantation that resonated with the essence of the land. The air shimmered with magik, and a resounding, echoing cry filled the sky. Moments later, the gryphon king swooped down from the heavens and landed beside them.

Alyssa didn't know what spell the wizard had cast, but she was grateful he had cast it.

"What? Why have I been summoned like a bad pixie?" King Hubert asked, preening his feathers which looked like molten gold in the current light. His fierce, intelligent eyes peered down at them.

"We must leave, King," Edegast told him. "Danger lurks all around us. Where in Daegries have you been anyway?"

With a detached sigh, Hubert allowed the two magik-users to climb onto his broad back.

"I tried to find you on the beaches of the sea. All I found were sea creatures and sirens... and ogres. See to it you do not fall off my back," he said. "You have cost us quite a lot of time by wandering off, Sir Wizard."

"Gryphon, don't start now," Alyssa whispered, annoyed to have been right about his whereabouts. "To Half Moon Manor, quick as a bunny."

The gryphon let out a rumbling growl and launched into the sky with a mighty beat of his wings. They soared through the turbulent currents of the oncoming storm, dodging lightning bolts and gusty winds. Eventually, the gryphon flew lower to avoid the worst of the storm which seemed to sway even the sky.

There was no way for the riders to know if they were close to the home of Lord Bryon and his kinsmen. They had to trust the gryphon.

When Hubert spiraled gracefully downward, Alyssa gripped tighter seeing the tops of trees below them. The landing on the ancient stones of Half Moon's courtyard jarred her. They dismounted, and the gatehouse keeper came running at them, sword at the ready.

"Who goes there?" he shouted as he ran. They barely managed to lower their packs and look friendly before he was upon them.

Chapter Eight

Alyssa held up her hands and shouted, "We're friends! Run get Lord Bryon, and he'll tell you!"

The guard faltered in his haste, peering at the wizard. "You... I know you!"

"Edegast the Green, sir. We have traveled from the Meadowlands to see Lord Bryon. We need shelter from this storm. Be a good man and help us."

"Ah, yes," the man sheathed his sword. "Sir Hyer at your service."

While they followed him to the manor house, Edegast kept the man answering questions about any strange wanderers, and Alyssa studied the buildings. In light of new developments, the manor didn't seem as powerful as it might be, or even as she remembered it.

The manor's design included fortified walls, battlements, and a watchtower. It was built to withstand sieges and protect the residents during tumultuous times. None had arisen in time recounted, and Alyssa felt sure they didn't understand that danger rolled toward them like a siege engine.

Likely they ain't aware, or else they'd arm themselves with more than old Sir Hyer at the helm, she thought, taking in the forlorn state of the place.

Half Moon manor also had a moat around it for defense. But the drought had dried up most of the water. An enemy would get mighty muddy, but they wouldn't drown.

She glared overhead at the black clouds scudding across. *We all need a good drenching rain.* But none would fall. None had in quite some time, and Alyssa worried about her family and the farm she'd left behind. The drought had cost them food.

Hoping for a better subject to focus on, she cast a look to where Hubert had strolled.

The gryphon sidled over to the barn to get out of the way of the storm. She could hear the horses neighing in fright as he peered in at them. It sounded as if one leaped against the wooden interior trying to escape the unknown presence of the gryphon. Alyssa hoped he didn't cause them to have an accident.

Finally, they entered the manor house. Sir Hyer took them straight away to the great dining hall to rest while he announced their arrival to the master of the manor, Lord Bryon.

Alyssa itched to pull Shad out and see how the scarf had survived the trip, but when she patted the pack, it pressed against her hand, indicating all was well. If Shadow was faring well, it was a certainty that the Grim was also.

Edegast sat heavily upon a wooden chair and stared at the doorway where Lord Bryon might enter. Alyssa didn't speak. He seemed in a mood to be alone with his thoughts.

Presently, their friend Lord Bryon appeared. He strode straight to the wizard and clapped him on the shoulders. "Edegast, my friend. What are you doing here?"

Edegast moved aside and allowed Alyssa to approach.

"By the grey beards of my ancestors, Lady Alyssa!" he exclaimed, shaking her offered hand and smiling. "This is such a glorious surprise!"

Edegast waved for him to take a seat, laying his staff aside. "We won't be staying, sir. Our journey takes us to the high seat of wizardry, and we are in quite a hurry. The storm brewing over us is why we tarried here."

Lord Bryon nodded and spoke briefly with his steward who hurried away. "I've called for refreshments, Edegast. There is time for that, surely?"

The wizard inclined his head. "As we sit here, danger is forming all around. Have you seen the ogres? They are leaving Daegries, boarding rough sail ships on the Silk Sea."

Bryon frowned. "Ogres? No, there have been none. But they never travel this far north anyway. Do you mean they are crossing the lands—leaving?"

Edegast nodded. "Yes. Leaving. One of them told us that marauders from the north were coming down out of the mountains attacking their villages. This is a terrible sign, and one that I wish for my elders to decipher. And as we have witnessed, the merworld is also preparing for danger. Tide, the queen of the Mers, told us that war is coming, and humans will be involved. It is weighing heavily on me at the moment. I simply wish to get to the Snowclids. We will be gathering the wise ones together upon my return to Knowledge Hall. Alyssa has come with me on another matter, one of great concern as well."

Bryon didn't press him for explanations, but turned to his young guest and asked, "And Pappy Oh? How is he? Did he come along as well?"

She shook her head. "He's well as far as I know. He finally recaptured his full self, out of the box, I mean. We left in a bit of a hurry, so I can't say what's happened since then."

"And your grandmother? All is well?"

Lord Bryon had no news from the far south, so he couldn't know what happened after she returned from her search for the scarf. She made a mental note. *Don't mention having Shadow with you.*

Last year, Lord Bryon hinted that he would love to have the scarf for other more warlike reasons, since it was reported to have powers to protect its bearer in battle. She didn't want to have to have another discussion with the manor lord over it. Bryon and Hubert were two people who would forcibly take the scarf if they could.

"Yes," she said, clearing her throat. "Um. The gryphon king was most agreeable, and we've even brought him with us today. He's our transport, in fact."

Lord Bryon looked completely aghast. "A gryphon? Here?"

Edegast nodded and added, "Yes, but fear not. He is as harmless as a toothless snake. He has taken shelter in your stables, I believe."

Lord Bryon shook his head and blinked a few times but said nothing. A serving man brought tankards of spiced cider and fresh bread and cheese. They dug in and for a time nothing was said.

Then, Alyssa asked, "Lord Bryon, sir, could I take food to the gryphon? He's traveled as far as we have, and he might be more agreeable if his belly is full."

Bryon grinned. "No harm in that, I suspect."

She grabbed an apple and a hunk of bread and placed them on a charger. Her pack hung on her back, and she could feel Shad stirring. "Soon, my friend, very soon," she whispered as she took it off.

She left the pack sitting beside her seat at the table with a wave to Edegast to let him know what she was doing. She wouldn't do that normally but here among friends, she felt safe.

The manor bustled with activity, but she didn't bother anyone. She found her way back to the front door and slid out. The black clouds scudded away over the mountains in the distance and the last rumble of thunder went with them. She noted not a drop of rain had fallen. Again.

When she got to the barn, the gryphon had disappeared. She looked in every stall, pausing only to rub the soft nose of a lovely gray mare who whinnied at her.

The mare's eyes were big, and she switched her tail as though annoyed. Alyssa asked her, "Do you know where the King has gone?"

The mare nodded her head. At least that's what it seemed like to Alyssa. The mare turned and moved to the other side of her stall, putting her head over the barrier. The teen followed her direction and peered out of the other end of the barn. The gryphon lounged on his belly in the grass, looking up at the now mostly clear sky.

"King," Alyssa said in a loud hiss. "What are you doing?"

He sat up and struggled to stand. Finally, he moved over to where she stood, and quietly said, "The sky cleared, the rain didn't fall, I have taken a rest. And I still require more."

She handed the apple to him. He pinched the apple with his front claw and lifted it to his mouth. Between munching, he mumbled, "Thank you."

"Why do you require more rest? Seemed like you were wide awake while we flew here."

"I am not accustomed to having riders. It uses more of my energy than normal flying."

She didn't reply to that. When he finished the apple, she took the core and handed him the bread. "I don't think we're staying overnight," she told him. "Unless Lord Bryon insists, we should be ready to go soon. Rest while you can."

"Hm," said the King. And he chewed longer on the bread.

"Do you plan on staying out here in the barn?" she asked.

"Yes. I have no need of seeing a manor home that is smaller than my own."

She sighed at his rudeness before taking leave of him. She dropped the apple core in a refuse pile, cleaned the charger of crumbs, and strolled from the barn back to the manor house.

The gryphon was useless for now. He'd made it clear he would have his rest. Before she could enter the manor again, a familiar face came rushing at her.

"Lady Alyssa!" the tall man shouted as he appeared by her side. He lifted her and spun her around. "When did you arrive?"

She waited until he put her down to answer. Her cheeks hurt from stretching into the grin she wore.

"Fletch, as I live and breathe. It's so good to see you!" she said. Lord Bryon's liegeman had grown taller, and his brown hair needed cutting, but his twinkling blue eyes were the same.

"Wait until I tell Cerius." He tried to look like a proper gentleman, but Alyssa knew his true nature. He was as much a farm boy as she was a farm girl. In love with being outside, dreaming under a tree. And just as happy to see friends when they arrived––something that didn't often happen at her house.

"Where is good old Cerius?" she asked, peering around Fletch for the other liegeman.

"On guard at a border crossing to another realm. There has been some trouble," Fletch said, looking away. She understood he likely wasn't supposed to discuss that sort of thing with anyone.

"Well, it's sure good to see you!" she said, smoothing her hair from the whipping it had taken from the wind. "Will you come and join us?"

"Us?"

"Yes, Edegast and I are traveling together to Knowledge Hall. He has news that Lord Bryon needs to hear, and I've been feeding the gryphon. He's flying us." She kept her opinion about Hubert to herself.

"What? A gryphon?" asked Fletch, shock registering on his face.

She nodded and waved toward the barn. "Remember last year when he was threatening my farm and my granny? He's trying to be on his best behavior now. He's out behind the barn sunbathing if you want to see. Just be forewarned, he ain't pleasant, and you might get an earful of hot air."

Fletch laughed. "I'll see for myself later. For now, I prefer to hear what the wizard says. My lord will not be happy if there is bad news. A lot of bad things happened here since you left last year."

"We'll have to catch each other up," she said with a smile. They went into the house together. She gave him a few sidelong glances. He was the same Fletch but seemed older now, more worldly. She wished they were staying longer so she could spend more time renewing their friendship.

When they entered the dining hall, Fletch addressed his lord and got permission to sit with them. Alyssa handed the charger to a liveried man nearby and sat at the table by Edegast. Feeling thirsty, she drank from the tankard she'd left behind. The cider was cold and sweet and full of something that she assumed was cinnamon or clove. Her pack remained untouched and motionless.

"Alyssa, I'm glad you've brought Fletch back with you," Bryon said. "Edegast says there is news, and my liegemen will need to be informed. Cerius is not available right now, but we can let him know later."

Edegast nodded and leaned in toward the manor lord. "Yes, and foul news it is."

"Let's have it then," Bryon said, crossing his arms.

"Well, the unfortunate spell Alyssa created last year that resulted in the growth of portal plants has been a catalyst for the Dark Master to rise."

"Portal plants? The putrid ones? The ones I told you to burn?" Bryon asked, turning to Alyssa with wide eyes. "Please tell me that you did as I suggested!"

Alyssa nodded. "Yes, oh yes. But unfortunately, it isn't just the plants that we have to contend with. There are holes—"

"Ahem, Bryon, did you see any openings behind the plants once you destroyed them?" Edegast asked, interrupting Alyssa before she could go into details.

"Yes, but we filled in the holes."

"Have you assigned a man to watch over them since then?"

Here, Lord Bryon hemmed and hawed a moment. "Well, no. You see, I have used most of my men to roust out the hiding place of the Needlemount unpleasantness. Ragon and Madrid continue to be trouble in the realm, you see."

Edegast pulled on his beard and sat back. "Those two rats are long gone. I would not be surprised to find them somewhere around the ogres' territory by now."

"No. We have found their underground tunnels, and I believe we are getting close. We have only recently returned home for the fall harvest. My men are needed here, for now. But we will return." The manor lord frowned and sounded convinced. "There is much trouble brewing with Ragon and Madrid. And now the Dark Master? I fear the path is one and the same."

"How so?" Edegast asked, straightening his robes.

"The Needlemount men would love nothing better than to be in league with such terror." Lord Bryon's brow furrowed. "We have wondered about the tunnels. They are far older than Needlemount itself. Used by the men there but perhaps not created by them."

"Ah. Then, danger lurks beneath that castle. I can imagine nothing worse," Edegast replied, almost to himself. Then, gazing hard at Bryon, he asked, "Have you encountered any of the dreadful creatures that the Dark Master employs?"

The manor lord looked worried as he shook his head. "No. Please tell me that we will not encounter them either!"

Edegast looked down and shifted in his seat. "If you are lucky. My advice is with home and hearth first, for now. Securing the manor and grounds and those of your liegemen, most importantly. The trouble underneath Needlemount Castle drives the need to protect your realm. Tell King Carigo. Have him strengthen the forces."

The atmosphere shifted to one of shade and gloom.

"He knows," Bryon said. "At least the realm is united in that. But he won't send anyone to help us."

"Sir," Alyssa addressed Bryon, "Don't you think you should go visit where the plants used to be? I'm curious if the holes have reappeared."

Lord Bryon tilted his head. "Is this what happened with yours?"

She nodded and glanced at Fletch.

"I'll go, my lord," Fletch said. "It is a simple matter after all."

"I'll go with you," Alyssa added, hoping for more time with her friend.

Bryon shook his head. "No, we will all go. Too many plights about. I trust no direction at the moment."

Edegast picked up his staff and said, "Time is of the essence apparently. If Ragon and Madrid have discovered the portals, they may well be training with the Dark Master."

The group walked out of the manor house and, once they were in the courtyard, Cerius found them. He leapt from his horse and shook their hands, beaming at Alyssa as if she were a long-lost sister. He asked what they were about to do and sobered when they told him they were going to view where the portal plants had been.

"This cannot be a good thing," he whispered to Fletch as he fell into step between the younger man and Alyssa. "I'll be going too."

Alyssa was happy to have both of the men along. It was similar to how she'd felt last year. Cerius seemed not changed at all, even though the poor fellow had been hurt a couple of times on their errand to find the scarf. Shad shifted in the pack, and she was reminded of how dangerous the Greater Daegries could be.

Bryon yelled for his stableman to bring horses, and the group waited while he did so. Cerius let his horse rest while they waited. It was nearly an hour before the rest of them were atop their steeds and headed to the plants' resting place.

The ride was not long, but it did take them along the edge of the woods where Alyssa had encountered a dryad named Rylee. Time had softened the edges of that memory until Alyssa felt sure it was a dream. She would never feel the same about trees again, though, and always spoke to the trees when around them.

The portal plants had been up against the far end of the woods. They dismounted letting the horses graze in the dried grass. As one, they walked over to examine the area. None of the plants had grown back.

"Do you suppose the plants weren't able to grow back due to the shade from the woods?" Alyssa asked the manor lord, assessing the land.

Lord Bryon shook his head. "It did not stop them last time. They thrived in fact."

The charred ground looked as though nothing might ever grow there again. But Alyssa wasn't fooled. She'd seen it happen.

"Now," Lord Bryon said. "As to the holes... "

He pulled some weeds aside and revealed a few saplings that were burned behind them, but no hole appeared.

Edegast was not convinced. He moved through the brush and into the woods beyond. The others looked one to the other, wondering if they should follow.

His shouting brought them all running forward into the unknown.

Chapter Nine

They quickly looked at each other as if weighing the danger versus the lack of weaponry. Alyssa had her pack but no weapons, and Lord Bryon and his men had daggers sheathed to their hips but no longswords

"Edegast!" Bryon yelled, peering into the gloom before them.

Alyssa's heart thrummed in her chest as she took stock. Where had the wizard gone? He hadn't taken more than three or four steps... then she saw the hole.

"Wait! Lord Bryon!" she exclaimed, pointing at the darkness that was to the left of where they had entered.

"Great Gods," Fletch said with an exhaled breath.

They moved toward the hole and listened, but there was nothing echoing from within.

"Now what?" Alyssa asked, looking to Lord Bryon.

Cerius spoke up. "This is a dangerous situation, my lord. I believe we should return to the manor house and collect rope. We cannot be certain how to proceed without knowing how far the hole goes."

"No," Alyssa said, heart pounding in her ears. "I'm not leaving this spot. Edegast has traveled these holes. He'll know what to do."

"Traveled them?" Bryon asked, eyebrows raised. "What does that mean?"

"I can't tell you the story, sir. I don't know all of it. He got to my farm through a portal hole like this one; that's all I know."

Bryon stood a moment staring into the blackness and finally sighed. "This is where we never know what to do that will be helpful or harmful. Cerius, you and Fletch go back. I will stay with Lady Alyssa. Bring more men with you, armed to the teeth. And rope, and even bring the ladder from the stables. We will have to be prepared for everything."

His comrades nodded and dug through the overgrown brush to return from where they had come. She heard the horses neigh at the returning men.

She kicked at a bit of dirt and tried to think. *What on earth would Pappy do?*

Then, as if something turned on in her head, she could hear her grandfather's voice as plain as if he stood before her.

Now gal," the voice said. *Ain't you a magik-user? Ain't you my mage-in-training? Get a spell going, Lys.*

A spell! Of course!

She looked around for a few items to conjure with. Ferns, lichen, leaves, and ... *oh, goodness, is that yarrow?*

She hurried over to the thick brush with sprouting weeds of all kinds. Some people would mistake the herb she wanted for a weed, and no doubt.

Blowing in the breeze stood yarrow, tall and bright, its white petals dotted with yellow. Yarrow needed plenty of hot and dry weather to thrive and, for the first time, Alyssa thanked the drought that had plagued them for the last year.

She asked Bryon for his knife to cut one of the plants off near the ground. No need for a lot. When she had gathered her ingredients, she handed the knife back to Bryon, piled everything together, and pulled her pack off. She set it beside the pile and plopped down right in front of it, cross-legged.

"Lady, are you making a fire? I am not sure that is such a good idea," Lord Bryon said, watching her.

"No," she replied. "I'm making a conjure. I need to be able to see Edegast and know where he is."

She called forth her magik power and it came from her fingertips flowing into the pile. Soon a flame flickered to life, but this fire didn't consume the items gathered there. She muttered a chant over and over.

"Edegast come forth. Edegast... come forth!"

"My lady, you have been working on your magik, 'tis plain," Bryon said, excited.

She only nodded. It was true. Calling forth her magik was easy to her now. Both Granny and Pappy had encouraged her to hone the skill. She'd done a lot of learning on her own, too.

She ceased her intonation and watched the flames closely. They went from yellow and orange to a blue close to the center. Inside the flames, she could faintly see Edegast, turning around and around as though lost.

"Edegast!" she called to him. "Come back!"

He stopped moving as though he heard her. He cupped his ear and leaned toward the darkness. Bryon peered into the flames from over her shoulder.

"Come back!" Alyssa and Bryon yelled together.

Edegast shrugged and walked away, disappearing into the nothingness. When he didn't reappear, Alyssa looked back at Bryon. He took a step back, a frown creasing his brow.

Blue shot into the air from the fire, and it went out in a great flurry of sparks. The plants lay there wilted and smoking but whole.

"Well, that's that, I guess," Alyssa said.

"He seemed to hear us," Bryon acknowledged. "Not to worry now, my lady. The wizard is brilliant. He will not leave us wanting." The manor lord poured his water bladder onto the smoking pile. "Safety first, eh?"

Alyssa shrugged as she brushed dirt from her breeches. "What should we do in the meanwhile?" the manor lord asked.

Catching up her pack by its straps, she tossed it over her shoulder and stomped to the yawning hole.

"I think I should follow him," she announced. "He might need me."

"No," Bryon said, waving his hands. "That is not necessary, and meant most kindly, not a good use of wisdom."

She paced back and forth in front of the hole. Edegast wouldn't leave them like this. He would find a way to get back... unless he was captured.

Her heart leapt into her throat. What if he *was* captured? "Lord Bryon, Edegast could be in danger. What if the enemy has attacked him?" She lowered her voice. "He feared the holes were tools of the... you know."

His shoulders slumped, and his face became somber. "We have to wait for the men to come. Someone will have to go into that hole. Someone battle-ready."

"Me!" she insisted. "I can do this, Lord Bryon."

"No, my lady. Not you. I have my doubts about a grown man armed with protection in there. Let us wait a bit and see."

Alyssa felt as though she were being told to go play with a toy. Bryon wouldn't allow her to go now but especially not after his men returned. Men far better prepared for battle, in his eyes. He didn't understand magik.

Alyssa waited for her opportunity. When he stepped closer to the brush and looked through it for his men, Alyssa dove into the black pit.

Once inside, she couldn't see her hand in front of her face. A vicious, cold wind blew through the passageway. A *fell* wind, Pappy would call it. One that bode ill. Fear made her cling tighter to the pack straps as she took tentative steps forward.

From past experience in dealing with a dragon, something told her not to yell out for the wizard. She kept putting one foot in front of the other, shivering from the wind that wanted to drive her to her knees.

Ignorance of what lay ahead gave her another reason to shiver. And then, like the church bells in Mudden on a clear Yule night, she heard Pappy's voice again.

Use your magik, girl.

She stopped, lowered her head, closed her eyes, and thought. Convinced that Pappy was guiding her, the fear which had held her in its grips fell away.

Use your magik, girl.

Well, if Pappy said to do it, then she could believe it would be okay. She held her hand out in front of her and said, "Magik, come to me now. I need you."

Slowly, a faint green glow began to emit from her palm upward into a strong orb. It hovered over her hand and grew in strength. Shadow did a somersault inside of the pack.

Soon, the glowing orb shone brightly in the dimness, and she could make out shapes and things nearby. Her balance seemed off as she moved forward, so she stretched out one hand to anchor herself. Surprisingly, she touched a wall, rough and uneven.

Something solid. Something to lean on. Relaxing, she tried to be as quiet as possible. Her breath rasped in the eerie silence, and the tiny hairs on her neck twitched.

In the magik's glow, she paused, peered ahead, and moved forward. When the tunnel split off, going left and right, she stamped her foot in frustration.

Which direction to take? Edegast had to face this same dilemma. Which one did *he* take?

As she stood there, indecision filling her, faint whispers and fleeting shadows glimmered in the path to her right. She stepped into that path. Nothing happened. She listened to the whispers. Nothing discernable.

She walked down the path a bit to see if Edegast appeared. If she didn't find him in a few yards, she would come back and try the left side.

Then, a ghostly figure appeared far ahead. She could easily see through its thin form. It motioned for her to follow and disappeared into the inky depths beyond. Cold sweat broke out across her brow.

No way I'm following a specter. It might lead me who knows where.

When sudden loud, maniacal laughter rang out ahead, she turned and fled back the way she had come.

Heart pounding in terror, standing at the juncture of the two paths again, she waited to see if anyone or anything pursued her. The magik orb hovered over her awaiting her command.

Alyssa was at a loss. She had no commands to give it.

She pulled her pack off and allowed Shad to float out. The scarf wriggled and twisted as if to work out the kinks it had endured during the time it was bound. Low calling of her name issued from behind her, likely at the opening to the hole. Lord Bryon and his men would probably be coming soon.

"Shadow, we need to find Edegast. Look around and see if you can find the right way to go. I'm as lost as a goose in the high weeds."

The scarf hovered near the orb for a moment before floating cautiously ahead down the leftmost path. Alyssa lost sight of it for a few moments. Eventually, the scarf returned and quite soon behind it, Edegast came scurrying along, staff up and lit.

"Alyssa," he whispered on arrival. "We must leave here, now. Hurry!"

She didn't even get to answer before he was bounding back up the original path, heading out. "Get back in my pack," she told Shadow as she hurried to follow the wizard's bobbing staff light.

Shad nosed itself into the pack, curled around the Grim, and she pulled the strings tight. She recalled the orb, extinguishing it as they bolted through the darkness.

When they reached the mouth of the hole, Edegast muttered some words, and they scrambled out.

Once on the outside of the hole, Edegast let out a ragged breath and peered at Alyssa. "You should not have followed me."

"Well, if I had *known* you were going to hop into that hole, I wouldn't have worried. I couldn't let you disappear again. Look at what happened the last time!"

He nodded. Lord Bryon gripped his nearest arm, fear flowing off him like steam rising.

"Very good to see you back, Wizard. We were on our way momentarily. I was awaiting my men's return," he said. Then with a hand to his heart, he said, "Lady, you gave me such a scare. Please do not disappear like that again!"

Alyssa shrugged and wandered away a few paces. She needed to have some answers, but it seemed that Edegast was not in a hurry to give any.

She watched the two men interact and tried to hear what was said.

"There is no need to go inside the hole, Lord Bryon," Edegast was saying. "The darkness is complete and there is no way to breach it. The way has been blocked for one to go forth from the inside to its next stop in the world. I fear coming through to here may still be viable. You would be wise to post a sentry. Be prepared for the utmost wickedness to ooze out."

Lord Bryon's eyebrows lifted in curiosity just before he turned at the sound of horses approaching. He pulled the brush back to wave at Cerius and Fletch returning.

Alyssa had no idea how long she had been in the hole, as the blackness ceased all sense of time and space. It must have been enough time for the others to gain help and return. She looked at the lowering sun and wondered how the gryphon would take the news that they were not going to make it out of the Heightlands today.

Soon, Cerius, Fletch, and ten other men fully garbed in chainmail stood around them, all carrying swords that looked immense and dangerous. Alyssa felt a tiny prick of comfort.

Shad shifted in her pack, wanting out. She turned her back to the crowd and whispered, "Not now. Soon."

But the scarf wasn't waiting. It nosed the pack ties aside and poked out to peer around.

Shadow was halfway out of the pack as Fletch strode toward Alyssa. She caught the scarf as it slid toward the ground, shoved it back into the pack and yanked the ties tight. Fletch knew about Shad, but she didn't want a whole lot of questions about what it had been doing since they last met.

"We've returned," he said as he came to a stop beside her. "What transpired in our absence? The wizard is safe?"

"Yes, he's safe. The hole held nothing but a deep foreboding darkness that he couldn't get through, so he came back." She neglected to tell of her treacherous journey into the hole.

Without a word about Shadow, Fletch lifted an eyebrow and shifted his gaze to the pack. Alyssa gave a quick shake of her head, and he didn't say anything, instead shifting his attention in a totally different direction.

He looked at her closely. "Are you feeling well, my lady?"

"Yes, why?"

He reached out and removed a large blob of gelatinous goo from her hair. "You seem to be appealing to the worm. You went into the hole, eh?"

She shrieked and patted her hair. She didn't hate worms; they were useful for fishing, but she didn't want *that* in her hair. Satisfied that there was nothing more atop her head, she felt her cheeks grow warm at the way Fletch grinned.

"Stop," she said. "You wouldn't like it either."

He coughed to hide a laugh. "It was such a nice bit of worm refuse, too."

She joined in the hilarity, and the sound of it carried on the wind.

Chapter Ten

E degast brushed off questions with a wizardly wave and announced that they needed to be off. He wanted to get some rest and see if the gryphon would carry them northward at night.

If Alyssa had been a gambler, she would have bet against that happening most emphatically. Hubert was like a lazy cat. He wanted to lounge and stretch rather than work these days. But after their arrival back to the manor house, to her great surprise, Edegast strolled from the barn with King Hubert at his side.

"Are you ready to depart?" he asked.

She had been chatting with Cerius and Fletch and quickly nodded. "I am, but I thought you were going to rest?"

"No rest for the weary," he replied with a shrug.

"Did you finish telling Lord Bryon and his men about the hole and what to do with it?" Alyssa asked.

He shuffled his feet and looked down. "Not exactly. There is no fixing the situation here. The Heightlands are riddled with evidence of the Dark Master. I have suggested that they keep a guard over it. We must be away. Quick now."

She didn't reply. He was on a mission to get back to his home and wouldn't admit the portal situation was as dire as returning to the Snowclids, but it most certainly was.

Without a further word, the wizard strode into the manor house and left the gryphon and Alyssa waiting in the courtyard. She said goodbye to her friends and turned to glance at the gryphon in embarrassment.

"Rude," King Hubert muttered watching the entrance where Edegast had disappeared.

"Be quiet," Alyssa admonished. "He's got bigger fish to fry right now, as my Pappy would say."

"Impudent!" Hubert hissed. She tilted her head considering if she should reply. After a momentary pause, Hubert said, "I am not happy about flying through the night like a horned owl."

His sentence explained his prickly demeanor. "That makes two of us," she told him. "But there it is. We ain't doing this for us, are we?"

He fell silent and scratched in the dirt with his claws. Presently, Edegast returned, and Lord Bryon was with him.

"Lady," Bryon said, holding out his hand for her to clasp. "I cannot tell you how good it was to see you. I hope there will be time for more of a visit when you return."

She smiled at him and allowed him to help her mount the gryphon. "Thanks. I'll be happy to have this journey behind me. A cup of nice, mulled cider and a warm fire will be welcome, Lord Bryon. Good luck with finding those rotten scoundrels from the castle."

Fletch came hurrying back at that time, and Alyssa noticed his muscular arms and legs striding smoothly. Gone was the lumbering, boyish gait.

"Lady, I wanted to say goodbye. If you should need anything..." His voice trailed off and his gaze lowered momentarily before he looked into her eyes.

"Thank you, Fletch. I'll be sure to send word as soon as I'm able. I hope that the troubles facing you and your friends is only temporary. Say farewell to Cerius for me."

He winked at her and whispered, "Take mind for the precious cargo you carry. I will be most anxious to hear the tale once the journey is behind you."

Her shoulders relaxed, grateful that he had the good sense not to mention what the cargo consisted of. She nodded and waved goodbye.

The young man said farewell to Edegast, who was finally ready to go, and moved aside for the wizard to climb aboard. Once they were situated, they waved to the lord of Half Moon Manor and Fletch. Hubert rushed toward the tower and the open plain beyond and they lifted into the air. The gryphon turned to face the mountains, the final frontier before they reached the northernmost tip of Daegries.

The Heightlands were as majestic as ever but, from the rider's vantagepoint, didn't seem any different from any other range. As she purveyed the landscape below them, Alyssa wondered where the Yetis were. With their snowy coats, they would blend in so well she wouldn't be able to see them anyway. She wondered how Bred and Fred and the others were faring. They'd been kind to her and Pappy when they were there last year.

Pappy had mentioned starting up some form of trade with them again, but his efforts were hampered from his life in the jack-in-the-box. Maybe now that he was free from it, he could make that happen.

In another hour, Alyssa saw the outline of Needlemount Castle in the distance and wondered what the Heightlanders would do to the rogues of the castle. She didn't like the Needlemount men. They'd earned every bit of hatred the Heightlanders had for them. Ragon and Madrid had made her journey to find the scarf more difficult as well.

Lord Bryon's men sought revenge, and she could think of nothing that would make a man pursue an enemy more. Even into the tunnels beneath a castle. She hoped the Dark Master hadn't taken the scoundrels in and made them any worse. They didn't need help with wickedness and evil.

At dusk, they passed over a massive forest, and Alyssa remembered the kind elves who had tended her hurts last year. Could it be this forest? From a gryphon's back or a bird of prey, the viewpoint seemed different. This forest disappeared and reappeared through the clouds, brooding.

She might well be half elf, she recalled. After her last journey, she imagined living with the elves, as wild as the lichen growing on the trees. Now seeing the forest beneath them, a longing to go there smote her. Shadow moved inside of her pack, rearranging itself and the Grim. The scarf might be feeling the pull of the forest creatures as she did.

Alyssa planned to talk to Edegast about journeying to find her lost parents, but so far there had been no good time. Maybe she would have a chance to discuss it, once the Grim was safely entombed at Knowledge Hall. She wanted to find a way to get back to the phoenix and enlist her aid also.

She took a deep breath, remembering the hitch in her plan. The Dark Master might be a problem. Disappointment filled her. She would speak to Edegast about what could be done, if anything. All he could do was say no.

When evening fell, there was no moon to light their way and Hubert descended lower, barely skimming the mountaintops. If she leaned far out, she could touch the uppermost tree branches. She wanted to ask why the gryphon was so low, but the cold wind would throw her words backwards away from him.

She pulled her hood up and tried to stay warm with thoughts of a hot mug of tea or cider upon arrival at Knowledge Hall. A bite of crusty bread, a hunk of cheese...

Alyssa dozed for a time because she jerked awake with her chin to her chest. They were settling down in a thick patch of snow. Edegast leapt from the gryphon's back, and she offered her hand for him to help her dismount. He pulled her off at such an angle that she stumbled to keep upright. With childish abandon, Edegast threw a snowball at her, laughing maniacally.

"We're here! We're here!" he cried out. "Hubert, find shelter as soon as possible or your beak may freeze! Come along, Alyssa. Home! Sweet home!"

He whirled around and headed for the shadowy castle behind him. A strong snow blew drifts against the walls painting the dull gray stone in brilliant white.

She remembered Edegast's warning to her grandparents about the weather. They probably wouldn't be looking for her anytime soon.

The Oh farm had big snows, but nothing like this. She couldn't marvel at it enough. Finally, with a deep chill embracing her, Alyssa hurried to catch up with Edegast before he could disappear into the depths of the citadel. Her movements were slowed by the depth of the snow, but she trudged hard through it.

Once inside, Edegast skidded to a stop and brushed snow from his person. She entered behind him and stood taking in the view of Wizard Hall.

There was a long foyer of sorts, with round settees in the middle of it where one could sit and remove outerwear. Carved trees with upturned branches for hanging wet clothing sat along the walls.

The high ceiling had painted colors in swirls appearing to move as you stood looking at it. Upon closer examination, Alyssa decided that some unknown magik moved through it.

A suit of armor to the right gleamed as if recently polished, and Alyssa admired it. She turned around and around, seeing things for the first time. Edegast allowed her to gape.

"It is quite a lot to take in," he said, removing his gloves and stamping his boots to remove the snow that clung to them. Then he added his cloak and hood to the ones hanging on the trees. She followed his actions, seeing snow on her own feet, and breathed a sigh to finally be free of her wet outer clothes.

"Now, where is everyone?" Edegast asked, absently.

He took off again, and she had to hurry to keep up. He made it to the end of the entry hall, turned to the right and down another corridor with paintings of wizards lining the walls.

"Who are all these?" Alyssa asked as she sped along. "Friends of yours?"

He shook his head. "No. More like ancestors. I will give you an official tour later with better explanations."

They went down a short staircase and, when they reached the bottom, they ran into a collection of people. Edegast stopped so suddenly that Alyssa almost ran into him.

A short man with a balding pate, dressed in brown robes tied in the middle with a strong rope, stood conversing with a woman dressed in a red robe. She seemed irritated and sighed more than once at what he said.

Edegast stepped up to them and asked, "Where is Trudor?"

The couple and a few others turned to stare at him. "Where indeed!" the woman replied. "That's why we are all gathered here, Edegast the Green. You should not go off on matters of no interest to the Wise. Then you would know what is what."

"What *is* what?" he asked, ruffled.

The short man lowered his voice. "A party of the Wise went out to meet with the Elders. The snow began falling shortly thereafter. Our dear leader is with them. None have returned, and we do not know if they cleared the Snowclids or not. We are about to go into the meeting hall for a council."

Before Edegast could reply, the group filed into a great hall with long tables and two fires, one on either side of the room.

A silent Alyssa followed them and took a chair next to her friend. She pulled her pack off and rested. Once she set it on the ground beside her, Shad wriggled inside, bumping up and down.

She pulled it open a little, made sure the book was still there, undamaged. She pushed Shad away, closed it, and patted the pack, her hand remaining on it for emphasis.

The scarf must have gotten the message. The pack fell into a slump and stilled.

A wizard in a pale-yellow robe walked to the head of the table and rapped a mug for quiet. The voices all went silent.

"As some of you may know, Edegast has returned. We welcome you back, my brother, and hopefully someone with the whole tale can fill you in," he said, smiling at Edegast.

Alyssa didn't know if they were real brothers or if that was simply a way to say friend. Wizards, like elves, had a language of their own.

"The matter before us now is how to get our family back home," the yellow-robed wizard continued. "The snow has gotten so deep that it may be days before they can pass over it, no matter where they are. We do not know as of yet if their mission was fulfilled or if they fell into troubled times."

The woman in the red robe had green eyes that snapped along with her words. "Troubled? I would not say the times are troubled. Nay, Salas, I would say they are terrible. Certainly not suitable to send our most valued leaders off into the elements. Whose idea was this anyway?"

Salas inclined his head. "They made the decision amongst themselves. But, as you say, Horoc, times are not the best we have ever seen. Weatherwise or otherwise. But they would not stay here and ignore our alliances. They would never do that, do you see?"

She crossed her arms, agitated. "Indeed, I do see. I was not consulted, and this grieves me. This is precisely why they should never have gone to the Auld Forest. How shall we find them now? Does anyone know where they have gone? What if their mission failed? What if they are in grave danger?"

Salas listened as she ranted on and on.

Another wizard, who looked to be the youngest gathered there, stood and cleared his throat. "If I may...?"

Salas waved for him to continue.

"Trudor and the others were headed to see the Elders. They may have encountered poor conditions in the mountains and are simply waiting for it to clear. Likely they will return home and try again on another day. No wizard in his right mind would attempt to cross the plain into the forest with weather such as this."

Alyssa wondered if by Elders they meant Elves.

Salas gripped the staff he held. "Their journey was of the utmost importance. Trudor would not dismiss it so easily."

Horoc closed her eyes and scowled. "Again, I should have been with them. Old wizards have no business being in charge of important business anyway. Even if they make it through the mountains, there is the matter of the dangers..."

Salas straightened. "We shall not speak of that here, Horoc. Edegast, please give us your thoughts. You are Trudor's heir. What do you say?"

At this Alyssa's eyes went wide. Edegast was their leader's heir? This was news! *Likely not Salas's brother then*. She peered at the wizard and tried to assess his age. Then she looked around at the others. None were her age. Trudor must be aged beyond measure.

Edegast's quiet voice said, "My thoughts are in alignment with Mani the Yellow, but first, I need to know how long the party has been gone?"

Horoc quickly answered, "Since the full moon."

"The moon is faceless," Edegast said with a sigh. "Close to two weeks. That is barely enough time to... to find the Elders. They likely have been delayed," he said, measuring his words.

"You are not fearful for your father?" Horoc asked, tilting her head toward him. Her green eyes were inquisitive as if his answer would solve a dilemma for her.

"We are living in peril, daily. I fear for all of us," he replied, dryly.

"Very well," Salas said. "If you feel that there has not been enough time to even make it to their destination, then I shall sleep better tonight."

Edegast nodded and the others turned to stare at him and the young girl beside him. "This is my young mage in training, Alyssa Chance Oh from the Farmlands. I promised Trudor I would bring her for an examination with the prospect of her becoming a lower-level wizard."

Alyssa's mouth fell open, and she gaped at him. Mage in training? How was that never spoken of before now? He didn't mention the scarf's arrival either, so she made a mental note to keep that to herself also.

Horoc narrowed her eyes. "Indeed? A trainee you say?" Her words brought all eyes back to Alyssa, and she looked down, uncomfortable at the scrutiny. Horoc covered her head with her hood and turned away.

Edegast didn't elaborate but instead asked for food and drink to be brought for them to celebrate his homecoming.

Serving men hurried out to fulfill his request.

Salas bowed to Alyssa. "Alyssa, this is mostly a calm gathering within these walls. You should not take anything you may have heard here to heart. We are simply concerned for our brothers and sisters who have gone on a journey to a neighboring realm. It is wonderful that you have come to us. Edegast, how did you get here during such a storm as blows outside?"

Edegast pulled on his beard and thought hard. "We flew on a gryphon, and I'm afraid in my excitement to be back, I have all but abandoned him. I hope he found a way into shelter."

"A gryphon?" Horoc asked, sitting forward.

"Yes, from the Meadowlands. He is a king in his realm, so please be mindful when you encounter him. I suppose I should go and tend to his needs. He is a stranger in a strange land."

With that the wizard rose and strode to the doorway. He disappeared the way they had come, leaving Alyssa alone with the others.

She gazed about nervously, wondering what to say. Thankfully, the first course came around at that time and she finally got to sip something warm and delicious, a hot cup of cocoa. The man served it in a tin mug, so the warmth of the metal gave new life to her frozen hands.

Salas smiled at her, and she noted he had kind gray eyes. "My dear, I know you have had quite a time getting here. I have sent word that you should be put in a room on my floor. Your comforts will be attended to as well as we can provide. Unfortunately, Knowledge Hall wasn't built for luxury."

While she watched the men bringing platters of food around, she wondered where they got their supplies. The Snowclids were the farthest mountains in the Upper Daegries. Who brought goods this far north?

She addressed Salas. "Sir, can I ask a question?"

He nodded.

"How do you get something as precious as cocoa this far north? Who supplies you way up here?"

He laughed and the edges of his eyes crinkled. "You are a breath of fresh air, Alyssa. Yes, we do have trouble getting foodstuffs up here sometimes. We store up supplies all summer and fall. If we don't have it by now, well, we will go without until the spring thaw."

He made it sound as though winter in the Snowclids would keep anyone from coming there. If that was so, then getting out of here might prove difficult also. And it didn't bode well for the travelers from Wizard Hall. He also neglected to answer her question directly, she noted.

Mani the Yellow spoke to her. "Alyssa, tell us about your homeland. I have never seen the Farmlands except in our books. Is it very big?"

This was something that Alyssa could talk about for days. She smiled at the curious wizard and said, "Oh, not terrible big. It's got a lot of land to it, but mostly there's food being grown there. We have a few towns dotted around. I actually don't get out that much. I live with my grandparents, and I help out on our farm."

He nodded, interested in her words. She decided to continue. "Yes, our farm is near a town called Mudden, and the folks there are pretty advanced, so far as ideas go. Not so much toward healers and such, no, but more like in farming and politics. Least, that's what my pappy tells me."

She ducked her head as she realized no one there knew anything about Pappy or the fact that he was the one who had the Grim. Those who knew anything about the situation were likely the ones traveling.

"Are you a healer, then?" Horoc asked, listening to Alyssa's explanation.

She nodded and took a good look at Horoc. "Are you a healer too? There's something about you..."

Horoc laughed and looked across at Salas who had taken a seat. "No, no. Not a healer, I would say. More of a w... witch to be honest."

This intrigued Alyssa, because Granny had been called a witch by Mudden folks and it wasn't complimentary.

Horoc finished, "I am visiting the castle to... eh... take a sabbatical, in a way." She hid her face by pulling the edges of her hood closer and now Alyssa knew it was on purpose. She wasn't that cold.

When the soup was served, Alyssa dug in. It tasted delicious, filled with onions, parsnips, and savory herbs. Silence descended on the room as everyone ate.

Finally, Edegast returned and reseated himself. A serving man brought him a bowl of soup which he slurped into his mouth taking care not to slosh any into his beard. But despite all precautions, a drop fell into it, and she hid a smile.

When he finished his soup, platters of meat and vegetables were served, and Alyssa selected a few potatoes and carrots with one hunk of what she hoped was venison.

Edegast passed a platter to his left and said, "King Hubert is doing well. He came into the front hall, but it was not to his liking, so he has selected the barn and a nice pile of hay for his resting place. I didn't tell him that the temperature would be terrible tonight, as he insisted that he would be fine. Salas, perhaps we could offer him some blankets?"

"I will see that it is done," Salas said with a nod.

Bet old Hubert thought the hall was too sparse for a King. His clawed feet would be cold in that barn, she mused.

Alyssa smothered a smile at the thought. She leaned toward the wizard, and asked, "Edegast, how will we get out of here? The snow was really coming down."

He shrugged. "I am not at all certain we will be able to for a time. If Solly the Sun smiles down on us for a few days and the snow stops, maybe then we can fly away. Good thing you came prepared for a stay. I warned your folks that it might be a good while before we returned."

She took a deep breath of acceptance, but still worried over the constable who had been at the door when they hurried off. She wondered what on earth that old grump had wanted.

One of Granny's sayings came to mind. *Worrying about things you can do nothing about is like being in a rocking chair. You rock and rock, but you don't get nowhere.*

Chapter Eleven

After dinner, Alyssa grew tired and asked to be shown to her sleeping quarters.

Salas volunteered. Edegast stayed behind to talk with his friends. She wondered where his room was in the castle. It was a massive place, and wandering around in it to find him would be a mistake.

In fact, getting to her room by following Salas was difficult. The castle was cold, too. Bitterly so. She longed for a warm fire and a heavy quilt to lie under to thaw out her frozen limbs.

When they turned yet another corner and strode down yet another corridor, she asked Salas, "Sir, I hope you'll escort me to breakfast in the morning. I don't think I'll ever find it alone."

He laughed. "Oh, never fear, my dear. I will come for you, or Edegast will. Maybe you should spend the day tomorrow touring our home to become familiar with the lay of it."

She didn't say so, but she thought that she likely would do that very thing. There was no way of knowing how long she might be snowed in, and knowledge was power, she had learned.

Finally, they obtained a hallway with rooms on either side. Salas used a large keychain and searched for the right key. When he found it, he unlocked the heavy wooden door.

The room inside was exactly what Alyssa had been dreaming about. It was well-lit with candles, had a fire roaring in the fireplace, and the bed, a nice four-poster with heavy coverings on it. The curtains around it were open. In the corner was an earthen pot to relieve oneself in, and in the other, a nice wooden screen to dress behind. The window, an arrow slit, was open with no sash, but it had a banner hanging over it to block the worst of the weather.

Alyssa sighed in relief. All the necessities had been thought of and she approved. She grinned at Salas, and he nodded with a returning smile.

"Please know that I am next door if you should need anything, my dear."

She set the pack down and collapsed in a chair in front of the fire.

"I'll be fine, thank you."

He murmured something and left quietly as she sat in front of the fireplace, soaking in the solitude. Knowing that the kind wizard was close by gave her a sense of peace.

Eventually, she heard the pack bouncing up and down and realized that there was no reason Shad should remain hidden any longer.

She pulled the drawstring open, and the scarf floated out, twining itself around her ankles as if to beg her not to stick it in the pack again.

She petted it like she would a dog. Finally, it settled on her shoulders after she pulled off her heavy coat and boots. She had been wrapped as tightly as she could but the cold permeated everything. She was happy to wrap in the woolen blanket lying across the chair and warm her frozen toes in front of the fire.

With Shad across her lap, she was so content, she dozed. She didn't know how long it had been when a knock sounded on the door. She shushed Shad to be quiet and threw the blanket over it.

Edegast stood there. "My lady, if I may have a word with you before retiring?"

She pulled the heavy door aside slightly and admitted him in. The wizard had been outside again. Remains of snow were on his cloak. "Where's Hubert?" she asked.

The wizard strode to the fire and stood before it to warm himself. "Oh, this is so nice."

She reseated herself and motioned toward a matching chair against the wall. He pulled it over and sat, his robes billowing around him.

"Where's the gryphon?" she asked again.

"Oh, he's in the stables. He wanted to be outside. Why, I do not know."

"Maybe he's afraid to be in here with so many humans? He hasn't been around that many that I know of."

Edegast shrugged. "Perhaps. He would be infinitely more comfortable inside, however. I left it up to him. He could come inside whenever it pleases him. He seemed dissatisfied when he came inside earlier. As if there was something wrong with the castle."

She nodded and looked back at the flames in the fire. A gryphon from the Meadowlands would certainly find such stony, damp accommodations unworthy, she imagined. Edegast cleared his throat and finally got to why he had come.

"So, Alyssa, you didn't have a chance to say anything to me at dinner. I know that you were not aware of the possibility of training as a mage, but the thought is there. I feel certain Trudor will agree."

"No, I didn't have time, and you should let a body know before you say something like that. I nearly choked."

"My apologies."

"So, why did you come here to my room? Not just to apologize?"

He straightened his collar and pulled on his beard. "No, not just that."

She waited. Was he about to confide in her about something else? What else could have him in such a dither?

His eyes misted over, and he grew solemn. "The party of my family, Trudor and the others, has been gone for too long. I lied to the others; may the gods forgive. The journey should have been over by now with the whole party safely returned."

She blinked a few times trying to understand.

"They have not returned, and my fear is that they have fallen into some evilment. I have come to you for the Grim. If they are not coming back, and that may be the case, then it should be protected."

She stared at his nervous movements and asked, "Why are you so fidgety about this?"

He twisted his hands together. "I am afraid to handle it. That book is the essence of magik for all time. It is believed to be able to stop the Dark Master, and for one to even be able to touch it is a privilege afforded to few. I only used it at your house. I did not handle it."

She had never seen him this way. "Well, I've handled it. Pappy's handled it, and I bet your daddy has handled it plenty. What makes you think it's something you can't touch?"

He smiled a small smile. "It isn't that I cannot. It is that I should not. I am not special enough."

She stood, stretched, uncovered the scarf so it could be free to float around the room, and went to the pack to dig around. Finally, she found the book and hefted it with one hand. She peered at the cover before taking it to the wizard. It was only a leather-bound tome, thankfully, not wet or torn.

"Here you go, Edegast. It's not special, neither to me nor mine and I suspect not to you either. There ain't no reason to feel less than you are. You're a wizard and more powerful than any of us."

She held it out to him but, when he went to take it, the book fell out of her hands onto Shadow who had parked itself at her feet. The scarf wrapped itself around the book like a final farewell hug.

"Shadow, release the book," Alyssa said.

The scarf held onto the book, tighter.

Edegast used his sternest voice. "Scarf, let go of my book."

Shadow lifted one corner as if to peer at him.

The wizard then reached down to pull the scarf from around the book. Alyssa reached down to pick up the book.

The scarf decided they would not separate it from its new friend, and rose to the ceiling, holding tight to the Grim.

Alyssa thrust her hands onto her hips and glared at the scarf. "I'm your owner, Shadow. You have to obey me."

Reluctantly, the scarf lowered until it floated waist high. It unwrapped itself from the book enough so that Alyssa could take the book.

"I declare Edegast, I don't know what's gotten into Shadow. Never had this happen. Usually, it's happy to do my bidding."

"Ah well," Edegast replied. "The scarf has been on a journey as we have. Perhaps it is overtired."

"Scarf did hear the story about you-know-who, remember? Wonder if that has anything to do with it?" she asked.

Edegast lifted his brows in surprise. Alyssa reminded him that the scarf had been his magik tool as he made points in his story to the Oh family.

"Oh, yes. Quite right," Edegast said, nodding.

Alyssa frowned at the offending scarf, and Shad flipped itself into a roll before flopping onto the bed in defeat. Alyssa handed the book out for Edegast to take.

He extended his hand, and his fingers tried to grip the book. But the tome flipped in his hand like a live fish, and he dropped it again.

Alyssa scooped up the book, and he waved her away, refusing to try a third time.

"Perhaps it should remain in your care for a little longer," he said, staring at the scarf. "Sometimes magik has a way of letting us know when we are overstepping. Or stepping over... something."

Alyssa shrugged and placed the book back in the pack. It was safer out of sight for now. Then she repositioned her chair to feel the heat a little less and sat.

"What is the plan, Edegast? Are you going to see me safely back home with King Hubert, or am I staying until the weather clears? Do you have something else entirely in mind? I feel a little like a mushroom over here being kept in the dark."

Edegast paced the floor in front of the fire, stopping occasionally to reheat his hands. Finally, he answered. "Alyssa, I do not know how to answer. I want you to meet Trudor. He is the wisest of us all. He is getting aged, and death could come at any time. I will ascend to a higher-level wizard when and if that occurs."

He paused to look at her. "It is our custom to find a replacement when either ascension or death occurs. Better done early rather than late."

"But what about my—" she began.

"Your farm and family will be looked after, I promise. My word is good, you know that. But this matter is dire. With the Dark Master alive, albeit in what condition I do not know, I must go ahead with plans to act against him. I am not holding you captive, please know that. But I need you here, my dear, to keep up with the Grim and have Shadow handy if it should be needed. Apparently the two are inseparable." He stared meaningfully at the scarf.

At that, Shadow slipped down and into the pack.

She took a long moment to digest his words. What about Pappy and Granny and the fact that she and the wizard had practically left them to be arrested? "Couldn't I go back home, make sure things are good there and then come back?"

He sat again on the chair next to hers. "There is so much danger in the world of Daegries right now, Alyssa, I dare not even consider sending either of you, King Hubert or yourself, anywhere. Not to mention fall has already turned into winter as you have seen."

She crossed her arms. Her voice sounded petulant even to her own ears. "Edegast, I have to go home! My folks don't have anyone else but me. You've got wizards everywhere that you can choose. Why me?"

He reached over and patted her arm. "Because none of them has the blood of the Iefyr running in their veins. You, my dear, may well be a major reason we will win against the Dark Master this time and put an end to him forever."

"How could I be the one to defeat him?"

He shrugged. "That is a matter still being deciphered. Suffice to say, he has weaknesses, and you have strengths."

"And a scarf that is protective of me," she added with a sigh.

He inclined his head, tapping his finger against his temple. "You must begin to change your thinking from Mudden-way to Wizard-way. Things here are not like back home. You..." he paused waiting for her to finish a large yawn. "You are tired."

"Yes, I'm tired. Aren't you?"

He nodded. "Let's revisit this tomorrow."

"Okay. Maybe there'll be something we can do to help my family and the world at the same time."

He strolled to the door. "There really is not. I have contemplated long and hard over this matter. But if Trudor returns soon, we will ask for his counsel. He is far wiser than I."

"Those words sound hollow, Edegast. You seemed to think they weren't coming back earlier."

"We shall keep a positive outlook, my dear. Keep hope until hope is lost."

Edegast opened the door with a loud creak and closed it behind him. Alyssa had no idea where he was sleeping, so she gave up wondering about it. Instead, she pulled off her breeches and tunic, dressed in a long nightshirt, and crawled into the bed. It was filled with pillows and deliciously heavy covers. Before she dropped off, she remembered the strange way the Grim had acted, and she wondered why. Soon, she sank into a deep sleep and worried thoughts turned into dreams.

The next morning the sun rose, and Alyssa was blissfully unaware of it. She slept so soundly that she didn't hear Salas's knock. She also didn't hear Edegast as he creaked open the door to peek in on her.

When she finally did rise up and stretch, the day was fully underway.

"I need something hot to drink and food to stop my belly from grumbling," she declared to the scarf who had snuck up the bed and curled near to her. "And you, dear one, must get under the covers so that no one sees you. It's not time to introduce you yet."

She rushed over to add wood to her fire and pull her clothes and boots on. Shad inched along, digging into the bedding until completely hidden within its folds.

When she had the fire toasting her room once more, she used the pot in the corner and found a stand of wood that held a pitcher and a towel. There was a bowl of water there as well, so she dipped one edge of the towel into the cold water and wiped her face.

It would be an excellent experience to have a nice hot bath soon, but she wasn't hopeful. Wizards wore oversized robes, which masked their body smell somewhat, but not completely, she remembered wrinkling her nose. Baths might not be even possible. Although if wood could be brought in, and snow could be melted… they could do it, she figured.

Edegast's words returned to mind, and she pondered over what would be required of her to be a mage in training. Maybe she'd get her own staff and wear robes like the others. Maybe staying in Knowledge Hall wasn't a bad thing.

Then she recalled why they had even come to the Snowclids: to hide the Grim. And she thought of the reported wickedness that was spoiling the Greater Daegries.

"That old Dark Master— I'll show him what's what," she muttered pretending to take a stab at someone with an imaginary sword. She'd get to learn how to wield a sword too, she assumed. Everyone in the entire world would have to learn how to use weapons. Everyone would need to be armed.

But is there a weapon that can be used against the shadow arts of magik?

She strode over to the pack and reassured herself that the Grim was still safely tucked inside. Then, on second thought, she pulled it out and sat with it on her lap. She flipped through the first few pages and found diagrams of things she didn't understand and languages she didn't know how to read.

"Great," she muttered, closing the book. "The source of all that is good in this universe, and I can't even decipher it."

She placed it back where she'd found it and loosely closed the pack so that Shadow could get inside if it so desired.

Time for food and drink, she thought as her stomach let out a loud grumble.

She pulled open the heavy door and stepped out into the hallway, closing it behind her. She heard Shad struggling with the bedcovers and knew as soon as she shut the door, it had flown across the room to be with her, one moment too late.

She didn't stop but went directly to the room next door hoping to find Salas.

She rapped hard on the door, bruising her knuckles, and waited patiently for him to respond.

Nothing.

She knocked again and again, but Salas was not within.

"That's lovely," she murmured wearily. She took off down the hall the way she thought that they had come. It was hard to remember. She had been so tired and distracted.

Soon, she came to a turn and took a left. The stairway led down, and she became disoriented. Did she climb up stairs last night? She didn't know, and what would be the harm if she got lost? She'd be honest about it and find someone to help her.

She took the steps quickly at first, but soon, the steps seemed to go down and down and she knew that she had gone the wrong way. While she paused at the bottom of the staircase trying to decide if she should turn around, she heard a loud moan.

Someone is hurt! She wouldn't ignore suffering of another, ever. She was a healer after all and, if someone needed her help, she would give it gladly.

The corridor she found herself in was dimly lit by a few guttering candles. Apparently, whoever was in charge of keeping them lit had gone to breakfast and not returned.

She heard the moan again. Up ahead, and on the right.

She hurried her steps and soon found the reason that the candles were going out. A wizard lay on the cold stone floor of the castle with a bleeding head wound. A candle snuffer lay nearby.

She put her hands on his head and told him she was a healer and that she was there to help him. He didn't say anything coherent, so she didn't ask more. The tunic she wore had a long tail. She pulled it out of her breeches and ripped a long strip from it.

Then she dabbed the injury, wiped away the blood, and peered at it to see what the damage was. It turned out to be a cut that would need to be sewn up. But she felt like she could get things started by using her magik.

She called forth her power and laid her hands on his head. Then, Alyssa closed her eyes and focused all of her attention on the injury. She could feel the healing heat go from her to him.

The only problem with giving another person your power is that it depletes you, she thought, sitting back, weariness taking over.

The man opened his eyes and stared at her. "Who are you?" he asked.

"My name is Alyssa Chance Oh. I'm from Mudden. That's a pretty far piece from here, but I'm glad I was here and not there. I hope you feel some better?"

He nodded gently. "I will be all right eventually. Can you help me up?"

She stood and offered him her hand. The hand that grasped hers was not human. She gulped hard and looked at the face before her. It had changed swiftly and now did not appear human in any way.

Her last coherent thought was, *How did that happen?*

Chapter Twelve

Alyssa awoke in a bed in a room with an immense amount of sunlight flooding it. She licked her lips and found them swollen and sore.

She tried to move but didn't have the energy to even lift her arm to bring it above the blanket. Something had happened to her, but she couldn't figure out what. It didn't matter though because she fell asleep as soon as the thought came to mind.

When she woke again, the sunlight slanted in the room leaving long shadows. Solly had gone across the sky and was heading to his resting place. She tried to turn her head, but again, it took too much effort.

She wasn't sleepy this time and determined that if she wanted to get up, she would have to begin to move around. She slid her arm out from under the blanket and dropped it heavily across her chest. Then she worked to free the other one.

By the time she accomplished this, sweat rolled from her brow down into her hair. She tried to quiet her breathing from the exerted panting that had started with the effort of moving, leaving her winded and tired.

This is not good, she thought.

She didn't intend to fall back asleep, yet her body was in control, and she couldn't fight it. In a short time, darkness fell, and she knew nothing more.

Alyssa dreamed strange dreams and only barely remembered someone speaking to her softly, wiping her face with cool water.

When she awakened the next time, Edegast was there with someone who was familiar to her, but she couldn't recall why. Edegast leaned close and asked her if she knew who he was.

She licked her dry lips. "Ed-e-gast, "she managed to say.

He stood beside the bed, face drawn from lack of sleep and worry. "Very good, my dear. That's enough for now."

She felt a cup of tea lifted to her lips and drank the cold liquid deeply. Soon slumber came for her again.

This time, she remembered the dream and struggled up from it to tell Edegast. They were all in dire danger.

She opened her eyes and tried to sit upright. The Iefyr woman who sat beside her in a wooden chair came hurrying over. Her face was the same face as when the wizard had been there before.

"You mustn't rush yourself," she told Alyssa. "There is nothing to fear now."

Alyssa's eyes darted to the door. "Where is Edegast?"

"He has gone for his bed. 'Tis very late, Mistress."

Alyssa tried to see out of the covered window slit but no light came from around it. The room was now lit with only candles.

"Who are you?" she asked, slumping back against the pillows and pulling the blanket up to her chin. "I don't know where I am, or who you are."

The woman stood beside the bed and reached over to take her hand. She felt her forehead, too. "My name is Feagus, I am a healer. I will be taking care of you while you recover."

"But... but... you're Iefyr. How did you get to Knowledge Hall?"

She smiled at Alyssa. "I live here in the winter. The wizards have need of herbs and such. We bring medicines, mostly herbs, to them during the growing season. Then since we grew them, and know the most about them, one of us comes here to administer them as needed."

"I guess it was my good fortune that you were here then," Alyssa said, tiredly. She closed her eyes and tried to recall what happened to her after the strange creature rose from the ground. "What happened to me?"

The door to the room opened then and Salas entered. He strode silently to her side. "Ah! So happy to see you awake, Alyssa."

She opened her eyes and smiled at him. "Salas. I'm sorry to be so much trouble."

He patted her shoulder. "No trouble, my dear. You've been through a terrible ordeal."

He turned to the healer. "I am only checking on her as I go to bed. I will return in the morning."

The healer nodded and brought the cup of liquid over to her patient. "Here now, you must drink this to keep yourself calm."

Alyssa nodded and sipped from the outstretched cup. "What is it?" she asked, wrinkling her nose. "Not tea, surely?"

The healer set the cup on the table beside the bed, taking care not to bump the candle which was dripping wax onto the cloth beneath it.

"No, not tea. It is an herbal healing draught."

Alyssa started to say that she was familiar with those and to ask what herbs it contained, but her mouth wouldn't form the words, and her brain shut off all communication at that time.

The next day, Alyssa woke feeling much stronger and it was then that she saw the bandage on her arm. She lifted it to find bite marks beneath it. There were two sets of them as if whatever attacked her didn't get enough the first time.

The healer was not seated where she should have been. Alyssa sat up slowly, hoping that she wouldn't be dizzy. When nothing of the like occurred, she looked around at the room.

It was almost like an herbal apothecary. There were glass bottles lining one wall and a wooden table where someone had been chopping herbs.

The healer had been called away, Alyssa decided. She tried to make out the names on the bottles but couldn't tell from the tiny handwriting. It seemed like from her vantagepoint that the bed had been placed in the room as an afterthought. Likely the healer's bed, she thought.

Alyssa was about to climb from her prison when the door opened and Edegast strolled though.

"Alyssa! So happy to see you awake," he exclaimed, taking her hands and looking closely at her. "You seem better."

She nodded. "I am. I feel myself again. I think that whatever the healer has been giving me has done its job."

"Excellent news!" Edegast smiled and let go of her hands.

"Tell me what happened. I don't even know what it was that attacked me. I see the bites, though."

Edegast sat in the wooden chair and straightened his robes as if taking time to word the answer carefully.

"You were attacked, that is true. By a creature that no one in this castle ever expected to be here."

"What was it?"

"A hobgoblin. A nasty one."

She looked at her arm. That much was obvious. "Why did it attack me?"

"Well, for one, you were not protected. That is to say, you had no weapons, no charms to repel it. It likely found you easy prey. Fortunately, although it may not seem like it, the creature didn't give you much attention. It could have done far worse. Hobgoblins are warriors mostly, and tools, we believe, for the Dark One."

"Tools?"

"He is amassing an army. Hobgoblins and all the other creatures of Daegries that have been long hidden and nursing a hatred of humans are beginning to appear again."

She groaned. "That's not good news."

"We believe ourselves lucky that you were found, alive and still in the castle. It could have taken you captive and we would still be looking for you." He paused to flick at something on his sleeve. "Why in the name of all that is magik would you be down in the catacombs anyway?"

She shrugged. "I didn't know where I was, and I got more and more lost with every step."

He looked at her and kindness spread across his face. "I am so sorry to have been such a poor host. I did check in on you, but you slept so soundly that I refused to wake you. I never believed you would try to go exploring alone."

She patted the bandage. "That was not exploring, Edegast. I got lost trying to find the dining hall. What is a catacomb anyway? And is that where... you-know-who was brought for you-know-what?"

He looked shamed. "Yes, the place of our dead. It is the honorable burial place for wizards and those who have served the world." He sighed, casting his eyes downward. "Be that as it may, for now, what a hobgoblin was doing there, I do not know. But rest assured, we are working to uncover the mystery."

Edegast lifted his gaze and stared at her as her stomach made an enormous rumble.

"Pardon me!"

Edegast covered his mouth to hide his grin.

"Can you lead me to where food is? I don't know how long it has been since I last ate, but my stomach thinks my throat has been cut."

The wizard laughed outright. "I will do even better. I will bring the food to you." As he rose to leave the room, he said, "Feagus, the healer, will be back soon with tea for you."

"I hope it's the regular kind and not something with herbs in it."

He waved at her and passed out of the doorway. In a few moments, the healer indeed did return with steaming tea.

"Feagus… please don't give that to me if it has something in it to make me sleepy. I want to stay awake, and I need to do so."

Feagus nodded. "It has no medicinal properties aside from being a tea."

Alyssa moved to get out of bed.

Feagus gasped. "You should not do that!"

Alyssa waved her away. "I'll be better off if I do." And she struggled to stand, her legs feeling like they had never held her before. She'd seen a newborn colt with wobbly legs and considered herself to look similar.

"Let me sit in that chair for a while," she told the healer who rushed over to take her arm.

Feagus helped her get into the chair and handed her the tea. Alyssa took the mug offered to her. It smelled like regular black tea with perhaps a tinge of something floral.

She took a long sip and sighed. "That will fix what ails a body and no doubt."

Feagus sat on the edge of the bed and watched her.

"Don't fret none, Feagus," Alyssa told her. "I feel much better. Stronger even. Thank you for all you have done for me. I hope I haven't been taking your bed this whole time. Speaking of time, how long have I been here?"

The healer counted on her fingers. "Two moon cycles."

"What?" Alyssa shouted, spilling her tea. "That's near on a month!"

"A touch over it to be exact," Edegast replied as he entered the room with a tray.

Feagus took the teacup while Alyssa tried to blot the stain on her gown.

The shock of being in Knowledge Hall for so long flooded Alyssa's mind. Edegast handed her the tray, and she didn't even look at the food.

"Oh, Edegast. My folks are going to be so worried about me. And what about King Hubert? Surely, he's dancing at the end of his tether ready to go home?"

Edegast shrugged. "He flew off during the night of our arrival. No wonder he wanted to stay outdoors. I believe he had planned it the whole time. "

She pondered his words. "And he calls me rude. I sure wish I could have gotten him to go tell my folks that I'm fine but staying here for the winter. They're going to be so mad at me."

"Pish, posh. I will stand in the gap for this. It is surely my fault and no other. They will not be cross with you, Alyssa."

She picked up a piece of crusty bread and began chewing. The tray held cheese and fruit and some sort of dried meat. She never said another word until all of it was gone. When she had cleaned the tray to the point of nearly no crumbs, Edegast took it from her and set it on the bed.

"Feagus," he said, turning to sit on the bed also. "Would you leave us alone for a while? There is much I wish to discuss with your patient."

Feagus nodded and stood. "If you should have need of me, I will not be far away. Just call."

They both inclined their heads. She truly was a kind soul.

"Now," Edegast began. "To catch you up. There is no reason for a hobgoblin to be in this place. It is even more dangerous than I can express in words. I must know all that you remember of the encounter."

She crossed her arms, putting one hand on the bitten area. Then she closed her eyes and began to relate what she remembered. "I was trying to find my way down there, to see what was there and get an idea of where I was. I hoped to find a corridor that would lead me to you or the dining hall. Instead, I heard a low moaning and, fearing someone was hurt, I followed the sound."

He took a deep breath in and exhaled slowly. "Go on."

She finished, "I saw what appeared to be a wizard, in robes of a color I can't recall, lying on the stones. A candle snuffer was nearby, and I thought the body was a wizard tasked with doing that. Then, I thought he or she had been injured, so I knelt down to lend a hand. I actually touched it, placed hands on it, trying to be of help. I wiped its blood..." She shuddered. "It grasped my hand, and its hand was something ghastly looking, but when I saw its face, then I knew I'd been taken for a fool," she said all in one breath. "Honestly, that is all I remember, my friend."

He clasped his hands onto the edges of his robes and stood, pulling them tight about him. "Oh, my dear. What a horrible discovery. Some Flesh Renders can appear to be one thing and resume their normal appearance when it no longer suits them. It didn't find you to be anything but a nuisance, thankfully."

She rubbed the injured arm. "I wish I could find it again. I'd show it what a nuisance is."

Edegast put his hands behind his back and looked down at the floor. "Oddly enough, I believe you may get that chance."

She lifted her head to stare at him. "What?"

"Yes," he said, turning to look out the window. "We are gathering a group of the wise to go down to the catacombs to search for your attacker. We thought that since Horoc was the one who found you, she would be the best to lead us back there, but if you are well enough, you would likely be preferred."

"What was Horoc doing down there anyway?"

"She says she was visiting the tomb of her mother."

Alyssa stared at his face and tried to read what he felt about Horoc's excuse. "Do you believe her?"

He turned back to the window. "The snow has stopped. You should try to get up and move about if we are to get you down those stairs again."

She didn't push him, but she direly wanted to know if Horoc was telling the truth. Someone as haughty as Horoc might be hiding something that could well have deadly consequences to her and every wizard in the castle.

Chapter Thirteen

It was more than a day before Alyssa ate enough and moved around enough to say she could travel any distance. Feagus had allowed her to sleep in her bed another night.

When she woke feeling fully rested, she took the bandage off her injury and asked for Edegast to be brought to her. In a few hours, the party gathered together to go in search of the hobgoblin.

Edegast remembered her ability with bow and arrows and had a nice set brought to her. "It may prove far too close down there to be able to use it," he explained. "But you might feel safer with it at any rate."

She shook her head. "Not as safe as if Shadow was with me. Can you take me to my original sleeping place? I left it behind protecting the Grim. I need to see that all is well."

Edegast closed his eyes and slapped his forehead. "I completely forgot about Shadow." Then he shook his head and waved for her to follow him. Feagus waited on a landing close by, and Edegast called her over.

"Return this bow and quiver to the bowyer. He will know what to do with it." He handed it to the healer who bowed slightly in acknowledgment. Then to Alyssa, he said, "I should remember your magikal abilities before making such plans. If you change your mind, they will still be available to you. You have only to ask."

Alyssa didn't comment but instead thanked Feagus again and again as they left, a wave of relief flowing over her to be leaving the medical room.

I'm too young to be confined to a bed.

Edegast took long strides to the far hall and then up one flight of stairs. He collected Shadow and her pack for her, while she worked her way along behind him. It was slow going and it irritated her greatly.

When the wizard returned to her, she was huffing and trying to catch her breath. He handed her the pack holding the scarf and book and her belongings. She released Shadow and draped the scarf around her waist like a sash, tying the end tightly. The scarf seemed annoyed at her but didn't act out, instead remaining docile as a scarf should do.

She patted Shadow and whispered to it explaining all that had gone on. "I've been sick in bed and not able to come get you," she said in the end.

At this, Shadow relaxed and curled around one of her hands in friendship. Then it blended into her clothing as if it knew not to try to stand out.

The wizard knocked on several doors on that floor asking his friends and brothers to come along to find the hobgoblin. Some were only too ready to be of service, while others hesitated, unsure whether they were actually needed.

Eventually, there was a group of five wizards, and Alyssa. Horoc was nowhere to be found, and again Alyssa felt a bit of uneasiness. She didn't say anything to Edegast, as this woman was a member of the wizard's world. Her unease might be completely unfounded, but she nursed it anyway.

Thoughts of her Pappy and his counsel in times like these assaulted her. She could hear him saying, "If it looks like a skunk and smells like a skunk, it probably is a skunk."

Horoc might be a skunk, for sure.

Salas was among the group hunting the hobgoblin. He had his staff, a heavily wooded piece with a dragon's head for the hand grip. He also took the lead, as one in the stead of the real leader would.

Alyssa wondered how that made Edegast feel. He was Trudor's heir and likely the next leader. She glanced at him as he strode along beside her. His face was unreadable and soon they had to go in a single row, and she couldn't see him anymore.

The others in the group seemed content to follow Salas's lead, and they didn't stare at Alyssa in curiosity.

Finally, when they reached the lowest floor of the castle, someone behind her said in a breathy whisper, "Ah, the catacombs."

Salas turned to Alyssa and asked, "Where did you encounter the Flesh Render?"

She took the lead and walked them farther into the blackness. A multitude of colored lights from differing gemstones atop staffs lit up the whole area as they went.

She stopped where she believed the creature had waylaid her. "Here sir," she told him.

Salas motioned for Edegast to come forward, and together they peered down at the ground looking for something.

"Aha!" Salas exclaimed at last, as he bent and picked up a shiny object. "This would be the turning stone."

He held it out to Edegast who didn't take it. Alyssa moved closer for a better look. In his hand it looked like a simple river rock. She'd seen a lot of them on the banks of Old Stony.

The other wizards moved in, crowding around, all trying to see what Salas held. Alyssa moved away from the group and stood off to the side, alone.

"What is it?" someone asked Salas.

"A turning stone," he answered.

"What kind?" another person asked.

"We will find out soon," came the reply.

Edegast came over to be with her. "A little overwhelming, hm?"

She nodded. "I feel ashamed to have been fooled by a stone. I guess I ain't a very good mage-in-training after all."

Edegast patted her shoulder. "It could have happened to anyone, Alyssa. No one expected such as this. It is a warning for us to be more careful."

She didn't reply but watched him as he worked his way back to Salas's side. Waving at the crowd, he said, "Let us continue on our mission."

Salas held up his staff and shouted to those gathered who were making quite a hubbub, "Quiet!"

All voices ceased.

"There is a creature in this area. You must use your magik to stun it, and then we will question it. Band together. "Then he motioned to Alyssa to rejoin them. "Come, you will be with us."

She nodded and moved to his side. "What sort of magik will be needed to stun this... creature?" She didn't want to call it by name since no one else had.

"Use whatever magik you have at hand. They are not hard to stun. They are difficult to kill or maim, so be mindful!" Salas told everyone. He looked down at Alyssa. "Use whatever you can, my dear."

She fingered the scarf and knew that this one item of magik was likely as powerful as any that they had, whether anyone, including Edegast, was aware of it or not. Before it had even come to her, it had a history of protecting its bearer in battle. She rather hoped that no one would even notice Shadow and ask questions.

Salas led the way with Alyssa in the middle and Edegast coming up behind. They went to every doorway on the lefthand side, and inside the rooms, where bones were laid with their hands holding weapons or simply crossed over their staff.

It made Alyssa uneasy at first. Then she remembered how Pappy had been arranged in his pine box. Cultures handled the dead in different ways.

On the fourth or fifth room's examination, there was a scuffling sound, and a blackness detached itself from the wall.

Salas held his staff higher and commanded his stick to bring greater light. The room appeared from the gloom and the creature before them bowed low.

"Who are you?" Edegast asked, holding his staff up to bring even more light. Alyssa immediately wished that he hadn't. The creature fell to the ground and began writhing as if in pain.

"Edegast, what is it?" she asked, shivering.

"It's a Funerial. You remember the story of the Dark Master, correct? They are beings who inhabit the final dwelling of the dead. Mostly harmless."

"Unless they're magiked," she muttered.

Salas looked at the marker to see who the dead person was and said, "It is protecting Erik the Brave."

At the name of its master, the creature rose and scurried over to drape itself over the bones laid on the bier.

"Be at peace. We wish you no harm," Edegast said, retreating. Alyssa followed and Salas brought up the rear.

"That was not what I saw down here," she told them. "But I'm making a mental note on what a Funerial looks like. Just in case." They nodded and the journey went on.

After many more rooms, she quit counting. The catacombs were endless it seemed. She couldn't believe the castle could have held so many rooms from its outward appearance.

Salas turned to them. "I do not think the creature is herein. It is my belief that the group who took the right turn might have found it already. Perhaps we should return and check before we get too far away."

Alyssa thought that was an excellent idea. Salas waved for Edegast to take the lead. They hadn't gone far when a robed figure stepped out of the gloom and murkiness and held up a club.

"That's it!" Alyssa screamed. Her arm where she'd been bitten ached like nothing she'd ever felt before. The creature bared its pointed teeth and grunted.

Salas stepped ahead of her, pushing her behind him and he and Edegast lifted their wizard staffs speaking words that sounded like an olden language. The dragon's eyes on Salas's staff burned fiery red, and Edegast's staff sent an ice blue flame. The power from the magik tools struck the hobgoblin fully in the chest.

Alyssa didn't know what she could do to help. All she had was glow magik that flowed from her in search of something. She was a healer, not a warrior. As if summoned, the other wizards arrived and chanted magik words as they pressed close to her making her uncomfortable.

At this time, Shad unwrapped itself and stood its end on the ground in front of her, blocking her view and protecting her from any stray magik. It also used its other end to face the remaining wizards behind her, as a warning.

She yanked at Shad to get it to lower itself, but it remained resolutely in place. If it had been a dog, it would have been growling.

"Be gone, you devil!" Salas yelled.

"Go!" shouted Edegast.

Alyssa held her arms out. The injured arm nearly fell back against her side as it was still weak. In spite of that, she called her power to come forth. "Scarf you better move now, or else you're gonna be in the way."

Shad rolled up from the bottom and hovered in the air waiting to see what she planned. In a moment, over the heads of the wizards a green fire spewed into the corridor and struck the hobgoblin directly in his eyes. The scarf skittered behind the group of magik-users.

The creature's screams were otherworldly. When he fell to his knees, his club on the ground, Alyssa recalled her power. Her hurt arm burned like it was on fire, and she grabbed it, gritting her teeth against the pain.

Edegast kept a spell going on the creature while Salas rushed to join the others in the event that there might be more than one.

Alyssa didn't cry, but she wanted to. She crept to Edegast's side and, without removing his eyes from the hobgoblin, he asked her if she was well.

"I've been better. Something about that horror... it's as if my arm knows the one who bit into it and doesn't like it one bit."

The creature threw its head back and emitted a guttural cry that made all the hair on Alyssa's head stand up. The pain in her arm intensified, shuddering up into her shoulder and across her chest.

She fell to her knees with a scream.

Edegast's spell wavered a moment as he tried to assess what her condition was and what to do for her, but only a moment. He called over his shoulder, "Scarf! Come and tend to your mistress!"

Shad floated over everyone's head and wrapped itself around Alyssa, especially over the area of pain. Soon, amazingly, the pain subsided, and Alyssa could once again speak.

She mustered the strength to say, "Thank you, Shadow."

The other wizards hurried toward them, staffs lifted, smiting the hobgoblin with their magik. The creature fell onto his back, unmoving.

Salas crept up to it with only a whisper of sound, double-checking to see that it still lived. He waved to the others. "Stop. It is barely alive, unable to disarm us."

Edegast lowered his staff, wiped his brow, and moved to Alyssa. "Are you well, lady? I could not stop to tend you while my magik struck the creature. Your glow magik saved the day!"

She nodded and asked him to help her to her feet. Scarf wrapped around her waist once more. Two wizards grabbed the hobgoblin's feet while Salas and another man lifted the ugly head and shoulders. They began the long trek back to the lived-in part of the castle where they could cast spells to contain the creature. They would then wait for it to regain awareness in order to question it.

Alyssa returned to her room on the floor next to Salas. She didn't expect to see him anytime soon and, because she was starving, pulled food from her pack. She crammed it into her mouth, praying for a quelling of the hunger.

A lesson in using magik: it makes you ravenous and bone-weary.

After she ate, she rested. Shadow sprawled across the bed near her as if it were taking a nap. She patted it lovingly. The scarf was the best friend she could ask for, as well as protector and champion.

In an hour or so, Edegast came for her.

"Come, we must eat and take drinks. Everyone is hungry after the hunt."

She nodded and said, "I took the liberty of eating from my pack, so I ain't really starving anymore. But I want to try and understand the direction to the dining hall, so I'll come along."

Edegast took a moment to pat the scarf. "Well done, Shadow, my friend. Well done."

Alyssa led the way to the door but looked back over her shoulder. "Shadow, stay and protect the Grim. Even though I know you will anyway."

She followed Edegast, memorizing the way they went.

They arrived in the dining hall in a short while, and she felt far more confident about returning to her sleeping quarters later.

"The day is waning," Edegast told her, pointing out of a window that was more like a slit in the stone. "Winter is nigh. Look!"

She stood on tiptoe to see what he pointed at.

Solly glimmered on the horizon filled with snow. Alyssa sighed. She'd been here far longer than anticipated. "Granny and Pappy are going to be so worried about me," she said, shoulders drooping

"I am sorry that word to your family did not go via the gryphon."

Alyssa frowned. "Just as well, I suppose. If Hubert goes anywhere near the farm, Pappy will probably try to hurt him. There was bitterness between them after the whole debacle last year. Hubert did save Granny though. Likely why Pappy didn't set a spell on him."

Edegast changed the subject. "I have planned for you to get some time working with a swordsmith. He will create a short sword for you."

She lifted an eyebrow. "You do recall that I don't know anything about swords or how to wield them, don't you?"

He shrugged. "Yes, of course. I intend for you to be trained as well. That may have to wait until the last snowfall, however, as it will need to be done outside."

She picked up the roasted meat with two fingers and took a bite. It was delicious, albeit a bit chewy. It prevented her from saying what she was thinking.

I cannot stay here all winter and until spring. I must get out of here.

Chapter Fourteen

There was no news about questioning the hobgoblin that night.
The next day, after only one sidestep in the wrong direction,
Alyssa made it to the dining hall alone. She left Shadow in her room
hidden in the bed linens with instructions to protect the Grim as
before.

Salas had already arrived and Horoc appeared shortly after Alyssa.
The sorceress wore a thick woolen cloak over her robes and her face
seemed pale. If she had come in from outside, she would be pink at
least in the cheeks, but no, her entire face was pale and her eyes seemed
sunken, with black circles underneath.

"Good morning," Alyssa said to her, trying not to stare.

Horoc muttered a low greeting and turned away with a bowl of
something that looked like gruel. Alyssa couldn't be sure, but it was
a safe bet that the wizards didn't have real oats or creamed wheat for
cereal.

Horoc sat as far from Alyssa and Salas as possible. They didn't engage her in conversation either. Soon, Edegast swept in and loaded a plate with food. He asked Alyssa how she had fared during the night.

"Fine," she answered. "My injury finally stopped aching. I guess it was poisoned from the bite and the creature reactivated it with his presence."

"Flesh Renders are famous for poisoning their victims," Salas agreed. "It would be a good idea to have Feagus look at it again to be safe."

Alyssa nodded. She'd been thinking the same thing. Besides she had some questions for the healer.

Horoc seemed mildly interested in Alyssa's complaint. "Girl, come here," she said.

Alyssa didn't want to be rude and refuse, so she got up from the table and walked over to her. The sorceress motioned for Alyssa to show her which arm it was.

"This one," she told her, pointing at her left arm.

Horoc took the arm and peered at the bites carefully. "I assume Feagus knows how to treat poisons, with at least a poultice. Surely, she has done so. This one doesn't look necrotic, so you will likely live. The poison leftover in your blood will always call out to its maker, giving you fair warning that danger is near."

Alyssa took her arm back and returned to her seat. She wasn't sure what necrotic meant but she was relieved she didn't have it. As to the statement that the poison remained in her blood, she wasn't worried about that either. She had Pappy's magik spell in her blood that would cross out anything else. The pain as a warning seemed like good sound advice to her. Although she hoped to never feel it again.

"Tis a pity we had to have a hobgoblin appear on the day you stumbled into the catacombs," Horoc said. "Evil folk. Make you afraid to get out of bed."

"Have you been visited by many?" Alyssa asked, trying to sound innocent. In truth, she was trying to find out how the sorcerer knew such a thing.

To Alyssa's relief, Horoc shook her head and turned away.

Instead of engaging further with the strange woman, Alyssa asked Salas, "Are you going to question the creature today?"

He looked at Edegast who only tilted his head to one side.

"Perhaps. Why do you ask?" Edegast asked her.

"I would like to be there," she said.

"No," they answered in unison, brows bunching over their noses.

Edegast explained. "It is too dangerous for you. You have been its victim once. No sense in taking a chance on something happening again. Even you have said the pain reoccurred when you encountered it earlier."

"Yes, but I'm going to see Feagus and perhaps she'll be able to give me something to fix my ailment. At any rate, the pain is gone now. I'd like to hear what the creature has to say for himself."

Edegast lifted his eyebrows and shrugged more to Salas than to her. "She should be taught these things," he said to his friend. "What good is it to be a mage if one is not seeking knowledge?"

Salas scowled. "True, but this is not a training, Edegast. This is a live creature with what manner of power no one can know."

"Would it serve for me to say I will stand in the gap? I can protect Alyssa. And besides, she also has the Scarf of Egladris, as you may be aware."

Salas smiled and nodded. "Yes, I have seen it. Indeed, a wondrous magikal item."

At the name Egladris, Horoc sat straighter and tapped the table. "The Scarf of Egladris? How is this even possible? That scarf left Daegries with the Dark One."

Edegast looked down at his hands, crossed in his lap. "Well, that is only one of the things I am here to report to Trudor. Oh, that he were here!"

Horoc sat back, a look of amazement and a bit of trepidation on her face. "The Scarf of Egladris... Edegast, I am sure you do not want to share this news with anyone before Trudor, but it *is* very intriguing. Perhaps Alyssa will show us her scarf sometime?"

The wizard patted Alyssa's hand. "Only if she wishes to. Not terribly necessary, Alyssa."

Alyssa watched Horoc's face slowly crease with the façade she wore most often. "Of course, only if it pleases you."

Salas, who had remained quiet during the exchange, returned to the idea of Alyssa sitting in on the questioning of the hobgoblin. "Go and see Feagus, my lady. Make sure she thinks the pain at the injury is not serious, and we will allow you to be there. But if there is any concern about your arm, you must take care not to expose yourself."

Alyssa nodded and said, "Yes, sir. Thank you." And she promptly stood. She asked which way to the healer's room, and they gave her directions that helped her remember where she had come from earlier.

Edegast promised to come for her when they were ready to go to see the creature which had attacked her.

She strode down the hall, peering at each of the faces on the wall as she passed portraits. She couldn't imagine so many wizards passing through this place. But there were many rooms with dead wizards and others in the catacombs. She shivered. *Not going back there ever again.*

When she arrived at the healer's room, she knocked on the door. Feagus answered, bowing to her and allowing her to enter. "My lady," she said. "How may I serve you?"

Alyssa wasn't used to the formality and waved her to sit. "I went with the hunting party to find that old hob—er... creature. When we found it, my arm burned and ached like I had a knife in it. Can you look at it and see what's wrong?"

Feagus nodded and pointed to the bed. "You take your ease, Mistress."

When Alyssa had gotten comfortable on the bed, the healer took her arm and touched the bites. She pushed on them and turned the arm over to see the backside.

"I can see nothing," she told Alyssa. "I treated your injury with anti-poison to stop it from growing inside of you. Then I used herbs in a poultice to pull out the poison. It is possible, I suppose, some moved inward before I could stop it. That would explain the sensation you speak of."

"Is it dangerous? Can I get sick or die from it?"

Feagus looked at the wounds again. "I do not know. I have done all I had materials or skill to do. If this continues, come back to me, and I will look for something else to try."

Alyssa sat up and draped her legs over the side of the bed. Feagus walked back to the chair and sat.

"Feagus, I wanted to tell you that I met some of the Iefyr last year. They were a small group in the woods, likely a hunting party. But I was told by one of the leaders that I might be half-elven through my mother's bloodline. Would you happen to know, or have you heard of, the Egladris family?"

Feagus looked away, staring at the wall for a moment. Finally, she replied, "That name doesn't sound familiar to me. I am sorry." When she gazed at Alyssa there was something bothering her. It was evident in the small lines creasing her brow.

Alyssa decided not to press her on the matter. Whatever it was about her family name that gave Feagus pause, she would learn about it soon enough.

"Don't be concerned," Alyssa said, standing. "I just wanted to ask. My parents have been lost to me for a good many years. I was told when I got ready to find them, I should start asking questions. I guess this is that starting place."

Feagus stood, clasping her hands in front of her. The tension that had been there a moment before, disappeared. "I will be happy to ask of my folk when I go back in the spring."

Alyssa smiled and patted the healer's shoulder. "Thank you kindly, Feagus. You can send word to Edegast if you find out anything."

She left the room, her heart torn with the thought that the healer knew something about her family, and it might not be good. She tried to recall how to get back to her own sleeping area. After a few moments she was on the right path and soon entered her room, calling Shadow out from its exile.

It floated up above her head and twisted into a roll before untwisting and settling across her lap.

"You sure have a funny way of stretching," she told her scarf, running her hand along the nearest edge. "You're going to be coming along with me to the site where my attacker is being held. I want you to protect me from it. He bit me and the bites hurt something fierce whenever I'm near him. The healer, Feagus, doesn't seem to understand what could be causing the pain. No matter, we're going."

Shadow unfolded until half of the length of it was standing upright. One corner gave a little salute to her before it collapsed back into her lap. They played tug of war for a time, but quickly composed themselves when a knock sounded on the door.

Alyssa left the scarf on her bed and answered the door.

Edegast stood there. He motioned for her to follow him and turned on his heel without a word. She started to leave and close the door behind her, but Shadow flew at her.

"I know I said that you were coming on this journey, but what about the Grim?" she asked it.

The scarf flew to the pack and tugged it up before attempting to shove it under the bed. Alyssa hurried over and helped, stepping back with a grin. The bed linens made a good cover for it.

Why didn't I think of that?

She wrapped the scarf around her waist and tied it like a sash rushing to catch Edegast.

They traveled to an outside building. She was immediately cold, her heavy overcoat still in her room and the wind winnowing into her clothing, icing her skin.

They were soon inside a wooden building that housed meats hanging to dry. The scent inside was woodsy and smelled of smoke and animal carcass. Her breath made puffs in the cold air.

The creature was tied up at one end, hanging from one of the meat hooks. It's head lolled forward and, the closer to it Alyssa came, the more her arm began to ache.

Shadow must have sensed her pain and fear. It unwrapped itself from her waist and draped over her shoulders like a shawl. The additional material over her body was a welcome warmth. She tucked her hurt arm under the scarf and kept it immobile.

Salas was there with them, as well as Horoc and another wizard who was unfamiliar to her. It was this man who poked the creature and made it look up at them. It bared its teeth and made a terrible moaning sound.

"What are you doing at Knowledge Hall? How did you even get in?" Salas demanded.

The creature only stared at him. This questioning was going to be far more difficult than they expected, and it showed on every face, save Horoc's. She didn't seem surprised. But she was occupied staring at the scarf most of the time.

Alyssa began to have her doubts about the sorceress. Where had she been when they were seeking out the creature? If it was such an important thing to her, where was she then?

"Answer him," Edegast said, poking the creature in the chest with his staff. The hobgoblin kicked at the wizard nearest to him.

Edegast shouted, "Lindon! Watch out!"

Then, Alyssa felt the black eyes of the creature on her. It stared at her as if memorizing every feature. And as it did, her arm began to burn as though a firebrand were being held to it.

"Ow, ow, ouch!" she cried, as she pulled her arm from beneath the scarf and grasped it with her hand in a way of protecting it.

Shadow bound itself around her hand and her arm as if to give her extra support. The creature yanked the chains downward as if to pull itself from the hook holding them.

Lindon hit the creature in the head with his staff. "Answer us!"

Black foamy blood seeped from the edge of its mouth on one side. At least that's what it appeared to be. With guttural sounds the creature tried to speak, and the wizards, including Horoc, had to confer to see if they even knew any hob languages.

While they were otherwise occupied, Alyssa decided to step closer and see what it looked like. The stench of its body beneath the animal skin it wore was horrible. She wondered if the animal had been one of the creature's unfortunate victims. The hobgoblin had a mark or burn on its chest of a crooked river going into a mountain. Alyssa gasped.

Through some trick of the light, the creature's red eyes glowed, and Alyssa took a step back. When the flame shot from its eyes, Shadow had already unwrapped and took the brunt of the attack.

Horoc, standing closest to the creature, took a dagger from her waist and slit the creature's throat. Shadow fluttered to the ground.

Alyssa cried out and ran to Shadow where it lay on the straw, smoldering. Edegast knelt beside her and watched as she patted at the burning cloth and tried to get the scarf to rise.

"Shadow? Come on now, my friend. Come on," she said, softly, lifting one of the limp ends. "Come back to me, Shadow."

But the Scarf of Egladris was either too weak to respond or damaged unto death. She turned frantically to Edegast. "What do I do? How can we heal it?"

But it wasn't Edegast who answered.

"Sing to it," Horoc replied, falling to her knees beside Alyssa. "Magik comes in all forms. Pick the scarf up, carry it to the healer, and sing to it all the way. Hurry now, be quick!"

Salas and Lindon stood nearby, stricken by the sight of the magik scarf so still. Their faces were glum and that, more than anything else, spurred Alyssa into action.

The girl gingerly lifted Shadow and carried it like a precious banner, draped across both arms. Edegast led the way, moving everything that tried to block their path.

She began singing one of Pappy's silly tunes. The one that Pappy sang when they were out in the sunflower garden.

Here Willy Nilly, here Tilly Tilly,
Sing silly silly and bring joy into the day.
Here Billy Billy, here Dilly Dilly,

Call Filly Filly and let's be on our way.

Alyssa kept saying the words Willy Nilly and Tilly Tilly all the way to the healer's room. Edegast rapped sharply with his staff and the door opened.

"Feagus, you have to fix my friend! It took a flame from the creature! Please fix it, Feagus!" Alyssa sobbed and gently placed Shadow on the bed. The scarf didn't move at all.

Feagus touched the scarf, and a glow came from her. Alyssa's heart was filled with hope. She stood beside the healer, recalling she was perhaps half-Iefyr, and the fact that this people and culture had created the scarf.

If anyone could heal Shadow, it would be Feagus.

The Iefyr's healing magik lit up the whole room with a golden glow. Fear of doing something wrong kept Alyssa from moving. She stood like a statue, eyes on the seared scarf.

Edegast grabbed her shoulder, startling her, and she briefly looked up at him. His face was drawn, and tears slowly slid down his face.

When Alyssa looked back at Shadow, darkness had engulfed it. A biting chill filled with dampness descended on the small room chilling all who gathered there.

Feagus turned to Alyssa, her shoulders slumped, horror on her face.

"I am so sorry, Mistress Alyssa. There was nothing to be done for it."

Alyssa stared incredulously at the healer and then back at Edegast. "What? What are you saying?"

Edegast pulled her away from the bed. "It's no use, Alyssa. Shadow is gone."

She yanked out of his grasp and flew to the bed, throwing herself over the scarf, sobbing its name. She bunched the scarf and yelled into the material. "No! No!" and no one could convince her to move. She cried so hard that she had the hiccoughs, but she still remained.

Chapter Fifteen

When at last Alyssa left the healer's room, she clutched the scarf to her. The scent of burnt follygrass filled her nostrils. Her head throbbed from sobbing so hard as she grieved her friend.

Onward to her room she went, her feet moving like a puppet being manipulated by another. They landed woodenly on the ground, step-by-step. Her restless mind couldn't accept this fate for her Shadow, her scarf.

How can this be? This is not real!

Edegast led her to her room where she could be alone and grieve the loss of her friend. She threw herself on the bed and scooped the scarf against the curve of her body as if she would never let it go.

Her tears wet the singed place where the flame had burned deepest. When she had emptied herself of tears, she held the scarf gently and laid it on the bed. She arranged it in the position Shadow usually chose. She did the best she could, but the scarf was now a much different form, scorched and burned

She went to get her pack thinking she would put the scarf in it, where it would be safe until she could get back home and bury it properly. But something stopped her in her tracks. After it had given her such joy—literally giving its life for hers—the thought of never seeing the scarf again made her ashamed to hide it away. Instead, she pulled the Grim out and carried it with her back to the bed, heartache filling her.

I'll bring Shadow back, just like Pappy.

She stood wiping her eyes, staring down at the Grim. Could she even bring an inanimate object back from the other side? She'd certainly never heard of such. She knelt by the bed, placing the book on one unburned edge of the scarf, and laid her head beside Shadow, silently begging for the heartbreak to end.

"Shadow, you were my friend. You saved my life. I owe you everything. I wish you were still here. Please come back to me, old friend. I l-love you!"

The tears were erupting anew when she placed her hand on the scarf, thinking of hugging it to her breast again.

Something happened. A ripple went through the scarf. The burned area lifted from the bed, and it moved to her face, wiping her tears. Then, it wrapped itself protectively around the book, as it had so many times.

Then, the material glowed, and the damaged area began ever so slowly to repair itself. Alyssa watched in amazement as the scarf came to her again and again soaking up her tears to use them to heal itself.

After a long while of this, the glow faded, and Shadow unwrapped itself from the Grim and draped around her shoulders in a gentle hug.

"Shad!" she exclaimed. "I was so sad. I didn't think I would ever have you again!"

The scarf tapped her on the head as if to say, "Why would you think such a thing?"

Then, it slid off and flopped onto the bed as if exhausted. She patted the end of it nearest her and pulled the covers back to lay them gently over her friend. Shad must have fought a terrible battle to come back from death.

She stared at the Grim, a foreboding filling her.

This book had the power to return a dead person or entity to life. That was now the most obvious thing she had ever known.

And the Dark Master must not get it. Ever.

Her first inclination was to find Edegast and tell him, but instead she gently placed the Grim in the backpack and lay beside Shadow, trying to understand what had just happened. She kept her head on the scarf until she fell asleep.

When Alyssa rose the next day, Shadow rose with her. The scarf seemed even more determined not to let her out of its sight. If she was going to get anything done, she would have to take Shadow with her.

"Let's have a talk," she said, petting the now-healed edge where it lay on the bed. It lifted one end and propped itself up on a bed pillow.

"You are supposed to be dead," she said. "I might want to take advantage of that for a little while. Some of the folks here would enjoy stealing a magik scarf if it would enlarge their own personal business." Horoc's face immediately came to mind.

Shadow flipped its other end as if annoyed.

"It'll be fine, Shad. We can sneak out sometimes. But for the next little while, I think we would be better served if you stay here and play dead."

The scarf lifted off the bed and floated over to cover her head. She moved it aside so she could see.

"I know what you must be thinking—that I need to be looked after in the case of folks looking to do harm. But I ain't met nobody yet that I'm worried about, not even that old hobgoblin, now that I know what it is. That Horoc woman might be a little on the mean side, but I don't reckon she's dangerous. She killed the creature in defense of you. But... she did show a lot of interest in you, for good or bad, I don't know. So, for now, you gotta stay here and stay hidden. I don't think I could stand losing you again."

Shadow slid from her head and pooled in her lap. She picked it up and took it to the pack. "Stay close to the Grim, Shad. That's the item that needs protecting the most. It is quite fond of you, so it would seem."

Shadow went limply inside the pack, and she smiled. It would do as told.

She washed her face and pulled on clothes that had been stripped off helter-skelter. She would find out about a bath today. To go all winter with no wash was a bad idea for anyone, and especially her.

"Keep this door locked and barred if possible. I don't want anyone coming in here while I'm gone," Alyssa told the scarf. She heard a scuffling after she closed the door and knew that Shadow was moving the pack to use as a barrier.

She headed to the dining hall to see what she could find out about the questioning of the hobgoblin.

Edegast was sipping a hot mug of tea and poring over some old parchments when she arrived. He looked up and studied her for a moment.

"Are you well?" he asked.

She nodded. "As well as I can be."

"Shadow was a good friend. It gave its all for you. You should be proud to have had such a fine magik item."

She poured a mug for herself and sat beside him. No one else was in the dining hall, but she leaned close to the wizard and whispered in his ear.

"Shadow is not dead."

Edegast leaned back and his wide-eyed look told her everything she needed to know. This man was trustworthy. There had been no malice in his actions from the beginning.

"It's true," she whispered. "It healed itself."

He set his papers aside and grabbed his staff. "I want to see this for myself."

She patted his arm. "Soon. Not now."

He reseated himself, staring at her, questioning.

"There is no rush, and I think for the time being, we should keep this news quiet. The less people get interested in my belongings the better, if you get my meaning."

He inclined his head in agreement.

"Let's say someone in this castle was not all they were supposed to be. Perhaps they're out for their own interests. Do you know anyone like that?" She meant Horoc, but Edegast could draw his own conclusions.

Edegast frowned, his bushy eyebrows coming nearly together over his nose. "No. I cannot think of anyone."

Alyssa didn't know how to get the information without coming out and asking. "Tell me the story about Horoc. She killed the creature. Is she someone who would do that in defense of us, or to keep us from getting information from it?"

Edegast turned his whole body toward her to stare at her. "Are you saying her actions were questionable? What would make you say that?"

"It may be my suspicious mind, but I think it's my intuition. Something about her doesn't add up."

"Seems to me that she killed the creature out of protection. It had just killed the scarf. Further damage to any of us would be unthinkable, and so she acted out of protection rather than malice, I believe." He turned away again to sip his tea. "She is an honorable person."

"We'll see," Alyssa said, turning to her own mug. "I would rather not be left alone with her, if you don't mind."

He nodded. "Certainly. You are my guest here, my pupil, if you will. I will honor whatever your wishes are." He stared at her again, his thoughts unreadable. "You are far too young to be so suspicious."

"I've seen a lot, remember?"

He shrugged. "True, but still..."

She changed the subject. "Speaking of tutoring me, when will that start?" Her heart fell a little when she remembered her family and the fact that King Hubert had flown home. She would now have to wait for the spring thaw to go home at the earliest.

"It will begin as soon as we get word from Trudor and the others. I am truly hoping they come home soon. The road is treacherous on a good day but now, with winter upon us..." He trailed off.

Alyssa saw the sudden stiffening of his shoulders and the slight trembling of his hand as he held his cup.

The wizard was afraid.

"What if they don't?" She set her cup aside and took a deep breath, watching him.

He closed his eyes and pulled on his beard in frustration. When he opened them, he dragged the parchments closer. "That is why I have been reading these." He pushed them over to Alyssa.

They were pages filled with tight script that spoke of how to elect a new Head Wizard.

"You're afraid your father is dead?"

"We live in perilous times," he said with a sigh.

"What would it mean for you to take over Knowledge Hall? You would be in charge over everything here, right?"

He nodded. "Yes. And the terrible thing is, I don't want to. It's expected due to my lineage, but I fear I am not ready."

She sipped her tea and thought about what he had said. She hoped that the party of wizards that had left would come back hale and hearty. And soon.

After a lull in the conversation, Alyssa inquired about a bathing place, and soap and a cloth. Edegast found a young mage in training and had her help Alyssa. To say the hot water filling the scented tub was a miracle potion would be an understatement. She lingered there as long as she thought was allowable and finally dressed in a clean linen tunic, and a long skirt with a belt that held a spot for a dagger or sword. The maiden mage was happy to take her soiled laundry and have it cleaned.

Alyssa collected her coat and went to explore.

She wandered through the halls of the castle and happened upon the kitchen quite by accident. It was literally outside the castle but connected by a long hall with openings on each side that let in fresh air and sunshine.

The view from the hall was beautiful, and she stood there, admiring the mountains for a while, before strolling ahead toward the kitchen.

Her mouth watered long before she arrived, as the smell of baking bread floated toward her.

Inside the kitchen were two large brick ovens, where items like bread and vegetables were being placed on wooden trays. She had devoured tea and a few biscuits with Edegast, but this was truly making her stomach churn for some solid were.

"Excuse me," she addressed the two men preparing food. They turned to see who was there, and one stepped closer to her from across a large wooden table where flour and other baking goods were strewn.

"I am Edegast's... um... friend, Alyssa Chance Oh. I was wandering around trying to get my bearings. I didn't mean to interrupt, but it smells so good in here I had to follow my nose!"

The man, wearing a white apron around his wide middle, smiled at her and said, "We have heard of you, Lady Alyssa. We prepared special soups for you when you were ill with poison. I trust you are better now?"

The other man, dressed similarly, smiled at her from over his shoulder before turning back to a large kettle of something bubbling.

She was elated that they knew of her. "Yes, much better. Thank you so much for your kindness."

After a few more compliments to their talents with food, she left them and headed back to the hallway.

As she stood admiring the view again, she turned at the sound of shuffling feet. Salas strode toward her. He had a long cloak over his robes, and his hands were tucked into the sleeves.

"Alyssa!" he greeted her. "I wanted to see you today to tell you how sorry I am about the Scarf of Egladris. Such a terrible loss!"

She nodded, trying to look forlorn. "Yes. I am very sad. But we must continue on, yes?"

He agreed and patted her shoulder in passing. "I will speak with you later. The cooks need an itinerary for our meals today."

She watched him go into the other building to confer with the cooks. Salas was doing many of the duties of his superior in his absence, so it would seem.

On the journey back to the inner sanctum of the castle, she saw Horoc, lounging against a wall, a sword easily visible beneath her cloak. When the sorceress caught sight of Alyssa, she stood away from the wall and hurriedly pulled the cloak over the weapon, as though she didn't want her to see it.

Alyssa didn't think that this look suited the sorceress at all. It was more of a Lord Bryon feel, and she knew he was more than a little reckless.

She's got something to hide, all right. Sure as rain, as Pappy would say.

Alyssa went straight to her room to check on Shadow and the Grim. Her fears about a rogue member of Knowledge Hall ran through her head all the way up the stairs and down the corridors.

When at last she entered the bedroom, she caught Shadow doing something that she never expected to see. It was undulating and changing colors near the pack seated beside the bed now.

The follygrass scarf was normally a rustic sort of green, but now it turned into several hues of brown before the color was leached right out of it.

"Shad," she whispered. "What in Daegries is wrong with you?"

The scarf fell onto the pack, covering it protectively. Alyssa strode to where it lay and picked it up, hugging it tightly.

"I'm not mad at you, Scarf. Only trying to understand. You've been through something pretty awful, and I want to know that you're all right." She pulled it away and stared at it. "Are you ill?"

Shadow lifted one end and waved at her as if to say all is well. Still, she was struck by its ability to change color. She had known it could change size and shape, but this was new. Did the near-death experience change its structure?

She settled herself into the chair with the scarf in her lap and spoke to it. "Shadow," she began. "I don't know what all you went through as you traveled between this world and the next, but I can see you are different. Now, I have to know… can you possibly become invisible? What I mean to say is, lose *all* color?"

The scarf rose up until it was eye-level and then slowly the color of the material lightened until it was virtually impossible to see it. Soon, the color returned, and it flopped back into her lap as if this feat was no big deal.

"Oh, boy! This is great!" She laughed and stood with the scarf in her hands, dancing around with it. "You are the most amazing scarf I have ever seen!"

"We're going to have some fun with this," she told it, grinning. "Let's go."

She wrapped the scarf around her waist and commanded it to go invisible. Soon, she could feel Shadow's weight and, when she touched it, she could tell it was there. But to the naked eye, the scarf could not be seen.

She went first to the dining hall, but she found no one in attendance, so she wandered down the hallway that led outside, to the entrance of the castle. There were rooms on either side of that hallway, and she decided to go into the first one she came to, a parlor, or drawing room.

There were tables with chairs and settees and a fireplace. The fire was delightful, and she decided to stay there until someone passed by whom she could question.

The furnishings were much more what she was used to than what her Pappy had remembered, when he told her tales of his time spent at Knowledge Hall as a young man. The wizards had come a long way since then, comfort being the highest priority.

Warming her hands by the fire, she heard the heavy front door screech open, and she turned to catch a glimpse of a wizard scurrying by.

His hood was off, and she saw his long blond tresses and beard. She hurried to the drawing room's doorway seeking a better look. But he had either gone into another room or out into an adjoining hallway.

She waited for a moment, hoping to catch sight of him again, but when he didn't reappear, she went back to the fire and warmed her backside. The scarf flipped its ends toward her middle to get away from the heat. Fear of fire was going to be a consideration, she realized.

Soon, footsteps came from the direction the wizard had gone, and she hurried back to the doorway for another look. He wasn't alone. Salas, Edegast, and Horoc were with him, and they were in such a hurry that no one even acknowledged she stood there.

Long moments passed. Alyssa thought perhaps they had reentered the castle through another door, and she was just about to leave the room, when they returned from outside. There were several more wizards with them. This group was scraggly and sick-looking, and they were being helped and half-carried by the others. Their clothes were torn and bloodied, and the haunted look in their eyes told a tale that others dreaded to hear.

But hear it they must, and so Alyssa quietly followed them into a room which had been locked on her earlier journey past. This massive room was likely where the wizards held their councils.

They were so involved with the weary and injured arrivals, they didn't admonish her for coming in uninvited.

Those injured ones lay down on the floor and someone hurried out, yelling for Feagus. Some who had fared better than their friends sat at the benches, heads in their hands.

When the healer arrived, Alyssa rushed to her side. "Feagus, I can help you. I have training."

The healer nodded, and they laid hands on the sick ones and uncovered what sort of ailments they had. Alyssa put hands on one man and felt the inside of his body quiver and shake.

"This one has inside injuries that I won't be able to tend, aside from giving pain relief," Alyssa said sadly.

Feagus switched places with her, and Alyssa went to work on a young sorcerer with a deep gash in his side. Her patient stared at her, his eyes darting around like a trapped animal.

"My name is Alyssa. I'm going to try to give you some healing now. What is your name?"

The young man writhed a little and didn't answer.

"That's okay," Alyssa told him, placing her hands on the injured area. "Let's see what's what."

As the two healers worked, Alyssa listened to the conversations going on around her.

"What has happened?" Salas asked a man who sat with his head in his hands. "You left us as a party of almost two score and now return with less than a half dozen."

The man shook himself out of his daze and gave Salas a determined stare. "Weren't fit for man nor beast out there."

Edegast paced behind the men gathered there. "My father? What news is there of Trudor?"

The wizard with blond hair and beard, who had hurried past the drawing room earlier, came to stand at Edegast's side.

"I am sorry, friend. Sir Trudor did not survive."

A terrible hush fell over the entire room, and no one moved.

Edegast's face paled into a dreadful shade of white. "He is... gone? My father is dead?"

Chapter Sixteen

When the young sorcerer managed to sit up with one scarred hand on his side, Alyssa patted his shoulder, then hurried to Edegast. The wound healing was easy compared to what the young girl from Mudden now faced with her friend.

"Edegast?" she asked softly as she drew near. "I am so sorry."

He stood staring without seeing. Alyssa wrung her hands, horror-filled at the terrible news now being explained by the survivors.

"He slipped down the mountain," one said.

"It was an avalanche. Many were caught and fell," said another.

The injured man Alyssa had worked on dropped his gaze to his injured hands. "Gone. Every last one of them. We tried to dig them out..."

Out of thirty men, only five had survived. The ranks of Knowledge Hall were woefully lower now than ever before, when every man was needed to fight the darkness covering the land.

The change in command would have to take place immediately, and new wizards established in the hierarchy, Alyssa thought before turning back to her friend.

Maybe not today, though.

Edegast sat heavily on a stool brought to him, leaning on his staff gripped with both hands. "This cannot be," he said over and over. "I feared this, but still held onto hope."

Alyssa knelt before him and placed her hands over his. "Dear wizard-my friend. Don't you let this tragedy overtake you. You know what all I've experienced. You know where there's a will, there's a way." Then she whispered to him, "We still have the Grim."

Edegast looked at her, tears wetting his cheeks before disappearing into the sides of his beard.

He shook his head. "I cannot do that, Alyssa. He would not want it."

"Yeah, well. Pappy might not have wanted it either, but I did it anyway. Sometimes it's necessary. I would say this situation is one of those times."

"You had no reason not to try. We do. The use of the Grim at this time, when the darkness is growing, would only serve to draw out the evilment. We need time to prepare for the war about to arise. No, we cannot use that spell."

"I reckon it's time to have a talk with all your folk here and let's plan what we *are* going to do then."

He nodded, his head remaining low. His grief was deep, and she knew she should walk away and let him have his time.

"I'm going to be in my room," she said. "But you know where I am. If you need me for anything, please let me know."

His shoulders shook and Salas came to the old man to comfort him. Feagus motioned for Alyssa to rejoin her. The two healers worked together on the final two patients, and then Alyssa took her leave of the gathering, pity filling her heart for Edegast and the loss that she knew hurt so much.

When she returned to her room, she had to talk it out. She paced in front of the fire she had created and spoke to Shadow like a sounding board. Of course, the scarf already knew all that she spoke of. Even though it wasn't visible during the excitement, it was still alert.

Shadow lay on the bed, color fully returned, rolled into a tube-shape, and propped up on a pillow. She never knew if Shad listened to her fully, so she stopped once in a while and asked, "Did you hear me?"

The scarf always lifted a corner and waved as if to say, "Of course, why do you ask?"

She prattled on for a long time and eventually, when she had talked herself out, she sat on the chair facing the fire and fell silent. Without Trudor, no answer would be forthcoming. Edegast would now have to make all decisions.

Shadow came to her then, and they sat in comfortable silence together. She allowed the scarf to drape across her shoulders like a snuggly kitten, and she pondered possible next steps.

It was late into the night when she finally decided to pull out the Grim and read. Without Trudor to guide Edegast in the entombing of the book, she wasn't at all sure what he would do about it. At least, there was nothing to be gained or lost in reading it. She didn't intend on using it for a spell of any kind, but she might well learn something valuable in it.

She hefted the heavy book and plopped down on the bed. Shadow slid from her shoulders and curled up beside her. She read as she slowly turned the pages.

Casting a spell several times is acceptable as long as it is the time of the full moon. This may be necessary to achieve the desired results from the manifestation. The repetition of a spell does not denote failure in the first or even second iteration of the spell.

Alyssa paused reading to consider these words. She had performed the spell to bring Pappy Oh back from the dead a number of times, calling on different things, performing different acts. She couldn't remember if it was done the same way twice or not.

"Amazing to me that I ever got him back on this side of the dirt, even as a voice," she told Shadow. "And I'm pretty sure that it wasn't the full moon when I performed it, because ole Hubert the Gryphon wanted me back by the time of the full moon. So, either this is not quite right, or these spells are up to individual actions."

Shadow flopped backwards as if to say the information was far too much to take in.

She tapped her finger against her chin and remembered what Pappy had told her about spells.

"Intention is the critical ingredient," he'd told her.

My intention was pure, and my belief was strong.

Shadow wrapped around her head and made itself into a jaunty witch's hat, complete with a pointed end.

She laughed at the scarf's antics and decided to read more another time. Edegast would have to have a conversation with her tomorrow if he was available so she could tell him her thoughts.

She carefully put the Grim back in her pack, pulled off her breeches, crawled into bed and fell asleep with her friend, Shadow, now in its normal shape, curled up at her head like a purring cat.

The next day dawned slightly overcast but a little warmer. Icicles hung outside her window dripping with a constant sound. She stared out at the approaching clouds on the far horizon. A short-lived thaw maybe. More snow was utterly unwelcome.

She had no idea what day it was or even what month it was. How long had they been there? She had been sick with the hob's poison for nearly a month.

She focused on this. "We left Mudden around the end of the grain moon. It took us several days to get here and then, after a few days here, I took ill. That was nearly a month out of mind, so it may be mid-September. If I'm wrong it's only worse, but I think we may be nearing Samhain... or already in it." She paced the floor.

Samhain was when the frosts deepened back home, covering Pappy's pumpkin patch until it looked like snow. She paused her pacing to look out the window slit again, this time letting her gaze travel across the hills. In the past, Samhain represented when they laid a place at the table for her parents, to honor their memory. But now, she believed the phoenix who had said they were still alive. She would not mourn them yet.

She moved away from the window and considered her choices, and how to find a way to get home. It was almost a certainty, even to her, that it would be necessary to wait until spring. Her grandparents needed her at the farm right now, she thought. They were getting too old for harvest without help.

As her brow furrowed in thought, Alyssa drew a deep breath. She couldn't leave Edegast now. He needed everyone to be with him, helping forge a new Knowledge Hall. Besides, she would never convince anyone to allow her to travel alone or with a party in any direction in these mountains.

It's too dangerous, Lys.

"Oh, Pappy! I wish you had come with me. I miss you!" she whispered to the voice she kept hearing in her head. But she heard the words and understood them. It *was* too dangerous. If a party of experienced wizards couldn't avoid tragedy, what made her think she could?

"What do I do now?"

She waited for a response, but none was forthcoming. She scooped Shadow up. "Dear scarf, how about you turn yourself invisible and let's go check on things? Edegast might need a friend right about now."

Shadow allowed her to wrap it around her waist and tie it into a jaunty bow, before disguising itself like a chameleon and blending in with her clothes. She took a long look down and tried to discern things, but it was impossible to tell where the scarf began and ended.

"Good," she declared as she pulled on the door to leave the room. She went into the dining hall and had a mug of tea, hoping Edegast would appear. When he didn't, she went in search of his room. She found Salas standing outside of a doorway and approached him.

"Dear Salas," she said. "Where is Edegast?"

Salas jabbed his thumb over his shoulder at the door behind him. "Here, within. He is not accepting company at this time."

"But I really want to see him. I want to let him know that I'm here for him."

Salas shook his head and crossed his arms. "He knows, my lady. He needs time and quiet to process his loss. He will return to us when it is time."

"What should I do in the meanwhile?" she fidgeted, wondering how she could get around the wizard and see Edegast. She felt rather than saw Shadow unwrap from her waist. She only saw a small glimmer as it flattened and slid under the door of Edegast's room.

"Seek out our swordsmith and have a short blade made for yourself." He closed his eyes before looking skyward. "Never did I ever think we would have to resort to weapons!"

"I'm living proof the danger is real. Why do you think you need weapons? Isn't wizard magik the most powerful?"

He crossed his arms and peered at her with his clear gray eyes. "The ones who seek to do us harm are mostly might and not magik. Sometimes magik is not usable against creatures of the night."

That statement sent a shiver down her arms. *Creatures of the night?* And what manner of creature was it that didn't succumb to magik? The only time she'd ever heard that was around a fire when Granny and Pappy were telling tales of their youth.

She swallowed hard. "Do you mean... real... creatures of the night or something conjured up like out of a nightmare?"

He nodded his head once. "Both. But conjured from a nightmare is a very apt description. The Dark Master is fond of creating evil things."

"What are we talking about here? More hob—um, creatures?"

He uncrossed his arms and took her by the shoulders like he would a young child and turned her to face down the corridor from which she had come. "Perhaps. Perhaps worse than that. Please go and find whatever you might be able to use to arm yourself. Even a hoe, or an axe is preferable to nothing at all."

She turned back to face him. "Sir, I am a mage also. I have magik. I'm not scared to use it either."

He scowled. "Yes, child. But you are not strong enough to withstand any more attacks. We cannot count on your magik being fully there yet. It wouldn't do for you to fall victim to another creature."

Guess you forgot I have the scarf— And the Grim, the spell book to beat all spell books.

She tried to control the eye roll she wanted to give him but failed. He waved his hands, dismissively.

"You'll give my regards to Edegast?" she asked, giving up the conversation as a lost cause.

He assured her he would. She hesitated then, until she felt the invisible Shadow land on her shoulder, and she took off down the hall, heading to her room. Once there, she checked on the book and found everything in order.

"All is good," she said aloud, before turning to the scarf. "Shad, tell me what you saw."

It always seemed to enjoy this game with her. It flattened itself out and floated forward from the door as it must have done once inside the bedroom where Edegast rested.

Then it soared up and hovered over the bed.

"You snuck in and took a look at the wizard who was on the bed?" Alyssa asked.

The scarf waved one end as if nodding affirmatively. Then it floated to the foot of the bed and slid up from there, turning its edge from left to right in a sneaky movement.

"Measured his condition, and then what did you find?"

The scarf's end dove toward the pillow and curled up next to it before lifting and floating to the door and stopping.

"He was asleep, and you left?"

Another affirmative wave.

"Was there anything out of the ordinary?"

The scarf flew to her tea mug and dipped inside of it, then flipped over and collapsed on the bed.

"He's been drugged?"

The scarf bent in the middle to fling its ends out in something of a hands-out shrug.

"You're pretty sure but not fully?"

It waved affirmatively before settling beside her. She paced a moment, thinking.

"Salas could have had Feagus give him a sleeping draught, that's likely." She put her hands to her mouth and considered what to do.

Shadow sat up and waited expectantly, like a dog for a biscuit.

"Could you slip into his room again and keep watch over him? He might be unsteady after having something to help him sleep. You can remain colorless, or you can be your normal self. He wouldn't mind either way, I'm sure. I'd like to know he ain't being drugged in a bad way. Though I'm pretty sure Salas is on the friends list and wouldn't harm a flea. But that aside, no matter what nobody says, he shouldn't be alone."

The scarf floated over to her and draped across her shoulders, one end stroking her cheek.

"Don't you worry about me none. I'm going to do what Salas suggested and go find the swordsmith. And if I'm lucky that bowyer, and a fletcher, too. When wizards, the greatest of magik-users, fear the bad ones running about, there's cause for alarm. Besides, Edegast already has a bow and arrows waiting on me," she told her friend as she fingered the material lying so close to her face.

In a short while, she and the scarf hid the Grim before they parted company. Shadow disappeared from view as it went invisible, and she followed her instinct on where a weapons master might be found. She arrived at the long building that housed the weapons and those who handled them just as Horoc was leaving.

"Alyssa," the sorceress greeted her, surprise registering on her face. "Why are you out here?"

"Salas sent me. Said I should get armed for everything that might go bump in the night." Alyssa stared hard into the earthen green eyes.

"I thought that was what the older, more experienced folks were doing? To protect the... um... less powerful," Horoc said, tapping her longbow onto the ground lightly, measuring her words.

"I'd prefer to be able to sleep at night knowing that my protection is beside my head, thank you very much."

Horoc made a sound of derision and passed by her.

Alyssa turned to watch her storm away and realized that she didn't like Horoc at all, and that fact left her heart sore. She'd never had an enemy before, but she was fairly certain this person could be one. A powerful one, in fact.

She longed for Pappy's input on the sorcerer, but he was silent, and she had too much to think about to dwell on it for long.

Chapter Seventeen

Alyssa found the bowyer, the fletcher, and the swordsmith and spoke to them all. The fletcher was a young man about her age, of ogre descent, named Kaarok.

He told her to call him Rok. He remembered Edegast asking for the weapons for her and when they were returned to him, kept them safely put away. He brought them out now and taught her how to keep her arrows from being damaged in the quiver, and he set up a target for her to practice hitting to make sure the aim of the arrow was true.

It wasn't long until Rok gave her a grin of praise. "Milady, you are gifted with the bowstring. How long have you been shooting?"

She paused to wipe a strand of hair from her brow. The exercise had made her warm in her heavy coat, and she found beads of sweat rolling down her cheeks.

She told him, "I reckon I picked up my first set about ten. My granddaddy took me out to find a bird for our Gratefulness meal."

"Gratefulness…" He gazed out at the distance and a faraway look come over his face. "I haven't had a true meal with my family like that in… well, far too long."

"If things don't go sour, we may have one here at the castle. Looks like I'm stuck here due to the conditions around these mountains. I'll talk to the cooks and see how the land lays," Alyssa told him, shaking the quiver to get the arrows to settle properly.

"Mind that you do not upset the delicate balance of your arrows. Do you shoot with your quiver on?" Roc asked, watching her.

She nodded. "Yes, why?"

"It could cause you to not be in the proper placement for your shot. Here let me show you."

He came over and situated his quiver as hers was, and then placed his bow over his back like she had done hers.

When he pulled out an arrow, the shift of arm and or shoulder caused the bow to be in a different position.

"Do you see?" he asked.

She admired his knowledge and wanted to tell him so, but instead, what came out was, "Yes. But I only do what comes naturally to me. If I'm after a rabbit or a deer, or even a turkey bird, I don't think; I just pull my arrows and shoot."

He smiled at her. "Genuine intuition, eh?"

She shrugged. "I guess. I don't know what to call it. I do what I do. Never gave it a lot of thought before."

He nodded and packed up his gear. "I have to get back. This has been fun, though. Thank you for spending time with me. There's few here our age, and sometimes I feel like I'm in the company of my parents and grandparents. Always watching my words. You understand what I say?"

She laughed and nodded in agreement. "Do I ever!"

They walked back to the castle together in an amiable silence that she found both fascinating and fun. He waved goodbye as he turned from the entrance and went left.

Upon entering the castle, her stomach churned and grumbled, so she headed directly for the dining hall. Salas was there, sipping tea and speaking to one of the other wizards. She recognized him as Lindon. He had been with them during the questioning of the hobgoblin.

His voice was low, but she could hear him say Edegast's name a few times as she poured a mug of tea.

"Salas," she said with a nod, as she made her way to the table to sit. "How is Edegast?"

He waved Lindon away and the man hurried out of the dining hall.

"He is as well as he can be, given the circumstances. I am glad to see you here. I have something to discuss with you." He shook out his robes and picked up his staff, leaned on it to stand, and she could see him mentally picking his words.

"What is it?" A serving man set a bowl of soup in front of Alyssa.

"The book. You still have it safe and sound, I pray. We, as a unified gatherment of wizards and magik-users, should have a council as to what the plan for it is. And the sooner the better."

She tried to decipher the look he gave her and to judge if he was being friendly. Her gaze fell on the bowl as if she studied its contents. Understanding the intentions of others in the castle was hard without Edegast to part the waters.

"Yes," she murmured, lifting her spoon. "I have it well-protected." She hoped that would dissuade Salas from trying to get to it. Although, as a magik-user, a wizard of any class could get the book easily, provided the Grim wanted to go, and if they could convince Shadow to release it.

She spoke in between bites. "Edegast and I spoke briefly about it, but nothing was decided. We were waiting for his father and the others to return—"

"—and as that is now a terrible ending, the fate of the book falls on the rest of us," he added quickly. "Perhaps you should bring it to me and let me keep it for you until something can be decided."

She dabbed at her mouth with a piece of cloth and measured her words. "No sir, it was given to me to take care of like my Pappy before me. I'll keep my hands on it until that decision is made on its future. By Edegast, whenever he is ready."

She didn't look up at him, not wishing to seem confrontational. She felt his eyes boring into the top of her head.

"Very well," he sighed, moving away to leave the hall. "As you wish. I would prefer you try to discuss the book with Edegast as soon as possible."

She did stare at him now. "Exactly my thoughts, Salas, exactly my thoughts. You let me know when it's a good time to see him, and I'll do that very thing."

After he left, she considered his words. Nothing would suit her finer than to talk to Edegast about the spell book.

"*Ain't nothin' holdin' you but gravity,*" Pappy's voice said inside her mind.

And he was right, too. She finished her soup and took off for Edegast's room. When she got to his door, she was surprised to see it standing open and Edegast seated on the side of his bed within full view.

"Edegast?" she asked, softly.

He looked up at her and waved for her to come inside. "Please close the door," he said.

She did as he asked. "Are you feeling better?"

He sat up straighter as if to shake himself out of a reverie. "I left the door open for fresh air. I am well enough. How are you?"

"Fine as frog hair, as Pappy would say. Shadow and I have been concerned about you. It's good to see you up and alert."

"I have been prostrate with grief," he admitted, shaking his head. "But I know that my father would not carry on this way if the situations were reversed. He would give my passing out of this world its due time of grief, and then he would get up, brush his beard and get back to the business of living. I shall do likewise."

She nodded, peering closely to see if she could see Shad. It was nowhere to be found with the eye, though. Either it was lying about being invisible, or it had left the grieving wizard alone.

"Could we talk for a minute?" she asked, pulling a chair close to the bed.

He nodded. "Most certainly. I am sorry that I have left you to manage these dark days without me. It seems that an old man does not know how to entertain a young girl properly in a cold and forbidding castle but leaving you on your own was thoughtless."

"I've done fine, Edegast. But the time has come for some important decisions to be made. Salas has asked me about the Grim. Whether I still have it and if I am protecting it properly. That Horoc, has questionable intentions too, if you ask me."

"Questionable intentions? How so?"

She squirmed a little. Horoc had done nothing untoward to her. It was more of a feeling.

"I've got a little bit of my Granny's intuition. That Horoc gives me a bad feeling. I ain't sure I like her yet. Her eyes gleam whenever the scarf is mentioned. Can't imagine her attitude when she hears about the book."

"Horoc is not a bad person," Edegast told her, a mysterious note to his voice. "She is not a social creature, true. But she is rather good at what she does."

This gave Alyssa food for thought. "What *does* she do?"

"I cannot tell you all. Horoc is a private sort. I know some of her history, but... if you mean what part does she play in Knowledge Hall business, I can explain that."

"Yes. What is her special skill? I'm a healer, a mage-in-training, if you will. You're a magik-user, a wizard. What is she? Is she only a healer? A sorceress? She called herself a witch—"

Edegast was about to answer when someone knocked on the door. He told the visitor to enter. It was Lindon.

"Sir Edegast," Lindon said, stammering a bit when he saw Alyssa there. "Sir Salas has sent for you. There is to be a meeting of the wise this evening after our meal. Your attendance is required."

Edegast stiffened and Alyssa heard his sharp intake of breath.

"Very well, Lindon. I shall do my best to make it to the meeting."

The corners of Lindon's mouth lifted briefly and then he was gone. Alyssa stared at the door for a while, unsure what to think.

Edegast stood and apologized for cutting their visit short. "You can rest assured that whatever this meeting is about, I can handle it. I am getting stronger every minute."

She nodded and smiled at him, feeling Shadow wrap around her shoulders. She resisted the urge to reach up and pat her scarf. "That's comforting to hear. Be prepared for the meeting to be about the book."

"That is not a matter for him to take upon himself," Edegast said, frowning. "Now that my father is gone, that is a matter for the new regent, and I shall handle it in my own good time. And while I am saying so, I do not like being commanded to attend a meeting that I should be holding." He took up his staff and tapped it on the ground almost angrily. It seemed to Alyssa that he stood taller, though, full of determination. She approved of his new backbone.

She pulled open the door and said, "Yes, well, be on the lookout for the reason for the meeting. I'll give the Grim to you, if you want it, but you said you didn't trust yourself with it. And honestly, it ain't too thrilled to go to anybody. So, I'm ready to keep it if that's how it has to be. I don't recommend letting anyone handle it, either. The Dark Master is still behind the arrows flinging out in all directions of Daegries, and who knows who is on whose side?"

He nodded. "We will have more answers soon, Alyssa. Thank you for stopping by, my dear." He placed his warm hand on her shoulder as Shadow slid away from her to avoid detection.

She turned with an afterthought. "You reckon I should be at that meeting? I mean, I *am* the heir of Egladris. I've got the scarf. I'm a person of value to this place, and I possess the Grim. If anyone would be required, it would be me, don't you think?"

Edegast took a deep breath and gripped his staff before moving to stand before her. He stared down at her, assessing.

"Right you are, Alyssa. Right. You. Are. Meet with us after the evening meal."

And they left the room together, strolling down the corridor, each lost in their own thoughts. When Edegast excused himself to go to Salas's quarters, Alyssa understood. He would need to set some boundaries around castle life now that his father was gone. Especially with Salas.

Later, Alyssa took Shadow back to the room and instructed it to protect the book. "It's in high demand now, and some folks might not have the same good intentions that others have. You've done a good job so far. Keep at it."

The scarf draped over the pack and became invisible. She left her new bow and arrows also, feeling certain there would be no need for them at the meeting. It occurred to her that she needed a good hiding place for her belongings. There was no place satisfying. Finally, she piled the pack on the far side of the bed, with the quiver and bow, and hoped no one would be so brave as to try to take any of it.

She still had time to go to the sword maker and see how the man fared with making one for her. She planned to ask for a few moments of training, which she felt certain she would need before being even a tiny bit safe with a sword.

The swordsmith, unlike Lord Bryon, was fairly tall and had deep auburn-colored hair that he kept bound back with a bit of cloth. She had spoken to him earlier and learned his name was Jet Arum, and he was a new addition to the family of wizards. He specialized in metal magik, and the wizards held him in high regard.

"Sir Jet," Alyssa greeted him as she came into the hut where he did his work. "How is the work on my blade?"

He looked up and wiped his brow with the back of his hand. So deeply was he involved with the beating of the blade he worked on, it took a moment for him to recall her face and put a name to it.

"Ah, Lady Alyssa, the blade is coming along. I should have it for you soon."

"Is that it?" she asked, as she moved closer to see what he worked on. "Can I see?"

He motioned for her to take a look. She saw that the blade had a good grip for a two-handed swing, which she was certain she would need to employ.

"Looks mighty," she said with a grin. "Could there be any way you or someone else could teach me a thing or two about swords? I told you before that I can handle a hoe handle and an axe handle, but a sword is different, and I could use some training."

He grinned in return. "I'd be happy to be your guide."

"Much obliged, Jet, much obliged. I'll be back soon to see it and maybe take possession, if you 'll allow it."

"Most certainly, milady. It's yours after all."

She smiled again and backed away a step or two, feeling the heat from the fire he had stoked in the makeshift earthen oven nearby. She watched a moment more as he took the blade and placed it in the fire to soften the metal for more precise attuning.

Then, satisfied that she would be in good hands with Jet teaching her, she left that area and made her way back to the castle to get ready for the council that Lindon had spoken of.

As she walked, she thought of what a war with the Dark Master meant to both realms of Daegries, the Greater and the Lesser. Her family and her home, Lord Bryon and his kinsmen, the Yetis, Haldors, and Iefyr were all going to be embroiled in the conflict, right along with the wizards. No one's homeland would be left unscarred. No matter what, she would fight to the death for her farm and her family.

She entered her room to change clothes and clean up before making her way to the dining hall. The scarf didn't move from its place with the Grim. Soon, she was on her way to the dining hall.

The evening meal was consumed and taken away when Salas stood and tapped his mug with a dagger.

"Good family, we are called here to have a meeting about the book that was taken south nigh on seventy years ago. If you are unfamiliar, and some of you might be, this is the grimoire which has been in the safekeeping of a mage in the south. His granddaughter, Alyssa, is here with us now, and she has brought the book along with her."

An elderly witch pounded hard on the table to get attention. "Salas, what is the meaning of this? Trudor sent that tome south for safekeeping. It should not be here. Especially now," she yelled.

Someone close to the witch spoke directly into her ear. "Pridalf, please do not shout. They can hear you."

"Well, I cannot hear them," the witch answered.

The kerfuffle continued until she turned her back on the one trying to quiet her.

Salas acknowledged her presence and addressed her concerns. "Pridalf, I know that you have had a special interest in this subject for some time, so I will allow your outburst. Please know that Edegast is about to take over the meeting and he will not leave you hanging on tenterhooks."

With that Salas moved away, and Edegast stepped up.

"My fellow magik-users," he began. There was a lot of pounding on the table and shuffling of feet as people tried to let him know they appreciated his being there.

Many said, "Here! Here!" and waved their wands or staffs.

Edegast smiled out at the crowd and tried to get their attention onto the matter of the meeting and off of his appearance.

Soon, when the room resumed order, Edegast began again. "Dear folk, we are here tonight to discuss a few items of great importance to us. One, the loss of our leader, my father, Trudor the White."

"Long may he be remembered!" voices shouted.

Again, Edegast had to wait for the room to calm. Once he had their attention, he said, "Dear ones, please contain your exclamations and outbursts until I finish, otherwise we will never get to bed tonight."

The old witch turned to the wizard next to her. "What'd he say?"

The information was repeated and Edegast continued.

"So, as you may know, Alyssa Chance Oh is the keeper of the Grim, as it has come to be known. I brought her here to get the book back to where it belongs. But that was before the hobgoblin was found on our property. With the ability of such creatures to get inside this castle, I am uncertain as to what the best plan is yet. Perhaps Knowledge Hall is not the safest place."

"Burn it!" came someone's reply.

"We cannot burn it," Edegast told them.

"Hide it!" came someone else's reply.

"It has been hidden all these years. Do not think that I did not consider leaving it where it was. I did. My thought was it is a magik-user's book, one full of knowledge such as this world needs in these trying days. What better place to keep it than here amongst those who can use it best?"

"Then what is the problem?" Salas asked, his brow furrowed. "How is having it here such a danger if we all can use it?"

"That is precisely the problem," Edegast said. "We most certainly cannot use it."

"Why is this?" Lindon asked. "We have never been told we were not allowed to use any of the books at Knowledge Hall."

"The Dark Master has arisen again," Edegast said simply. This sent a ripple of concern through the crowd.

"The D-Dark Master has been dead for a long time," Lindon said, face turning white. "I am young, but I know the history."

Faces became blank as some deciphered his words. Silence fell, and Edegast knew he finally had the attention of every person there.

"Some of the history is fallacy. My words are true. I have seen evidence and have found the path the Dark Master is using to come forth and take over the world of Daegries. That is his intention, I can assure you. I told Trudor some of this before my last journey. I was going to seek his counsel on my return but, as we all know, that is now impossible. The appearance of the creatures here in our most vulnerable place is even more evidence of this coming evil."

"Trudor shared nothing with any of us about this," Salas said to Lindon by way of explanation. "I have only learned of this danger recently myself."

Edegast nodded and continued shoving his hands into hidden pockets in his cloak. "As per my instructions. I did not want everyone at Knowledge Hall to live in fear in our home if it was unnecessary. But now, with the evil being so obvious, well, if we do not prepare and protect these items that are defenseless, we will lose everything. Which is why I now question the thought of the Grim being here. It is the one thing that the Dark Master seeks over all else. We are sitting here in our castle as though we are impenetrable, and that is a lie."

"True enough," Salas agreed, nodding. "The creature that came among us proves that. How did that even happen, good Edegast? How did a creature like that make it into the inner sanctum?"

Edegast paced a moment before turning back to the crowd. "For those who do not know, we had portal plants to appear, as did many others. They were short-lived as the weather is too cold to sustain them. The holes that opened in their midst, however, were not affected by the cold. And once opened, the way in is ever available. I suspect an entrance is still open somewhere in the catacombs."

"Why don't you fill it in? Close it up?" Lindon asked. He sat near the witch who was hard of hearing. He had to repeat his question to her.

"It will only spew the fill dirt out and be as it was before, mostly unchanged. Wooden barriers are useless as well. There is little that can be done to bar these holes from being passages to the Dark Master's domain. Or to other points in Daegries."

Alyssa digested his words. If the portals, once opened, were always open, then no place on Daegries was safe.

The crowd looked one to the other, then all eyes turned to Edegast.

Salas spoke the question everyone wanted to ask. "Then how do we protect ourselves and our work?"

Chapter Eighteen

- -

Alyssa stared at Edegast right along with everyone else. She hoped he had an answer, because no one so far had succeeded in closing the portals. Shame reddened her cheeks at the thought of her part in this terrible drama unfolding.

"We will have to consult with the Iefyr. They are the elders of this realm. They have seen the many devices of the Dark Master recently and have always recorded them through time. They have been busily traveling the Greater Daegries to see the portal plants and to speak with those nearby to learn what they have witnessed. As have I, " he said.

Alyssa frowned at his words. It was he, himself, who had done these things.

"Charge into the Underworld and kill him," Pridalf said. "We took a chance on him in the old days and look where that got us. He deserves a vicious death."

"That would serve his purposes nicely, Pridalf. No, we shall consult the Elders. They will know what to do. I feel certain that this is why my father and his group were going to the forest. To seek out the wisest of the Iefyr to see what they knew about the plants and the holes and dark magik."

"We should not do that until the thaw," someone said in a worried voice. "No one wants to end up buried in snow... again."

Edegast blinked at these words but continued on. "No, we should not. Not now. So, that is why we are going to band together here in this castle and keep watches. I will need the strongest among us to take two-hour stands. Twelve for day and twelve for night. No one watches alone, and there will be a watch of two at the minimum."

Here Edegast paused to look out at the shock on the faces before him.

"I am sorry, my family. This is a terrible time we are living in. But take heart––we have the Grim, we have our knowledge. We will be the guardians now as in the old days."

"I ask again," Salas said. "Why cannot we use the book to fight the Dark Master? We have the solution to the problem with our guest here." He waved at Alyssa.

Edegast seemed a bit nervous as he glanced at Salas and quickly looked away. "Salas, my heart is heavy. But, magik once released, has very dangerous consequences. I fear the Dark Master can track the magik that comes from using this book. If we try to magik him with it, he will find us and conquer us, down to the last man."

Terror rose in Alyssa's throat, closing it. Her mind tumbled over the fact that Edegast had used the Grim to bring Pappy Oh back. The very spell that might be looked for by the enemy.

"Edegast!" she said, hoarsely. "What about Pappy?"

He knew what she meant. He closed his eyes and dropped his chin to his chest, his beard splaying out. "We can only hope that the constable will keep things protected."

"Did you ask Murray to call on the farm that day?" She could barely form the words, let alone say them.

He quickly moved to her side. "No. Oh no, Alyssa. I would never do such a thing. I only meant that if the folks were being watched by the constable, then trouble, if it comes, will be dealt with swiftly. We do not know that *any* actions on *anyone's* behalf has brought destruction to them at this time. It is only possible as the taint spreads."

Alyssa wiped tears away and said nothing as a large lump had formed in her throat.

"*Ain't your fault, gal,*" Pappy's voice said.

A wizard in a deep purple robe stood, and with a slithering sound, he pulled out a sword from a scabbard under his cloak. "For the Snowclids!" he shouted.

Others followed suit. Soon cries "For the Snowclids" and "Wizards unite" rang throughout the castle. Many of the wise carried arms, and those who didn't had staffs and wands, and they were not afraid. They would protect what was theirs to their dying breath.

Salas led the throng from the meeting room to begin setting up watches. Alyssa was certain he had encouraged them to take up arms, as he had encouraged her.

She turned to Edegast and said, "I'm not ready for this. I've ordered a sword to be made for me, and I've taken a few quick lessons with the fletcher. But that's not enough to make me feel safe against an age-old enemy or his armies. I'll be forever sorry for my messing in magik that started these wicked plants to begin with."

"Do not berate yourself, young lady. It was an honest mistake. You were trying to bring your grandfather back and did not know about magik. Or its backlashes. By the way, our bowmen and swordsmith are quite adept at training with weapons. You only have to ask."

She fell silent. She *had* asked. She would really have to follow through now. Perhaps even spending long days practicing with someone.

"Do you reckon the Dark Master will attack the castle?" she asked, musing. The skin on her arms was prickling like it always did when she was on edge. She added softly, "Or my farm?"

He stepped back to the dais and picked up his staff from where he had left it before the meeting. "I would not tell anyone that it was a possibility unless it truly was. His creatures have made it inside this castle once. There is nothing to say they will not continue the attempt."

"Somebody'll miss the creature that Horoc killed, sooner or later," Alyssa said, looking at her feet. "I reckon the enemy forces will be coming to find him."

"I hope it is later, and I hope they do not figure out where he was when he disappeared." Edegast waved to her for them to depart.

She realized how exhausted she was as she trudged along behind him up to the stairs to her room.

"Where was Horoc tonight? I didn't see her anywhere."

Edegast switched his staff to his other hand. "She is off patrolling. She wanted to see the place where the portal plants had been. She may be examining the holes. I am not certain."

"Don't you think that is a bit risky and especially at night?"

He tilted his head and put a finger alongside his nose. "No, not really. Horoc is well-prepared for any attempt from the Dark Master. She has had much training. Perhaps you could talk to her about sparring with you."

Alyssa didn't say anything, but she didn't want to be that close to the sorceress. She certainly didn't want the well-trained woman coming at her with weapons. She frowned at Edegast. Why did he know so much about Horoc and relate so little?

"Keep a close watch on the Grim," Edegast told her, face downcast. "If we are attacked, it is the one thing we must save at all costs. I really must decide what to do about it."

She nodded and turned to go up the stairs, heart as heavy as her feet.

When she reached her room, she noticed that Salas's door was closed and there was no light coming from beneath it. He had gone to set up watches. Perhaps he would take one as well.

She entered her room and called to Shadow. It immediately rose from where it had draped itself over the pack. In a brightly colored green hue, it flew to her wrapping her in a big hug.

She laughed. "I missed you too, Shad. I missed you too."

The quiver and bow remained strung over the bed post. She fingered one of the arrows and considered if she could shoot a human, or other creature, for any reason that was not food related. Her mind and her heart warred over it until she fell into a dreamless sleep.

The next day dawned, bedraggled and dreary. The snow started early, falling from the sky in great waves, and the clouds thickened oppressively.

Alyssa left the scarf protecting the Grim, before heading straight to the swordsmith, scowling at the snow as it fell in earnest. Jet greeted her with a smile and pulled the sword out for her to examine.

She tried to control her dismay. The blade was long and not suited to her ability to wield it. "This looks wonderful to me, Jet," she lied, "but I'm afraid I might not be the best judge. As I told you, I need some training."

"Here," he told her. "Take it. And, as it so happens, I am free right now. May I help you?"

She grinned, taking the sword and holding it, measuring the weight of it. "What great timing I have! Yes, please do show me!"

He nodded and took the cloth apron from his middle, laid it aside, picked up a blade that looked to be a bit worn from use, and they went outside together.

The snow kept them under an overhang to practice. Jet showed Alyssa how to stand with her feet planted, and how when a strike is made, it can be extremely jarring to the arms and shoulders. They tapped swords a few times so she could understand how to grip, and he allowed her to stab into a target he dragged over from a tidy corner of his work area.

Lifting the heavy blade to punch it into the target took all of her effort. Slicing and parrying Jet's blade sent her on her backside more than once. When they finished the lesson, her arms ached from muscle weariness.

Finally, they went back inside, and Alyssa wiped snow from her coat and boots. The blowing snow was worrisome, and Alyssa asked Jet how to protect her weapon from the elements.

"It would be best not to try to use it in bad weather, but sometimes one cannot choose what happens during a battle, so be sure to dry it well before putting it away. Blades will bend and break in extremely cold temperatures. And of course, keep your scabbard well-maintained and oiled to prevent damage to the weapon when covered."

She nodded and promised to do as he asked. He handed her the sword in a leather scabbard after he took the time to dry the blade and make sure the holder was in good shape.

"You might be able to get someone good with leatherworks to make something that fits you better. This is all I have at the moment," he said.

"This is perfect, Jet. Thank you so much for all of this. I am awed at your knowledge."

He gave her a wink and watched as she attempted to fling the heavy scabbard over her shoulder. "Wait," he said, moving to another pile of leatherworks. He pulled out a strap like a belt. "Let's create a makeshift holder. If you can soldier it onto your back and fit it down behind your arm like this…" He placed the blade in its scabbard so that the hilt was near her ear. "There. You can touch the business end there by your side."

She grinned and thanked him again, knowing full well she would never be able to pull the heavy blade from the holder quickly enough to use it. She would need to practice a lot to get the action down to a fine point.

"You're welcome. Here take these," he said, handing her some copper coins. "It's fitting for anyone receiving a weapon to get money with it. For good luck."

Alyssa accepted the coins and waved at him as she took her leave. She wondered if Lord Bryon could make a leather scabbard for her that was more secure. She would ask if she ever made it back to the Heightlands.

Her path took her into a curtain of falling snow, and she had to brush it away from her face to see. The weather was not fit for anyone to be in, so she increased her speed.

Somehow, she managed to get inside but it was by way of a different entrance. She had gotten off course from the blinding whiteness. Relieved to be inside and out of the weather, she stood a moment to allow her vision to clear.

Nothing appeared familiar. She had entered the castle at a place that she hadn't known existed. She turned to stare at the wooden door. Not nearly as heavy or well-made as the one at the front of the castle, nor was it fortified, or manned.

Perhaps I'm near the catacombs. As big as that place is, they likely have more than one entrance. If I can find the stairs leading up, I'll be able to get back on track.

She moved ahead in the gloom. Candles in sconces on the wall glowed dimly but none appeared in the hallway she was heading toward. It didn't feel right to her, either.

There is no light to guide me.

"Magik, come to me now," she said, holding her arms out in front of her. The green glow issued from her fingertips, and she flattened her hands straight out, balancing the magik on each hand. There was nowhere to go but forward, but her intuition caused her to stare into the gloom before her.

A wizard stood there, illuminated only by Alyssa's magik glow. His cloak hid his robes and any weapon he might have. The darkness hid his face, and she could tell nothing about who she addressed.

"Who are you?" she asked, voice trembling.

The wizard pulled his hood away and Alyssa lifted her hands higher. A creature from her worst nightmare stood before her. It appeared as a giant rat with a long snout and sharp teeth that glistened when he grinned at her.

Ragon and Madrid had been in rat form when she'd been in the dungeons of Needlemount castle, but they had been bewitched by Edegast and were normal-sized.

"Be gone!" she said as powerfully as possible. "Don't make me release this magik."

The creature didn't make a move, either to harm her or to leave, so she forcefully blew the glow magik directly at its face.

Unhappy with the glowing orbs, it swatted them away. They only returned, making the creature angry with all of the undulations. While it was otherwise occupied, Alyssa struggled to remove her sword. She tugged and tugged, and it refused to budge.

Finally evading the magik orbs, the creature rushed toward Alyssa. Its bony hand brandished a dangerously tipped pike.

Its robes never touched the ground, and Alyssa had never seen anything move that fast. With the sword useless on her back, she flung her arm out and sent all of her magik directly into its beady eyes.

A yell sounded from behind the creature, and suddenly Horoc was there. The sorceress stabbed her sword into the creature's back, and it crumpled, a flurry of rats fleeing from under its robes and down a nearby corridor. Horoc chased them as far as she could.

Alyssa bent to examine the creature. It looked rat-like with whiskers and black eyes that stared dimly upward. The ears were farther down on the head but also pointed like a rat.

When Horoc returned, Alyssa rose to her feet. "Thank you, Horoc. You saved my life."

The witch's eyes flashed like twin bolts of lightning. "What in Daegries are you doing down here? Was one encounter not enough for you?"

"I—I didn't mean to be here!" Alyssa said, voice rising. "It was an accident. The storm had me confused as to which door I was entering through."

"Fool of a girl!" Horoc spat, breath heaving. "Stop wandering around this castle, alone and unarmed. You're going to end up being on the wrong end of a pike—or worse!"

When she said "unarmed," Alyssa's temper flared. She yanked her sword from its scabbard, anger giving her extra strength. The blade fairly hummed as it left the leather. Her arms, already weary from the lesson with the swordsmith, couldn't carry through with the act, however, and the tip of the blade went down.

"I am armed!" she ground out; her teeth clenched as she tried to right the blade.

"Then do better about using it," Horoc answered, wiping her own sword on the cloak of the creature before sheathing it again. The woman had no problem handling her blade. It looked as easy as breath.

Must have grown up using one, Alyssa thought.

She heaved her sword up and struggled to put it back in the scabbard. Frustrated, she finally pulled the scabbard from her shoulder, shoved the blade in, and slung the sheathed sword back over her shoulder. Her back throbbed from the effort. Then, in a shaky voice, she asked, "What is this evilment?"

Horoc glanced at the creature as if she was familiar with it. "It is a Phank. Raised up in the abandoned tunnels where the Haldor used to live. An abomination of the Dark Master's."

"Is it human or animal?"

"Who knows? It keeps company with rats, so mostly rodent, I suspect."

Alyssa wanted to say something cruel about the creature but refrained.

Horoc waved her forward. "We shall go back out into the yard and come around. It is safer that way."

Horoc dragged the creature along behind her. Alyssa didn't want to know where she would put it, so instead she asked, "Why does the castle have so many openings and no one watching them?"

"I was there, wasn't I?" Horoc asked, glancing at her.

Alyssa couldn't deny that the woman's timely appearance had been her boon. Maybe that was where Horoc's magik truly lived. She was always where protection was needed.

When they arrived at the doorway, Alyssa tried to prepare for the onslaught of the weather, but no amount of preparation could stop the cold that seemed to penetrate every layer. She huddled deeply into her coat and followed Horoc's footprints. The brave sorceress veered off toward the left from the castle's front door, leaving Alyssa to hurry inside alone.

She didn't even acknowledge my thanks for her saving my life. Alyssa shrugged at the insensitive sorceress and focused on something she could control, like a mug of hot tea and a roaring fire. She found both in her bedroom.

Edegast waited for her there, also.

"Alyssa," he greeted her as she entered the room.

Shadow waved from its perch over the pack. She waved back.

"Is there something you want to tell me?" Edegast asked, lifting a thick eyebrow.

She thought quickly. He surely couldn't know about the attack so soon. "I ain't sure I know what you're talking about."

"Shadow come over here," Edegast said. The scarf floated over and curled up on the bed beside him.

"This magik scarf can make itself invisible. Did you know that?"

Drat! How did he find out?

"You mean you didn't know?" she asked, innocently. *Let him think that this is common knowledge.*

"No, I did not," the wizard declared. "But seeing as how it can do this, and you are not at all surprised by it, I can only assume you have known about it for some time."

"Yes, I've known. What's wrong with that?" She tried to make her voice sound concerned as if Shadow had a malady that caused it to go invisible. "Is the scarf in danger?"

Edegast closed his eyes and tilted his head back for a moment. "No, no. Not at all. In fact, the scarf has become one of the most interesting and provocative magik items in the castle, it would seem. Since you have to keep the Grim safe for a while longer, I would advise you to do the same with the scarf."

"Why are you so worried about the scarf?"

"Why are you not?"

His quick response set her back on her heels a moment. Finally, she said, "Because Shadow picked me, Edegast. It's my scarf and was always meant to be mine. The Iefyr told me as much, hence why it is called the Scarf of Egladris. I don't think anyone *could* steal it now, not without a fight. So, the scarf protects the Grim, and they both stay in my room. Easy, yes?"

He stared at her, then stood and prepared to leave the room. "Nothing in this life is easy at the moment. I want you to be extra careful."

"I hope you are equally as worried about me," she said, pulling her coat off. She draped it over the chair in front of the fireplace to dry.

"Certainly, I am," he said, softly. "You are very important to me, Alyssa, as is the entirety of the Oh household. But you must remember that I am currently about a bigger cause, and while you are a piece of that and have a part to play, you are not the entire cause. I will reveal more soon."

With a mighty effort, Alyssa pulled the sword out to show to him, hoping to change the subject. "Look at this. Maybe it will give you some comfort. I feel more secure anyway."

He took the blade and examined it. "I do not believe that this sword is well-suited to you. And I would prefer it was treated with a spell or two to make it even more shielded."

Ignoring his observations, she took it back and replaced it in the scabbard. "Almost had to use it today," she told him.

His brows came together in a worried frown. "How so?"

"Best you hear it from me," she said, crossing her arms. "Horoc had to kill another creature down around the catacombs, I think. Exactly where we were, I ain't entirely certain. I was confused when I entered by the wrong door. The creature came straight for me, so I didn't have time to get my bearings."

"Another one?" he whispered. "The same? A hobgoblin?"

"No, this one was something that she called a Phank. It looked like a giant rat and there were real rats following it around. She chased them away after killing the creature."

"Oh my. This is terrible news," he said, shaking his head. "I have to go to attend to something, but I will be back soon. You need to know a few things. I cannot divulge it yet, but... well, be looking for me in an hour or so."

And out the door he flew, his cloak revealing his long graying hair where it flew back from the whoosh of air as he went.

Chapter Nineteen

Alyssa did as Edegast requested, even though the day was waning, and she was hungry. When the wizard returned, she was grateful to see a platter of dried fruit, cheese, and bread in one hand and two goblets in the other.

He placed the platter on the bed, and the goblets on the floor while she pulled the chair around facing him. She poured water for them from the pitcher in the wooden stand.

They sat on the bed and Edegast spoke. "I have returned as I said I would, to tell you a few things that you need to know. I did not intend on having to do this chore as I believed my father would be here and would be overseeing everything. As it is, I am going to be the one doing all."

She nodded as she popped a fig into her mouth.

"First, these creatures appearing inside the castle bode ill in ways that even the wise cannot comprehend. They are, as some might call them, harbingers of far worse still to come. The fact that the Dark Master is alive and sending them forth like torches in the night, well, that says much to me. It also reminds me that the Needlemount men remain unaccounted for. It would not surprise me if this creature, this Phank was not from the same place."

"Horoc said they were known to live around the Haldor's mountain. Is the Dark Master sending out these creatures to try and find the Grim?" Alyssa asked, a piece of cheese in each hand.

Edegast stared at her. "In a word, yes. Alyssa, I had hoped that my father would be here and would advise us on what to do with this grimoire, this magik book. Since he is not... well, I must do what must be done."

"You're sounding as dark as a thunder boomer overhead."

The edges of his mouth lifted. "You are a very perceptive person."

"What do you mean?"

"I mean, you always get to the bottom of a situation right away. You do not wait to slide around its edges. Directness, I believe is the proper word."

"Why would I waste time on dancing around an issue with you? We have no secrets."

He placed his goblet on the floor, tore off a hunk of the bread, and chewed thoughtfully.

She went on. "So, the Dark Master is seeking the Grim, and he's using the portals to travel to and from. And he's looking here first. How's that for guessing?"

He laughed and brought his goblet back up to sip from it. "Excellent with one exception. He, himself, is not using the portals. He is using his force of creatures to explore the land for him and find what he seeks. He is preparing for battle the only way he can. You see, he is no more than a shade himself. He needs the Grim and its magik to bring him back to his full form."

"Ah," she said, taking a sip of water. "I had forgotten that."

"Yes, so, the Grim is important to him. We must find out a way to protect it and keep it away from him, or else destroy it."

This took her aback. "Destroy it? What's your idea? You must have one or we wouldn't be talking right now."

Edegast stood and walked to the fireplace, staring at the guttering flames, his goblet held tightly. "Indeed. I do have one. No one is going to like it though. Salas, in fact, hated it."

Alarmed, Alyssa asked, "What? What is it? Tell me." She got up and walked over to him and tugged on his arm. "I'm not a child anymore, Edegast. I can handle whatever you say."

The edges of his eyelids wrinkled. "I was hoping you would say that. I have decided to leave the Grim with you for the time being. Nowhere in this castle would be nearly as safe. The Dark Master has no idea who you are yet and, therefore, is not seeking you. He certainly cannot have any idea that his grimoire is under the protection of the Scarf of Egladris either. And that, my dear, is a very good thing."

She silently nodded at his words.

They continued talking in low voices late into the night, rebuilding the fire and going to the dining hall for tea. When Alyssa finally fell into bed, her mind was exhausted. Great planning took time, she'd discovered.

The next day, the snow had stopped but drifts of it remained around the castle. Someone set a few of the younger wizards to the task of digging a pathway.

Alyssa sat alone in the dining hall sipping hot cocoa and trying not to think about the frigid air permeating everywhere in the castle, unrelenting. She was grateful not to have to wear a dress with only a cloak to keep her warm.

Edegast's plan from last night had left her wondering. Their conversation returned to her, and she turned the words over in her mind.

The wizard wanted to send out a new group to find the Iefyr and warn them, as had been his father's intention, however misaligned it had been. He felt they had to get the word to the Iefyr about the Dark Master and what he might be up to.

Edegast told her that the Iefyr were the most vulnerable of all the races, because their magik was not like his or hers, but more like keeping goodness and light for the balance and harmony in nature. They were also the wisest and likely the best prepared for battle in many ways. But if their realm should fall, then more evil would be arriving in the world of Daegries, and the wise in Knowledge Hall could never allow that.

But if they were lucky, the Elven leader might divulge the whereabouts of dark elves. "A sect of Iefyr that they call Nithereen. Those elves have more knowledge about warfare and weapons, and especially about the Dark Master, who the elves have fought before.

During their planning the previous night, Edegast had told her, "We will be lucky to find the Nithereen and even luckier to survive the meeting." He had a faraway look in his eyes.

"Why can't the Iefyr contact them for us?" she had asked. "Why do we have to do it?"

He straightened and said, "Because the Iefyr and the Nithereen do not communicate any longer. The Nithereen have been using dark magik for some time, and the Iefyr swore them as enemies once it was known. The Nithereen were not known as such until that time. They were accused of stealing away Iefyr and corrupting them."

Alyssa hadn't liked the sound of that at all and now, sitting in the dining hall, she felt dread creep into her belly.

She asked for clarification. "You mean they were taking the Iefyr as hostages? Why?"

"Mostly as bargaining chips. They could force the Iefyr to do many things for them if lives were at stake."

She whispered, "That makes them as bad as the Dark Master."

Edegast paced the room, as he was wont to do. "Perhaps it is only a rumor, after all. But now the Dark Master could be using the dark elves for his own purposes. If that is the case, we may be in far worse trouble than we think."

"The Nithereen are working with him? Well, that's a lot of scary times ahead if you ask me," she replied.

"Indeed. The trouble I see at the moment is, we do not know anything. We do not know about the Iefyr, the Nithereen, or anything else. It is beyond time for a parlay."

Alyssa spoke the words that were going through her mind at the time. "And we want to go and find scary elves? What if they *are* with the Dark Master? What if they steal *us* away?"

Edegast put his hands behind his back and stared into the fire. "We have to know for certain. Also, the Iefyr will know what to do with the Grim. If it should be kept and hidden or destroyed. In good faith, I cannot make that decision alone."

"Do you really think it needs to be destroyed? And how would we even do that? It's a flighty book, Edegast."

Aside from saying that the Grim was safer with her for the moment, he had said nothing about its future. There was really no answer to her question. They had no idea what was going on in the various dominions, and whether the Grim had a part to play or not.

When he left her, she stared at the scarf for a long time where it lay draped over the pack.

Coming back to the present, seated in the dining hall, Alyssa sighed and sipped her cocoa. She shivered but it was from fear, and she watched the doorway hoping that Edegast would come in and bring some better news.

As she rose to leave, she heard voices raised out in the corridor. She eased to the doorway to listen. When she recognized the voices, she peered out.

"You cannot be serious, man!" Horoc was saying, disbelief written on her face. "Do you forget so quickly the losses we have already incurred in this accursed weather?"

Salas stood in front of her, head bowed as if he were afraid to look her in the face. He shuffled his feet as her onslaught continued.

"Tell me that you are still negotiating this. Tell me, Salas!"

At that, he lifted his head and stared at her. "No. There is nothing more that we can do. We cannot remain idle while the enemy sends his forces here to decimate us. We must act while we can."

"That remains to be seen!" she hissed, shoving past him roughly. She headed down the corridor away from Alyssa, and Salas went up the stairs toward the floor where his room was.

Edegast has had his talk with Salas, she decided. *Now Horoc knows about the plan, and she's upset.*

Alyssa reasoned that if she had been told such news, she would be upset, too. The Magik-users would have to battle the elements to find the Iefyr, who didn't usually allow any such thing, to let them know their lives were at stake. And also to beg the Elves for the location of their sworn enemy. Sounded like madness to her.

Because of that fact, she decided to give Horoc a bit of forgiveness. The woman *did* save her life, even if she wasn't very gracious about it.

It seemed obvious to Alyssa that since Edegast was telling folks about the plan, he must be making the move to enact it. Soon she would need to get packed and ready.

She trudged to her room, walking slowly up the stairs, deep in thought, until she arrived at the door. Absolute shock filled her. The door was standing ajar.

She pushed it open the rest of the way with the toe of her boot and looked within.

"Shad?" she asked, softly, approaching the pack.

Nothing moved. She ran to the pack and found it empty. The Grim was missing, and her beloved follygrass scarf along with it.

She snatched up her quiver and bow and hefted the sword over her other shoulder against her back and ribs. "Somebody is going to pay!"

"Edegast!" she shouted as she ran down the hallway where his room was located. "Edegast!"

He stuck his head out of his room, and her angry face caused him to step out. "What? Alyssa, calm yourself. What has happened?"

She slid to a stop and took a moment to catch her breath. "They're gone!"

"Who is gone?"

Through a heaving breath, she cried, "Shadow and the book, of course! Both gone! Stolen!"

Edegast pulled her into the room and set her on his bed. "What? Please tell me that you are poking fun at me."

"No! I'm not. They're gone, Edegast! I have no idea who could have done such a thing." She waved around at his room. "I was hoping you had them."

The wizard put a finger against his lips to quiet her. He closed his eyes and held his hands out in front of him, fingers out, palms down.

Alyssa felt energy rush from him, blow over her head, and out of the room into the castle. This act of magik reminded her what a powerful wizard he was.

He didn't even have to command it, she thought.

His keen eyes stared after the magik, and a frown pulled his eyebrows together over his nose. He stayed that way for several moments until a chill wind chewed at Alyssa's knees. The wizard lowered his arms.

"It is well, Alyssa. The scarf and the book are with Salas."

"What?" she exclaimed. "What does he need them for? And why would he go into my room, uninvited, to get to them? He could have asked me. He could have asked *you*. What is happening?"

"Not to worry, my dear. He is planning on going on the journey to the forest. He will keep the book safe."

She resisted the urge to jump up and down. "And what about my scarf? Why does he need that?"

Edegast placed his hands on her shoulders, calming her. "The scarf is invisible. It is protecting the book without form as you likely have asked it to do. Salas may not even know he has it."

Alyssa glared at Edegast, sliding the sword onto the bed. "All the talk about hiding the book here made me think y'all had a well-protected library where it would be stored, and no one but wizards and powerful magik folks could get at it. But... I guess that describes the Dark Master, doesn't it? He has powers, of a certainty."

Edegast nodded, pulling on his beard. "And wisdom like one of us. He has had years in exile to learn things about the world and how he can twist it to his benefit. The only good thing is his weakened state."

Unsettled, Alyssa said, "Yes, you said that. This is terrible news, and we don't want the book to fall into his hands. If Salas has your permission to take the book to the Iefyr, that's your business, and I will let him have it. What I won't do is manage without my scarf."

He crossed his arms and said, "Shadow is indeed a different matter. Let us go and see to that at once." And with those words he strode out of his room, Alyssa jogging along behind him trying to keep up.

Eventually they found Salas in his room, packing. Alyssa mentally kicked herself for not checking there first.

"Did you—?" Edegast began.

"Yes," Salas answered quickly, giving him a strong stare.

Alyssa's temper rose. "Why didn't anyone ask me to get it for you? Why did you do it so...sneaky-like?"

Salas took note of the bow and arrows. "We are working against time, my dear. My sincere apologies if my cutting through the niceties has offended you. There is nothing to fear from me, I assure you."

Alyssa felt Shadow, silent and invisible, wrap around her shoulders, and she instantly relaxed. "I forgive you, Salas. But I think talking things over with a person is better than acting with no warning."

"I fear 'tis better to ask forgiveness rather than permission, I fear in this instance." He bowed to her in apology.

Out of the blue, Alyssa heard Pappy's voice.

"Tell them you're going along."

"Uh, Edegast," she said, stalling, trying to understand why she had to go.

The wizard stared at her, waiting.

"I... um... I think I need to go along on this journey. I am half-Iefyr. I could be of help to the group. I'm a healer, and I've got magik abilities." She paused, not knowing what else she should say. Then, finally, she added, "That book has been in my family for a long time, too. I feel responsible for it, and well, I'm going—if for no other reason than to make sure it is safe."

Edegast looked down at his feet and then nodded. "I wish I could go too, Alyssa. Truly I do. But with my father and so many others gone, and now losing Salas to this venture, well, there is no good way to accomplish our objectives here *and* there."

Salas nodded also. They were on the same page.

"I guess I didn't make myself clear. I *am* going," she said, emphasizing her meaning. "With permission or without."

The two wizards looked at each other.

"There's only Horoc and me, so far," Salas said.

"I am sure others will agree to go," Edegast replied, crossing his arms.

Then they both looked at Alyssa, judging her resolve. Edegast nodded, refusing to meet Salas's eyes. They could not keep her at the castle.

"Well, thanks for not telling me I can't go. I didn't want to have to fight for this. Oh, and by the way, Shad has returned to me, so all is well." Alyssa patted the scarf's edge, and it returned to its normal color so the others could see it.

"That is a miracle and no doubt. You should have let the Wise know, however. I got a terrible fright when I encountered a scarf, presumed dead," Salas said, frowning.

"It was for Shadow's protection," Alyssa answered. "Edegast knew."

Edegast cleared his throat, embarrassed.

"I see. Fine, then. Grateful I will be to have you on this journey, Alyssa. Truly, a magik scarf and the spell book will be most welcome," Salas said, returning to his packing. "No one knows what awaits us."

"*Get that book back,*" Pappy said.

Alyssa waited a beat before doing so. "Uh, Sala... You can give that book back to me, now. Unless Edegast says you are the new bearer of it, of course. But you should know, Shadow protects it better than anyone else could. Speaking of which, how did you even get *to* the Grim? The book usually won't go to anyone. And Shadow was protecting it."

Salas drew himself up taller, and said, "I threatened the scarf with annihilation from wizard's magik if it didn't give me the book."

"How did you even know the scarf was there? It can make itself invisible... as you have seen."

"Oh, it was at first. When I stuck my hand into the pack, it wrapped around my arm like a vise. I couldn't even get to the book. When I pulled my hand out of the pack, the Scarf of Egladris was wrapped around it like a falconer's gauntlet, nearly cutting off blood flow. That was when I threatened it."

Alyssa stared at him dumbfounded. "And then what happened?"

He shrugged. "I told the scarf that I was taking the book for its own protection and there was nothing to be done for it. The scarf turned into a violent green, as if angered, and dove into the pack. I thought I would have to go in after the Grim a second time, but then, the scarf flew out of the pack carrying the book, evading me so that I could not retrieve it. It waited for me to open the door, and when I did, it flew here straightaway. It placed the book straight into my pack and hasn't left it since."

Alyssa was more than a little proud of Shadow. It had protected the book as she had asked it to. But Shadow would allow a wizard to take it, and that could never work, she thought. She'd have a word with it about that. No one could be trusted anymore. Not even wizards.

Salas attempted to pull the tome from his pack, but it bobbled and fell to the floor. When he attempted to pick it up again, the pages flew open and turned like mad.

He attempted to grab the book mid-turn and received a vicious cut on his finger for his efforts. "What in the world has gotten into that book?"

Alyssa bit the inside of her cheek to keep from wearing a gloating grin.

The scarf unwound itself and went to cover the book as it had been doing. Alyssa walked over and scooped them both up. Salas's shoulders sagged.

"As I said, it's a little picky about who can handle it," she told the wizard.

Salas shook his head and said nothing.

Edegast pushed his hands into the folds of his cloak and said to Salas, "Very well, we will leave you to your packing. Alyssa must prepare as well."

They left Salas and went next door into Alyssa's room. She didn't miss the slight smile that Edegast wore. Small victories, she thought. He promised to bring her sword to her before they left. She took the Grim and Shadow to her bed and got them packed away for another journey.

The whole group traveling to the forest were not able to get ready that night. It was after daybreak the next day before they could leave the castle.

Edegast paced back and forth, his frown deepening with every passing moment. When they finally gathered at the front door to the castle, he gave them all one last word as he leaned on his staff. Alyssa's sword was draped in its scabbard across his back. He looks the part of a powerful wizard today, she thought.

"The forest is not far, my friends. I pray you make it from our mountains to the plain and to the forest without incident. Please know that I will be using all methods to insure you have a somewhat easier journey. If you should encounter prohibitive weather, please find a safe place and take cover. Remember, it is easy to get lost!"

The small party of four moaned and groaned at his words, remembering the ones already lost, but the warning did not fall on deaf ears. Alyssa especially didn't want to get lost in the Snowclids or even anywhere between them and the forest.

No one had any idea what to expect. The few who returned from the first party led by Trudor had little to contribute as to a way forward. They had gotten hopelessly lost and suffered mightily because of it. And none of them volunteered to go again.

The group set off to a blue sky over them, but the temperature was frigid. Alyssa had been given a new set of warmer clothes to wear including a cloak with a lined hood to cover her head. With her coat, her cloak, and her scarf, she was warm enough, but the best gift was from Edegast. It was a pair of fur-lined, thick-soled boots, perfect for mountain trekking.

"They are my own boots, and I expect to see them again," he'd told her, half jesting, half serious. "I have resized them for you. They will serve you well as they have always done for me." He bent down and spoke a word to the boots, and though Alyssa couldn't understand the strange language, she got the intention.

He stared at her for a long time before finally slinging the sword from his back. "It is not suited to you, child. You have Shadow and the Grim. And a bow with arrows, items which you are excellently skilled in using. If you are attacked, I expect the others will assist you, but nothing with this sword. You will be in danger with such a massive thing weighing you down, and I do not wish to lose anyone else in the mountains."

Alyssa felt bereft of the protection once he resettled the sword on himself, but she knew he was right. The Phank had been on top of her before she could even pull the sword for use.

Edegast drew a dagger from his belt and handed it to her. "Place that in your boot. Keep it close at all times. May the gods help anyone who gets that close to you."

Now as she strode along behind Horoc, watching her straight back move and sway with every slick step on the mountain trail, she thanked the gods for her friend, Edegast, who did his best to insure her safety.

At least she was on the front line and actively involved against the Dark Master and not at the castle wandering around. At least she knew the people with her were well informed and prepared for what may come. She felt the bow and quiver shift on her back and thanked the gods for weapons, too.

Hopefully, the folks back home are safe and sound and not facing any hobgoblins or ogres or worse. She had left Edegast with a command to let her family know she was safe as soon as he could.

Once they had left the castle and could only barely make out one of its tall spires behind them, the journey began for real. The trail took a marked turn upward for a long time. The snow fell in starts and stops and by the time they decided to take a break and eat something, it was falling in earnest.

"There's an area over there," Horoc said, pointing. "We can take shelter."

They followed her lead and once they were there could see the mountain had a small cave-in, and the tumbled-down rock formed a rather large overhang.

The group took this opportunity to eat as they sheltered there, waiting on the snowfall to lessen. Alyssa was certain that dried meat and bread had never tasted so good.

"We should conserve water as much as possible," Salas told her, giving her the small bladder. "It will be next to impossible to melt snow and ice on this trail."

Alyssa took a drink and handed it back. "Salas, I can make fire happen without too much trouble. Let me help."

"It isn't the fire that is troublesome," Horoc said, putting her hand out for the bladder. "It is the dangers of who might see it and come along to join in its warmth."

Alyssa peered at the area outside. The snow would definitely make finding their tracks harder.

"Who lives in these mountains?" she whispered.

"Frost giants and trolls, most likely," Horoc answered. She gave the bladder back to Salas. "We should move on soon. The snow is easing."

Alyssa shouldered her pack again. Shadow had wriggled inside. She supposed even magik scarves might get cold in the mountains, so she helped it along and then secured it.

Horoc took the lead after that, and little was spoken. She seemed to be sure-footed and hardly ever slipped. Alyssa stepped into her footprints. This became a little game of hers and kept her mind occupied as they went.

When the trail tilted downward, staying on one's feet was no longer a game, but a life-threatening reality. The snow had melted in places, refreezing into ice. It ran down the mountainside creating massive stalactites.

Alyssa was grateful not to have the sword. To be off-balance in such terrain would have terrible consequences.

They traveled single file, Horoc in front and Alyssa in back.

The sorceress called a halt after she and Salas, and another wizard with them named Japher, all slid into one another.

"Japher, you must stay far enough behind me not to tumble into me!" Horoc scolded.

"I am so sorry!" he apologized. "It is very hard to stop my feet."

Salas agreed with him. Alyssa remained quiet. She was grateful to be on the backline. The others scuffed up the icy surface enough that she could manage easier. Edegast's boots had been magiked also, she was pretty certain.

Horoc took out a long piece of rope and tied it around her waist. Then she handed it to Salas who now fell into second place behind her. He tied it around himself and passed it to Japher. After he tied it around his waist, he turned to Alyssa, but she didn't want to be bound to them.

"I think it might be smart to keep one of us loose. If y'all take a tumble, everybody will either go over the side together or slide down this mountain together. Either way, somebody needs to be free to save you."

Horoc laughed. Her laugher echoed off the mountains until it became a mocking sound.

"Alyssa, you are a bright girl, to be sure." The sorceress turned and started ahead once more. "And full of humor, too."

Alyssa didn't know how to take the phrase, so she shrugged and trudged ahead.

Japher, a slender nervous type, kept up a constant humming, as if his mind were anywhere but on the trail. Alyssa almost wished she could do the same.

Every part of the landscape looked so alike that Alyssa felt her mind would run to madness. The path they followed, if one could even call it so, wound down and down and down. It was snow covered and icy, and Horoc told them more than once to mind the places she slid in so that they wouldn't do the same. Jagged rocks appeared on either side at times, and Alyssa found herself pushing or pulling on them to give herself a bit more forward motion.

When the sun rose above the tallest peak, they knew that noontide had arrived. It would be near to impossible to hide themselves with the sunny spots they encountered. But it wasn't long until they crossed over a bit of land misty with clouds, and the sun didn't penetrate the gloom there.

Without the warmth of the sun, Alyssa found herself drawing her clothing tighter around her to keep her body heat in. "Why has it gotten colder? If that is even possible," she asked out loud to anyone who cared to answer.

"The mists. We are in a little valley, and the mist is covering it. The mist is heavy with water, as are the clouds. We will be soaked to the skin if we stay out here much longer," Horoc answered. The sorceress looked around, trying to peer into the gloom. "I see a spot where we can shelter. It won't keep the wetness from weighing on us, but we may find the sun burns off the mists in an hour or two."

Alyssa pondered again how Horoc could see so well and know so much. She meant to ask her when the time was right.

They made for the spot Horoc had seen, and everyone tried their best to protect their heads and clothing. Alyssa wished heartily for a quilt or blanket that she could cover herself with.

As predicted, in another hour, the sun climbed over the mountain and chased the shadows away and the mists lifted.

"Thank the good gods," Alyssa said looking up. "And you too, Solly."

Horoc suggested they could get a few miles in that day if they moved their feet. "The caves of Uratod lie between us and the lower mountains. I would like to shelter there this night."

"The caves... isn't that where... the... " Japher stammered.

Horoc cut him off. "Yes, it is."

Alyssa, already on sensory overload, looked questioningly at Horoc.

"Never mind, girl. You don't need to know."

Salas bent down over his boots with a pretense of wiping off the snow, and whispered to Alyssa, "No need for worry."

This made Alyssa even more curious. What was the sorceress hiding?

Alyssa brushed the wetness from her clothing and boots as much as possible and hoped the sun would dry her out enough to make life bearable.

They moved forward, every small step a challenge, every step toward their goal a win in this treacherous game.

Chapter Twenty

W hen the sun touched the mountains on the other side of their trail, the group finally arrived at the Uratod caves.

Alyssa stamped her feet to release the accumulated snow. Everyone looked around at the area where they stood, but there was not much to see.

It was a deep hole dug into the side of the mountain with barren trees around the entrance, likely hiding the cave mouth in the warmer months.

While the others pulled off their packs and prepared to make some sort of a fire, Horoc stood at the entrance, her sword gleaming in the last rays of the sun. Alyssa thought she looked like the Goddess of travelers, capable of protecting them with her own life.

Alyssa freed Shadow and it draped across her shoulders, invisible, trying to tickle her chin, playfully. She set to helping build a fire. There was a small amount of wood lying buried beneath the snow to use as kindling. Alyssa took what she could find, along with dried leaves and small thatches of fur from some animal that had floated into the cave.

She struggled with the damp wood, finally resorting to magik to light it.

Once Alyssa got the fire started, she left Japher to maintain it. Something he seemed quite skilled at and happy to do.

Salas stood nearby, sorting out foodstuffs.

"I have some food to contribute as well," Alyssa told him. She hurried over to her pack and rummaged around for the dried meat. She wasn't sure how much longer they would travel and the food she carried was sure not to last, but she shared it anyway.

Salas walked to Horoc and had a quiet word with her. She nodded and moved outside the cave. Swishing sounds came to Alyssa, and she quickly realized that Horoc was moving through the snow doing something.

Salas returned to his task, but Alyssa was curious and stepped to the cave mouth to see what task the sorceress had taken on, aside from guarding.

The air outside was thick with enchantment and slight silvery tremors. Bare echoes hinted at the presence of other magikal beings nearby.

Fear gripped Alyssa instantly. *This ain't right, oh great Wizard's Beard*!

She turned to the right, out of the cave, and tried to say something to Horoc, but the back of a misty figure appeared in front of Alyssa, its arm raised as if to strike Horoc.

"Stop!" Alyssa shouted, sending her magik streaming at the figure. The green glow lit up the mist and a horrific creature became visible within its camouflage. Shadow, now fully visible, flew at it, diving down underneath it at the last moment.

This scary tactic did not work. The creature turned toward Alyssa, surprised at the attack. She could see its face, completely skeletal. The eyes burned a fiery red and the upraised arm with its deadly intention found a new mark.

Alyssa's resolve faltered at the terrible form staring at her. It came at her with such a ferocity that Alyssa was unprepared for the onslaught. Shadow rolled into an arrow and went straight through the center of the creature, tearing a hole in the mists that shrouded it.

The creature issued a hollow scream when Shadow wrapped around it like a coiled rope, some ancient magik causing small issues of fire to flare within the folds of its misty body.

Horoc, in a wide stance, swung her sword beheading the creature with one great swing, sending it away to its maker severed head and all. Shadow fluttered like a hummingbird to right itself once the mists were dissipated. It changed from the bright angry color to its usual dull color once again.

Shaken to her core, Alyssa dropped to one knee. Shadow flew to her, wrapped around her protectively.

"Alyssa, are you hurt?" Horoc asked. She pulled on Alyssa's arm to help her gain her feet.

"I'm not hurt. I'm scared plenty though. What were you doing out here?" She scowled at the sorceress. "And while I'm at it, just who on Daegries are you? You ain't no simple sorceress, and that's for sure."

Horoc frowned at her a moment. Her earthen green eyes bare of feeling. "It is not who I am that should matter to you, lady fair, but *what* I am. For now, simply know that I am your guide and protector, as Edegast would have been. As you can see, well-made steel kills them. Your dagger would have served you better than magik."

"That'd be a mite too close for me."

Alyssa felt the hand on her shoulder in passing but her mind was adrift with questions. Shadow straightened like a blanket before her, awaiting her to sit upon it and rest.

She didn't say I was wrong about her, at any rate. She bent and patted the blade in her boot against her ankle. She would have to learn what creatures succumbed to magik and which were too far advanced to even attempt it.

Alyssa plucked the scarf from the air and went back inside the cave where the fire burned brightly. The flames changed colors from red to green to purple and orange much too quickly to be her magik. It didn't matter much, as long as the fire burned all night.

She stood in front of it, warming herself, quiet with her thoughts. Shadow slunk over to the pack, covering it softly.

Horoc stayed apart from the rest, keeping close to the entrance. Alyssa couldn't stop thinking about the creature they had encountered.

Finally, she went to Horoc and spoke in low tones.

"Thank you for saving me," she said. "I was trying to do the same for you, but as you mentioned, magik didn't seem to bother it none, aside from Shadow."

Horoc tilted her head in an offhand gesture. The woman didn't take admiration or acknowledgement well, it seemed.

"Might I ask what exactly we're faced with here? I'm betting this is a haunted hill and that ain't the only creature rambling around out there."

Horoc nodded, a small movement of her head. "Yes. This is the Cave of the Uratods, the Undead. I didn't tell you before, hoping not to scare you."

"Ah, so that creature, that was an... Undead. What was it before it was undead? Was it ever alive?"

"Yes, of course it was. Undead creatures have to be alive to become undead," Horoc replied, her brows knitting into a frown. "However, these poor souls are enchanted by the Dark Master. A bit like doubly undead."

"When you kill them, as you did that one, do they find peace again? Being a servant of the Dark Master seems like a terrible way to exist, in any form."

Horoc shrugged. "I do not know the answer to that, Alyssa."

"Is there any chance that newly Undead are around?" Japher asked. He had been sitting quietly near the fire, listening to their conversation.

Horoc let out a long breath. "Possibly, Japher. But it will do no good to dwell on such."

"Why would you ask that?" Alyssa questioned him, curiosity loosening her tongue.

Salas straightened beside his friend, as if to intervene. Horoc shrugged and allowed Japher to answer.

"Uh, our family members who perished, did so here," he said, his gaze on the fire.

Alyssa's jaw dropped. "What? Trudor and the others? Here?"

Horoc moved back to the fire and kicked a bit of flotsam back in from where it had floated out of the circle. Anger lined her body. "Yes, here. The Undead assaulted them. They were near the ledge trying to fight their way back into the cave and the snowbank above them gave way, sending them over the side."

"So that was the avalanche that was spoken of," Alyssa said, softly, nodding as she understood the whole event now. No one had told her everything. "I didn't know. I'm very sorry for your losses."

Japher and Horoc nodded at her apology.

Salas came to Alyssa. "The survivors did not relate the whole tale to anyone until Edegast heard it first. Likely, it was better for you not to hear the whole terrible story. But now you know."

So, they were protecting me by not telling me? Alyssa sat by the fire and had a long talk with herself. These wizards were a clannish bunch. All of them had secrets. She didn't even want to know what sort they might be harboring, but she well knew they had them. This was only a taste of it.

Pappy's voice came to her. *"Let this be a guide for you, gal. Don't trust everything you see and half of what you hear."*

She closed her eyes and imagined she could smell Pappy's pipe smoke. He grew some aromatic herbs and put them in his pipe and the smell was familiar and comforting to her.

Ah, if only, she thought, opening her eyes, losing the illusion. Then, the others gathered around the fire to discuss the next plan of action.

"Are more of those creatures around?" Alyssa asked to no one in particular.

Salas nodded and answered. "Yes, I am sure they are."

Japher poked a bit of burning wood, Sparks flew up and disappeared into the cave's roof. "Our company are so few in number, I fear for our safety."

Horoc stared into the flames. "Japher, we *are* few, but we are mighty. Alyssa has a weapon that the Undead cannot match. Perhaps you have heard of the magik scarf that travels with her?"

Shadow unfurled from where it had been lying and flew over to drape across Alyssa's back. The scarf became as bright as it could, glowing against her skin.

"The Scarf of Egladris is powerful enough to keep us all protected while we are on this mountain," Horoc said. "It was the scarf that slayed the Undead creature that we encountered. I dispatched the spirit into the Underworld, but the scarf took the kill. We must hurry after our rest now, before word reaches the Dark Master. We must remain vigilant and be prepared for an attack, however. Surely bad news travels faster than good. It will not be a long trip to the lower level and the plain, but it may be treacherous."

This brought about complete silence and individual contemplation. No one asked what might happen if the Dark Master had now been alerted to the Scarf of Egladris, but Alyssa certainly thought about it.

Nothing good ever comes with power, she remembered Pappy saying one time. She added to that saying: *Nothing good comes with power when it was misused.*

Soon everyone began pulling off pieces of dried meat that had been heated on the end of a long stick that Horoc had brought in from the mountainside. There was only the one stick, so they had to take turns. Alyssa allowed others to go before her. Her grandparents would tan her hide if she were not showing proper respect to her elders.

After they ate and shared water, they each took their straw mats from their packs to sleep on. The finely woven straw weighed nearly nothing, so it had not been burdensome. Alyssa smiled to herself as she remembered the gryphon king trying to make friends with the horses in the stables where the straw likely came from.

She worried for a time about King Hubert and hoped his journey home had been successful. Then, she worried for a time about her family. They were unprotected at the farm. Because the Grim traveled with her, there was nothing for Pappy to use for spell-making or for protection either, aside from his normal conjuring books.

She felt comforted by the fact that he was pretty smart and likely didn't need a book to work from. Not like her. Even though she hadn't done that properly either. She tossed and turned for a time and it was nearly dawn when she finally slept.

Horoc woke her by nudging her arm with a boot. "Wake up, Mudden girl. The road awaits."

Alyssa sat up and rubbed her eyes. It was cold in the cave, but not nearly as cold as outside where snow had fallen through the night. She peered out at the whiteness beyond the cave's opening. No flakes fell that she could see, but they were deep inside the cave.

She stood and adjusted her clothes for maximum warmth, took Shadow and draped it around her shoulders like a shawl, and folded her mat to go back into the pack. While she was rearranging things, she checked on the Grim.

She still didn't understand why they were sending it to the elves. There may have been something in it that the elves needed for protection. She wanted nothing more than to be able to sit down with it and read. There had to be spells in there that she could learn and use.

Why didn't I do that when it was safely tucked away at home?

She continued to chastise herself as she shoved it deep into her pack and covered it with everything she could find. No way to keep it safe, aside from Shadow, but she needed the scarf for warmth.

The group moved out of the cave. Horoc stood for a few moments looking around, especially overhead. Everything seemed quiet. Maybe too quiet. The extremely charged atmosphere from last evening was missing, making Alyssa feel more secure.

The girl shook her head. If danger should engage them now, there was nothing they could do. They had to get off this mountain as soon as possible. The Undead could attack easily sending them over the ledge just as before.

She shivered as icy fingers of wind tried to pry into her clothing. Horoc moved ahead and Alyssa followed.

Up ahead, the whiteness of snow, deep and fresh, nearly blinded them all. Horoc led them slowly through the thickest part which happened to cover their trail ahead. When she threw up a hand to make them halt, Alyssa's heart thrashed in her chest.

Horoc bent low and peered at something in the snow.

"What is it?" Alyssa whispered.

"Tracks."

The woman did not say more, and Alyssa did not ask, but she could see for herself they were not human tracks. They were flat and bare, without trace of shoe or boot. Horoc moved closer to the mountain and farther from the ledge and waved for the others to follow suit.

As they went, Alyssa noted that some of the tracks appeared to be animal. Something akin to what the Yeti's wolves' tracks had looked like. Whoever walked about in this unfavorable terrain with no foot covering had a four-legged creature with them.

Soon, the sun came out and beat down upon them. The cold wind and layers of snow all around them gave no room for warmth, however. Solly's happy rays did make them relax for a short while and they moved quicker.

Nobody wanted to be on the mountain any longer than was necessary and making haste while the light was strong was a good plan.

They followed Horoc as she picked a path that slanted steadily downward. Eventually, it widened enough for two people to move together, and that brought an audible sigh from the group.

Even Alyssa, unused to such travel, blew out a breath she'd held in. She looked up and around her for the first time in a long while. The footing was still snowy but not as icy and she felt like she could walk without looking down all the time.

As they traveled toward the plains, it became apparent that this area had not been spared the drought. The front line of trees leading to the forest were bare and white and looked utterly bedraggled.

The group took a few moments to rest and collect themselves. Alyssa approached Horoc to ask about the trees in the distance.

"What happened to them?" she asked, pointing at the withered timber.

"Nothing," Horoc replied, a curious note to her voice.

"But they are not green, or brown, as I expected. They are white. There must have been some dreadful event to strike them down like that."

Horoc laughed softly for a moment or two. "No, Alyssa, they were not stricken at all. They are birches. A tree valued greatly by the Iefyr. When they are in full bloom from spring until late fall, they are as green as any other. In fall, their leaves turn brilliant yellow and red, and they fill the forest with color. It is only now, in winter, that they cover themselves with the barrenness of white."

Alyssa pondered this. "I reckon I never saw a birch before. Not even last year when I came through the Greater Daegries. At least, not this kind. They are sort of pretty in their white coats."

Horoc nodded and motioned to the others to fall into line again. Alyssa followed suit, but she kept her eyes on the trees before them, drawing ever closer. In the brilliance of the snow, an animal or person would be seen even at this distance.

Unless they were cloaked in white.

Chapter Twenty-One

They were nearly at the birch tree line when the first whistle came, clear and as melodic as birdsong.

Horoc stopped, holding her hand up. The others came to a halt behind her. She listened closely. The whistle sounded again. She cupped her mouth and sent out a returning whistle. It was so similar that Alyssa was a little surprised. She had learned how to whistle when she was a child, but it was mostly to get the attention of someone working in the garden. This was a whistle like none she'd ever heard before. One she wasn't entirely sure she could ever mimic.

In a matter of moments, there appeared a hooded Iefyr dressed in white robes. It was as though they had been a part of the birches, because one moment they were unseen, and the next they were seen.

In the land of Mudden, these were known as High Elves and of course, they had their own magik in a physical way. They could leap great distances, bend their lithe bodies in many ways others couldn't, and they were excellent archers.

This group, armed with long bows and quivers of arrows on their backs, were some sort of protective force guarding the Iefyr kingdom, Alyssa supposed.

She took in their piercing slanted eyes and glistening blond hair. And strangely thought how she looked like them in some ways. Maybe not the pointed ears, as hers were rounded and stuck out a bit like Pappy Oh's, but there was something about them...

Shivers went through her then, and Shadow sensed her unsettled feelings. It lengthened itself until one end was near enough for Alyssa to grab, which she did for comfort.

She had been at an Iefyr camp on her last journey, and it was pretty standard, only meant to be temporary. Something that could be packed up and moved at a moment's notice. The ones standing before them now were a whole lot more foreboding in appearance and attitude. This was their land, and now Alyssa and company were trespassing.

She stood quietly as Horoc and one of the Iefyr spoke in low tones in the Elven tongue. Alyssa couldn't understand it, and she was amazed that Horoc could speak it so well.

When the sorceress bent her knee to the Iefyr leader, the elf placed a gloved hand on her head and in the most incredible way, the woman began to glow. From her bowed head to her booted feet, she became a glowing ball of light.

"What evilment is this?" Japher cried, throwing his cloak aside to pull out a dagger.

Salas stepped forward and pulled on his arm to stop him from rushing forward. He whispered something in his ear.

Alyssa threw her hand out to block them from advancing. If Horoc was subjecting herself to this magik, then she must approve of it. Alyssa turned to stare at the wizards standing beside her who had now put away their weapons. When she faced Horoc once again, she was not prepared for the woman who gazed placidly at her.

"Hail, Alyssa," Horoc said, nodding her newly crowned head of white hair, a trademark of these woodland folk. "I am sorry for deceiving you, but it was a necessary device to protect you."

"Who…Who are you? Protect me? Me?" Alyssa stammered, pointing at herself. The woman who had once appeared as little more than a female wizard, now showed herself to be something more--a wholly different person, clad in the same garb as the Iefyr, strangely transformed.

She smiled at Alyssa. The girl from Mudden gaped at her, voiceless.

"I am known as Ina to my people, the Iefyr. I am one of many princesses."

"Ina? I thought your name was Horoc? You… you're an Elven… wizard?" Alyssa finally managed.

The tinkle of laughter filled the wood. "No. I am an Iefyr warrioress, a shield maiden. I am sworn to the house of Egladris, to be certain."

"Why didn't you tell me this? Because this deception seems a little unnecessary to me," Alyssa stammered, shaken to her core. She clung to Shadow who had circled her waist and made itself available to protect its mistress at a second's notice.

"We will have plenty of time to discuss my motives and everything that goes with it. For now, please continue to trust me as you have done. I mean no harm for this group, as I have shown, and would never harm the heir of Egladris nor the scarf she bears. I swear my crown on it." She smiled a gentle smile, touching the coronet of flowers. Then

Horoc, now Ina, nodded to Salas and Japher before turning to have a short word with the Iefyr leader in Elvish. Soon, they all moved to go into the woods.

Alyssa kept Shadow handy and only shrugged at Japher and Salas. Confusion crowded her heart. Why had Edegast kept her in the dark? Knowing who Horoc really was would have made things so much easier. And if she could have known that the woman was sworn to protect her, well, that made a lot of difference even now.

She could only trust that more information would be forthcoming. So many strange things had happened to her on this journey, she was no longer surprised at anything.

Magik danced within the forest. The trees were lit from within by hundreds of tiny lights bobbing back and forth. As Alyssa drew near, the lights became hundreds of fireflies. These tiny creatures had been a boon to her on her adventure last year, and she smiled and waved at them, remembering. They illuminated the dim interior of the forest like welcoming beacons. A path appeared and it was lit by the same lights, golden and glowing.

The temperature was much warmer in the thickness of the trees, and Alyssa could smell the scent of food wafting out to her every few steps. Her stomach grumbled at her neglectfulness.

In the distance, Alyssa heard the sound of water rushing down a stream and many voices lifted in song. The song caused an ache to rise from within her chest and soon she was amazed to find tears on her cheeks.

The girl from Mudden relaxed for maybe the first time since leaving home. She fought back a wave of homesickness for the farm but allowed the soothing sounds and sights of this place to quiet her emotions.

"Home is where the heart is, gal."

"Thanks Pappy," she whispered, wiping at the tears.

When they found themselves in a valley surrounded by the forest, with a rocky stream hurrying nearby, Alyssa understood Pappy's words. She marveled at the wonderment of it all, the scenery, the scents, the warmth that filled her spirit. Her heart belonged here as strongly as it did at the farm.

Salas and Japher stopped beside her as she breathed in the fresh air, feeling the mist on her face.

"I do love this place," Salas said. "I have since my initiation as a wizard."

Like a fire brand burning through Alyssa's cloudy mind, his words struck a nerve. "You knew Horoc was Iefyr! You've been here before!"

"Yes," Salas admitted, nodding. "I was sworn to secrecy. It was not my tale to tell. Horoc... er... Ina wanted to tell you in her own time."

"And Edegast too," she said.

He nodded. "No one intended on keeping things from you, but the castle became so dangerous, we had to switch paths quickly. There was no time."

Alyssa shook her head in disbelief. There had been time for a simple conversation, she thought, but refused to say more. She had a lot of questions that needed answering.

Japher remained silent also, too surprised to give voice to anything he might be feeling as the latest member of the deceived party. They continued to take in the beauty of their surroundings.

Ahead of them, Ina stood like a silent sentry, allowing the impact of the moment to wash over her. "*Dra'y'sray, ruzani, obasi fiefin,*" she said, breathlessly.

"What does that mean?" Alyssa asked, coming to a stop beside her.

"Draysray, Motherland, peace and love for all," Ina translated. "In Mannish it is Draysray. In Elvish, it is *Dra'y'sray*. It is my home. And yours for now."

The Iefyr princess said it as though she offered Alyssa the world on a gilt platter.

Alyssa smiled. "Guess so," was all she said. She patted Shadow and moved to follow the elves once more. The others fell in line.

Before long, they arrived at the Iefyr village. It was much more stationary and spread out than the encampment that Alyssa had seen on her last journey. Here were actual treehouses and huts and children playing in the yard.

Alyssa had never seen Iefyr children before and it was a little amazing how they seemed much the same as humans. They played with wooden sticks and rolled wooden balls to and from each other. They had beautiful blond tresses like the adults and were slender and agile as green saplings.

Ina pointed out an apothecary, a healer's hut, and a large outdoor kitchen. Alyssa drew in a deep breath appreciatively as they passed these places by.

Ina took the company to the largest treehouse perched atop a hill overlooking the village and the rushing river.

Alyssa gazed on the scenery and nodded. The view was astounding. The people seemed happy and uncaring about the events going on around them in the other parts of Daegries. They likely didn't even know, Alyssa thought sadly.

Tragedy waiting to happen. If the Dark Master had his way, this world would never be the same. These folk would either cease to exist, or else exist as his slaves.

Alyssa resolved to fight to protect these folk from such a fate as she followed Ina's straight back into the living tree and up the steps inside to the actual dwelling.

At the top of the great tree there were platforms that looked out over the forest and surrounding areas. A long table was set out on one such platform, and at the far end of it sat an Iefyr leader. The forest's canopy was the roof, and it seemed endless.

It was plain to see the elf seated at the table was considered one of the leaders (perhaps *the* leader) due to the crown that he wore upon his head. The crown was made of woven branches and leaves and had bits of berries in there too, and Alyssa couldn't stop the smile that plastered itself on her face. Here was the Elf of the Woodlands that every storybook talked about. He was truly convincing in his grass green tunic and breeches and berry brown foot coverings. He wore a deeper green cloak and hood to protect him from the cold. The sheer look of wisdom and knowledge in his eyes, and the placid countenance he wore made her feel instantly safe.

His hair was long and braided, white as snow. Alyssa almost felt compelled to bow before him, but he waved to the group to be seated.

"Please take comfort; you have traveled far," he said in a voice that soothed and gave solace to a weary mind. Alyssa wanted to pinch herself, fearing a sort of magik being placed over them. Everyone relieved themselves of their packs and gear, preferring to rest at the table.

Shadow settled into her lap and seemed as happy as a scarf could be, so she pulled off her pack and placed it at her feet, under the table. The bow and quiver followed.

"Ina, you are well?" the leader asked.

She nodded and smiled. "O Eldon Bryndar, I am ever so grateful to be home!"

Alyssa made note of the leader's name. Eldon. She was still thinking about names and the power they can have when you know them when she was addressed by the High Elf.

"Alyssa Chance Oh," he said in his calm voice. "We have waited to meet you for a long time."

She didn't know how to respond. How long had they known about her? A long time sounded like her whole life when he said it.

"K-King Eldon," she said with a stammer. "I ain't never seen this place before. How can you know me and want to meet me?"

He smiled a smile that would send moonbeams dancing. "The Iefyr make it their business to know everything that is important to their kingdom. I was given information after your journey last year with the scarf. And of course, our dear Edegast has kept us informed."

She made an 'oh' shape with her mouth. "I see."

"And a fond welcome to your company. Master Japher and Salas, I trust you are well?"

The two men nodded but did not reply. Alyssa wondered if they were as awed as they seemed. But who could be anything else in the House of Eldon, King of the Iefyr?

Several bubbling dishes were placed before them, and Alyssa could hardly contain herself. The smells were making her stomach growl even more fiercely.

"We have prepared some hearty stew, savory bread, and a

warm drink for you. Please take as much as you desire," King Eldon said.

He didn't have to prompt any of them twice. The stew was on par with Granny's, but the bread was a little dry. Not that she cared. She used it to sop up the leftover gravy in her bowl. Then like a true Farmland girl, she ate a whole apple for dessert and eyed a second one.

When the meal was finished, and the dishes were whisked away, King Eldon leaned toward his guests and stared at them with a seriousness in his eyes that felt both frightening and protective at the same time.

"Dear friends, it was not for nothing that you came to us. There is a matter to be discussed which holds all of our realms in dire circumstances."

Alyssa nodded. "The Dark Master, no doubt."

"Alas, the news has traveled?" Eldon asked, lifting his eyebrows.

Ina sat back in her seat. "Yes. Edegast has informed us as best he could. The portals are actively being used by the enemy. The men and wizards are doing their best to cover them over or at least set a guard over them, but no one knows the extent to which the enemy has planned offenses against us. The portals will make it much easier, unfortunately. What is the plan, my king?" she asked. "Is it to be war, then?"

Eldon didn't answer right away. He steepled his fingers together and rested his chin on their tips. Finally, he said, "We are prepared to engage in battle with these creatures, but maybe not so much with their maker. It is our belief that the Black League needs to be told of what is going on. They have a say in what happens here as much as any of those living in the forest."

"The Nithereen?" Ina asked in a hushed voice, looking around furtively. "Surely they know the dangers lurking behind every tree."

Alyssa chose that moment to insert Edegast's words. "Edegast said we would benefit if we could gain the Black League to our side. Their knowledge and magik would turn the tide in our direction, he said."

"They are anathema!" Ina said in a hiss.

Alyssa persisted. "I ain't rightly certain what you mean by that, and Edegast seemed worried that they might kill us as easily as join us, but no matter what, it would be worth the effort to try, he said."

"They would never kill us," King Eldon said. "They are our brethren, regardless of our differences."

Ina sat back, dejected. "They have made slaves out of—"

"Yes. It is so, but perhaps even those plans can be used as tools to our advantage," Eldon interrupted. "Now may be the best time to recall our people. *All* of our people."

He gave Alyssa a long look and said, by way of explanation, "The Nithereen have a much dimmer magik that is not meant for this happy world. In the language of Men, they are called Dokalfar, the dark elf."

Alyssa had heard of Dokalfar. She might not have understood they were dark elves, but she knew enough to believe the tales told to scare children. She couldn't count how many times she had been told to behave or the Dokalfar would get her.

So many different names, cultures, and people in the world of Daegries! She couldn't wait to find out what the Nithereen were like. Just their name had her intrigued.

"I had hoped to dissuade you from using the Nithereen in your plans," Ina said, a furrow appearing between her eyes.

"But why, my child? Are they not included in this danger? Imagine the terror that will be inflicted if they are routed unaware. They have to be told. If they wish to join with us, they will be welcomed as would anyone in the realm who seeks us out in peace."

Salas spoke finally, his hands crossed over his middle. "I daresay all hands working on this situation will be needed. I suspect that your brothers already know about this situation. Few in Daegries, Greater or Lesser, are unaware."

Alyssa couldn't agree more and wished for her Pappy with all her might. As the elders talked, her mind returned home to Mudden, and when she came back to the conversation, everyone was looking at her.

"I'm sorry," she said, looking down. "I guess my mind wandered. I didn't hear what was said or asked. Since y'all are looking at me, I guess it was something I'm supposed to answer."

"I asked what news from the south lands you bring," Eldon repeated, his face placid and kind. "Has the taint reached your homeland too?"

"Oh, the evilness...? Not much has been seen in my local area. Mudden is pretty well protected by people watching out for trouble-makers and bad folks. Edegast and I traveled north together, and it seemed like there was more and more of the... taint, as you call it. I saw ogres leaving across the sea. Even the sea creatures, the merfolk, were worried. A leader of them said a war was coming."

"Did Edegast relate to you what he had seen on his travels within the portals?"

"Not really, 'cause he's a wizard and well, they're a little quiet on their business," she looked at Salas and Japher with a wince. "No offense."

A chuckle went through the crowd.

"None taken," Salas told her. To Eldon, he said, "Edegast found evidence of the Dark Master's stirring, and we have witnessed many of his evil ones at the castle. That is what has so many frightened. It is about as bad as we can imagine. We came with young Alyssa to bring the Grim for the Elders to look over and decide how we can best use it."

This made Eldon sit back, cross his arms, and fall deep into thought. "The Grim," he said, his voice soft as though he were about to fall asleep. "Such a book as the world has never seen..."

"What do you think is going to happen now?" Alyssa asked Eldon. The Elven leader lifted his head.

"Now, we can only prepare and wait. There may be more to share with our people, and your company, but I think that is a conversation to be held in the brightness of day. You have traveled far and through many dangers to bring the Book of Spells to us. Our people will need to look it over and decide what is to be done. If it were so easy to rid the world of the Dark Master with something from that book, it would most likely have already been done."

This gave Alyssa pause. *Should I tell them that the book is missing information?* Her reanimation spell showed how flawed the Grim was. It had failed spectacularly. Missing information could lead a magik-user into a lot of trouble if they didn't have the right conditions.

But Edegast had healed Pappy Oh using the spell. He'd known something that she didn't, and it had worked. This fact made her hold her tongue. Eldon, being the leader of the Iefyr would most likely know some details she didn't either. She'd be quiet for now and be a good guest.

Ina called for drinks to be brought, and the shadows grew long around the gathering. Alyssa had sweet mead and soon felt herself nodding.

The elves started their nightly ritual of song under the moonlight. She followed her group to watch for a short while, but when Shadow began writhing and twisting, wanting to be a part of the music and dance, she asked for her bed.

Ina led her and Salas and Japher to a quiet glen near the water where a cabin with three beds was nestled. A glowing fire had been built and it was warm and welcoming.

The wizards waited outside for her to have some privacy, and after a few moments of getting undressed and into a long sleeping gown, Alyssa fell onto one of the beds and into a deep sleep.

Chapter Twenty-Two

In the lingering shadows of the night, right before the dawn, Alyssa woke. She was disoriented with the surroundings where she lay, and all she could think of was the smell of Edegast's pipe tobacco. When she heard snores from the other two beds, she remembered, relaxed, and gave over to her wondering mind.

She recalled the meeting with Edegast at her family farm. Edegast had sent her from the room for tea when he was performing (or preparing to perform) the spell on Pappy. Looking back, she realized this was likely done on purpose.

She mentally kicked herself for not asking more questions. Not that Edegast would have been under any obligation to answer her, but asking would not have hurt anything. As her mind went back to her home, it naturally settled on how she'd gone off and left her grandparents.

She tried to combat the homesickness and worry by pulling on her clothes under the covers. She took her pack and grabbed the Grim to have a look at it.

This book holds keys to upend Hektor, the Dark Master. But how? She read the first spell. More like a manifestation for money.

Bah! Who needs coins when the whole World of Daegries is at stake?

She turned to the second spell.

Pretty words about creating a spell jar.

In despair, she turned to the spell she had botched while trying to bring Pappy Oh back.

Make the circle... sprinkle bits of bread... jump on the bed... recite the words...

The next few pages were mostly about the importance of using consecrated items. She certainly hadn't done that when creating the spell for Pappy.

She sighed. None of it made sense as far as saving a realm or even ways to keep the book from being destroyed, which had begun to rattle around in her head. After flipping through a few more pages, she gave up with a sigh. She shoved the tome back into her pack and told Shadow to protect it. Time to get up and move.

She wanted to find a spot to watch the sunrise. She walked a short distance to a quiet stretch of the stream facing a wide expanse of forest. Nothing could be prettier than the setting where she found herself.

Shade obscured the glen, but she could see the first tinges of daylight as it lightened the mountaintops. She found a large flat boulder by the water and faced the coming sun.

The ever-present cold chilled her, but Alyssa filled her mind with the peace and love that Ina had spoken of, and soon she thought only of the sounds and scents of Draysray.

She sat on the boulder for a long time, until the sun was up over the mountains and shining down on her.

"Solly, Solly, round and jolly, what will today bring?" she asked the glowing orb. The sun didn't answer, but simply continued to warm her and fill her with happiness.

When she heard the little cabins and outbuildings stir with life, she turned to look back at where she'd spent the night. Japher was just coming outside, his robes looking a bit wrinkled.

He strode to where she sat and tilted his face back to appreciate the sun. "Because of snow around us in the mountains and that cold wind, this is so needed. It's been too long since we had any solid sunlight," he acknowledged. "I hope it continues!"

She nodded. "Maybe it will melt some of that snow on the mountain and we won't have such a bad time going back."

The mage's deep brown eyes stared at her a moment. "If we go back".

"What?" Alyssa felt fear creep up her chest. "Why wouldn't we go back? Edegast needs us. We've left Knowledge Hall really unprotected."

He shrugged. "Not for me to say. Let's see what today brings. Perchance we will hear more about the road ahead."

Once again Alyssa felt like she was being left on the outskirts of a situation that directly affected her.

Japher wandered off in search of food, and she rose to go back to the cabin to collect her belongings. Her stomach rumbled at the thought of food and made her hurry.

Back inside the cabin, Alyssa noted that Salas still slept. She had no idea how old the wizard was, but it would do him good to get more rest after the recent mountain trek. His soft snores were slightly muffled by his blanket.

She collected her pack, bow, and arrows, and the scarf which hovered beside her. Not wanting to wake the old man, she motioned Shadow to be still and quiet and not stir around too much.

The scarf wrapped itself around her waist, and she tied it like a sash. Best to be close to her and the Grim. She trudged out of the cabin and down the incline, turning at the cobblestone path that led to where they had met and supped with Eldon.

The smell of food wafted out to her, and she skipped up the few steps to enter. She sat at the table, nodded to Japher who was nearly finished eating. He left shortly after she arrived.

Ina was not present, nor was Eldon, so she tucked in and ate her fill of eggs and roasted meat. Also, bread slathered with butter and honey. While she drank a mug of tea, she patted Shadow absently.

The scarf flitted under her fingers like a tremble went through it. She stared down upon the cloth, trying to figure out what the movement meant.

Suddenly, one end lifted to point surreptitiously toward the doorway. She turned to look back where she had come into the building and saw Salas enter. He looked tired and his clothing hung on him like he'd lost weight.

He came to where she sat and patted her shoulder. An elf with pointed ears that stuck far out from his head poured him a mug of water to drink. Salas thanked him, taking a long chug.

"How do you feel?" Alyssa asked. She hoped she didn't sound as concerned as she was.

"As though a juggernaut has run me over."

Alyssa was unfamiliar with the term and frowned as she turned to look at him.

"A powerful force. Like a wave spell," he explained. "Something that runs through you without stopping."

She nodded, understanding. The wizard waved to the elf and asked for food. Alyssa had served herself. This inability to even get food for himself worried her.

"Do you think you should see a healer?" she asked.

He shrugged. "I am certain it is nothing that a long rest will not heal. Being here, in this place, I have everything I need in that direction." He noticed the frown she wore and added, "Not to worry, Alyssa. I will recover soon. The magik that I have used in the recent past has depleted my strength. That is all."

She took a deep breath, patted Shadow, and rose to leave. "I'm going for a walk, but I'll gladly get you anything you need. Rest in our cabin and get your legs back under you."

He thanked her, and she hauled up her pack, and bow and arrows, slung them across her shoulders and left the dining hall.

Outside, the land of the Iefyr came alive. Someone shook out a blanket, someone else built a fire, and children chased one another in front of a treehouse. Life here seemed so normal to Alyssa. She felt as though she belonged. Their language and mannerisms were different from hers, but she liked them all the same.

Sunlight dappled the trees in the forest ahead, and a feeling of longing shot through her. She passed the buildings and headed for the woods. In a few moments, Ina called out to her. The warrior elf was no longer wearing a crown and robes. Instead, she wore hunting clothes much like Alyssa remembered her wearing in the Snowclids.

"Alyssa," Ina said, hurrying up to her. "Where are you going?"

"I thought I would go into the woods a short way. I love the forest so much."

"Not without me," Ina said, a frown deepening lines between her eyes. "No place is safe right now."

"Suit yourself," Alyssa answered as she took off again. Ina kept up easily, and soon she took the lead into the woods, holding back low-hanging branches for the smaller teen. Alyssa was grateful for the walk as it stretched out her sore muscles and cleared her head.

Once fully into the forest, they moved slower. Alyssa admired every tree, even those felled by wind. The pungent smell of pine, and the earthy odor of fallen leaves gave off a damp, fresh scent. She bent low to peer at tiny mushrooms growing on the fallen trunks.

Sure is a lot of fungi to admire.

Alyssa wanted to collect some of it to take back to Granny Gert, but she held off. Perhaps there would be time later when she had something to collect them in. She remembered dried mushies were still quite usable, oftentimes even better than fresh.

Ina kept a watchful eye while Alyssa studied the land and its inhab-itants. A white fox stared at them for a moment before darting off into the thickest part of the forest.

"Snow fox," Ina told her. "Likely come down from the mountains to hunt. The drought has not been as bad here as near your home."

Alyssa's eyebrows rose. "Have you been to Mudden?"

"No. I have only heard about it from Edegast."

The two continued walking and soaking in the feeling of oneness with the woods. Finally, when time seemed to have gone by effortlessly, they turned for the village and the others waiting for them.

"Sorry for taking up so much of your time," she told Ina as she moved to head back.

Ina shrugged and stepped in front of her to lead again. "The woods are my home. I have missed it. Time is nothing to me when I am here."

"I feel really comfortable here myself."

They had not gone more than a few yards when a loud crash sound-ed off to their right.

"What was that?" Alyssa asked, holding Shadow down with one hand, shoving her clothing aside with the other to be able to gain the dagger in her waistband.

Ina held up a finger to indicate quiet and slid her bow to her hand. Quietly, she pulled an arrow out and placed it near the string. They stood still, watching and waiting for whatever it was to show itself.

Another crash filled the air, followed by the sound of a falling tree. Now Ina nocked the bow with the arrow and sighted it in the direction the sounds had come from. Whatever it was, moved toward them.

Alyssa saw the blur of white fur, seconds before Ina pulled the string back for shooting. She yanked Ina's arm down and caused the arrow to go wide.

"What are you doing?" Ina hissed.

"It's not an enemy!"

"It's not a fox either!"

Alyssa stepped in front of Ina and watched as the big, hairy, white creature stepped around the trees, trying not to knock any of them down.

Her heart pounded in her chest as it came closer and closer. Then, in a moment of recognition, she grinned and waved at the creature.

"Dopple? Dinger? Dangle?" the creature asked, coming forth to put out its big paws in greeting, its worried face turning into a grin.

"Grindel, grapple, granger," Alyssa replied, smiling up at it. She'd studied some of Pappy's books about the Yetis and learned the fairly simple language. She stepped into the Yeti's hands and was lifted to eye level.

"Bred?" Alyssa asked, although she already knew it was the Yeti who had made food for her and her company on her last trip into the mountains.

The Yeti nodded. "Gremlin." Then the two proceeded to carry on a conversation in Yettish with a few words thrown in of Mannish.

Ina shifted from foot to foot. Finally, she asked, "What on earth is this snowman doing this far south?"

"Snow woman," Alyssa corrected. "And she's scared and here to ask for help. Let's get her back to King Eldon."

"Help?" Ina asked, shock written on her face.

Bred settled Alyssa back on the ground, then she pulled a young Yeti out from behind her. The youth's eyes were wide, and it nestled back against its mother, a hairy paw held to its mouth.

"A baby?" Ina asked, wonder on her face.

Alyssa, filled with excitement, smiled at the young one, and said hello. "Grumpkin."

"Grump'n," it answered quietly as though it was uncertain if an answer had been required.

"We're going to take care of you, both of you," Alyssa told them.

At this point, Ina turned on her heel and led the way back to the settlement of the Iefyr. Alyssa tried not to show her concern. One Yeti would be reason for questions, but a Yeti *and* child meant something was desperately wrong in the mountains to their southeast.

Back at the long table with King Eldon, everyone sat with Alyssa, including two Iefyr hunters, all waiting to hear something important. She would translate for the Yeti folks, if needed, and hoped the Elvish words spoken would be translated for her.

She smiled to herself as she recalled the turmoil it had created when she'd insisted on the Yetis being led up the tree to the King's table. It had been a slow trek, but they made it. The tree groaned at the massive bulk that climbed through it, but it stood rooted to the spot.

"Do you know what brings the Yetis so far south?" Salas asked Alyssa.

"Something happened in their home caves. Bred and her baby were heading to safety after the menfolk sent the young ones and mothers away. But they were separated from their group and got lost in the woods."

"Where are the rest of them?" Japher asked.

Alyssa repeated the question in Yettish. Bred looked sorrowful and shook her head.

"She doesn't know where the rest are, or even if they are alive. After the evilment came upon them in the night in the caves where they live, they scattered for their lives. They have no weapons to speak of. They are a peaceable folk." Alyssa patted the Yeti child's hand.

Eldon leaned close to Bred's son. "Grindle, grapple, grum, grum?" he asked. Alyssa smiled. Of course, the King of the Iefyr would know Yettish.

The boy Yeti grinned up at the King and nodded. Eldon waved for a mug of apple cider to be brought for the child to drink.

Bred spoke to Eldon, and he seemed to understand her. Finally, Eldon sat back in his seat. "The evil has come down through the Yeti mountains and either enslaved them or killed them. At least as far as this female Yeti knows."

Alyssa felt a lump form in her throat. She'd gotten attached to the Yetis when they'd come to her aid last year. So many were good natured and helpful. Now she didn't know if any remained.

Tears fell down Bred's furry cheeks. "Drimmel, dum, dum, hubby taken from me."

Her Mannish was limited but everyone understood her that time.

"We'll get him back," Alyssa told her, defiance in her voice. "We'll get them all back."

Ina's ice-blue eyes blazed. "And how on Daegries do you expect to do that?"

Alyssa returned the shield maiden's glare. "We're going to fight them. Every man or elf of us against every ugly troll and goblin of them."

Salas and Japher exchanged looks.

"Perhaps it is time we unveil a plan for the situation we now face," King Eldon said. He pulled out a map and motioned to a man sitting away from the table. The short stocky man strolled over. He was garbed in a colorful tunic and breeches and was armed with a short sword that had been tied off.

Alyssa's mouth dropped open. This was a man of the Haldor! In fact, she knew this man as one of King Vernon's. He had been kind enough to show her the Wellspring where the phoenix lived.

"Sir!" she exclaimed. "I don't remember your name, but I remember your face. And your kindness to me."

He smiled, his eyes nearly hidden beneath his bushy eyebrows. "And I do remember you, milady."

King Eldon introduced him to the others. "*Nishish a' Dwarven.* This is Noggor Stonedigger, from the Haldor halls. He goes by Nog, if you will. He has brought us news most concerning. Nog, please tell them what you told me."

Alyssa had wondered how Eldon was so well-informed before their arrival, but now she knew others had been here with similar news. None of the Iefyr seemed surprised.

The dwarf looked around the table and allowed his gaze to fall on Alyssa last.

"An army of goblins attacked us in our caves, right up to our forge, about a week ago. They were fiercely armed, with long knives, maces, and many axes. We kept them at bay until they realized to attack us in our lair was a bad idea. We are capable of much mayhem there, so they fled. We followed them as far as we dared without leaving our women and children unprotected. I came here to ask for the Iefyr's help. We have no ill will with anyone and cannot decipher how this can even happen."

"And that is why we are gathering here today to each tell our tales, and make a plan," Eldon told him.

"This sounds like the work of—," Japher began.

"Shh. No need to use that name. To even utter it gives him power," Ina interrupted, shaking her head.

Alyssa felt her heart thud in her chest. She'd felt homesickness, joy, peace, sadness, loss, anger, and now trepidation all inside an hour.

What were the Iefyr even contemplating? And if it was to be war, how could she help with a small birch bow and a quiver of arrows against maces and axes?

A dejected and fearful air fell over the room.

Chapter Twenty-Three

Silence fell for a long spell. No one knew what to say. Finally, when Eldon cleared his throat to speak, everyone listened carefully.

"My friends, we have gathered here, with enough knowledge on the circumstances of Daegries at this time, to warrant a banding together for protection. The entire realm of both the Greater Daegries and Lesser Daegries hangs in the balance. Every last man and woman is needed to fight against this evilment."

Ina added, "*Dra'y'sray cut halid.* Our trek here was filled with danger. I suggest scouting parties to look at our road ahead and even more importantly to scout the entire forest around and about us."

Alyssa watched as every head nodded. Consensus was achieved already, even without taking a vote. Even when some of those gathered didn't understand all of it. She could see a big problem with this plan already.

She said, "King Eldon, if you send scouts over to tend to the troubles with the Haldor in their halls, then your own forest is left wide open to attack. If you send them to mind the Yetis' troubles, same problem. She inclined her head toward Ina. "I'm assuming you don't have enough scouts to take on every issue across the realms of Daegries. And surely you don't intend for the wizards to participate in this? Good magik is excellent for protection, but oftentimes best used at home. I have witnessed how magik won't work against some of these creatures."

A murmur went through their midst.

"How many forces do you expect the Dark Master to have at hand?" Ina asked Eldon.

He deferred to Nog and Bred. They both indicated that the wickedness was greater than their own kind could fend off. Alyssa knew that both factions had large numbers, so this sent her fears even higher.

The murmuring turned into full-blown conversations, some in Elvish, some in the Common Tongue. The noise level rose. Finally, King Eldon stood and tapped the table with his knife.

"My friends, my kin, we certainly have a problem as Miss Oh has pointed out," he said. Turning to her, he added, "For one so young, you are exceedingly wise. Rest in the fact that our wood is filled with enough warriors to keep the evil at bay for now. We are calling on all our forces which are around the realm to return to us. If we could send out a scouting party to take note of what lies around us, and perhaps to go to the southern fringe, to the Nithereen... well, that should be sufficient for now."

The room quieted down. He continued, "Now, gather around me, and let's have a look at this map."

Everyone stood and created a circle around the table. Bred was tall enough to see over Nog's head so she stood behind him.

King Eldon proceeded to point out places of interest to the group. "Here is where we stand in the woods of Draysray. To the northwest of us are the Snowclids. To the east of us is the realm of Men, and to the south of them, Yetiland and the Heightlands. Farther northeast of the land of Men are the halls of the Haldor. If you follow this path, you can see how the Evil One has built forces somewhere between the Yetis and the Haldor."

"And it's spreading south and east," Salas said, a bit under his breath. "If not stopped, the heart of the Greater Daegries will be taken."

Alyssa felt as though the wind had been taken from her. It seemed quite plain. Hektor was sending out his forces from somewhere in the vicinity of Needlemount Castle and the mountains around it. And his reach was getting bigger.

"*Them rats at that castle are involved in this, sure as rain,*" Pappy's voice said.

Alyssa nodded slightly, even though she knew he couldn't see it.

"The land where I'm from isn't mentioned," she said, pointing at the bottom part of the map. "But my homeland is about here, and over here is the ogres' swamp. They have been leaving in packs recently."

"The foul taint is that far south and west," Ina told Eldon, her brow furrowed, stabbing the map with her finger.

He nodded. "Yes, it is quite possible. It seems as though the whole of Daegries has fallen into a stupor. Even the wise ones have not known of the spread, save Edegast. Long may his beard grow."

This news sent many of the group back to their chairs. It was bad enough to hear of the dangers, but to see how it had spanned out gave them tremors.

"I wish Edegast was here now," Alyssa said under her breath. Eldon heard her and nodded. The wizard was the only one with complete knowledge of how vast and wide the enemy had grown.

"Until more can be known," Eldon said, "we must prepare. To what end, no one can know, but we have been idle long enough. We need to know the land around us. How the evil has spread in this area. And, to seek the minds of the Nithereen. Enlisting their aid is necessary. Does anyone have anything else to add?"

Alyssa took a deep breath and said, "King, I want to know, when the time comes, who's going south to the Farmlands to protect my folk? They're wide open and innocent."

King Eldon sat back and crossed his arms. "That is a fair question, Alyssa, but I have no one to spare, my friend. Can you find anyone close enough to band with them?"

She thought about the men of the Heightlands. They were still too far from her home. The sirens were closer but much more dangerous. Her people around Mudden wouldn't trust any creature that looked different or acted differently from them. Finally, she shook her head. "No sir. I guess there ain't nobody."

Ina raised an eyebrow and looked at Eldon. "Sire, there may be a way."

He shook his head curtly. "Let us not discuss that now, Ina."

"But we have to go to the Nithereen encampment anyway," she continued in a hushed whisper. "If what is being said is true—"

"Rumors. You are counting on rumors."

She closed her eyes against his comments. "Rumors often have truths in them, my king."

Eldon gave her a slight shake of his head before he glanced over at Alyssa. "We need you in this party. I understand you have healing abilities?"

She nodded. "Yes, sir."

"The Nithereen have folk who are ill, due to too much absorption of dark magik. It may be advantageous for us, if you were to go and try to use your magik, light though it may be."

Alyssa didn't bother to fill King Eldon in on how much she had learned over the year since she'd been at the Iefyr encampment. She was no longer a mere apprentice.

"Dark magik doesn't scare me none. I'll go, gladly," she replied. "Scouting out the land is probably not a bad idea, although I suggest leaving Salas and Japher here to protect. Their magik is more powerful than most."

Eldon smiled. "Our forest is amply provided for, but the wizards are more than welcome to keep us company with their good cheer."

Alyssa silently stroked the scarf who had saved her life more than once. She would not be afraid. Not many creatures in the world of Daegries could hurt her unless they went through Shadow first.

Salas and Japher shuffled their feet, embarrassed to be the center of the conversation. Soon, they took their leave of the gatherment. In a short while, the others followed suit and before long it was only Alyssa and Ina and a few Iefyr archers left. She smiled hesitantly at them, knowing they would not understand if she spoke.

King Eldon refolded the map, and Alyssa took the opportunity to ask what his plans were concerning the Grim.

"Sire, what about the book? It wouldn't be smart to have it within reach of a goblin or worse. You mentioned your elders having a look at it."

Eldon set aside the map and took a deep breath. "Yes, I did. The conflict with that is, they are all in the scouting parties and managing them. I suspect I am the best for this particular duty. May I have a look at it?"

She hesitated. The Grim was so particular about being handled these days. Refusing the King would not be wise, though.

She dug into her pack and pulled the book out. "I'm going to give it to you, but you need to have your hands out. It wants to flip around a little."

Eldon smiled and held his hands out obediently. She moved closer, rubbing the cover gently. When she stood right in front of him, she held the book out. It trembled in her hands, vibrating violently.

"It may not go to you, Sire," Ina told him, eyes glowing with wonder.

He laughed and said, "*Agno nigh, nigh.*"

The tome lifted and floated over to the elf. He took it and looked through the first few pages. He whispered to it, "*Berenor aloda hough.*" He went through the pages, slowly at first and then quickly, pausing to observe many of the spells. At the end of his search, another sigh came from him and a sad look crossed his face.

Alyssa's mouth fell open. The book went to him like it knew him. None had been able to do that before now.

Eldon handed the book back to her. "It is indeed a mystical and magikal book, Alyssa. But one I am afraid we know very little about how to decipher. Why didn't Edegast keep it? All of the encyclopedias of the Wise are at the castle. Certainly he could have used them for this."

Alyssa ducked her head shyly, feeling like he was attacking her friend. "He lost his father, sir. Trudor fell in the mountains. His biggest concern became getting word to you."

At these words, Eldon quickly sat back to stare at Ina.

"It is true, my king. Trudor's party traveled to bring tidings to Draysray. An Undead attacked them, and I believe the one killed for attacking us was one and the same."

"Justice served," he said, worry lining his face. "This is grievous news indeed."

Alyssa spoke up. "Is there anything that we need to know about the Grim or its contents that can help today? I feel like it needs to be hidden. Even if, as Edegast has said, the Dark Master is not looking for the book to be found with me, it won't take a schoolteacher to explain it to him. He'll figure it out sooner or later, and I'm not sure I'm capable of fighting him for it."

The king lifted an eyebrow and nodded. "You are correct, Alyssa. The book needs to be hidden until such a time that it is useful. I have given it some instructions. It will behave for you."

The fact that the Iefyr had created the scarf made her suspect that they knew something about the creation of the Grim, too. She waited patiently for him to finish.

When it became apparent that he wasn't going to say more, she asked, "King, who's going to hide it? And where? I've been the care-taker for a long time now. It's a special thing to me. I'd like to be a part of its history, however that comes around, but I brought it here for the Iefyr to help me with it," she said, peering at the faces staring at her. "It has been said that we should either protect it, or... well, destroy it."

He placed the map in a leather pouch. "As far as the Iefyr are concerned, the bearer of the book has all the reasons to keep it and hide it and protect it. It will be up to you, Alyssa Oh. Do with it what you will, as wisely as possible. Tell no one where it is, and make sure you put it in a place where it is secure, and do not forget where!"

This last was said almost jokingly, but his eyes were deadly serious.

"We cannot take the time now to go over the Grim and decipher its contents. That would be a better job when Edegast can join us—"

"Or if—" Ina interrupted.

"—let us not count on ghosts." Eldon shook his head and frowned at her.

Ina crossed her arms and looked away.

"Mayhap you will be able to read it and understand it on your own," Eldon said gently. "It should reveal itself to the right person. It only needs coaxing."

Alyssa squinted at these words. *Coaxing? Coaxing for what?*

Eldon continued. "Just know that if the situation becomes dire, destroying the book will have to be done."

This made Ina sit up straighter. "You mean...?"

He looked at her with a piercing gaze and answered, "Ina, if what you believe to be true can be proven... well, that is all the answer we need, is it not? But if your thoughts turn into fallacy, Alyssa will have no other choice."

Now Ina turned and stared at Alyssa.

The girl felt heat rise in her cheeks as she spoke. "I don't know what you're talking about, but if you could tell me where to hide this book I'd be ever so grateful, because I think that might be the best move right now."

"There is no place safe," Eldon returned. "Let your heart guide you. I would begin in the woods of Draysray. Placing it in nature would please it. There are many deep silent places here."

"You mean... bury it?" Alyssa whispered.

He smiled again and handed the map in its case over to a tall, young elf standing nearby.

When the king didn't respond to her question, she took a step back. Her thoughts returned to his words about the deep and mysterious woods of Draysray. Unless someone saw her put it in the ground, they would never find it there, for sure. And she would need to take great care so that she, herself, could find it once more.

She hefted her pack and took off without a word to anyone. Ina soon followed, however, and Alyssa turned to stop her.

"Princess, I know how devoted you are about protecting me, but it seems to me that responsibility ended when we got here. You can take a rest and forget about guarding me. I've got a calling of my own at the moment."

Ina closed her eyes against these words as though they were painful. "No, Alyssa, it will never be so. I will guard you with my life until I am dead if needs be. You cannot go off on your own with this danger so close. It is not only my duty, but also my desire to protect you. Something that my kind does not do often for those of the mortal world."

Alyssa took a deep breath. "Be that as it may, I need a little privacy for a while. Please give that to me. "

Ina began shaking her head, but Alyssa held up her hand to stop her. "No. I mean it. Don't follow me. If I get into trouble, I'll yell so loud this entire village will come running."

"It's my duty—"

"Duty's not worth a wooden nickel except to those at war. Or so my Pappy tells me."

Ina didn't argue with her logic.

"I know we may be at war soon, but not today," Alyssa continued. "I'll be back in a short while. Stand here and watch for me if you have to. Otherwise, trust that I can handle things on my own."

The she-elf's mouth moved to protest more, but Alyssa turned on her heel and strode away. She didn't look behind her, but she didn't hear any footfalls either. Once she reached the tree line, she looked back and saw an empty trail.

"Thank the sun and moon she gave up," Alyssa said with a released breath before trudging into the woods.

"Now what will be a good mark for the place to leave it?" she murmured to herself. "Need to have something to remind me."

She stood among all manner of trees and could name the most common ones. But occasionally a white birch tree would appear, and it would be the odd man out in the grouping. This made her decide to hide the book beneath this type of tree. She stood with one hand on the tree's trunk. Thinking a dryad might be living within, she decided to ask for permission.

It wasn't in any book that this was a proper thing to do, but Alyssa knew it would never be refused if the request was given nicely.

"Dear birch tree, with your bark so white, if a creature lives within, please hear my plea. I need to plant something close to you, and I ask permission to do it. I promise not to damage anything. At least not intentionally," she said, looking at the bare branches. "And if you can protect this bundle for me until I return, I'll forever be in your debt."

When no one appeared to refuse her request, she began digging. It was not too hard to do since the ground was pretty moist beneath the decaying leaves there. She dug a hole as deep as she dared, without doing any damage to any root system nearby, and took a tunic from her pack to roll around the Grim.

Shadow floated over her head, twisting its edges over what she was doing.

"I know you and this book have gotten close in all this time, and you likely ain't too thrilled with leaving it behind. But I promise you, Shadow, the Grim is going to be safe. As safe as I can make it anyway. I know you heard King Eldon say to destroy it, and well, if it comes to that... well, we'll do what has to be done. I ain't too certain how you destroy a magik book, though."

Alyssa placed it in the hole and covered it with dirt. Finally, she scattered leaves over the site and looked around to find something to remind her where it was placed. She didn't want to have to dig around every birch in the forest.

She noted an oak tree beside the birch, and it had a knot on its trunk that looked to be bigger than her two fists placed together. "I'll remember you," she said, touching the knot.

Then she gazed about to make sure there weren't two oaks with big knots. And made a mental note of how far from the path the tree stood. In fact, she walked and counted the paces.

Finally, assured that there were none other than the one before her, she took a deep breath and nodded. This would have to do for now. She heard something moving through the trees, something big, and was afraid of being discovered, so she threw the pack over her shoulder, situated her bow and arrows, and climbed into the branches of the oak tree. She hoped the few leaves still on the tree would be enough to hide her.

It turned out to be a massive stag with many antlers. She remained quiet and waited for it to leave. It stilled below her and stood sniffing as if he could smell her scent. Then, he lowered his head to the ground right where she had placed the Grim. He let out a loud snort and began pawing at the hole.

It didn't take long to paw, however. Soon it was using its antlers to help, and Alyssa feared it would uncover the book and potentially damage it. Why it would want the tome, she couldn't say, but the Dark Master had all manner of ears and eyes and the likelihood of this stag being magiked for evil purposes was high. She looked for a brand on the deer such as she'd heard about, but she saw nothing.

A fear to disturb the stag, and even worse, not to, filled her. For the first time, she realized that Ina was more needed than she wanted to admit.

Eventually, the creature decided there was no time to continue its seeking under the oak and moved off in the direction of the stream. Alyssa let out the breath that she'd been holding.

She noted his direction and climbed down.

To leave the Grim buried where a creature as powerful as a stag, or anything else enchanted, could find and uncover it would never do. How did she know that the book wasn't sending out signals to be found? It was a magik book, after all.

Even a resourceful squirrel could spoil her plans. She quickly set aside her pack and dug the book out. The tunic was dirty, but she didn't care. She pulled Shadow out and told it to guard the book. She shoved it into the pack and felt Shadow twining around it as she pulled the ties.

Alyssa did the best she could to cover the hole. She said a few words of thanks to the trees before setting off to follow the large male deer. It was going to water and that was the way she needed to go also as the village was by the water.

She took one last long look at the area where she had attempted to bury the Grim. Every step away from it gave her heart a twist. What would she do now? She couldn't leave it in the care of anyone else. She would have to take it with her for the rest of the time she was in the Greater Daegries, no matter how dangerous that proved to be.

But I ain't got to tell nobody I still have it. Maybe Eldon and the others will assume I buried it.

When she returned to her room in the cabin, she was exhausted and dropped her belongings on the floor before she tossed herself onto the bed. The quiet of the village and the solitude of the cabin soothed her to sleep.

Someone pulled on her arm, calling her name.

"Alyssa!"

She moaned and tried to roll over. She didn't want to be awakened. It was so warm and cozy…

"Alyssa!" the voice rose with urgency.

She finally opened her eyes, blinking at Japher who stood over her, his face a mass of concern.

"What?" she asked as she rolled into a sitting position. "What has happened?"

"King Eldon has sent out scouting parties to survey the roads around the forest. When they return, we will hear when the group going south will leave."

"And this news had to be told to me now?" she asked, temper flaring.

"Well," he began. "Yes. King Eldon asked that every person be informed, even if they were not yet needed. He wants everyone on guard."

Alyssa nodded, relenting. "Oh. Thanks then. What is happening now?"

"I believe that the elves of Draysray are gathered to speak with Eldon now. He is preparing them for attacks that may come."

Alyssa wanted to hear some of what was said, so she grabbed her pack and weapons and headed for Eldon's platform. Once she neared the area, she knew she wouldn't have to strain to hear. The elves of Draysray were gathered on the platforms and on the ground. A large contingent of them, all listening to their king carefully.

His words were being translated by a plainly dressed Elven man for those like herself who didn't understand the language of the High Elves.

"My kin, you will not be unprotected. When the company goes south, warriors will still be within the forest to bear arms against any attacks," King Eldon said.

"*Ashunder ash*? Shall we bear arms, as well, my king?" asked someone with long blond braids down his back. "We are not unaccustomed to fighting, Sire. Only a little leaf-covered due to unuse."

King Eldon smiled down at him. "It would be wise to brush off the leaves. Why don't you begin a list of arms we have among us? Nothing is unimportant. Every bow and arrow, ax, shovel, and cookpot counts."

Alyssa watched the plain elven man turn to the others and tell them to help him create the list. Every household would have to put something down.

She started away from the crowd when she heard her name being called. She looked around and finally up to the platform. Ina stood there, waving to her.

Alyssa forced her shoulders down and tried to relax as tension filled her. She headed for the stairs that led up to King Eldon's platform. She had to look into the interior of the tree house, however, as he and Ina had moved from their original place.

She found them in a quiet book-lined room with chairs and a table where maps were tacked to the wooden walls. Blank eyes revealing nothing peered at her as she approached.

"The Alliance has been formed. Please sit, so that we can plan with you." Eldon waved to the nearest chair, and she sat heavily, dropping her pack and weapons at her feet.

"Who will go?" she asked.

"You, Salas, Ina, and Japher. Bred and Nog may remain here until we decide if the Nithereen will be with us, or, against. They may share your road," Eldon said, dropping his gaze to his hands. "We have a great deal of uncertainty at this time. It is my hope that your efforts will turn the tide and the Nithereen will be convinced to join us as a matter of their own self-preservation."

"Me too," she replied softly, wanting to ask what they would do if the dark elves refused, but decided that she wasn't prepared for the answer.

"Let me tell you what this journey may bring," he said, waving at the nearest map. "This land here is all Iefyr; that includes Draysray, and the forest far south, the old one where you met the Iefyr first. We have contingents like that throughout the Greater Daegries."

Alyssa nodded, following his finger.

"This small clump here is where the Nithereens reside. They chose to break away from us. Not so far as to be unreachable as you can see. For such a short trek, it is likely the most dangerous of all."

She took a deep breath and stared into his eyes. "Why so?"

"They have certain... other powers, as I said. They have enchanted their forest and all of the creatures within it. It would be unwise to think they would not be aware when you approach the woods. Likely hours in advance."

"And we are asking them for protection? Sounds like we need protection from them, more like," she said, shaking her head.

"Ina doesn't think they are as bad as I say. She can fill you in on her thoughts later. For now, try to be as prepared as you can for every possibility. If not for the Nithereens, then the Dark Master's legions may lie beyond this safe haven. You all are far too valuable to lose to either faction."

"Why am I more worried about the Nithereens than the Dark Master?" Alyssa asked, fear rising like bile up her throat.

"There is good reason to fear all, but I believe our brothers will be easiest to convince to join us and not spar with us."

"I sure hope so," Alyssa answered, her voice tiny in the light of the Elven home.

Chapter Twenty-Four

Listening to Eldon, it had not taken long for Alyssa to realize that her magik was not sufficient for what was going to be required of her. She longed for a stronger, better-made bow that fit her stature and ability. All she had seen thus far in Draysray had been long bows hewn from deer antler, or wood, some even from the birches. King Eldon had concluded his meeting with a warning to be quiet and to travel under the cover of night.

As she stood in her cabin, contemplating what to use for defense, if it came to that, someone knocked softly on the cabin door.

"Come in," she whispered. Ina entered, dressed in black clothing. A wide band hid her ears, which would have been a giveaway to anyone seeing their pointed tips. Another cloth covered her hair, muting it. The woman had looked so different at Knowledge Hall that Alyssa almost gasped every time she saw her now.

Her tunic and leggings were also black, and bristly with fur. Alyssa suspected it came from a bear but didn't ask.

"Are you ready?" Ina asked, striding to Alyssa. The clothing Ina wore made no sound either, and she could have passed for a shadow. "The scouts have returned. There have been individual bugbear sightings, and one troll. We must make good use of our time. The taint has begun to get a foothold even here, it seems."

Alyssa looked at her own worn tunic, and leggings held up by a rough belt. The pack lay on the ground not completely filled. Edegast's boots were scuffed now from all the walking she had done, and she could feel the chill beneath her feet already.

Ina pulled Alyssa by one shoulder so she could look her over. The elf shook her head and leaned down to whisper in Alyssa's ear. "You need darker clothing. Do you have any?"

Alyssa shook her head. Ina nodded and sprinted out of the cabin. Alyssa pulled Shadow out and it wrapped around her, as if it were as fearful of the trip as she was. No way she could leave it behind, nor the Grim either. No one would know that she had the two items. She would keep them well-hidden.

When Ina came back to the cabin, she had twin outfits for Alyssa. One to wear and one to have in case of rain, and they were both identical to Ina's clothing. Alyssa sent Shad into the pack, and she took the outfits from Ina.

The Elven princess waited while Alyssa went behind a dressing screen and changed. When she came out, Ina handed her a pair of butter-soft black boots with thick soles of leather. After Alyssa pulled on the boots, Ina pulled a long scarf from her waist and draped it over the girl's head. Then she pulled a band out and shoved it over Alyssa's head and ears.

"The Nithereens dress this way," Ina whispered. "They will not see us if we are as murky as their woods. And if they do, they will think we are one of them at first. We will need that element of surprise. Also, our clothing has been magiked by our High Lords. It will be hard to pierce through it. I would wear the Scarf of Egladris around myself if I were you. There is magik in that scarf that we do not know all about."

Alyssa didn't doubt that at all.

"But before we leave," Ina paused and pulled a sturdy bow made of black horn and a quiver woven from black material from her pack. "I had these made for you. They will be a good weight and not too hard to use."

Alyssa grinned at her and took the bow, black as ebony. The arrows seemed to be of normal make and size, but something told her that they were also filled with some sort of spells. Alyssa couldn't have been more thrilled to leave her other bow and arrows behind.

"Will someone here be able to take care of what I leave behind? I might want them again when I return, if I ever do. Besides, those boots belong to a special wizard friend of mine."

Ina nodded, a slight smile of understanding on her face.

Once they felt everything was in order, they slipped out of the cabin and down the path until it neared the woods. Japher and Salas waited there, wizard robes and cloaks with hoods barely visible in the gloom of the forest.

Many of the elves who lived with or near King Eldon were not out celebrating this evening. The big fire was still unlit, and the revelers who always seemed to incite Shadow had not begun their songs. Too much trouble around them, Alyssa thought.

No one spoke, but Ina led the way with Salas behind her, Alyssa behind him, and Japher bringing up the rear. Alyssa noted that Salas was using a staff to help on the inclines. Japher did not, but he did have a heavy pack that seemed to pull him backwards by the shoulders.

In about an hour, with Draysray behind them, Ina took a short break and gathered them together to tell them what to expect on the road ahead.

"We are not far from Nithereen land. It used to be a part of Draysray but somehow was cut away. Perhaps that was their intent. At any rate, we will need to skirt the clearing that lies ahead. Stay with me and stay close to the trees."

They all had some water to quench their thirst and plunged ahead, following the Elven warrior. When at last they reached the clearing, it was plain to see that something foul had been through there and left a burned circle which separated the trees of Draysray and the forest of the Nithereen.

Ina motioned for all to be silent and to follow her. They turned right and stayed in single file as they edged the burned area. Without warning a great swoosh was heard, causing all to look up.

Ina pulled Salas back unto the trees and everyone followed quickly. Overhead a large bird soared, circling, perhaps for food. The bird was far larger than even an eagle and its underside appeared black.

It didn't take long for it to tire of seeking out prey in the area between Draysray and the other forest and it flew away to the south.

"An emissary of the Dark Master?" Salas asked Ina.

She shrugged. "Perhaps. It isn't a usual thing for birds of prey to hunt at night. If this is so, this creature has perfect sight even in the darkness."

Alyssa shuddered. She had ridden on a Bop, or bird of prey, and she knew how massive and mighty those were. Why one would be this far south with no friends, she could only guess. She'd never seen them flying solo.

Ina stepped back toward the circle and stared up into the now-empty night sky. She waved to them, and they took off in a bunch, staying close to one another.

She traveled about halfway around the circle before plunging into the woods once more. Soon, they heard the large bird's wings flapping overhead again. With the trees to shield them, they felt covered and safe.

Its cry sounded like a throaty *creak* that sent cold chills down Alyssa's arms. It called out over and over as it sought its prey. Alyssa hoped elf, wizard, or farm girl were not on the menu and hastened her stride.

The group made good passage through the Nithereen woods for a short while. Then the terrain took a more difficult turn, and the path become less marked and more heavily burdened with viny grass and weeds beneath the lighter layer of snow.

A chill wind blew up from nowhere and they all pulled their cloaks tighter. Alyssa noted the path, now mostly obliterated, took them through a thick stand of trees old and gnarled with low-hanging branches.

Moss grew on the boughs and some of it hung down like green hair. As they traveled beneath these trees, Alyssa could imagine whispers coming from the trees through the hiss of the wind. She shivered and followed Salas's staff which was now aglow with a dim blue light.

Suddenly, the entire group fell to a stuttering halt. Voices chattered all around them, and strange languages were spoken. Some laughed, but the sound was not happy.

Alyssa turned back and forth trying to figure out where the voices came from but to no avail. The voices belonged to shadows and ghosts as far as she could tell.

Ina called out. "*Mar on elain alron!*"

Salas held his staff aloft and repeated her words.

Alyssa could only guess at their meaning.

Japher turned to Alyssa with fear in his eyes when there was no return call. There was only shuffling and skittering in the woods all around them.

They were surrounded.

Ina hissed, "Do not move a muscle. We are waiting. They will come to us when they are ready."

"I thought you said we would be like shadows to them dressed like this," Alyssa hissed back.

Ina snorted softly. "We made it farther than I thought we would so that was indeed the case."

A flare lit up the depths of the woods in front of them. A tall Elven warrior dressed all in black lifted a torch high and took a few steps toward them.

"Peace, you bring, peace we accept," the strong male voice said. He moved to Ina and stopped a few feet away from her. "Who are you?"

"We are from Eldon, the Iefyr leader. We would ask a parlay with your leader."

"You will have to be bound by sight."

Ina gave Salas a nervous glance and nodded. The Nithereen motioned for someone to come forward. The warrior came with black strips of cloth and bound their eyes so they couldn't see anything. Satisfied, the Nithereen company placed one guard behind each of them, and each guard prodded them in the back to get them to move.

Ina was the most sure-footed among the group from the Snowclids. Alyssa heard Salas stumble, and she stumbled also, her Elven guard yanking her arm to prevent her from stepping on him. Traveling through the remainder of the Nithereens' woods was tedious and slow.

Japher actually fell a few times, and someone grunted and growled as they had to haul him back to his feet. Alyssa felt as though they were being herded like pigs to a pen.

In the end, they were all scratched, muddied, tired, and irritable. Alyssa's anger at such treatment rose with every step, and for entertainment, she imagined what her Pappy's tongue-lashing for the entire company of elves would be like. He wouldn't take this treatment quietly.

After an hour of stumbling through the woods with impatient elves assisting them, they were pulled to a stop.

The bindings were removed from their eyes, and they got a look at the Nithereen's homes. Built on the ground rather than in the trees, the homes were made almost as part of the forest. Trees sheltered their homes with low-hanging boughs, and vines twisted around them holding up the rickety looking structures.

Candles in holders illuminated everything on trees and on the ground. Alyssa wondered how on earth the trees didn't catch fire.

Magik, if tended with care, can bring about amazing things. Alyssa heard Pappy's voice in her head and nodded at the words. She remembered the Danglebugs and the magik she and Pappy had created together.

The company had brought Alyssa and her friends to the leader's home, apparently. The older sylvan leader stood leaning on a massive staff of ash, peering at them from under graying brows. His eyes were the clearest brown Alyssa had ever seen, and she felt his gaze upon her and saw his curiosity.

He knew Ina in some fashion, because she strode to him and bowed.

"Father of trees," the elf said to him, breathlessly.

"Daughter, why have you come this way?"

Ina rose and Alyssa noted that the two were almost eye to eye. Ina was a lot taller than Alyssa, so the striking contrast of the Nithereen leader's height was noticeable. They appeared like twin saplings.

"We bring ill tidings from Draysray," Ina told him. "It is most urgent to have a parlay with you. Bring the best archers in this land. They need to hear me."

He hesitated only a moment before turning to the nearest elf, and in their tongue, sent him off to bring others. He waved to the travelers to follow him and led the way inside his home. Alyssa vowed to learn some Elvish so she could communicate better.

The immense interior of the wooden structure caused Alyssa's eyebrows to rise. The only similarity to a tree was on the outside. The house became a rough-hewn burrow inside the tree. It went for a long way underground. Rooms turned out from each side of the burrow and the main passageway was lit by metal sconces filled with candles.

Melted wax scent filled Alyssa's nose. She tried to look into some of the rooms they passed, but there was some form of magik protecting every one of them, and she could see nothing but a wavery brown haze. The darkness ahead was like looking through a cloth. She could make out Ina's back before her, and her feet beneath her, and that was about all she could see.

Soon, they came to a room created beneath the large tree's root system. The roots dangled overhead and made perfect ropes to hang things like lanterns, cookware, and other necessary items for a kitchen.

Impressed, Alyssa wanted a house like the dark elves lived in. So simple yet so complex, she thought.

Salas remained his stoic self, unfazed, but Japher ogled everything, making sounds of wonder.

The elven leader sat at the head of a large wooden table and waited for everyone else to arrive. Once they were seated, he asked Ina to begin.

She related to him everything that had happened at Knowledge Hall over the last moon phase, and how, on their journey to Draysray, they had been attacked.

She concluded with saying what Eldon had told her to say. "The entire realm of Daegries has fallen into a web of dangers, and the Dark Master is the spider lying in wait. He seeks a return to this world and is sending out evil emissaries to aid him."

At that, she turned to Alyssa. "This is Alyssa Chance Oh. She owns and protects two items of magik that you may find interesting. She hails from the far south and the farmlands."

Alyssa felt the piercing brown gaze of the Nithereen leader upon her. She ducked her head and pretended to be pulling her pack off. What she was actually doing was getting the bow and arrows more readily available should the need arise. The whole group had been herded here under painful prodding, and she wasn't going to forget that anytime soon.

"Alyssa," the leader said softly. "You are welcome here. You have nothing to fear from us. We have traded with the southerners before. Our warriors are less than welcoming sometimes, but they are sworn to protect this wood. They have to harden their hearts to enable their duty to be fulfilled."

She looked into his eyes and terror filled her. Could he read her mind? Finding her voice, she said, "Then why do I feel so uneasy around you? I don't know nothing about the Nithereen people. They are remembered in my land as night horrors whisking children off, never to be seen again."

Ina frowned as she turned quickly to see Alyssa's face.

Alyssa shrugged. "I'm being honest, Ina. I don't know these people. I barely know you. I have a stake in what happens in the realm of Daegries because my people are in as much danger as anyone. But I ain't going to be nobody's slave."

The Nithereen leader's smile was cold and fleeting. "Your honesty will be rewarded, young one. I am Anfalen Dorjor. I have been the leader of these people for a long time. We are not completely immortal. Not like the High Elves, such as Ina and Eldon, who have that ability."

Alyssa nodded. "Nice to meet you, King Anfalen."

He gave me his full attention. "No, I am no king. I am no better nor lesser than the greatest of my warriors."

The room filled with archers dressed in the colors of nighttime, heavily armed with bows and arrows. Some had long swords tied down. Where they came from, Alyssa didn't know.

Once the swish of cloth was silenced, Anfalen spoke again. "What would Eldon have us do? You have told us tidings of the Evil One trying to raise his forces, but not the solution. I warrant you do have one..."

Ina cleared her throat and looked around at the many gathered.

"We are to prepare for war, Anfalen. We can stop him, but we will have to take out his armed men first. Those who are unfortunately situated between us."

"Where do we begin?" someone standing behind Ina and Alyssa asked in a gruff voice.

Salas and Japher said in unison, "Everywhere."

Chapter Twenty-Five

After the meeting with Anfalen and the others broke up, Alyssa remained in the treehouse. Anfalen and Ina wanted to speak to her alone without anyone else around.

"Alyssa," Ina said, a softness in her voice. "There is need of the Scarf of Egladris in all of this."

Alyssa tilted her head, listening carefully. "Why?"

"We know the creator of it," Anfalen said.

The room, although underground, went completely silent, and Alyssa felt as though the mud walls were going to cave in. Her special ability, to know when the other shoe was about to drop, kicked in. "Who is the creator of the scarf?"

Ina and Anfalen shared a look before they turned to her.

"Your mother wove the scarf of Egladris with her own hands from the follygrass that grows in the clearing. It was her way to unite the

High Elves and the Nithereens. It was never supposed to leave her care."

"I received the scarf from a phoenix, and it had been in a bunch of hands before me. Why didn't it stay with her?" Alyssa scratched her brain to remember all that the beautiful phoenix had told her.

"When you are ready to find your mother..." The phoenix had known who Alyssa's mother was. And her father, who was alive, too.

"Where's my mother?" Alyssa asked, suspicion in her voice. "And for that matter, my daddy? He is missing too! You folks must know. You both look as guilty as a fox in a henhouse."

Again, the two exchanged a glance.

"Your mother is in a protected place. She is well, as is your father who refused to be parted from her," Anfalen said.

"I want to see them," Alyssa said, nearly choking on the lump in her throat. "Where are they? I'll take the scarf to her. My mother can do whatever is needed."

Ina put out a hand to stop Alyssa from rising and storming out. "Calm. Calm is needed, Alyssa. You can accomplish nothing with so much emotion. You must remember your magik now. It is necessary."

The phoenix had said much the same to her. She told her to practice her magik. Well, she had more or less. She tried to make spell jars and learn about potions from Pappy, but he was the mage in the house. She let him take over as he had when he had been fully alive. She only helped him when he couldn't do something due to the constraint of the jack-in-the-box. Now she wished she'd done more.

"My magik is for healing and seeking out things. I have no real magik, not like a wizard such as Edegast or Salas. Heck, even Japher has more magik than I do."

Anfalen shook his head, a furrow creasing his brow. "You do not know what you have inside you, girl. Never doubt your powers."

Alyssa wanted to laugh in his face. She couldn't keep the derision from her voice. "Oh, you mean the power to bring out a green glow to find things hidden in the dark? Or maybe the way I can put my hands on people to know what ails them? That's about all I have, Anfalen. I'm not special! But if you have a purpose for any of *that*, well, let me know."

Ina patted her hand. "You do not give yourself enough credit. With your healing abilities, along with the scarf, and potentially, the spellbook..." She gave her a raised eyebrow that asked more than her words. "It is possible that you are far more powerful than you know."

Alyssa sat like a stone. No one knew where the Grim was. Ina probably thought it was hidden in Draysray just as Eldon had suggested.

"You'll have to show me what power you think I have. I can't believe how any of what you said makes a difference up against trolls, bugbears, and worse." She refused to name the Dark Master.

"I had hoped you would take that view. We can provide some training for you. Tomorrow, if you're ready?" Anfalen asked. One eyebrow tilted as though he wasn't going to take no for an answer.

"You sure take a lot on yourself in supposing," Pappy said in Alyssa's head. *"Watch that one; he's slimy."*

Blowing out an aggrieved breath, Alyssa said, "Anfalen, I'm here under strange circumstances. War is about to break out everywhere, yet my people are unarmed and unprepared. Nobody seems to care about them, either. I came here with the Draysray folks hoping that the Nithereens would join forces with us. For the whole realm, including my own. I ain't rightly sure I have time to learn how to do battle like you want."

"It isn't a matter of what he wants," Ina replied. "It's a matter of what you might be called on to fight and how best to defend against it.

You are young and untried, Alyssa. Salas and Japher are training with you as their knowledge of these enemies is lacking as well."

What do I need to be shown that I haven't already seen? How much harder to catch a rat than to put an arrow into one?

Those questions showed on her face, because Anfalen leaned toward her and said with an expectant edge, "Never fear, Alyssa. I would not test you if I was not certain you would pass the test. Your friends are unafraid. You should be, too."

Alyssa had had enough of the sweet talk. "If I agree to this training, you have to promise to get me in to see my parents. You still haven't told me where they are. I demand to know right this minute!"

"They are not here," Anfalen told her, looking away.

Ina hissed her surprise. "Not here? The entire encampment at Draysray believed you took them!"

He shook his head. "I am sorry. We had them with us for a short while, but then, they escaped."

"So, you don't know where they are?" Alyssa gasped. Her fists doubled into balls as she tried to understand what he was saying.

Anfalen waved a hand for peace and waited a moment before answering. "Yes. We do. But you will have to remember that they left of their own free will at first. They intended to go home to your farm, Alyssa."

Her heart fell and tears sprang to her eyes. "Home?" she whispered and waited for him to continue.

"They were the first casualties in this conflict. In fact, they are in the Dark Master's dungeon right now."

Now Ina gasped. "No!"

"You said they were safe!" Alyssa cried, hot tears falling down her cheeks. "How could you let that happen?"

"I said they were in a protected place. And that is true. They are not exposed to the elements, nor are they being mistreated that we can tell. I have sent scouts to gain information, and they returned to say that for now, they are doing well. Your parents were captured, Alyssa. We tried to get them back, to no avail. The goblins who took them were well armed and traveled fast. They were back in the northern mountains before we could even get halfway there."

Ina closed her eyes, and her shoulders slumped in defeat. "Taken? When were you going to let Eldon know?"

"We have been in communication."

"He never said a word to me."

"Perhaps he was afraid that you would take matters into your own hands."

"I cannot believe he would keep— "

"—you have been away with the wizards, Ina. Perhaps he has been waiting for the best time."

Now anger lined her face. "Anfalen, you took them from Draysray as a bargaining chip. And you thought Eldon would bend to your will and exchange land for them. Everyone knows that. But now, they are stolen. Missing from all of us. Now you will never get your lands back!"

Her words hit the right mark. The high lord of the Nithereens wiped his brow. Her hard words had stricken him into speechlessness.

This was news to Alyssa. She had believed that Draysray belonged to the High Elves, rightfully. Did this mean that the Nithereens were the real owners of the beautiful wood? And her parents had been taken by the Nithereens, as a way to regain those lands? These folk would certainly pay for that by the High Elves. And herself, if she had the ability.

Ina's chin jutted stubbornly, and Alyssa believed that they were of one mind.

Anfalen noted the change in the air, and his archers shifted positions. "Before you judge us too harshly, know that this training will be even more necessary to find and gain release of your parents."

"I doubt that, Anfalen. You can either take me to my parents or have a company go with me to rescue them, and then we can talk about training. That's my bargain. Take it or not." She crossed her arms, defiance sending a thrill though her.

To her great surprise, the leader of the Dark Elves grinned and nodded. "Training is part of taking a company with you, do you see? It will not slow your journey. It will not stop anything. You cannot go to the lair of the Dark Master unprepared. Take the training, and we will go with you to rescue our people from their prison."

This news set Alyssa back on her heels. Ina turned to peer at her as if to ask for the next step. The girl from Mudden grinned at her. There would be another journey.

The next day, Alyssa was tired and moody. She'd spent a long time tossing and turning on the hard wooden bed she'd slept on. The bed was situated on a platform high in a tree where she feared rolling out too far and falling to the ground. Japher and Salas had been given accommodations in a nice burrow, and that made her grumpy, too.

She tried not to judge too harshly, as these people were doing their best to be kind to them. But with the whole training idea hanging over her, she wanted to scream and shout at every face. She wanted to be on the road in search of her parents. She had long ago written them off as dead. Thinking about them now, it seemed unreal.

How could the Elves allow them to be taken by the enemy like branches to a fire? I ought to be marching toward their hiding place right this minute! Why was I led to believe I would be healing folks with illness from dark magik? Balderdash! I'll have a strong word with Edegast when this is all over.

She paced the floor beside the bed, taking care not to misstep. How long had she lounged at the farm in ignorant bliss while her parents were in danger? Why didn't she act upon the urge to find them last year when the phoenix had told her they were alive?

Anfalen's words returned. Her parents had begun to trek home again when they had been taken. *They were coming home to the farm, to me, to the family!*

Her final thought was always: *Why didn't they take me with them when they left?* But now, looking at it overall, she felt different. She was free and available to save them and with help. That might not have been the case had she gone with them from the farm as a much younger child.

The training field, as it was known, was little more than a clearing in a sunny glade. She stood in the clearing and glared up at Solly. Where had he been when they were dying from snow and ice in the mountains? Her heavy coat and boots were far too warm for this day.

Shadow wrapped around her waist like a proper sash, and she tapped one end for comfort. The Grim remained in her pack tucked in the notch of the oak tree where she had slept. She'd done such a clever job of it, she couldn't even tell it was in there. Not that there was any need to protect her belongings today. Every person in the wood was prepping for war.

Soon, three of the Nithereens plus Anfalen, Ina, Salas, and Japher all arrived in the glade.

"Now," Anfalen said mysteriously. "We will train our friends in the Nithereen way."

Armed with staffs, Salas and Japher strode to where Alyssa stood with the bow and arrows Ina had given her. The three Nithereen warriors who had accompanied Anfalen and Ina disappeared into the woods.

"Are we to be ambushed then?" Salas asked, looking confused.

"Nay, brother. You must hunt them," Ina answered.

Japher looked at Alyssa, and she shrugged before nocking an arrow in the bowstring and stepping toward the tree line. "So much for healing magik."

Salas lifted his staff and said, "*Ecangl*!"

The staff sparked and lit. Japher fell back next to Salas. He lifted his own staff and said, "*Alangl*!" and the wooden stick did the same as Salas's had.

The three of them entered the woods, with the men on either side of Alyssa. The girl from Mudden took a few moments to allow her eyes to adjust to the gloom.

She listened closely for sounds of breathing, footfalls, or even whispering. Her hunter skills kicked in, and she became one with the forest.

The trees intertwined, and she doubted an opportunity to get an arrow to fly true. The path forward soon became a tripping hazard, covered with vines.

Alyssa lowered the bow and placed the arrow back in the quiver slung over her shoulder. She could not use them for fighting in these conditions. She took a deep breath and called forth her magik glow.

Shadow shimmered beneath the spell, warmed her waist, encouraging. Unafraid, she took a few steps forward. Here, at least, she could use her magik.

Japher whispered. "How do we know which way to go?"

Alyssa shook her head. "We don't. Be quiet and listen for them."

Then, off to the right, they heard the sound of scurrying in the brush. Alyssa stared in that direction. Nothing appeared.

"Go forth and find," she whispered to the green glow. It lifted over her head and blew outward with green tendrils dripping downward as though it were seeking something.

When it stopped over an area and gathered itself like a storm cloud, Alyssa pulled an arrow out and once again nocked it.

"You have been found," she said, simply.

The green glow covered the ground and one of the Nithereens stood in the light of the spell, grinning at her. "Well done, my lady. Know that this was but one of the trials. The first is detect, the second is disarm, and the last is defend. You may capture me now."

She motioned to the two wizards for one of them to "capture" the elf. Salas took a rope from a hidden pocket in his robes and tied the hands of the elf. Then he took him back to the glade.

"I thought this was training," she said to the elf as he passed her.

"It is a form of training. If you cannot detect, disarm, or defend, there would be no point in your efforts, true?"

She nodded and allowed them to pass.

Alyssa didn't think it was wise to stand there waiting for Salas to return, so she and Japher continued on. Alyssa recalled the green glow and tried to consider what else she would be able to do with the next elf.

Disarm. Hm. Probably won't allow himself to be taken with such a simple spell as I have.

Alyssa took a step forward, and she heard Japher shout in surprise and pain. She whirled around to see that her friend had been captured, and had a long knife against his throat. The Nithereen holding the knife was dressed all in black, and the part of his pale face that was visible looked deadly serious.

Chapter Twenty-Six

"What will you do now, my lady?" the Nithereen asked. "You cannot pierce me at this range with your arrow, and especially with him protecting my vital parts." He pulled Japher even tighter against him, and the wizard grunted at the action.

"Glow, come forth." Alyssa didn't recognize her own voice, so smooth and forceful it sounded.

The elf laughed. "A glow spell cannot harm me."

"True. But a spell can be twisted and turned into the will of its maker."

The Nithereen's eyebrows lifted.

Alyssa blew on her palms holding the green glow. "Burn," she whispered.

The green changed to orange, and the glow began to smoke. She bounced the flaming orb up a moment and allowed it to return to the few inches above her palm. It felt hot, but it wasn't injuring her. This magik had been most helpful when making fire at night beside the barn. "Do you want me to send it at your face now? I think you'll drop that knife pretty quick if your face is burning."

The elf allowed his hand to fall, and the knife was no longer at the throat of her friend. "You may capture me now," he said.

Japher pulled rope from his robes as Salas had done and tied the elf's hands. He pushed him in the back to get him to move.

"Alyssa," Japher said as he came alongside. "I do not like to leave you alone here."

She shook her head. "There's only one more test, Japher. Don't fret none. I'll be grand." To the elf she said, "Detecting your friend was easy; disarming with my brains instead of my brawn was pretty easy, too. I guess the next trial will truly test my mettle?"

The eyes beneath the black mask crinkled at the edges. "Yes. I believe you will fail the next one."

As she listened to their retreating footsteps, she tried to steel herself for the next trial. What had she been told? *Defend*. Defend what? Herself? She'd been told many times that the scarf would defend whoever was wearing it.

She reached down and loosened Shadow around her waist and softly said, "You may have to do the defending, my friend."

The scarf rose and rewrapped itself around her head like a turban. She laughed at the silliness and took a few steps forward, listening to the deathly silence of the forest.

Not even birds twittered. She kept taking small steps forward, senses on alert for any sign of the third Nithereen.

She gazed overhead but saw nothing. When she had walked forward a few yards, she stopped. Something was wrong. Why hadn't the elf made his presence known?

She heard rustling to her left and spun to face it. There was a bulbous monster coming toward her, and he had an inert elf slung over his shoulder.

"Defend, my foot!" she shouted. "What manner of evilment is this?"

The ugly gray face of the creature, a massive goblin, split into the most devilish grin she'd ever seen. He had long tusks for lower teeth, and she was certain he would use them to rend flesh if given the opportunity.

The way the creature stared at her with saliva dripping from its mouth... This was not planned. Was the elf injured? Dead? She could only hope he was unconscious and having a deep sleep. That, she could cure.

The monster paused to see what she would do.

Well, she thought, I'm supposed to defend. I reckon I'm defending that defenseless elf.

She pulled an arrow from her quiver and nocked it, then let it fly, aiming right for the forehead of the monster.

But it was no dim-witted creature. It caught the arrow in mid-air and broke it in two. It grinned again and advanced, shaking the elf's leg as if to say, "I got him. I'll get you too!"

"You only think you'll get me," she hissed between her teeth. "Scarf, protect."

Shadow unfurled itself and formed into an arrow, its frayed edge honed and dangerous.

When Shadow launched, it made no noise.

The creature, shocked to see the scarf coming straight at his face, dropped the unconscious elf and threw his arm up to fend off the follygrass arrow.

Shadow's slivers of frayed edge pierced the monster's forearm, and it released such a scream that Alyssa was certain the others would come running.

The more the goblin yanked at the scarf, the tighter it wrapped, needles of follygrass spiking into every finger on each hand.

The tusked creature took off running back the way it had come, arms in front of it, screaming the whole time. A host of elves appeared to stop its escape. And stop it, they did, with arrows flying.

Alyssa darted behind a wide trunk to avoid being hit. Shadow came floating along, barely visible, unafraid of the pinging of arrows all around. It rewrapped around her waist and looked like a normal sash to anyone looking.

"Well done, friend." She patted it proudly, and watched as the elves roped the monster and took it away. She ran to where the fallen elf lay.

She held her hands over him and discovered his head had been struck with something. He was bleeding a little from the wound, but the danger was internal.

When Salas and Japher came hurrying back to her, she told them, "His head is hurt. It's bad. We've got to get him to a place where he can be looked at by Iefyr healers."

They glanced at one another and then at Anfalen, who rapidly approached.

"What is his injury?" the elven leader asked as he arrived at her side, concern lining his brow. "Can you heal him?"

Alyssa stood. "No, I can't. His injuries are beyond my abilities. He needs an Iefyr healer. Is there one in your encampment?"

He frowned. "No. We don't have them here."

"Who does the healing for you when someone gets hurt?" she asked, shocked.

"We have ways and means to get healed."

"Well, please do tell me! This man might die in a few minutes if he isn't healed. His brain is swelling inside his head like an overripe melon. Are you hearing me?"

Anfalen bit his lip. Indecision clouded his face. To an elven warrior standing nearby, he said, "*Bris fris wis*. Hurry, come with a flat frame of wood to carry him on, and let's get to Draysray as soon as possible."

The black-dressed elf wanted to argue, but Anfalen cut him off. "*Nagis*! It will be his funeral bier if you linger any longer!"

The warrior ran back toward the Nithereens' camp, and Alyssa placed her hands on the injured elf's head. Shadow draped its ends over her hands. She focused sending all her healing energy into the injury. A strange golden light emitted from her hands.

Ina strode up then and gasped at the work being done.

"What happened?" she whispered to Anfalen.

"Alyssa was to do the final trial, but a goblin found Bale first. She succeeded in defending. Or rather, our men say the Scarf of Egladris did," Anfalen told her.

Alyssa sat back and allowed the spell to fade. She stood and brushed herself off. "Your man here, Bale... I don't know how he was injured, but that goblin was looking for a fight. Bale tried his best to give him one."

"Yes, he is a good man," Anfalen said. "You have encountered the real enemy on this day, Alyssa. Let us go."

Alyssa didn't like the thought of leaving the injured elf in such a vulnerable state, but others had joined the area, and she knew he was not alone.

She and the others followed Anfalen's rapid footfalls back to the encampment. The frame, carried by four elves, passed them heading back for the injured man.

When they arrived at Anfalen's home, Alyssa retrieved her pack from the oak, checked for the Grim, and went to find food. She took a steaming mug of tea and some meat and cheese from the table in preparation to leave the Nithereens' woods and return to Draysray.

"It would be advisable to stay here," Anfalen told her as he watched her rearranging her pack underneath the trees.

"Why?" She turned to face him and felt a sinking in her stomach. "Don't you want me to go with him, defend him, help heal him? Isn't that what the trial was about? Defending? It wasn't dark magik that did that to him, Anfalen. I was sent to protect and serve at the will of King Eldon, and I will. Unless you have elven ones who are sick with the dark magik I was told about, I'm leaving."

Anfalen twisted a ring on his left hand. "That was a half-truth. You are something of an enigma. Eldon did not know how you would respond to coming here. It was necessary learn the whereabouts of the enemy. The injury to Bale was not planned. I will always be indebted to you for protecting one of our own."

She scratched her cheek. "Not the first half-truth I've heard on this journey, not likely to be the last. Why'd you even want to set up the trials? What a waste it all was."

"Perhaps, but some girls would run into the woods screaming at the sight of someone being held against their will. We had to see—"

She cut him off. "I don't think so, Anfalen. And who are you to test me on how to detect, disarm, or defend? I believe that I showed you what was what today. I ain't running away, I ain't getting sick, and I won't scream or faint either."

"Truly, you did all that was asked for. But the attack so close to home by a goblin... well, that was more than any of us could have expected. These attacks are the pangs of pain that we have heard about from others. Until now, not seen here in our woods."

She tossed a water bladder into the pack and turned on the elven leader. "Exactly. You've suggested that you plan to fight with the High Elves against the Dark Master. Is that true?"

He paced a few feet before giving her his full attention. "Indeed, we have been estranged from our brothers in Draysray for too long. The land issue between us is no longer valid if all the realm is taken by the enemy. Today proves how much we should be united."

"Then pack your bags, Anfalen," she replied, hefting her pack onto her shoulders. "We leave soon for Draysray."

The Grim bounced in Alyssa's pack from the heavy stride she made. The scarf was inside wrapped around the book. The two had become partners in whatever this journey held. And like inseparable twins, they did well tightly together. She found her bow and arrows, added them to her heavy load, and went in search of Ina.

The elven princess stood outside the encampment, guarding. Alyssa strode up to her and stood beside her without saying anything. When the elf who had once been portrayed as a sorceress spoke, it was to the trees.

"*Anduii, fitge me.*" She stared up into the branches.

"What does that mean?" Alyssa asked softly.

"I am asking for forgiveness. I will not return until the bloodshed is at an end. My second home is in the woods. They are like a hallowed hall to me. I fear I may never see them again."

"I'll be with you, Ina. I won't come back here until it's over either. Alive or dead," Alyssa said, breathlessly. "You won't be alone."

The tall elf looked down at the girl from Mudden and smiled. "We are truly kindred, are we not?"

Alyssa grinned and nodded. When Salas and Japher shuffled up, they were carrying their staffs and leading the frame bearers who carried Bale. The injured elf lay still and pale on the frame, and Alyssa put a hand on his forehead. He was still alive, fortunately. His pulse was thready, and she knew time was not on his side. She nodded at the ones who were carrying him, and the party took off into the woods.

Anfalen, dressed in breeches and a tunic, followed in the rear of the company, hosted by a group of warriors to protect him. He had a long bow made of wood, and his quiver of arrows had deadly silver tips.

Alyssa hoped to ask him where they came from. She would bet coins they had been made by the Haldor.

The High Elves sure will be excited to see this group, Alyssa thought. Wonder how they will be received?

The trip was as treacherous on the return as it had been before. The only feeling of courage they could draw was knowing there was safety in numbers. And also, courage came from knowing the one leading them was the tall elven shield maiden who seemed to fear nothing.

Alyssa stayed on high alert the entire trip. She could have sworn she heard wolves howling in the distance, but she was certain they didn't live this far north.

Finally, convinced it was wolves barking, she asked Ina about the sounds.

"Not wolves, not this far north," Ina told her. "The Goblin-Master has bred packs with other animals and created a wolf-type that is both horrifying to see and turns the blood into ice to hear."

Alyssa scrunched up her nose. "Oh, ugh, that doesn't sound good. Are we in danger?"

"Yes," Ina said, before falling silent and trudging ahead. Alyssa thought she heard the elf mutter, "All the time, every moment."

After those quick words, Alyssa made sure to note from which direction the wolves' howling came. She would not be dinner for some hungry wolf-bear or wolf-badger.

They didn't stop that night for more than a quick rest in the clearing they had seen before. On first watch, Alyssa looked around for any trouble that might present itself. Nothing appeared.

After a rest and food and drink, the group plunged forward into the woods that would lead them to Eldon's people and healers.

As they picked their path through the thick underbrush, Alyssa tried to understand what the entire journey had wrought. Ina had found out something about the Nithereens, and Alyssa had found out something about her parents. That was all. The Grim still remained with her, for good or for bad.

How would she convince Eldon or Edegast to allow her to go find her parents? Yet, how could they stop her? She thought of all the ways Edegast would try to convince her to wait for the spring thaw. Eldon might consider the realm's need of her skills and decide in favor of that.

If her parents were being held prisoners by the same enemy that was trying to overtake the entire realm of Daegries, then she needed to be a part of the group going to fight him.

She had to find them and release them, if it wasn't already too late. The world's survival might rely on it. Also, Shadow and the Grim were key players in the rebellion which was fast forming. The scarf had properties she didn't even know about, and the Grim held all the answers that Hektor the Pale sought. She would find some way to use the book to overthrow that old Dark Master.

Nightfall arrived once they trudged up to Eldon's home. Lights were brought out and illuminated the way for the frame bearers to take Bale to the healers.

All King Eldon said to Anfalen was, "'Tis about time you came home. We will discuss more soon." Then he followed the others to make sure the healers were informed.

Ina and Anfalen went up into the tree where Eldon lived and made themselves at home. Alyssa went back to the cabin where she and the wizards had been before. It was deserted for a little while. She pulled everything out of her pack and allowed Shadow to float around to stretch out.

The scarf had not even been given any attention after the attack on the goblin, so Alyssa made a fuss over it. She truly was grateful for all that it had done on her behalf.

"I wish you were at home in Mudden, protecting Pappy and Granny," she said, wistfully. "But of course, they would likely refuse to let you even attempt to do that. They're so stinking proud."

Shadow undulated and landed across the bed as if exhaustion had claimed it. She followed suit, holding the Grim tightly to her as if it were a favored toy. It was quite some time that the threesome rested until the wizards, Salas and Japher, came into the cabin. Shadow flattened out over the book, turning itself invisible, hiding the Grim.

"You must come to the healer's abode. They have need of your skills," Japher said, as he gently shook Alyssa, believing her to be asleep.

Alyssa sat up and took a few deep breaths. Assured she was awake, the two wizards left the cabin to allow her to gather herself. She tucked the Grim into the pack and ordered Shadow to protect it. She very likely had nothing to worry about, as Salas had tried to take the book from Shadow before, and the result was not positive. He likely wouldn't try again.

As she strode down the stone-lined path toward the healers' hut, she muttered, "Hope they have food and drink there. This might be a long night."

Chapter Twenty-Seven

When she arrived, Alyssa was ushered to the bedside of the injured elf. She used her glow spell to illuminate the hushed abode and added light over the hands of those trying to save Bale's life.

She felt like a glorified torch.

The healers muttered strange words over the patient in their elven tongue and soon a flush showed on his cheeks. Alyssa's heart leaped inside her chest as Bale thrashed and twisted and moaned. A fine sheen of sweat covered his brow as he fought the injurious swelling.

When he finally quieted, all the healers, including Alyssa, took a deep breath of relief.

"The danger has passed," one of them said, motioning for Alyssa to extinguish her glow. Torches were placed around the bed, allowing the brightness of her spell's light to be replaced with their golden flames, softer and calmer.

"It will be a matter of his own body recovering now," the oldest healer said, nodding to the others.

"Alyssa, thank you," one said. "It was your quick thinking that saved him today. We are all grateful for your fast action and healing efforts that began the recovery before he ever arrived."

Her face grew warm. She had begun to take her abilities for granted, but truly this time it had been a boon for someone.

"I'll go now," she told them. "Please send word if you need me, though."

They all nodded, placing their hands together and bowing slightly.

Alyssa thought to herself, I feel special. I hope he makes it. What a terrible thing to happen. Everything works out like it's supposed to, I reckon.

The trials had been more like games to show her prowess to the warriors and ended up being a life-and-death situation that showed she had skills. Fortunately, she had been there when the goblin targeted the Nithereens.

"More to come," she muttered as she strode down the path toward her cabin. When she passed Eldon's platform, she saw bright twinkling lights around it. Maybe the elves were having a meeting. She hoped she wasn't on the menu. She wanted nothing more than go to bed and sleep. Using her glow spell took a lot of strength to sustain for a long period of time, but to do it twice in a day, with traveling a great distance through mountains and forests, was utterly exhausting.

As soon as she made sure that Shadow and the Grim were together and safe, she threw herself on the bed and fell fast asleep. She didn't know how long she'd been asleep when someone gently tugged on her arm.

She opened her eyes to the blackness and a form standing over her. A hand clamped down on her mouth to silence her. Terror filled her. But it was only Ina.

"Don't speak, only follow me," the elf's voice whispered near her ear. Alyssa was not usually one for the mysterious, but something in Ina's voice made the girl bolt upright and clutch her coverlet.

Ina moved away from the bed, and Alyssa slid to her feet to follow. Fortunately, she had not even undressed, and she crept out of the cabin behind Ina.

They didn't speak until they were in the woods away from the populace.

"I have been with the council of Eldon and Anfalen. They intend to make a surprise attack on the Dark Master in his mountain. Get him before his armies can get us. I thought you would want to know."

Alyssa rubbed sleep from her eyes. "Yes, thank you. When is this supposed to happen?"

"During the round face of Luna."

Alyssa leaned out to look up at the cloudy sky. The moon was not even visible. "When is the moon full?" she asked.

"We have almost an entire cycle to travel in," Ina said.

A whole two weeks, Alyssa mused. That wasn't much time, but she knew the elves could move quickly when they needed to.

"Does Eldon know I intend on going along? I ain't missing a chance to find my folks."

Ina nodded. "Yes, the leaders both discussed the likelihood."

"Nothing will stop me," Alyssa said with conviction.

Ina paced a moment before turning her attention to Alyssa. "They will leave on the morrow. Are you certain you are prepared? You have not been shown the slightest bit of swordplay. There will be little space under the mountains for bow and arrow."

Alyssa nodded. She'd been thinking about that ever since the trials. "You're right, Ina. Too right. It's not too easy to parry another's attack and slice back, is it?"

Ina grunted. "No, and longswords are heavy. You are a weakling when it comes to wielding one."

Alyssa wanted to argue but the elf wasn't wrong in what she said. "So, what do I do?"

Ina came close whispered in her ear. "We are going to find a sword that fits you. Well, I use the term loosely. A regular sword is not what you need. More of a short sword, I am thinking. Even a long-handled dagger would be better suited."

"Now?"

The elf nodded and Alyssa could make out her grin in the shadows. "Where?"

"The house of the Haldor. They will do it for you. They are masters at metal."

Alyssa didn't like that idea at all. First, it was a journey off the planned route to fight the goblins and Hektor. Secondly, it would mean Alyssa had to go alone.

"I ain't sure about this," she told Ina. "I don't even know how to find that old dwarven mountain to begin with, and even if I did, I might never be able to make it in time. It ain't like Draysray is right next door to it."

Again, Ina's face drew close. She whispered, "Birds of prey are nearby. I have acquired two for us."

Ina was going with her on Bops? "This sounds like a disaster in the making," she told the elf. "But I don't think I have much choice."

Alyssa went inside, redressed, and secured her pack. Shadow and the Grim were safely hidden away. When she exited the cabin, Ina took off toward the deepest part of the woods. Alyssa jogged to keep up with her long legs, questions bubbling up on her lips.

"Will we make it back in time to go with the group to fight the Dark Master?" she said, panting slightly.

Ina never slowed but only said over her shoulder. "Surely these creatures will understand our need for speed."

The elf's assumption made Alyssa's heart drop into her shoes. There was little the Bops understood, aside from feeding them fat calves.

They maneuvered through the trees and up and down hills until Alyssa was thoroughly lost.

"Ina, do you know where we are?" she asked, finally. "Are we lost?"

Ina stopped abruptly, holding up her hand for silence. *Screeek!*

Hearing the screeching Bops, Alyssa felt as though her blood had turned to ice.

Screeek!

Ina took off at a run, pulling an arrow and nocking it to her bow as she went. Alyssa wasn't armed with anything but the spells she carried in her body.

They stumbled into a clearing where the giant birds flapped their wings and pecked at a goblin attempting to whirl ropes around their necks.

Ina let arrows fly; some hit the tough olive-colored hide of the creature and bounced off. This sent it fleeing into the forest. The birds continued crying and flapping their wings even after the danger had passed.

Ina and Alyssa went to them using soothing voices and stroking to calm them. Ina spoke soft Elvish, and Alyssa spoke in the same voice that she used on her horse back home.

"Come now," she said in her gentle singsong. "It's all right, now. All's right in the world."

The fright the noble birds had encountered made Alyssa want to rush into the woods after the goblin. But she alone could do nothing, and they would likely injure or kill her.

"Don't we need to tell someone that a goblin is in these woods?" Alyssa asked.

Ina shook her head, patting the bird before her. "No, we haven't the time. Scouts will be coming this way. Hurry now."

The birds responded to her cooing and crooning, and soon they were ready to take on their passengers. Alyssa was uncertain even how to get on top of her bird at first, but Ina, always her guide, helped her before jumping on top of her own mount. It wasn't the first time Alyssa noticed the elves' powerful ability to leap and jump high off the ground. Ina was as lithe as a cat.

In a short while, they were flying over the forest into the dark night. Alyssa could not see anything definitively below her and held onto the bird's long feathers with her eyes closed.

It was during this flight time that Alyssa realized Ina had never answered her question about their location in the woods, and now there was no way to ask it again with the chilled air blowing at them. She could only hope Ina would know how to get them back again.

The air only got colder as they approached the mountains. Alyssa had on a cloak over her tunic and breeches, but it was not thick enough.

Her body trembled and her teeth chattered from the steep drop in temperature. Through watering eyes, she saw the terrain growing ever nearer. She could not tell if this was the Haldor home or not. Towering mountains appeared below, most of them in shadow and only the snowy peaks showed in the gloom.

She held on tight as the Bop made its descent. The wings flapped mightily and then folded back as the bird jogged a little way before coming to a complete stop.

Ina's bird did likewise, and they both squatted for their riders to depart. The elf spoke to the birds and patted them gently. Alyssa patted her bird, too, and wished him well in the only manner she could. He seemed to understand as he bobbed his head. Ina handed her a piece of dried meat and Alyssa fed the bird, taking care to keep her fingers out of the way.

Shortly, the elf waved for Alyssa to follow her. Alyssa's heart thrummed in her chest as they located the doorway into the mountain. The same door that Alyssa had exited through last year, she noted, while looking out over the mountains. She squinted and thought she could make out the valley and lake beyond.

Wonder if that old dragon ever got himself out of the den he's made. Wonder if the Haldor ever did anything about him at all.

She stood close behind Ina, who didn't even knock, only lifted her hand and said, "*Eldre, Aldre, highstone.*"

The door made loud rubbing noises as it moved. Just inside there were torches in iron sconces hung on a rock wall. Something the mountain had provided plenty of, Alyssa thought. *There will never be a shortage of rock.*

They strode down the passageway, cut directly into the mountain and followed it as it led down. Alyssa remembered the Haldor had led her to the door, but she had forgotten the way to get there. Her mind had been full of finding the phoenix.

"How do you know how to get into the halls of the Haldor?" Alyssa asked as the thought struck.

Ina smiled. "The Elven and the Dwarven nation were close at one time. I still have friends."

Alyssa marveled at this. Ina seemed more knowledgeable than even Edegast. She certainly got around, Alyssa thought to herself. She wondered how old Ina was. She seemed far older than she looked.

They made a few turns and found themselves in a great hall where burning candles dripped wax tendrils all the way to the ground. A broad man with an equally long beard looked up from a map on the table where he stood with two others.

"Well, blow me to Draysray, look who came to dinner!" he exclaimed, before heading toward them. He wore a pair of coveralls and heavy boots.

Ina grinned, and they clasped hands, staring at one another in wonder for a moment before the woman ducked down and hugged the man. She picked him up and tried to twirl him, but his girth prevented it.

The two friends laughed until tears of mirth filled their eyes.

"It has been too long, Bobleque," Ina said at last.

The other two Haldor men gaped at them. They didn't know her any more than Alyssa knew them.

"Time to get acquainted," Bobleque said, beckoning them to come to the table. "Bring drink!"

Soon, tankards of beer were brought to the guests. Alyssa declined, preferring to have her wits about her. The Haldor realized their mistake and brought her a steaming cup of tea. It was black and strong, but Alyssa added a splash of milk, and it was fine.

"Troubled times," Bobleque said to Ina after all of the names had been exchanged and salutations given.

The two Haldor men, one of whom had accompanied Alyssa to the phoenix's fountain last year, were introduced to her.

"Fain," the broad-chested, red-haired dwarf said pointing to himself. "And that's my brother Gain," he said motioning to the other man, nearly identical to him. "I remember you, my lady."

She smiled. "Thank you for that, Fain. I remember you both very kindly."

"What brings you under mountain?" he asked. "Dangers everywhere." He frowned into his tankard.

"That's for certain," Alyssa agreed.

Ina spoke up. "We have a request to ask. We have no time for reunions, unfortunately. A party of us will be leaving from Draysray at first light to go to the mountains around Needlemount Castle."

Her friend, Bobleque, pulled on his full black beard. "What sort of request? And I'll have to ask what you're doin', goin' to the teeth of this monster who sends out goblins into every corner of the Daegries. You've no doubt heard we've been victims of the Dark Master's army."

Ina sniffed a little and pulled on a sad face. "I have heard, and it is sorry I am for this. We plan to go to the teeth of the Dark Master's realm in order to take the fight to him. We cannot sit still while he overruns everything. You are correct about the goblins though. We encountered one accosting the Bops who waited to bring us here."

"Dark times, I'd say," he replied, and then before thinking asked, "What manner of creature would attack those feathered monsters?"

"Bold ones, and getting bolder," Ina told him.

"Are you here to request we join you?" Bobleque asked, his sable eyes peering at her closely. "Elves and Dwarves are not known to be easy bedfellows."

"Not because of lack of love for drink and song, however," Fain added, lifting his tankard.

Ina took a pull from her mug and set it down with a thump. "No sir. Not as of yet. A contingent may be coming here soon, to help your people. But you seem to be doing fine for now. I saw no security on the way here or nearby."

"It's only a farce, friend. How could we be doing fine with goblins on our doorstep and a dragon still breathing close by? What do the Elders have planned?" He wore a frown and clicked his tongue in dismay.

That answers that, Alyssa thought. "We're going to help you. But first, we need to know what the Dark Master is up to. And we have to try to stop him first," Alyssa said, soothingly like she spoke to the Bop. "If we can. If we don't die by the sword in the process."

"What on Daegries is Eldon thinking, sending women?" the Dwarf asked, sizing Alyssa up.

"I've got more about me than meets the eye," Alyssa answered, pulling herself up taller and trying to sound mysterious.

Fain said, "Truth, Bob. This little lady has been through the dragon's lair."

Bobleque gave her a nod of approval. "Not for me to dip into the Elven plans. I'm sure they wouldn't have you going if you weren't a scrapper."

Ina grinned and clinked mugs with Bobelque. "Indeed, she is. As am I. Do not forget, I am a warrior too."

"Oh, I haven't forgotten, Princess. But no one seems to know what the Dark Master is up to. They don't know how to plan defense when they don't even have a glimmer of the offense."

"You will know when the time is nigh. But first, we need something from the Haldor." Ina waited a beat before adding, "A short sword, or a long dagger made for a small- statured person, with protective markings on it."

Bobleque tilted his head and stared at her, before turning his attention to Alyssa. "Think that's doable." He tapped his tankard with two fingers as if trying to decide. "I s'pose we'll have to leave it to the king. Vernon will know what to do."

Ina fell silent and looked lost in her thoughts. Alyssa didn't say anything, but she felt pretty happy inside. She'd met Vernon the last time she'd been to Haldor Hall. He had taken a liking to her back then. Maybe he would feel the same way now.

"Can we go to him now?" Alyssa asked, finally. "We don't have much time, to be honest."

Bobleque issued a heavy sigh, motioned to Gain and Fain, and they led the way to the king's quarters. Alyssa didn't remember any of the passageways and had to admit that she could never find it on her own.

When they stood outside a heavy wooden door built into the rock, she felt her nerves twang. Something felt wrong about bothering the king for such a silly thing as a sword. Would he march them right back out again?

The king's steward answered the door, tiny spectacles at the end of his nose, and an attitude full of importance. Alyssa thought he looked like a short, stout school master.

"Yes?" he asked.

Bobleque hemmed a moment before saying, "We have need of an audience with the king."

"Not all of you surely?" the steward asked. His countenance never changed.

Alyssa pushed forward. "No sir. Just me and my friend," she said, motioning for Ina to come along.

They were admitted and the others left out in the passageway. Alyssa thought she heard the heavy trudge of boots leaving the area. She noticed Ina frowning at the way her friends were being treated, but she said nothing.

King Vernon sat on a cushioned, velvet chair near a wooden bed with a matching dresser and a chaise lounge. He yawned loudly and wiped at his nose, sleepily.

When he finally focused on them, he sat up straight. "You! You, girl! I know you."

She bowed to him. "Yes sir. I'm back."

"We never found Karnagal, the dragon. He still lives and breathes fire somewhere in these mountains. Are you here to lead a party to him?"

This took Alyssa back a step. She hated to put her unpopular thoughts first, but he had asked. "No. No sir. Why haven't you found him? I certainly didn't have any trouble. He's in your old throne room, or at least he was."

The king shook his head. "There was another cave-in and apparently your way in has been closed. We have another one, the same one where he landed through the ceiling of the cave, but it's not a safe drop for us to try. Perhaps you could be persuaded to do it?"

She shook her head. "No sir. I'm here on other business. Elf business."

Then he seemed to collect himself and looked at Ina. "I see."

"I'm here to ask another favor, King Vernon," Alyssa said, softly.

His thick eyebrows clashed together over his nose. "What this time?"

Ina stepped up at that question and answered. "Sire, we would like to acquire for Alyssa a short sword or a long dagger, which is protected with spell words for battle. The Haldor have always done the best with smithing and magiking swords."

"I'd take that as a compliment, Sire," the steward, who had stepped closer said. He smoothed out a dressing gown of silver threads and silk.

King Vernon sighed heavily and ran his bejeweled fingers through thick hair. "Very well, so it shall be done."

Ina gave Alyssa a smarmy grin and bowed to the king. The steward laid the sleepwear aside and led toward the door.

Alyssa turned to the king for a final word. "Sire, I will give the dragon problem my attention at my first opportunity."

She followed the steward out. He looked both ways down the hall and saw none of the men who had accompanied them.

"I will return soon, Sire," he said as he closed the door to the royal bedroom. "Follow me," he told them.

They followed him in the opposite direction from which they had come and, as had been her norm lately, Alyssa was horribly lost in no time.

Ina seemed to be able to follow the direction and didn't stumble in the dark. Alyssa was beginning to think that elves had superior night vision. At least, Ina did.

When they arrived at a heavy door with iron hinges, the steward used a key from a chain he carried and opened it. The staircase within led down to the fiery pits of the Haldor.

This is where I came to before, Alyssa thought. Only her approach had been on a lower level. She saw again the ore being turned into objects as the hefty men carried great pots of it to and from.

"Go down there and tell them what you want. Tell them that King Vernon approved this. Tell them that Simon sent you. That's me, and they are unlikely to go against it."

Ina nodded, and together she and Alyssa began to descend the stair. When she could, Alyssa looked around trying to find her entrance point from the first time she'd been there. Things looked a bit different as there were piles and piles of swords, shields, and armor stacked everywhere.

"Looks like they are preparing for war," Ina observed.

Alyssa didn't answer, but she agreed heartily. She hoped it was against the Dark Master and not the dragon. At least against the Dark Master they had a chance to win. With Karnagal, she wasn't so sure.

Once on the ground, Ina strode to the nearest dwarf and tapped him on the shoulder. The noise was great, and she had to shout.

He soon understood what she needed and waved for them to follow him. He led them to a pile of swords. It didn't take long for him to find one suitable for Alyssa. It was thin and light, and even she had to admit it was easy to handle. He placed it in an oiled scabbard and she slid the whole unit over her shoulder and down her back. It wouldn't be any harder to carry than the bow and arrows.

Ina grinned at him, took his hand, and shook it in thanks. Then she waved for him to wait, removed the scabbard and short sword and looked it over in the light of the massive flames of the brick ovens.

"Protective words!" Ina shouted.

"They're there," the man shouted back.

"Show me!" She handed the sword to him, and he pushed past a man who was bent over a forge. He beckoned them to come closer, and they did.

The heat felt like a dragon's fire to Alyssa.

The blaze lit up the silver of the blade and, in the fiery text, mystical words in an old tongue appeared.

"What does it say?" Alyssa shouted to him. He shrugged, took the blade out of the fire, plunged it into a bucket of water, and grabbed a massive piece of cloth to wipe it on. Once it had cooled, he gave it to Ina, and she returned it to the scabbard.

"Get the elves to decipher it. It's their language," the man said in Alyssa's ear before returning to his fire.

Chapter Twenty-Eight

Alyssa didn't remember anything about the trip back to Draysray except that it had been freezing, and she had been tired. The sleep she'd managed, before being roughly wakened at sunrise, was disjointed and unrestful.

After being led to the main tree in the center of the forest, she was given a wooden charger laden with fruits, cheese, and bread on it. She found mugs of water every so often on the table and chose one, before plopping down on the damp ground as others had done.

This would be a long and arduous journey fraught with dangers, and her nerves twanged at every sound in the woods around her. Ina was nowhere to be seen, but she did see one of the healers from Bale's room.

She waved him over. "Sir, how is the patient? You may be the only one who will bother to tell me."

He stared at her a moment until recognition took over, and he strolled to stand a few feet closer to her. "Ah, my lady. Bale is doing much better. He still has not opened his eyes, but you can rest in knowing that this will happen in its own time."

"So, the danger is mostly passed?"

He nodded and, without anything more to say, waved goodbye to her and wandered off. Once the business of getting rid of the Dark Master was over, she would like to spend time in Draysray learning from the Iefyr. They were mighty at what they did. She even dreamed of bringing Granny here. She wasn't sure who would be showing who how to heal, though.

A wave of homesickness spread through her, closing her throat and making tears spring to her eyes.

She wiped at the tears, rose from the ground, and brushed at the dirt on her backside. Her pack scraped heavily against her back, and the sword and quiver on either side of it made her feel weighed down.

Shadow had gone inside the pack to protect the Grim without any sort of fight. She missed their times together, but it would do no good for anyone if the scarf or the book were to be in danger.

When Ina appeared, outfitted in elven clothes, she looked like a part of the woods, all greens and browns. Her face and head were covered also with a wrap that hid everything but her eyes. Alyssa felt relief to see her.

When had the elven woman become so important to her? She couldn't say, but that was how she felt, and no doubt about it. Ina had protected her and, indeed, saved her to the point where Alyssa feared being without her.

Japher, Salas, Anfalen, and Eldon soon appeared at the edge of the wood. They all wore robes of varying lengths and colors, and they banded together as a company unto themselves.

Bred and her son (who Alyssa had learned was called Peddy), Nog the Dwarf, and many of the other healers stepped into the clearing as well. Alyssa tried to decide who was coming along and who was staying at Draysray.

Japher and Salas wore the same traveling clothes they had worn before, so they were geared up and ready to go. Anfalen and Eldon, fully adorned with crowns, looked much too regal to be traveling through woods and mountain snows, so she assessed they would likely be staying.

Peddy clung to his mother, and Bred kept a hand on his shoulder, comforting him. They spoke in soft rumbling voices of Yeti-speak, and Alyssa watched mother and son with a feeling of trepidation.

She's going off and leaving her boy? Alyssa shook her head at the thought. The child would be terrified after losing so much of his family in the mountains. He would be truly alone without her. But there were elven children for him to play with, if they would forget his size and language issues.

Nog was heavily armed with a two-handed sword in a sheath across his shoulder and tucked in beneath his pack. He was definitely going out to slay things.

Several Nithereen warriors, some Iefyr archers, who Alyssa hoped knew healing arts, and she and Ina. That was all who were going? A pittance against such a force as the Dark Master had. She drew a long breath. They had what they had. It would have to be enough. Smaller numbers might be safer and stealthier, she thought.

Her focus was on finding her parents. Nothing would keep her or stay her hand from that. Not even a half-dead creature, probably was once a Haldor, who roamed in her worst dreams at night.

But the girl from Mudden had begun to dread the words she'd spoken about getting back all those stolen from the realm. *"We're going to fight them. Every man or elf of us against every ugly troll and goblin of them."*

Once they lined up for a final inspection and pep talk from the kings of the elves, the company trudged forward into the heart of Draysray, headed to treacherous mountains filled with the Dark Master's followers.

In the talk, she learned that Salas and Japher would only accompany them as far as the edge of Draysray. They would take an Iefyr healer with them to relieve Feagus at Knowledge Hall, and they would fight their way through the elements back to the land of wizards.

Alyssa hated to hear this. Not only because the weather was still dreadful in the mountains, but she was certain she would need them and their magik. The wizards could cover her mistakes if she called upon magik that required tools. Their staffs could hold off a lot of wickedness.

She had nothing but Shadow, really. The Grim bore so much old-world vocabulary, she would not be able to decipher it quickly. And she could only hope she would not have to use the weapons she carried, as she truly was inept.

At least I still have magik.

Bred would accompany them up to the mountains, and then she and Nog would take off to see what could be done about her kinfolk. Peddy was already bawling at being left behind. If they found the missing Yetis, they would then go to help the Haldor fight the goblins trying to overtake their homes.

Yetis and Haldors fighting together sounded like a formidable force to Alyssa, and she smiled at the thought. She hated to lose such powerful folks to another cause, but stealth would be necessary to thwart the Dark Master's armed fighters. And stealth was something the Yetis were not known for.

After that, Ina, Alyssa, the Iefyr archers, and the Nithereen warriors were all that was left to go into the mountains around Needlemount and roust out the goblins and evil ones.

She closed her eyes and muttered a few words to the gods and goddesses of wars and warring factions. She hoped for success in all the battles that lay ahead.

When they moved through the trees, a quiet as deep as the heart of the woods descended. Alyssa felt a thrill go through her. Whether from terror or simply the unexpected, she would never know. Shadows darkened the heavy woods, and they all strained to see, hear, or smell anything that might be danger.

It was in that quiet interim that Alyssa heard Pappy's voice as clear as a bell ringing for dinner.

"Lys, you gotta get this done and get back here to the farm. Them old portal plants are growing again, and well, I ain't too sure they will allow any cutting or burning this time."

She desperately wanted to reply. It was simply a voice in her head. It wasn't real, but the thought of the old folks needing her brought fresh tears to her eyes, and she choked on the sadness that rushed through her. She looked down at her feet moving through the brush and refused to look anywhere else.

Is it truly you, Pappy? Or am I losing my right mind due to all the troubles ahead of me? If Pappy was concentrating on her coming home, then did that mean he wasn't in some jail in Mudden? If it was his voice, that was surely good news. She didn't know the real answer, but it comforted her to know that Pappy wasn't sending her messages about the terrible mess he and Granny were in.

She sent an answering thought that when she returned, she'd have her mother and father with her, and gods help those portal plants then.

When the company broke ranks to camp for the night, watches were set for every three hours. Alyssa, too keyed up to sleep, agreed to be in the first group.

She, Salas, Japher, and Ina sat together on the cold ground before a small fire talking in low voices about the road ahead. Salas and Japher were facing the worst dangers, going through the Snowclids alone.

"Do not forget about the dangers at the cave. We cannot afford to lose you," Ina said, frowning and pointing a finger at them. "Cold steel is the best method for the Undead."

"Oh, believe me, Princess, we will never forget that." Salas let his gaze fall to where his sword lay beside him. He clasped his staff even tighter.

"And when you get to Knowledge Hall you must inform Edegast of all that has gone on. Tell him that the danger from the gathering darkness is worse than even he believed."

Again, the two wizards agreed and promised they would. Ina stabbed her bow into the ground beside her and fell into a morose silence that no one wanted to interrupt.

Alyssa kept thinking about her family and friends. Did Lord Bryon even know what was going on? She wished she had some way to warn him. He could get his liegemen together and form some sort of armed force to protect his area from the goblins. But they were close to Needlemount and likely already knew the danger.

She pulled out a battered old journal and looked again at the map she'd drawn on her first journey into the Greater Daegries inside the binding. It was far too simple and didn't have the right distances drawn out. It was mostly for her sake, so she would know in the general direction things were located. She put it away and decided that if she lived through this, she would have a fine map maker design a real map of the Daegries akin to the one that King Eldon had.

After all, she'd be telling the tales of her adventures to her children and their children if the gods smiled on her. She'd need a good map to point out the way she'd traveled.

Her hand brushed the Grim in her pack, and she almost recoiled. She'd nearly forgotten it was in there. This reminder sent her thoughts tumbling over one another.

What if she was taken by the enemy? The book would fall into the very hands she had been trying to keep it out of. Shadow lifted up out of her pack and wrapped around her arm as if reading her unsteady thoughts. She shook it loose and forced it back into the pack.

"Tomorrow," she whispered to the scarf. "We'll fight those demons tomorrow."

Ina and the others were discussing potent poisons and Alyssa listened to the talk with no interest. The three hours passed uneventfully, and soon she was bedding down for sleep.

Sometime during the night, the fire guttered out and a stiff northern wind blew up, reminding them that winter had barely begun yet. The watch, held by the Nithereens, had been uneventful and they didn't restart the fire. They were creatures of dark woods and dark ways and preferred darkness over light.

Alyssa grew so cold that she thought her teeth would chatter. She pulled Shadow out of her pack and used it for an extra cover. Her pack became her pillow and soon she fell again into a troubled sleep.

Pappy was singing one of his silly songs.

We're hunting Gryphons
Hunting them through grass

We can't see them standing there,
Until the very last...

... last... last... the words faded, and Alyssa sat up to look around her, listening for the next verse. Pappy Oh was not there. Iefyr were there though, standing, staring up at the coming dawn. They had taken the last watch of the night, or the first watch of the day, to be exact.

It was their tradition to honor Solly the sun and Luna the moon, and Alyssa wondered why they hadn't sung last evening. Likely they would make too much noise for the area. Their ceremonies were like celebrations too, and there wasn't too much to celebrate at this time.

She scooped Shadow up to wrap around her shoulders and went to the elves to see what they were up to. They didn't speak to her but didn't refuse her company.

Alyssa looked up to see what they were so focused on. The wind in the trees blew their thinner tops sending them waving like flags at a bazaar. The trees where they stood were massive sentries, so tall that a girl like herself could never climb to the top.

Soon, the first vestiges of daylight shone through the trees and the elves spoke as one. Words Alyssa didn't understand but wanted to, as the heartfelt way they were said touched her.

When they once again lowered their gazes to the world around them, she asked the nearest one to explain to her.

"What're those words?" she asked.

He smiled at her. "Only the oldest language in Daegries. We always try to greet each day with thanksgiving for all that we are and all that we have."

"And the evening?"

"Much the same. It is a gift from us to the gods for allowing us to live another day."

He smiled at her again and turned away to follow his kin over to rebuild the fire. She went back to gather her pack and get ready for a long day of trekking over hill and through fen.

She hated to allow Shadow to revisit the pack, as it had proven to be quite a warm cover and a comfort too. But as the Grim was alone inside and in need of protection, she reluctantly watched as the scarf dove inside and curled around the book.

I sure could use some hot coffee or tea, she mused.

By the end of the next day, with unmatched sore muscles and tiredness, the company said farewell to Salas and Japher. The wizards, along with their Iefyr warrior/healer, would be leaving at first light and chose to camp in an area a little farther away than this night's chosen spot.

Alyssa went with them to say a private goodbye, knowing that she could easily find her way back by following the firelight.

"I want to send a message to Edegast, and don't want the world to know about it," she told the wizards. "If you wouldn't mind, let him know that I believe the portal plants are once again growing in Mudden at my family farm. If he should have the ability to travel there, well, I'd be beholden to him to help my kinfolk get rid of them again."

Salas nodded, putting his hands inside his robe sleeves. "I will make sure he knows, Alyssa. I will also let him know that the objective for you has changed. Are you ready to release the Grim to me for safekeeping?"

This took her back a step. He didn't know that Eldon had suggested she bury the book. As far as he knew, she still had it.

She remembered the Grim didn't go to another's hands easily, but he had experienced that before at Knowledge Hall. She pulled her pack from her shoulders, and let it fall to the ground before opening it to tug the book from its depths. Shadow came out with it, and she shoved the scarf aside.

She handed the book to Salas, who had a strange look on his face. Alyssa would have sworn it was amazement, but she knew better.

The wizard took his hands out of his robe and held them out. When she gently placed the book into his hands, his look changed quickly to one of terror and pain, and he cried out, dropping the book.

Japher, who had been standing quietly nearby, lifted his staff in defense of the older wizard as Salas carried his in a sheath on his back. The light from the staff illuminated the area, and Alyssa waved to him to extinguish it.

Salas hissed at the burns appearing on his palms. While Shadow flew to the book and covered it protectively, Alyssa hurried to the wizard and offered healing. He allowed her to place her hands on his palms.

Strange feelings went through her like she had touched a writhing fish, scaly and with pinpricks. It sent shocks through her, and she let go, sweat beading on her brow.

"Salas, I... can't," she said, her voice trembling. "Your magik...forbids..." She bent at the waist and Shadow lifted up, one half covering the Grim and one half patting her face.

Salas moaned and placed his palms together, saying words that she couldn't understand. Soon, it seemed the pain subsided, and he opened his hands. A white light sent a glow through the dimness around them, and he quickly waved it away.

"What... was that?" Alyssa asked, struggling to stand. She could still feel the prickles of sharp darts in her hands from his magik.

"The Grim transferred some form of evilment to me as punishment for touching it, I think. Then, you tried to use your magik on me for healing and of course, my magik revolted," he explained, returning his hands to his robes. "Quite a combination of wrong moves."

"Did you know that would happen?" she asked, scooping up the Grim and Shadow and returning them to her pack. "That was a terrible experience."

"No, I didn't exactly, but in the future, make sure the wizard's magik has been quelled before advancing with healing."

She nodded, a frown etching itself on her face. *I may not ever touch another wizard for healing if that is likely to happen.* "Well, I'm sorry the Grim isn't cooperating, but apparently it's chosen me just like the Scarf of Egladris did, and now it won't take to anyone else," she explained.

Salas shrugged. "Trying is worthy of failure."

She turned to go but his next words stopped her. "What will you do with the Grim when faced with the creatures filling the realm? The magik of the Grim may not go against the fools who follow its creator, or even Himself if it comes to that."

She paused mid-step and turned back to face him. "Tell Edegast that my Pappy's presence beside me on this journey would be most helpful." *Oh, if only he were here!*

And then she strode into the night, following a small glow to the fire of her company. His words haunted her enough to keep her awake long into the night.

What will I do if goblins try to take it? Do I chance the accursed thing burning them, too, or fight until death to keep it from them?

No answer came so she put her pack under her head and draped Shadow over her body slipping into another strange dream.

Pappy Oh wasn't singing this time.

Chapter Twenty-Nine

<hr>

The next afternoon, when the group reached the edge of the trees of Draysray, Bred and Nog said goodbye to them. Their journey took them to the caves of the Yetis farther south. Alyssa and her friends were headed straight ahead across the plains to where Needlemount castle stood with spires gleaming in the sunlight.

She wondered how the people of Half Moon manor were faring. The evil had surely tainted all of this land like the others. She hoped Lord Bryon and Fletch and Cerius and all of the Heightlanders were not under siege at this point, but it was entirely possible.

I wonder if Lady Pianna is well. How would Lord Bryon's mother manage a siege? Their small realm was unaccustomed to such things. They did have a King, though. Likely he's been called on for help, she thought.

The remaining group decided to have a quick meal before crossing the plain. A yeti and a dwarf might not seem too suspicious to anyone watching, as they were headed in the right direction for their kind. But a group of elves with one single young human heading to the mountains instead of the woods would be a target to anyone.

While they dined on cheese and meat and a sort of light bread, they talked about a plan for what came next.

"Has anyone ever gone under the mountains into the darkness before?" Ina asked.

"The Nithereens have done," one of the Iefyr archers replied. "At one time, history says they fought with the Dark Master."

Alyssa spoke the words before she could even stop them. "Is that why they're called Dark Elves?"

He shrugged and stood, waving to his comrades to prepare to leave. And they all rose to follow him.

Alyssa wondered what the dark magik was that the Nithereens were known for. Did they poison their weapons? Call on Undead creatures to fight alongside them? She was about to ask Ina when they came out of the woods suddenly, and a vast plain appeared before them.

That plain was a wide vista where the bright daylight shone down exposing all of them. Alyssa noted it right away, and Ina paused to peer out at the near-dead grass ahead. There were burrows and hills but, for the most part, only a wide-open area between the forest and the mountains.

The area around Needlemount lay ahead, the snow glittering off the peaks, and Alyssa was once again reminded of a resemblance to cake icing. The snow and ice ran down the sides into crevasses and drop-offs.

Alyssa recalled how it hadn't been terrible getting to the castle, but she was certain this trip would be stealthier, and they likely would find a way in under the mountains.

"How do you plan on getting to the Dark Master's home? Didn't you say he was the sort to go underground?"

"Yes," Ina answered. "Like a mole. He is a creature of the darkness."

Alyssa remembered what a time the farm had trying to get rid of real moles. "Harrumph. I know how to take care of moles."

The Iefyr archer overheard her and laughed. "And how is that?"

"You pour stuff down the holes. They hate that." She marveled that the elf knew her language.

"Yes. Imagine what quantity we would need to get rid of these moles," he said with a chuckle.

Alyssa nodded. A lot, she wanted to say, but that was a foregone conclusion.

"Well, we can either stay here until it is night, or we can forge ahead," Ina said to anyone listening.

"What say you, Princess?" the archer asked.

"I say let's go ahead. Only the Nithereens will be able to travel in the blackness. I'd rather fight in the daylight if I am to fight."

Alyssa didn't say so, but she was pretty sure that the Dark Master only had forces that liked dark and gloom. They wouldn't do well in the brightness of day. Or at least she hoped that. With all of her heart, she hoped it.

They hadn't gone even halfway across the plain when a group of three large, ugly, goblins rode toward them. They rode on giant rodents or rodent-like creatures. Their massive tails acted as rudders and kept them on track.

"What in Daegries is that?" Alyssa gasped, pointing.

"Oh, ye gods!" Ina moaned. "Trouble of the worst sort. Those riders are bad enough, but the bite of their steeds will poison worse than a scorpion! Prepare! They ride Thrustrats!"

The archers bent down and made ready to fire. The whistle of their arrows sang out. The arrows landed on shields that the goblins carried and bounced off the hides of the Thrushrats. The archers kept firing while the Nithereens pulled vicious looking blades from their sheaths.

Likely poisoned, Alyssa thought in her terror. Dark elves. Dark magik.

She had nothing but her glow spell and Shadow and a short sword she was entirely terrified to try to use. She pulled the scarf out and gave it an order to protect. It wrapped tightly around her. She called forth her magik, and it hovered over her hand for a moment until she sent it to blind, kill, or maim. Finally, she pulled the sword out. Obvious to her, arrows were not going to harm these creatures.

Ina joined the Nithereens and called out to Alyssa to flank her. The Mudden girl did as she was told, but it proved for no purpose. The enemy still advanced and the glow spell did not harm them any more than the arrows had done.

"For Draysray!" Ina yelled rushing toward the three.

"For Nithereen!" the others yelled as they followed her.

Alyssa didn't know what to do. The goblins slashed at the elves with longswords, and they all fell to injuries sustained. The Iefyr archers grabbed her and retreated back towards the woods.

"No!" Alyssa cried, fighting them. "We cannot leave them!"

But when she turned to look back at the Princess and her fighters, they were already being marched away by one of the goblins who held a wicked curved blade. They were headed in the direction of the mountains around Needlemount.

The other two goblins leapt from their steeds and entered the forest looking for Alyssa and her friends. The Iefyr climbed up into the trees overhead and nocked arrows to rain down on them.

Alyssa sheathed her sword and followed the elves, choosing a tall evergreen whose leafy top was so far up she could only barely see it. When the branches became too frail to hold her, she stopped climbing. Her heartbeat pounded in her ears, and she feared it could be heard by everyone around her.

It wasn't the evil ones that took notice though.

It was Shadow.

The scarf reached its ends up to pat her cheeks as if to encourage and calm her.

"I ain't so sure that we're going to survive this, Shadow," she whispered.

The scarf untied itself and opened to its full length and width, covering her, as though she was under a blanket. And it went invisible.

The goblins banded together below, seeking. Their scent, like fouled meat, rose to Alyssa's nose, and she winced at the sound of their guttural language.

Their heads were covered by metal helms, and they wore ugly battered armor with no place vulnerable save the folds down their sides. The elves, as precise as they were, could not harm the monsters from their perch overhead.

Instead, they took a silent breath and held it as the evil ones moved below. Then, a mischievous chilly breeze blew up, rattling the leaves, and the goblin underneath her tree looked up.

His long tusks clattered as he chomped his teeth together. "*Urg org glug,*" he said, grabbing his nearest comrade's shoulder. He pointed, not at her, but at the elves perched nearby.

She held tight to the branch she perched upon. The goblins didn't hesitate but set to work trying to figure out how to get them.

Before long, the elves had all been found. This meant Alyssa, although wrapped in Shadow, had been found as well, even though the goblins didn't know it yet.

The good thing was, the elves and Alyssa were in trees. The bad thing was, they were in *trees*.

The goblins were too heavy to climb the trees, and the trees were too old and tall to shake until they fell out, so the Dark Master's fighters did the only thing left.

They built fires to burn them down.

Alyssa didn't know goblin-speech and knew very little Iefyr, so couldn't communicate that well with her company in the trees.

She resorted to magik, sending tiny fireflies at the faces of the goblins who dared to look up at her. This only seemed to annoy them.

When the fires began, the Iefyr sent a volley of arrows down on the creatures but met with no luck, and they soon gave up the attempt.

Finally, afraid of the flames licking at the base of the trees, Alyssa called out to the dryads of the forest. "Help us, Tree-Spirits, or we're all going to perish!"

To the great amazement of everyone, dryads appeared and blew a killing frost over the fires, extinguishing them with a driving sleet storm. These creatures were not kind and noble this time, and their faces were as frightening as any Undead.

The goblins, terrified of the apparitions, and Alyssa's voice who had summoned them, ran to hop on their Thrushrats. But the dryads didn't appreciate the fires they had built to destroy the trees and sent a volley of sticks and stones at them, blown by an unseen wind.

The sticks fell away, but some of the stones made purchase and one of the goblins bent double when a perfect-sized rock hit him square in the side between the folds of his armor. The Thrushrat, spooked by all the objects flying at him, bucked the injured goblin to the ground and galloped away.

The others escaped across the plains and, after a while of waiting to see if any would return, the dryads returned to their homes, waving at Alyssa as they went. She supposed they could see her under the scarf. No need to stay covered now, she thought as she pulled Shadow away, and it wrapped around her shoulders.

The company remained in the trees for a while, waiting for the fallen goblin to get up and charge them. When it didn't, curiosity got the better of them, and they cautiously climbed down.

Alyssa pulled her sword, prepared to stab the goblin if it gave them any trouble. The weak side fold of their armor would not be forgotten.

The archers stood ready to shoot arrows into the creature, although it was pretty clear that option had no value. Alyssa approached the fallen warrior and gingerly toed him with her boot. He didn't move.

Then she noticed the dented helm and realized that the Thrushrat in its haste to depart had actually stepped on the goblin's head.

"I think... I think it's dead!" she cried, horror rising in her.

The nearest Iefyr deciphered the emotion in her voice and came forward to lift the goblin and turn him over. The creature's eyes were wide-open and unseeing.

The Iefyr warrior shook his head as he turned to motion to the others. He said a few words to them, and they joined him by the goblin's side.

Alyssa didn't know what to say or how to communicate with her company of elves. She made motions of dragging the body into the woods, but no one took the hint. Finally, she grasped one of the goblins booted feet and began tugging.

That got the rest of them moving.

They hid the body in the woods beneath a collection of leaves and dirt, but first they stripped him of his armor and weapons. Beneath the battered plate, the goblin was thick-skinned and hairy in places. Alyssa refused to look away. She wanted to remember what one looked like, battle-ready, or dead. They left the armor stacked nearby, but its weapon, a vicious-looking blade, they took with them.

Solly the Sun was disappearing into the horizon by the time the company could start anew. They had little trouble following the goblins' path. The creatures were nasty and dropped their garbage, as if their mama would collect it for them.

Alyssa watched for any blood as they went, fearing the worst for Ina and the Nithereens, but nothing appeared. She breathed easier but wasn't foolish enough to believe her friends were out of danger.

The mountains of Needlepoint lay ahead and leaving bodies behind would be easier for the creatures who lived beneath them. Fortunately, none appeared.

Shadow moved about, restlessly. Alyssa soothed it by saying how it had been very brave. Becoming invisible was exactly what she'd needed.

"Imagine their surprise when they looked up and saw nothing but a pair of boots with legs attached," she said, softly. "They were shocked, I just know it."

Scarf didn't move, only lay there as if it was considering her words.

"Don't worry," she reassured it. "You'll get another chance at those ugly creatures."

As the evening fell and they were still on the outskirts of the mountains, the elves kept going. She was tired and worried, but they couldn't stop out in the open.

When they strode up the first incline of the mountains, Alyssa wondered how these elves would find the opening to the goblins' caves. The leader turned and said a short word to his comrades, and they all turned away from the path and found a niche of an overhang to rest under.

As Alyssa tried to remove her pack and maintain a bow and arrow and a sword, the Iefyr archer who had discussed moles with her came over and assisted her. She smiled at him and said, "Thanks."

Surprisingly, he nodded and said, "Welcome."

"Where did you learn Mannish?"

With a wink, he whispered, "Some of us are well-traveled. But don't let anyone know. They would take me out of fighting and put me in a place to teach the young."

Alyssa, slightly astonished, asked, "What's your name?"

"Tangle. Tangle Fieldcress."

"That's not Iefyr. That sounds like a name from Muddentown."

"Yes. I've been living with the elves so long no one remembers that I'm human."

"So, you *are* human!"

He nodded, grinning. "Don't tell anyone."

"Well, Tangle, where on Daegries are you from?"

His face fell a little. "North of your kin. North of the Meadowlands, but not by much."

"I didn't know there were any settlements that way!"

He nodded. "We're small, but we're mighty."

That made her grin and took a lot of the tension away.

The other Iefyr archers made ready to resume the trek, so he waved at her and went to be with them. His presence gave Alyssa peace, and she didn't feel so isolated anymore. She did wonder how a Meadowlander had come to live with the elves and why he had stayed.

At night, Alyssa had trouble seeing the path, so she had to rely on the sharp vision of her company. The sky filled with clouds and rumblings that promised to unleash a storm. What they would do in that case, she could only wonder. The path was all uphill and there was no type of shelter to be found.

She didn't have to wait very long to find out. They rounded a bend of the path with a sheer cliff on one side and nothing but blackness on the other, when the skies opened up to pour down a frigid rain.

Every step Alyssa took slid either sideways or backward, and she feared being swept off the mountain into the bleak emptiness on her right. She peered up at the cliff, half-expecting someone higher on the ridge to be looking down at them, but no one was there.

The leader of their company waved them on, and she tried to get closer to Tangle who was ahead of her, in case there came a landslide from the storm raging around them.

When the rain abated, a terrible wind arose and turned the moisture in the air into a driving snow with ice embedded in every gust. Alyssa watched as the archers' quivers became ice-covered. Her own eyelashes and hood were so heavy with snow that it became hard to blink or protect her head.

She kept a constant watch for another overhang where they could shelter but even if one was found, the wind would not give them any respite.

She huddled under her cloak and hood and placed one booted foot in front of the other, watching her own steps fill the indentions of the elf in front of her.

They each placed a hand on the shoulder of the comrade in front of them, so that they each had a point of reference in the awful weather. It wasn't long before the wind died, and the snow lifted to a fine mist. Alyssa breathed a sigh of relief.

The leader of the company held up a fist and stopped their forward momentum. Alyssa thought he was going to tell them he had found shelter, and she shifted her weight.

He moved carefully to the side of the abyss and fell onto his stomach reaching his covered hand over the side carefully.

Alyssa couldn't imagine what he was doing until he pulled something back to his side and cradled it. Tangle inched up to try to see what it was, and Alyssa went with him.

The Iefyr in front of Tangle turned to him and even in the low light, she could see the terror on his face.

Tangle turned to her and in a kind, soft voice said, "It's Princess Ina's headcloth."

Alyssa moved him aside and crawled to the side of the Iefyr leader. He handed the band to her, and she sat up clutching it to her chest.

She closed her eyes and wanted to call forth her glow spell so violently that she actually trembled. There could be no magik glow now though. Not this close to the enemy.

She opened her eyes and noted that the snowfall thickened once more. They had to push on.

She pulled the band over her head and used it for a kerchief.

"Let's go," she said, motioning to the others. "Find the Princess."

Chapter Thirty

When they finally located an entrance to the underground of the mountains, it was only due to the scuffled markings of goblins' feet illuminated by a torch stuck in the ground. Nothing looked quite as large and unorganized as a group of goblins' footprints whirling around and wandering off with no direction in mind.

The creatures wore nothing for foot coverings except the tough hide on the bottoms of their feet. And the rocky terrain and snow and ice didn't bother them at all.

No mistaking the left-behind armor and trappings of the goblin army, however. Once the elves and Alyssa found the mountain's secret entrance, stealth was called for. The Iefyr archers led the way, and Tangle brought up the last of their company behind Alyssa.

Her anger had cooled significantly, and a healthy dose of fear and trepidation had taken its place. If Ina was being carried, she could have dropped the head covering on purpose. Alyssa held onto that thought with every dangerous step.

The interior of the mountain's belly was filled with grasses, rocks, and mud. A massive entryway had been hewn out, and there were multiple places where someone had built and burned a fire.

The creatures had not left a guard posted, and this worried Alyssa more than ever. Perhaps their intention for her friends was something the evil ones wanted to be present for.

The company eased past these places and headed down a narrow corridor that had been created by axe and shovel, and a great deal of curses, if Alyssa knew anything about such difficult work.

The mountains of Needlemount would never cede its strength for the likes of the Dark Master's forces. Not without a fight it wouldn't, and it looked to her like that was exactly the case.

Some of the stone walls were stricken with long claw marks that reminded her of a certain dragon in a nearby region. The marks seemed to drip blood in the half-light, but it was only the red rock. The smell that came from so many unwashed bodies passing through made Alyssa wrinkle her nose.

The faint light at the end of the corridor signaled an end to unoccupied terrain. Alyssa drew her sword, carrying it in one hand. Shadow draped around her body in a twist for easy detachment.

As they grew closer to the light, the company held a collective breath. The light source came from candles precariously stuck in the rocks of the walls, and the wax flowed like lava, leaving long tendrils on the ground. Someone in the goblin army had walked through it, smearing it.

The Iefyr leader held his fist up to indicate they should stop. He turned to face them and shook his head. They could not go forward unless they wanted to be the goblins' next victims. Even Alyssa could hear the rough voices and snarly laughter.

The company turned around and quietly retreated until they were outside the mountain and in a place safe from roving goblin eyes. It would not serve them for long, though, as groups of the horrible creatures came along on patrol regularly.

The Iefyr leader spoke. Tangle told Alyssa what was said.

"He wishes for us to go back down the mountain and plan an attack. We cannot simply walk into the teeth of the enemy's territory."

Alyssa grunted, frustrated. Why hadn't they planned before now? This was not going to help Ina and the Nithereens out of the goblins' clutches.

"Tell them that you and I will go into the cave of the enemy alone, and they can stay behind and come for us if we're taken. I don't think waiting and trying to figure out a plan at this late date is smart."

"He will not agree to that, my lady," he said finally, tilting his head.

Alyssa grabbed his hand and pulled him to the Iefyr leader. "I don't know his name."

Tangle nodded and said, "Galander."

Alyssa turned to the leader and looking him deep in the eyes said, "Tell him what I say, Tangle. Galander, kind elf friend, my name is Alyssa Chance Oh. I am related to the maker of the Scarf of Egladris, who I believe is held somewhere here in the clutches of the Dark Master. I ain't going back anywhere. I'm going forward. I'll find and release the princess, and my family alone if I have to. This I swear before you now."

Tangle's eyebrows went up, but he spoke the words.

Galander listened carefully and when Tangle finished, he waved at the Meadowlander for silence before asking a curt question.

Tangle lowered his gaze respectfully, and whispered, "Well, I guess the jig is up now," he said to Alyssa, reminding her that these Iefyr didn't know he could speak her language that well.

She could only hope her forwardness hadn't gotten Tangle into too much trouble. She watched Galander's facial expressions as Tangle answered his leader. They went from confusion to wonder and then to concern.

After a short silence, Galander addressed Alyssa. When he finished, Tangle translated.

"He understands your journey is different from the Iefyr's, but the end result is the same. He cannot in good conscience let you go on your own, even with me along."

New frustration and irritation rose in Alyssa, and she crossed her arms, fighting a pout that would be used to sway Pappy's decisions, but here, was ineffective.

"Tangle, make him understand. I ain't staying here. I have to go into that mountain and find Ina and the others. Then I'm going to find my parents, even if it's the death of me!"

Tangle translated what he could, but Galander interrupted mid-speech, and crossed his arms. The Iefyr leader glared at Alyssa in as near an attempt to mimic her own body language as anyone had ever done.

"*Goh. Dusiant goh.*"

Tangle nodded, let out his breath and told Alyssa that Galander had refused.

She closed her eyes and tried to understand. Galander was in a terrible situation. He wanted to get to his princess as much as anyone, but he was sworn to protect his fellows and her as well.

The only thing she could do at this point was to be kind. So she smiled at the Iefyr, who visibly relaxed, and she took a few steps away.

It would be hard to give up the protective cocoon of the elven army, but she had a journey of her own. She would take off as soon as these fellows were asleep or otherwise occupied.

The company moved several more times through the evening, until they found an overhang that hid a large outcropping of dead brush. It would have to do. No fire would be burned this close to the goblins' home, Alyssa knew.

They set up watches, ate a small portion of dried meat and drank water. Alyssa took the last watch with Tangle, and one other Iefyr. While others kept a vigil, she did her best to sleep. Her sword was next to her right hand, her bow and arrows were within reach, Shadow draped over her like a coverlet and kept her mostly invisible. Her pack served as a pillow and in a short while she fell asleep.

She would have wished for restful sleep, but that wasn't going to be the case. Instead, she tossed and turned and fought invisible enemies.

When she jerked awake hours later, the situation was perfect. Everyone was asleep, and the watching ones were standing looking in a different direction, or missing altogether, likely gone off to scout the area for goblins.

She quietly gathered her belongings and used Shadow as a shield to hide her as she took off down the trail toward the entrance to the goblins' lair.

Sleepy-eyed and weary of travel, Alyssa took few precautions as she entered the cave. Nobody had been within when the company had entered before, and she didn't expect anyone to be there now. She wasn't wrong.

The empty cave entrance greeted her with all of its messy ground. She stepped up to the pile of armor and tried to decide if any of it would fit her. Nothing would, she finally noted.

You're wasting time, Alyssa.

She eased down the corridor, past the bloody claw marks and stepped to the doorway. Apparently, goblins never sleep, she thought. The room beyond was massive and filled with milling goblin troops.

It was like being faced with the dragon Karnagul again. There was no way around the room to the places beyond. The only way to get to where she wanted was to fly across the area or slip right through the midst.

She could not slip through the goblin army. There were far too many of them. Suddenly, she understood the Iefyr leader far better. He didn't want to retreat to plan their next move. He wanted to retreat entirely.

As she stood there, trying to decide what to do, a shift of goblins entered the cave from behind her.

She turned terrified eyes to the narrow strip of land between her and them and realized too late her mistake.

She was trapped. Nowhere to go, nowhere to hide. The only thing left for her now was to be captured and hope to find her friends and family.

Sure hope Tangle and the fellows discover I'm missing and make it in time before these critters string me up and hang me over a spit. The scarf shifted, guessing her plan.

"Shadow, you have to protect. We must split up." It wrapped tighter, but she pulled it away. "No, there is no time now. Go invisible, protect the Grim, and when it is time, come for me. I'll likely be in a dungeon."

Then the creatures were on top of her. They jabbered and spit at one another and her.

One massive goblin yanked her by the arm and dangled her in the air. The scarf slipped unseen into the pack, and she knew it was wrapping itself around the book with all its might. The goblin deftly tossed her weapons and the pack aside, leaving her defenseless.

She muttered, "Goddess, save us" as she realized that the Grim was now in the hands of the very factions that she was supposed to protect it from.

The goblin tucked her under his arm like a sack of potatoes, and another one scooped up her pack, draping it over his wrist like a lady's handbag.

They marched right into the war room of the goblins' army with their bounty.

Alyssa held on, eyes wide open, hoping her captor would take her to where they held Ina and maybe her parents.

Here is the end of the first part of Alyssa's journey with the Grim. The next book, working title, Twin Terrors, will be part two. The events told in it will be separated into details pertaining to the rest of the World of Daegries and how the various realms fare during this dark time. It tells of the deeds and perils of all the members of the Alliance after Alyssa's capture, including Edegast, who plays a big role. There will be a fourth book in this series, currently untitled, which will tie everything together, and the story of the Great War will be recounted.

Thank you for being a reader of my work.

M. K. BROWNING

THE END

About the Author

M. K. Browning also writes under the pen name Kim Smith. Her works include, mystery, young adult fantasy, and small-town romance. You can find her at her website or at these social media sites: Facebook, Twitter, Instagram

If you enjoyed this book, please consider leaving a review!

Sneak Peek

Back at the Farm

When Pappy Oh reentered the house from the backyard, he heard Granny Gert talking to the constable and offering him some tea. Of course, the man refused. Pappy knew if he dared walk into the living room he would be in deep trouble with the constable.

He was supposed to be dead.

Rumors had been flying for some time around Mudden, and he was the object of the rumors. But for someone to see him in his own home, well, that would be the end of all speculation.

He decided at the last minute to again go out the back door and hide in the wisteria arbor. It had gotten even more overgrown and decrepit. The old coot, Murray, wouldn't think to look for him there.

He paced as much as he could with all the vines twining every which way. He needed a conjure to keep nosy people away. As soon as he could manage one, he'd do just that.

It wasn't long before he heard the front door slam and saw old Constable Murray walking away from the house. He gave it a few more minutes and hurried back to the kitchen where Granny awaited him.

Her hair was mussed all over her head from her pulling at it, and she looked like she was about to explode with anger.

"What was that about?" he asked, stopping beside the kitchen sink.

"He's following up on someone saying they saw you hoeing out in the garden."

"Who told him?"

Granny swiped at her unruly silver tresses and said, "He didn't say, but I'm mostly sure it was Tony. That man is the worst sort of snoop and informant."

Pappy went to her and patted her shoulder. "Don't worry none, Gert. I'll tend to Tony."

"What're you going to do about him? For all his faults he ain't a bad hand around here. He does help keep things running."

Pappy straightened his bent back and looked out the back window. "He has to go if he's been spreading stories in town about us. We don't need no one poking their noses in our business again. Remember when the kids ran off?"

She nodded and, with shaking hands, filled the tea kettle. "I guess he'll be talking again now with Alyssa missing."

"Not if I can help it," Pappy said. He opened the back door and picked up his hoe sitting right outside the door on the back porch.

"Pap, now don't go to doing nothing violent. You know well as I do that won't help nothing," Granny called after him. He kept walking for the barn where Tony was usually to be found.

"I ain't never killed nothing with my bare hands, and I ain't aiming to start today," he told her over his shoulder.

****

Follow M.K. Browning at Goodreads and BookBub

Also, you can follow M.K. at Amazon and find out when her next book will be released!